Boy Still Missing

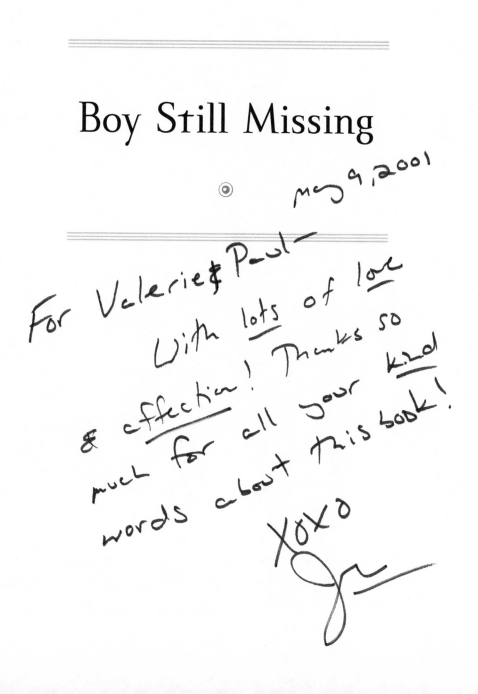

May 9, 2001

For Valerie & Paul—
With lots of love
& affection! Thanks so
much for all your kind
words about this book!
xoxo

Boy Still Missing

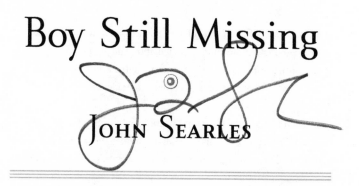

John Searles

WILLIAM MORROW
75 YEARS OF PUBLISHING
An Imprint of HarperCollins*Publishers*

BOY STILL MISSING. Copyright © 2001 by John Searles. All rights reserved. Printed in the United States of America. No part of this book may be used or reproduced in any manner whatsoever without written permission except in the case of brief quotations embodied in critical articles and reviews. For information address HarperCollins Publishers Inc., 10 East 53rd Street, New York, NY 10022.

HarperCollins books may be purchased for educational, business, or sales promotional use. For information please write: Special Markets Department, HarperCollins Publishers Inc., 10 East 53rd Street, New York, NY 10022.

FIRST EDITION

Designed by Nicola Ferguson

Printed on acid-free paper

Library of Congress Cataloging-in-Publication Data has been applied for.

ISBN 0-688-17570-8

01 02 03 04 05 QW 10 9 8 7 6 5 4 3 2 1

For my family,
Lynn, Keri, Raymond, John,
with love.

And for my sister, Shannon,
who left this world before she had the chance
to fulfill her dreams. Every single word of this book
is dedicated to her memory.

Boy Still Missing

PROLOGUE

Once a year I return to Holedo, Massachusetts, on a bus from far away. I watch out the window as we pull off Route 67 and make our way along Hanover Street toward the station. Holedo is nothing like the desolate, middle-of-nowhere place it was when I lived here. There's a McDonald's now, a 7-Eleven, a golf course, and a mammoth grocery store called the Big Bag, where skinny mothers shop in bulk, stocking their refrigerators like fallout shelters. Only one of the old town bars still stands. Renamed the Pewter Pub, Maloney's looks even more dismal than it did when I was fifteen, the year I tangled myself up with Edie Kramer and changed my life for good.

Even though my father stopped hanging out in bars ages ago, I find myself trying to catch a glimpse inside as we pass, but all I see is the bus's gray reflection shining back in the white light of a hot summer day. A moment later we're off Hanover. The bus rounds the corner, and we drive *by the Holedo Motel, owned and operated by my father since he bought it in a foreclosure sale. With the kidney-shaped pool out front, blue siding, and hedges trimmed in the shape of animals—a pig, a mouse, a puppy— the motel holds no trace of the dump it used to be. I glance up at room 5B, vacant since a winter day almost thirty years ago. Something in me pulls the way it always does when I first catch sight of that door. A sign the rest of the trip will turn out the same. After I settle in, my father and I will spend an entire weekend together, walking around the property, sitting at the table in the back of the office.*

Together, but not really together at all.

When he yawns and goes to bed for the night, this is what I do: lift the master key from its hook and climb the stairs to the vacant room, now used only to store mops and brooms, cleaning rags and linens. Inside, the air smells of an old woman's suitcase, a cheap vacation. I sit on the naked, lumpy mattress and touch my hand to the disconnected phone, spinning the rotary once or twice just to hear that forgotten sound.

How many minutes pass? Ten? Forty?

Time is the one thing that changes, but eventually I lift the throw rug by the bed and stare down at the stain on the carpet beneath, still there after all these years. The shape is a rounded triangle, a giant pear, a teardrop as big as a baby. Thoughts I spend all year pushing away tumble forward, and I have to hold my breath to shut out the stale air, the memories, the regrets.

If only I hadn't kissed Edie that first night.

If only I hadn't been so curious about Truman.

If only I could have stopped the most important person in my life from dying in this room alone.

One

June 1971

Whenever my father disappeared, we looked for him on Hanover Street. My mother drove us slowly along in our orange Pinto, gazing into shadowy windows. Between the rows of smoky bars glowing with Schlitz and Budweiser signs were slim alleyways where he parked his fender-dented GMC. My mother's best friend, Marnie, sat in the passenger seat, and I squeezed in the back. Marnie's job was to keep an eye out for my father's truck, but she spent most of the time applying foundation, darkening her lashes, and glossing her thin lips in the visor mirror. Marnie had recently read somewhere that all men were intrigued by Southern women, so she adopted the appropriate lingo. Besides the occasional "y'all" and "yahoo," it meant a lot of nicknames. Peaches. Honey pie. Cupcake. At fifteen I considered myself practically a man, and the sound of all that food coming from her mouth did nothing but make me hungry.

Tonight Marnie was in the middle of plucking her eyebrows when she said, "Is that his truck, peaches?"

"Where?" I said, sticking my head between them. I loved being part of Find-Father-First, and when she spotted his truck, it pissed me off, because I felt I had lost somehow.

"There," Marnie said, tapping her nail against the windshield. "There's the bastard."

I scanned the narrow parking lot. Datsun. Ford. Plymouth. Ford. GMC. My heart banged away, thinking of what usually came next. My mother hated bars and would almost always send me inside to nab my father. "A person could waste a whole life in one of those places," she liked to say.

For me there was nothing better than stepping inside the crowded brick caves—the smells of wet wood, stale beer, and smoke forever mingling in the air. I loved being surrounded by the cracking of pool balls, women with tight jeans and cigarette voices. They were so opposite from my mother with her smooth, young skin, flowery blouses and chinos, timid movements and soft hum of a voice. My mother had the air of a churchgoer, even though she never went to church. She was Sunday afternoon, and those women were Saturday night. Whenever my father saw me, he would pat his heavy hand on my shoulder and introduce me to all his pals. My father was like a movie star inside a bar, probably because he wasn't bald or potbellied or sloppy like the rest of the guys. He had straight teeth and a wave of dark hair, muscles and a flat stomach. He wore the same rugged denim jacket all year long and held his cigarette like a joint. While he paid his tab, I'd grab a fistful of straws so Leon Diesel and I could twist and snap them at the bus stop in the morning. Some nights I'd shove my sweatshirt pockets full of maraschino cherries and a couple green olives for Marnie. The neon fruit stained my hands and the inside of my pockets a strange artificial red that never completely came out in the wash.

The thought of the whole routine made me smile when my mother signaled and braked. We all squinted at the truck parked between

Maloney's Pub and the Dew Drop Inn. Even in the summer, faded garland Christmas bells and angels dangled from the wires that hung between buildings and across Hanover Street. Every December the Holedo town maintenance crews put up new decorations, only to let the weather slowly take them down the rest of the year. Under the wiry remains of a golden bell sat the truck Marnie had spotted. Red and silver. Snow chains on the tires even though it was June. "No," my mother said in the softer-timbre voice she used for disappointment. "Roy's truck has that dent in the fender. And he took his chains off last March."

"Honey," Marnie said, "that man took his chains off long before that."

My mother glanced in the side-view mirror and pulled back onto the street, not laughing at the joke.

"Get it?" Marnie said. "Ball and chain."

Neither of us smiled. After all, none of this was funny. For the last two days my father had been on what we called a "big bender." It meant he left for work on Wednesday morning and hadn't been seen since.

I took the opportunity to dig at Marnie for picking out the wrong truck. "Those weren't even Massachusetts plates." My voice cracked a bit, which took away from the slight. I had the froggiest voice of any guy my age and was glad the magic of my long-awaited puberty was finally beginning to deepen it. Marnie looked at me and shrugged like she didn't care. But we both knew she had lost a point or two in the game.

She went back to her eyebrows, and I tried not to be distracted as she plucked. Hair after hair. Hair after hair. She was one of those women who had great faith in the transformative powers of makeup and jewelry. Marnie was so different from my mother, who kept her thick, soot-colored hair in a neat little headband. My mother had tattoo-green eyes and a smile that didn't call for lipstick or gloss. On her ring finger she wore a tiny silver band with a diamond no bigger than a baby's pinkie nail.

We rolled to the end of Hanover Street, where the entrance ramp led to the highway out of Holedo. The bar lights blurred behind us, and my mother started checking and rechecking her watch, probably realizing how long we'd been searching. I stared out the window at a row of gray apartment complexes, an auto body shop with a half dozen mangled vehicles in the lot, the steady row of streetlamps that cast white light and shifting shadows inside our car as we moved. Marnie clicked on the radio and left the dial right where she found it. Whatever was playing when she hit the button—country, rock and roll, Bible preachers telling her she was headed straight for the pit of hell—suited her just fine. Tonight the car filled with the sound of violins. My mother was too distracted to care, and when I reached to change the station, hoping to catch the last inning of the Red Sox game, Marnie brushed my hand away.

"We're not fussy, sweet lips," she said. "Let's just listen."

"My name is Dominick," I told her, but she was already entranced by the music and didn't seem to hear. I could have hassled her some more, but I wasn't dying to listen to the game anyway. Just trying to follow the Sox so I could keep up with my father, something I hadn't done all season.

We cruised to classical, and I thought of Leon at the bus stop. Every Friday morning the band kids lugged their clarinets and flutes to school in black cases like miniature caskets, and it set Leon off. "That's the problem with this fucking town," he said. "They waste time teaching pansies how to play useless instruments. Give me an electric guitar, and then I'll join the band."

More than once I had suggested he take up drums because he seemed genuinely troubled by the lack of cool instruments in our high school. But Leon said he wasn't interested in playing backup for a pansy band.

I had known Leon since the first grade, when his family moved to the basement apartment downstairs from ours. In that time he had grown to be one of the toughest guys in school. His body had transformed into a lean muscular form. He kept his wispy hair perfectly feathered with the help of a wide-tooth comb carried in his back pocket, the handle forever jutting out of his jeans. Leon's biggest badge, though, was the slight trace of a mustache above his lip. For some reason he didn't seem to notice that I had ended up a lot like those band kids, with my thin voice and splash of acne on my forehead. Over the last year I had shot up in height, but I was reedy and long-legged, which left me feeling awkward all the time.

"Look at you," Marnie said whenever she caught my eye in the visor mirror, her lipstick dried into the wrinkles around her skinny lips. "You're such a doll."

That was my problem. I was the type of a kid that weirdos like Marnie, old ladies, and nuns found attractive. "He is so gorgeous," they would say to my mom. "He must be a real lady-killer." Leon had already fooled around with half a dozen girls and even claimed to have finger-fucked one. I had yet to kiss.

The violin rose and fell. A car with one headlight passed. We were alone on the highway, moving toward our exit. A police car was parked off the road in the parking lot of the Holedo Motel, behind a scattering of raggedy pine trees. The inside car light glowed yellow, and I caught a glimpse of the officer's mustache. If my father was cruising by, he would start muttering his usual speech about all the cops in this town being crooked, that they were a bunch of lazy cowards banned together in their own little boys' club. He'd light a Winston and then his speech would work into bitching about President Nixon, tax increases, and layoffs. My mother just glanced at the cop car, looking too worried for someone going fifty-five.

"Maybe it's time to start a new life," she said absently.

Something always shifted inside me when my mother talked like that. Before I was born, she had slipped from life to life the way some people changed jobs. The biggest proof of her aborted existences was my older half brother, Truman, who lived in New York with my Uncle Donald. "Someday," my mother used to say, "when things settle down with your father, Truman might come live with us."

I had never met Truman. Every month or so my mother took a train to New York City to see him. But for reasons no one would explain to me, he didn't visit. I guessed my mother wanted to keep Truman away from my father. Or maybe if Truman came, it would be too hard to send him back. Since I didn't like the idea of her old life cluttering up her new one, the arrangement suited me just fine.

Still, I was curious.

"Tell me about Truman's father," I said after Marnie leaned against the window and shut her eyes. The other day I'd found some pictures under my parents' bed while I was snooping. None of Truman, but one of a man with bushy black hair and firm white skin stretched across his face like a mummy's.

"Oh, Dominick," my mother said, "let's not talk about that now."

"What should we talk about?" I asked, sticking my head between the bucket seats.

Two of my mother's front teeth barely overlapped each other, but it was enough of an imperfection for her to have mastered a lips-together smile. I was sure other people thought the expression was sweet in a shy kind of way. To me it always looked like an odd cross between happiness and sadness. "Let's talk about my life when I lived in New Mexico," she said and smiled in her way.

This was one life my mother loved to discuss. It was full of bright memories, as annoyingly cheerful as one of my old children's books. Page one: My mother woke up one sunny New Mexican morning. Page two: She let out a big New Mexican yawn. Page three: She made a hearty New Mexican breakfast. It was so unmysterious I grew bored, but I let my mother talk because I knew it made her feel better.

"I used to make these breakfasts," she said, "with cilantro and fresh tomatoes, eggs and tortillas."

"Sounds great," I said, feigning enthusiasm.

"It's funny. When I made those breakfasts, I used to think I'd always make them. No matter where I lived or who I lived with."

"So why don't you?" I asked her.

"I don't know," she said. "Grocery stores are different around here. Everyone in Massachusetts eats pancakes and French toast in the morning."

My mother kept talking, walking me through the canyons she used to wander. As she blathered on, I thought about my father. Most of the time I'd flip-flop between trying to side with him and feeling bad for my mother. At the moment, though, I felt bad for me. After all, who the hell wanted to drive around aimlessly half the night listening to my mother's narrated tour of New Mexico? If my father wasn't on Hanover Street, it meant he was with his latest girlfriend. And if we were really planning on finding him tonight, we might as well look there. "We could drive by Edie Kramer's house," I said, interrupting.

My mother tightened her hands on the wheel and stared intently out at the highway, as if we were making tracks through one of her canyons at that very moment and she needed to concentrate. I had the urge to roll down the window in hopes that a fresh breeze might loosen things up again. More than once I had heard my mother accuse my father of sleeping with Edie. It seemed ridiculous that she didn't simply assume it to be true. Edie was the ex-wife of Stanley Elshki, the owner of the plastics factory where my father worked. Over the last few months there were three nights like this one when we couldn't find him in any of the bars on Hanover. When my father returned home near dawn, he explained that he had been playing cards and lost track of time. Last week he claimed to have fallen asleep in the factory parking lot.

"Imagine," he had said. "I stuck my key in the ignition, rested my head on the steering wheel a second, and the next thing I know it's four in the morning."

"Now he has a sleeping disease," Marnie had said when my mother told her his story.

Since my mother ignored my suggestion, I leaned back and opened the window. The car filled with cool summer air, and Marnie stirred in her seat. "Could you shut that?" she asked.

I closed it partway.

Marnie looked at my mother, her full-moon eyes widening above her chicken-beak nose. "Terry, Dominick's got a point. I mean, if you have your heart set on finding Roy, we could see if he's at Edie's."

"And what if he is?"

"We don't even have to stop. We'll just roll on by, and if his truck is in the driveway, you can tell him to shove his line of bullshit once and for all when he comes home."

We all knew—or at least I did—that there would never be a once and for all when it came to my mother and father. Here's how it would go down: My father would walk in the door; my mother would hurl accusations and promptly burst into tears; she'd let him sweet-talk her into the bedroom, where they'd fuck their brains out. Loud enough for me to hear. Loud enough to turn my stomach. After that, my mother would act like nothing ever happened. She'd smile and ask me, "What would you like for dinner?" or "How's school anyway?" And that's what I hated most: When my father was on her shit list, she acted like I was a grown man, her partner in all of this. But the second he won her back, I was a simply a boy again, their son.

My mother pulled off the highway. She cut across Hattertown Road and over the narrow wooden railroad bridge to Gringe Farm. There were no streetlights in this part of town. All I could see out my window were the shadows of leafy branches against the dark sky, the string of sagging telephone wires from pole to pole. Pegluso's swamp reeked like a septic tank as we passed. Soon we were driving up Barn Hill on our way to Edie's. She lived in a large Victorian topped off with a slanted and spiraling roof, painted lemonade yellow but peeling since her divorce. A couple of times when Leon and I were hanging out in the parking lot behind the Doghouse, shoving fries and foot-longs into our mouths, we spotted Edie. She was tall and leggy, with shampoo-commercial hair the color of a Twinkie. Leon knew she was divorced, and for him that added an element of sluttiness to her. Whenever we saw her, he spent hours afterward speculating about her sexual appetite, the way she liked to do it, the number of men she rolled around with.

As we reached the top of the hill, my mother slowed down, and the car made a slight squeaking noise in the night. We chugged by the place, staring out the car windows. The house was pure faded glory, a majestic frame naked with tired paint. Suddenly the idea that my father was on a drinking bender didn't seem so bad. If he wasn't here, we would drop off Marnie and head peacefully back to our apartment until he rolled in.

"Do you see his truck?" Marnie asked.

Edie's circular gravel driveway was empty except for a white Cadillac.

"He's not here," my mother said, letting out a sigh of relief. "He's not here."

At the end of the street she turned the car around and made one more pass on our way home.

"Wait," Marnie said. "Slow down. Slow down."

My mother hesitated, as if she didn't really want to stop. It was fine with her to believe my father wasn't there. He was drinking with his friends. He was playing poker. He was asleep in the factory parking lot. At the same time Marnie and I spotted his GMC on the other side of the house in a driveway that led to an old barn.

"There's his truck," we said in unison.

My mother stopped the car dead in the street. She stared at the truck, and the dark headlights glared back. A dozing giant, lifeless in the night.

"Honey pie," Marnie said. "You can't just sit in the middle of the road. We might get hit by a car."

My mother leaned her head back, and I could see that her cheeks were wet with tears.

"It's okay," I said, trying to calm her. "There's probably an explanation."

"Yeah," my mother shouted. "Like, maybe he's screwing her."

She seemed to fold in on herself, and the tiniest croak came from her mouth. A moment of nothing, then a fit of sobs. The sound made me think of dark birds frantically escaping the wet nest of her stomach. Flapping and flapping. Marnie stroked her shoulder.

"Do you want me to go in and get him?" I asked.

My mother coughed. "I couldn't make you do that, Dominick."

"Really, I don't mind." My voice sounded too high and stretched, the way it did when I consoled her. Crack, I thought. Deepen and change.

"All right," she said, and her crying stopped. "Go get him."

"Wait a minute," Marnie said, holding her hand out, flat and even, a mime against an invisible window. "If you want Roy, just march right up to that door and knock. Don't send Dominick to do your dirty work, Terry."

"I am not facing that woman. Dominick will simply get his father and we'll be on our way."

"But—"

"Marnie," my mother said. "Trust me. Dominick doesn't mind coming to his mother's rescue."

I was a pro at fetching my father from bars, but I was beginning to realize that his girlfriend's house was a whole new deal. What if I interrupted them in bed? What would he say to me? There'd be none of his pals to introduce me to. No cherries. No straws. I put on my Sox hat and tried to look brave.

As I walked the driveway, tiny white stones crunched under my feet in the swell and hush of a breeze moving through the willow trees like a whisper. I went slowly around to his truck and, even though I knew better, peeked inside to be certain he wasn't there. I could hear it now: "I gave Edie a ride home, then fell asleep as I was backing out of the driveway." Maybe he did have a sleeping disease like Marnie said. But he wasn't inside, so I turned toward the house. In the corner of the lawn a red maple shimmied like a cheerleader's bushy pom-pom against the black sky. The air smelled like jasmine and reminded me of a sense exercise I did the one year my parents bothered to send me to catechism. Blindfolded, every kid had to guess what they were smelling. Chalk. Shampoo. Dirt. The game was simple until you reached a strip of cloth Gritta Alexander had brought in. "Jasmine," she had said proudly when no one could guess. The nun said, "All these are smells God created." But it didn't seem God would ever create a fuck-me smell like that. Now something like jasmine lingered around me and mixed with the lemony scent of summer grass. I thought of Gritta, who was all breasts and belly now, with a big curvy ass. I checked my watch, almost twelve. When I reached the front porch, I looked back at my mother and Marnie in our bubble-shaped car. In the shadows I could see Marnie fixing her makeup, my mother with her head bent against the steering wheel.

I padded up the steps, took a breath, and knocked—soft at first, then louder. No one answered. I stood in the silence, wondering what to do next, and Leon came to mind. All year he had been after a girl named Jennifer Bilton. When her parents were away in Acapulco, Leon found her house key taped inside a wind chime on the back porch. He claimed to have let himself in and walked right into her bedroom. "Where there's a will," he told me, "there's a key to get in."

I lifted Edie's mat, then checked under a rusted milk box and behind a barren cement planter. No key. I put my hand on the knob and turned. The door opened without the slightest creak. In front of me a long hall led into the heart of the house, the walls lined with shoes. High heels in dozens of colors. Flats. Sneakers. I closed the door behind me and stood for a moment, letting my eyes adjust to the dim light. Not knowing where to go next, I decided to follow the path of shoes. The flowered wallpaper seemed alive with more jasmine and summer scents drifting in through the tall windows. A clanking sound came from the back of the house. I walked toward the noise, and the farther I went, the more shoes I found. Only now there were work boots and cleats, bowling shoes and ballet slippers, all resting in shoe boxes with tissue paper and price tags. When I rounded a corner, I spotted a crack of light beneath a door. I paused, then pushed it open.

At the stove Edie stood stirring a pot. My father was nowhere. The room smelled like warm milk and cinnamon.

"Mrs. Elshki," I said. Then, remembering her divorce, "I mean, Miss Kramer."

Edie gasped and whipped around, holding a wooden spoon in front of her like a weapon. "Who the fuck are you?"

Her blond hair hung straight down to her shoulders, where it broke into thick chunks of curls. She wore a lacy nightgown that stopped just below her ass. Her long legs were a bit dimpled, something I never noticed when she stood in line at the Doghouse. Her breasts hung full and round, with quarter-size nipples pressed against the soft material. In the bright light of the kitchen, I could see that her eyes were red. She had been crying like my mother. Or drinking like my father.

"How the hell did you get in here?" Edie said.

"The front door," I told her, deepening my voice and trying to sound businesslike. "I knocked, but you must not have heard me. I'm Dominick Pindle, and I'm looking for my father."

With that explanation she seemed to calm a bit. She lowered her spoon. "You scared the shit out of me. And your dad's not here."

"But his truck is parked outside."

"Aren't you a Sherlock? Just because his truck is here doesn't mean he is." Her voice had a raspy sound to it that made me think of a singer in an all-girl band, the way she might sound the morning after a killer show. Edie turned back toward the stove and started stirring again. Her arms were long and lean, and I could see her muscles as she moved that spoon around and around.

"Do you know where I can find him?" I asked.

"Try Hanover Street. Maybe he crawled inside a beer can and died."

"That's my father you're talking about," I said, my voice still low. It felt odd to defend him, but I wasn't sure what else to say.

Steam rose from the pot and licked at the curls of hair that rested on her shoulders. Edie turned to me, and her expression softened. She had eyes that pulled up at the corners like a cat's. A thin nose. When she smiled, I could see that her teeth were small and even, framed by her thick lips. She reminded me of that pregnant actress who had been butchered to death a few years back in those Manson murders. I couldn't remember her name, but Edie was a dead ringer for her. "Forget it," she said. "I've had a rough night."

We stood there a moment, not knowing what to do next. I suppose she was waiting for me to turn and leave, but I found myself thinking of all the things Leon imagined about her.

She likes it doggy-style.
She likes it every night.
She'll do it with anyone.

"Well, I guess I should go," I said finally, even though I wished I could stay longer. I walked toward the kitchen door, that hallway of shoes.

"Dominick," Edie said. "Wait."

I turned back to look at her. Leon was right. Everything about Edie was beautiful. Her tan arms. Her long nails. And especially her tits. I could just hear him when I announced that I'd met Edie Kramer and she was wearing nothing but a skimpy nightgown. He'd flip. "Yeah?" I said.

"You could stay a minute," she said, her voice still raspy. "We could talk."

My mouth went dry. "You want to talk? About what?"

"Anything. The weather. The news. You." She paused. "Your parents."

Even if she was the most fuckable woman on the planet, my lips were sealed when it came to spilling info on my parents. "What about them?" I asked.

"Nothing in particular. Actually, I don't know why I even said that. We don't have to talk about them at all. Why don't we just get to know each other instead?" Edie crossed her arms in front of her and rubbed her elbows, smooshing her tits together so they grew even larger. "There's nothing lonelier than waking up in this big old place with no one to keep me company."

I looked from her perfect chest to her perfect face and decided that maybe she didn't want dirt on my parents after all. Maybe she did just want to talk, like she said. I thought of all the times I woke in the middle of the night and listened to my mother carrying on with my father in the next room, when only a few hours before she had been bawling to me about him. Her panting always left me feeling betrayed, lonely, too. I thought of all those times my mother talked about starting a new life, the way I used to wake in the morning and wonder in the silence of our cramped apartment if she had left, deserted me.

"Do you want some warm milk?" Edie asked.

Now I was the one betraying my mother, but I sat at the kitchen table anyway. In my head I still heard scraps of Leon's gravelly voice — *three fingers, all night long, blow job.* Afraid Edie would catch on somehow, I pushed his words from my mind. "Why do you live in such a big house if it makes you feel lonely?" I asked.

She poured our milk into two thick mugs. As her fingers gripped the pot handle, I noticed that her pinkie nail was broken and chewed, unpainted. Instead of being taken in by her nine other red nails, I found myself staring at the short, imperfect one. "I was raised as an army brat," Edie said. "My dad was an officer, and I lived in something like twenty-six different military apartments growing up. So I like the feel of a big house. The security. Even if it's lonely sometimes, neither me or the house are going anywhere."

"You like Holedo?" I asked, curious because no one else — especially my mother — ever seemed to have a nice thing to say about the place.

"I've lived all over the world," Edie said, putting a mug in front of me and giving me a closer look at that one undone nail. "Holedo is just as good a place as any. It's quiet here. Peaceful."

I decided she was right. Who needed canyon walks and secret trips to New York? Holedo was just as good a place as any.

Edie pulled a bag of Chips Ahoy! from the cabinet and settled next to me. Her smell was milk and skin. She was Gritta Alexander all grown up.

"So what's with all the shoes?" I asked.

"Oh, those," she said, waving her hand toward the hallway. "I guess you could say it's a moneymaking scheme."

"What kind of scheme?"

"Well," she said. "I want to start designing shoes."

The cinnamon and sugar turned Edie's concoction too sweet, but I drank it anyway. "You made all those?"

"No. I bought them. It's a good idea to know the whole playing field before you get in the game. Right now I'm just buying up every shoe I see. I'm still trying to figure out what kind I want to make."

She'll make you hard, Leon said. *Make you come.*

"What kind do you think?" I asked, shutting him up. Something about her business plan didn't sound quite right, but what the hell did I know?

"Actually, I'm partial to men's shoes. They're so sensible. It's not fair that women have to clomp around, teetering on heels all the time."

I thought of my mother's white sneakers—the hushed, shuffling sound they made against the cracked linoleum in our kitchen. "Women don't have to wear those things."

"If they want to get somewhere, they do," she said. "I have to wear them."

I dipped a cookie and took a bite. The milk was making me sleepy, and I knew that my mother and Marnie were probably getting anxious, that was, if Marnie could stop looking in the mirror long enough to wonder what was keeping me. Thinking of them waiting outside guilted me into steering the conversation back to the reason I was here. "So why is my father's truck in your driveway?"

Edie blinked her cat eyes and looked away without answering. The question seemed to have flown from my mouth up to the ceiling, somehow missing her ears. "Let me see your feet," she said, changing the subject.

"My feet?"

"Don't be shy," Edie said with a sudden giggle to her rock-star voice. "Let me see them."

I decided to let go of the whole thing about my father and put my sneaker on the table, because I didn't really want to think about his truck outside anyway. Edie loosened the laces, tugged at the heel, and pulled it off. I had taken to not wearing socks lately, and my toes wiggled before our faces. Never before had my feet felt so private.

"Footwear can transform you," she said, pinching my big toe, then brushing her fingers along my arch, making my leg go stiff as I fought my ticklishness. She held up my sneaker and shook it. The once-white tongue kept still, but the laces dangled at her wrist. Baby snakes slithering around her soft skin. "Take a look at this. How are old are you anyway?"

"Seventeen," I said, adding two years to see if I could pass.

"I thought so. You're not a boy anymore. You're a man. And a decent pair of shoes can help you look like one."

I nodded and pushed the mug and Chips Ahoy! bag away.

"I want you to come with me. I've got just the right shoes for you."

With one sneaker still on, I walked behind Edie to the hallway lined with shoes, staring at her ass the whole time and memorizing details. I could touch it, I thought. I could lift her gown and run my hands along her skin. Edie bent over and dug around. She tossed aside a clear plastic shoe that reminded me of a glass slipper. Cinderella. "Hmm," she said. "They must be downstairs."

We walked to the basement, where unmarked cardboard boxes filled the room. A flickering bare bulb hung from the ceiling, dizzying itself in a circle after Edie had yanked the string. The walls were constructed from round gray rocks that made me think of skulls, dull crowns showing, hollow faces sealed into the cement forever. A single sketch of a strappy sandal was taped to one of the round rocks that jutted from the wall. In the far corner sat a tattered mattress, striped orange and yellow like a circus tent and covered with fluffless pillows. The air smelled of earth and cobwebs, water underground.

"Is this your work?" I asked, pointing to the drawing of the sandal.

"Yes," she said.

"It's beautiful," I told her. "But not as beautiful as you."

It was something Leon might say, not me. But it actually sounded pretty good. For all she knew, I was a lady-killer.

Edie looked at me and smiled. She touched my cheek with her hand. "Like father, like son," she said, then caught herself.

My father. I could have called her on that, but being with her was too much of a good thing. After all, if Edie were a girl my age, she would never even notice me. But in her dark basement, in the middle of the night, I started to think I had a chance. Again I thought of Leon and the way he asked girls if he could kiss them. "You ask, and they say yes or no. What's to lose?"

I cleared my throat and said, "Edie?"

"Yes?" She was standing in front of me with her head tilted, lips together.

"Can I kiss you?"

Edie laughed. Things like this worked for men like Leon and my father. Not for me. Then she said, "Why would a handsome young man like you want to kiss an old woman like me?"

There was that word again. "Man." It was my chance to be one. "You're beautiful," I said.

"I'm trouble," she told me. "Besides, you must have dozens of girls chasing after you."

"Not really. Actually, none at all. I've never even kissed a girl."

"Never?"

"Never."

Edie looked at me, thinking. "Well. One little kiss wouldn't hurt. But if I let you, you have to do something for me."

I could see it now—mowing her lawn, scraping the dried yellow paint off this big fucking house. Still, it was worth it. "What do you want?"

"I haven't decided yet. But I'm sure I'll need you for something soon enough. So you have to promise you'll be there for me when the time comes."

"I promise," I said. "Whatever you want. Whenever."

"All right, then." Edie puckered her lips, like we were going to have a showy stage kiss.

I stepped forward. My heart stomping in my chest like one of these new, unfamiliar shoes. Before she could back out, I put my lips against hers. She felt less soft than I would have imagined, and I could taste alcohol under the milk and cinnamon. The combination tasted strange but delicious. It was as if I were kissing a statue, though, because Edie just stood there, stiff. My heart was pounding fast enough for both of us. I felt like I had swum deep under water and everything was muted and slow, the way it is at the bottom of the ocean. No sound. No quick movements. Just our bodies. Just our lips. Blue all around. From somewhere far away I heard a dull humming noise. As hard as I tried to shut out the sound, my body swam toward it, back to the surface.

My mother's horn.

Edie and I stopped and looked up at the rafters of the basement. Red and blue wires dangled above our heads like veins.

"I have to go," I said.

"Remember," she said, her voice serious. "You owe me."

I nodded yes. She could have asked me to build her a whole new house and I would have agreed.

"Wait," Edie said as I turned to go. She rustled around in a dark corner and produced a pair of men's work shoes. Steel-toed and black. "They may be a little big. But you'll grow into them."

The horn was still blaring. No doubt it was Marnie pissed I had been gone so long. My mother would be too concerned about the neighbors to make all that racket.

I raced up the stairs, Edie trailing behind me. "I'll show you out," she said. "It's a big house, and you might make a wrong turn."

But I rushed ahead of her. Up the stairs and down an unfamiliar hall. I must have veered off course somewhere, because the horn was coming from behind me. I opened a door to my right. A closet filled with empty hangers. I turned and opened another door. A canopy bed, lacy peach curtains and pillows. Lying in the bed with his shirt off, hairy chest exposed, passed out, was my father. He rolled over at the noise, and I froze in the doorway. I had settled so easily into the idea that he simply wasn't at Edie's, and the new development confused me. I had finally kissed a woman, and I didn't want it to be his girlfriend. Instead of waking him and telling him to come home, I closed the door and went back into the hall.

Before I knew it, Edie was standing right behind me, though she might have been there all along. "This way," she said and led me through the maze to the front door. As I stepped outside, she ran her fingers along my chest. The motion made the smooth, hairless skin beneath my T-shirt burn.

"Sharon Tate," I said.

"What?" Edie asked.

"That's who you look like. That pregnant movie star who was stabbed to death." I never read the paper, but the headline with her name came to me out of nowhere. I remembered her smiling photo, too.

Edie folded her arms in front of her as if to stop a chill. Somewhere in her house a clock was chiming. "I'm sorry," she whispered.

I wasn't sure if she was referring to the fact that she looked like a dead woman or if she was sorry that my father was in her bed. Maybe, I thought, she was sorry I couldn't stay longer. Whatever she was trying to say, all I could do was keep walking.

When I got close to the car, I saw it was Marnie honking, just as I suspected. My mother was trying to pull her hand off the horn. For the first time they looked pathetic to me, like Lucy and Ethel bumbling along on an adventure, only without the laughs.

"Honey," Marnie said, "you've been gone so damn long I've gone gray. And what's with the shoes?"

"Never mind," I told her, pulling them against me like a trophy from the other side. One foot was still bare, my sneaker left behind on Edie's kitchen table.

"Did you find him?" my mother asked.

I swallowed hard and climbed into the backseat. "He wasn't there. Edie borrowed his truck to move some furniture. She doesn't know where he is." I figured my father could deal with my lies if my mother called him on it.

"What kept you, then?" Marnie asked.

"It's big in there. There are lots of places to get lost." My voice cracked again, and I couldn't help but smile. I sounded just like Leon and my father, I thought. Just for a moment I sounded like a man.

Two

The morning Edie decided to call in her favor, I was standing under a tent at the Holedo policemen's auction with my mother. It was a cool, drizzly November day, and the sound of raindrops on canvas made me think of knuckles cracking. Over and over.

"Do you think we'll get what we want?" my mother asked. She was wearing a yellow plastic kerchief over her head. Beneath it, her hair was pulled back in a bun, leaving a funny-looking lump in the plastic.

"Probably not," I said, practicing my new routine of telling her the exact opposite of what she wanted to hear.

The taxpayers' association had funded a brand-new police station—or pigpen, as my father called it—on the other side of town. The new place had turnstile doors, a six-car garage, and an intricate emergency switchboard. After three years of on-again, off-again construction, the station was finally up and running, so the cops were selling off all their old crap. For the first hour we watched people walk away with wooden desks, torn vinyl office chairs, coffin-size filing cabinets, even the titles to three souped-down squad cars and a badge from Holedo's first sheriff, Will Warner.

But my mother wasn't interested in any of that crap. What she wanted more than anything was the old station itself. With its single-story design, ivy-covered brick face, and rooms lined with barred cells, she had convinced herself it would be the perfect home.

"Don't be so pessimistic," my mother said. She ran her hand over her kerchief, and it crinkled like a sandwich bag. "It's our chance to own a place. Do you want to live in that apartment the rest of your life?"

This opposite thing was so easy with her. "As a matter of fact, I do."

Since my father had taken a job driving a truck for Edie's new shoe business three months ago, apartment life was better than ever. He was gone most of the week, trying to make sales to independent shoe stores up and down the East Coast. If the business took off, I had heard him explain to my mother more than once, Edie would hire more drivers and he would get to be the dispatcher. That meant he'd make a lot more dough than he used to bring home from the factory. All I knew was that with just me and my mother around during the week, I could watch television whenever I wanted, drink soda, and eat chips in the living room.

"You'll change your tune once we spruce it up," my mother said.

No matter how much we fixed the place, it could never be a real home. Last week Officer Roget had given us a tour. Between twisting the bristly tips of his mustache and listening to my mother giggle over all his cocky jokes, he explained that no one had ever spent more than a single night in a Holedo cell. It was really just a holding pen until criminals were sent to a real prison or set free. The news left me disappointed. If we were going to move to a jail, I wanted it to have a dark and dangerous history. I tried to imagine murderers on death row, planning their escapes before their brains got fried in the electric chair, but I found that impossible with the smell of Roget's stray cats, the emptiness of the jail cells, and toilets that were as filthy as forgotten fishbowls. The place felt more like the Franklin Park Zoo outside of Boston. Still, my mother was convinced it was a great fixer-upper. My Uncle Donald had sent a fat check from one of his latest inventions, and buying the old station was the way she was going to spend it.

But we had competition.

After the cars had been auctioned off, the only people left standing under the tent were Vito Maletti and Grover Payne. Vito owned Peaceful Pizza on Water Street by the bus station. Grover owned the Town Auto Body on Hanover.

"Peaceful Pizza Two," my mother said.

"The Town Auto Body at a new location," I said.

She sighed. "What happened? I thought we got rid of the competition."

For weeks my mother and Marnie had gone store to store, tearing down auction signs from community bulletin boards, as well as calling local radio stations and disguising their voices to announce a change in date. "Excuse-a me," Marnie would say, switching off her southern. "Ze oction 'as-a bin chenged."

"You couldn't have expected everyone to fall for your tricks," I said.

"Why not?" my mother said, her beige raincoat practically swallowing her. "All's fair in love, war, and house hunting."

This was her idea of a joke. Ever since that night at Edie's last summer, my mother's jokes had begun to annoy me. It was as if Edie's kiss had aged me ten years, and I saw my mother in a different way. I wanted her to stop wasting time with Marnie. I wanted her to stop chasing after my father. I wanted her to stop putting on the normal mother act every time he won her back.

Across the lot a skinny girl was single-handedly protesting the auction. She was about my age and my height, with long, flat brown hair that made me think of a "before" picture in a Wella Balsam ad. One of those pretty-faced models looking dismal until the shampoo blessed her with bounce, luster, and a glowing smile. She held up a sign that said HOLEDO MUST PRESERVE HISTORIC BUILDINGS, but no one seemed to be paying much attention to her.

"Who is that girl?" my mother asked.

"Don't know," I said, because I had never seen her in school before. "But I think she wants our new home to be a museum."

My mother looked her way and said, "Well, I always admire a girl who fights for what she believes in."

"We are opening bidding on the former Holedo Police Station," Officer Roget announced, stealing a quick glance at my mother. His face was saggy and pouched, set off by a crooked nose and thin lips. The face of a skinny man set atop a muscled body. Something about the way he kept putting his fingers to his mustache, like it was a costume that didn't fit quite right on his face, made him seem shifty to me. Or vain. I wasn't sure which.

"He sure is handsome," my mother whispered.

I looked at his gorilla chest stuffed into a blue uniform. His holster rode high on his waist, the pistol jutting out like some inflexible part of his body. "Maybe without his head," I told my mother.

Roget fingered the black nest of his mustache, then touched his badge and prattled on. "This six-room office building has housed Holedo's finest since 1923. There are hardwood floors, a galley kitchen, and three bathrooms. It's well suited for a business. Of course, it could easily be renovated into something else."

"I feel like I'm on *The Price Is Right*," I said.

My mother didn't respond. I knew she wished Marnie had come with her instead. But Saturdays were Marnie's big day at the hospital, where she was in charge of television rentals for patients. Most of the week she made her way from room to room, gathering crinkled dollar bills from sick people with bedsores on their asses and nothing to do but watch *Mary Tyler Moore* and listen to Marnie's personal line of bullshit. On Saturday mornings, though, Marnie was the Bingo Lady. For a full hour her face was broadcast over the hospital television system. "B one. G fifty-five. I know there is a winner out there somewhere!" The way she dolled herself up and carried on, you would think she was a guest on *Carson*.

"We will open the bidding at fifteen thousand dollars," Roget announced. "Do I hear fifteen thousand?"

Grover waved his faded and fingerprinted cap in the air. Vito counterbid. The two of them went back and forth until Roget reached fifty thousand.

"Why aren't you bidding?" I asked my mother.

The air around us was flashbulb blue and smelled of fireplace fires. Her face looked puffy, heavier than usual, in the morning light. Her cheeks were red. "I'm just letting them lay the groundwork. When things get serious, I'll make my move."

Vito bid at fifty-five thousand.

"Sounds pretty serious to me," I said.

"Do I hear five thousand more?" Roget asked.

"I'm out," Grover mumbled, folding in a high-stakes card game.

The three of them were in Monte Carlo. Marnie was in Hollywood. And my father was hauling his girlfriend's clodhoppers all over New England—the bombshell girlfriend I had kissed but not seen since. All last summer I kept hoping to spot Edie at the Doghouse or the Cumberland Farms Quick Mart. I had ridden my ten-speed by her house a few times in the fall, desperate to catch a glimpse. When I didn't see her again, I started to blame my father. Of course Edie preferred him over me. He was all about beer, big muscles, and his big mouth, and I was none of those things. Whenever I fetched him from a bar after that night at Edie's, I tapped him on the shoulder and pointed to the door. No more intros with his buddies. No more hanging out while my mother waited in the car. That was how much I had changed.

"Do I hear five thousand more?" Roget said.

"How much did Uncle Donald give you?" I asked.

"Never you mind," my mother said and raised her hand to match the bid.

Vito didn't wait. He shot his hand in the air.

"Sixty-five thousand?"

My mother raised a finger.

"Seventy thousand?"

Vito waved.

"Seventy-five thousand?"

"Mom," I said, unable to stop myself from stopping her. "We could buy a real house for this much. Think about it."

"Not now, Dominick," she said.

"Seventy-five thousand?" Roget asked.

"Mom," I whispered. "Let him have it."

Finally she seemed to hear me and hesitated. Her hand stayed by her side.

"Going once," Roget said. "Going twice."

My mother bit her upper lip but kept her hand still.

"It's better this way," I said, deciding to ease up on the opposite routine for a while.

"Sold. To Mr. Vito Maletti."

My mother put her head down and turned toward the car. Her crazy plan had been let loose into the air like a balloon caught in the wind. She untied her plastic kerchief and slipped it inside the pocket of her raincoat. When we climbed into the Pinto, she pulled a gum wrapper out of the unused ashtray. Inside the silver paper was the piece of Juicy Fruit she had been chewing when we arrived. She stuck the piece back in her mouth and put the wrapper in the ashtray again. Whenever I bought gum, I blew through the pack in under an hour. But my mother worked on one piece forever, saving it in a wrapper between chews as if there were an international gum shortage.

We drove out of the parking lot of the new Peaceful Pizza, where Vito was shaking hands and that girl with the picket sign was packing up her protest. My mother stayed quiet all the way across town, and I rolled down the window and let in the earthy, late-morning air. The rain had stopped, and somewhere, someone had managed to start burning leaves. Finally my mother said, "All I want is a little round thing on the wall so I can control my own heat. I want a kitchen where I can keep the trash can beneath the sink."

Ever since she had heard about the auction, my mother had been going on about the flower boxes she wanted to put in every window, the wicker planters she planned to buy, the braided throw rugs for the hard-wood floors. But she never mentioned removing the bars from the cells or dealing with any of the other setbacks that came with buying a police station. "Uncle Donald would have to have invented a time machine for us to afford that place," I said.

My mother twisted the knob on the radio, and the car filled with noise from a football game. The Eagles versus the Patriots. Or the Saints versus the Cardinals. I could never keep them straight anymore. "Well," she said, "if those fellas hadn't shown up, we would have gotten the place for dirt cheap."

We were on River Road, about to pass the new police station. My mother kept her eyes on the road, but I stared out at the green rectangle of lawn, the shining windows, the three-story layout. An officer stood on the tarred river of sidewalk—hand to his forehead like a visor or a salute—gazing up at the face of the building as if awestruck by the design. Now *that place* looked like it could have been a home. Seeing it made me feel sorry for my mother.

"You can save the money for something else," I said.

My mother reached for the radio again and pushed the hard black buttons. Classical. News. More football. Weather. Nothing seemed to make her happy, so she turned it off. The road snaked its way through the center of Holedo. Redbrick buildings on either side. A gold flashing light winked at us as we skirted beneath. The skeletal frames of last year's town Christmas decorations—two angels and a star completely stripped of their garland—blew back and forth in the wind. The air from outside smelled different here. No more burning leaves; now it was factory smoke. I rolled up my window, hushing the sound of spin-ning tires.

"I'm going to tell you something, but you have to promise not to tell your father," she said.

Sharing secrets with my father was never a temptation. Besides, when my mother made up her mind to trust me, my word was a mere formality. "I promise."

She glanced away from the road toward me. Her face looked puffy still, and I thought of moist air trapped beneath her skin. The tight fist of hair behind her head left her ear naked and exposed. Without jewelry, the pierced hole was a miniature mouth opening toward me in a yawn. "I have a little money put aside," she said. "Not enough to buy a decent house yet. And God knows I'd never get a mortgage with your father's job. But if something should happen to me, I want you to use it for yourself."

I thought of her life in New Mexico, a waitressing job in San Francisco she had told me about, Truman. She once said that she left her old lives quietly, like she was ducking out of a party without telling the host or the other guests good-bye. I imagined myself as one of those hosts, eyeing her from the corner, watching her gather her coat and shuffle toward the door. "Are you going to leave?" I asked, as a worried feeling mushroomed inside me.

"I'm not going anywhere, Dominick. I just want you to know I have a little security blanket for you and me in case of an emergency."

We were pulling onto our street, Dwight Avenue. Row after row of rented three-story houses with jigsaw-puzzle roofs and torn-screened porches. Our apartment was in the only five-story complex on the block, built on an old neighborhood baseball field. Outdoor stairways led to each floor. The brown aluminum siding was streaked and stained from the leaky gutters. For the first time I saw this place the way my mother must have. Mustard instead of sunny orange. The muddy brown of a pond when she wanted the blue of a sea.

I've lived all over the world, Edie said in my head. *Holedo is just as good a place as any.*

"Why did you come here?" I asked my mother as she scoped out a spot in the lot behind our building.

"What do you mean? I married your father, and we moved here together."

My next question could have pushed her secret sharing session a bit far. Still, I asked, "But why did you marry him?"

We parked in front of an overloaded Dumpster, and my mother

turned off the car. A sign said NO PARKING, but we could get away with it until Monday. There were empty milk cartons scattered at our wheels. Cream soda and RC cans. A flattened bag of chips. A pigeon clenched a thin disk of potato in its beak, complete with green slivers of chive. My mother sighed. Her exhalations were often heavy, weighted things, the sound an old woman might make if she looked back unhappily on her life with no more time to make things right. "It's like those breakfasts in New Mexico," she said.

Here we go again, I thought.

But then she said, "When I met your father, I thought he was the most handsome man I had ever seen. He loved to have a good time. Driving around on his motorcycle together. Staying out all night. Before him my life was such a tangled mess, and everything with him was one big party. I guess that's exactly what I needed."

I tried to wrap my mind around the image of my mother on a motorcycle, staying out till the sun came up. It made me wonder if she changed personalities when she changed lives. After all, she was always warning me to be careful on my ten-speed. I asked her what any of that had to do with those breakfasts.

"I only mean that your father was perfect for a certain time and place in my life. But taking it further didn't exactly work the way I had hoped. We had you, which was the best thing that ever happened to me. But I thought your father would change when our lives did. Settle down. I thought we'd buy a real house—"

She stopped, and I knew she must have been thinking about the police station, on its way to being a pizza place instead of her dream home.

"Looking back," she said, staring out the car window past the metal Dumpster, spilling over with its dirty insides, "looking back, I realize I should have paid attention to the signs."

"Signs?" I said, not getting her.

"Signs. Life lays them right in front of you. One. Two. Three. All you have to do is look, Dominick. You'll see as you get older. If you step back and take in the world around you, there's always some sort of guidepost. Something telling you which way to go. He drank too much then. He lied then. But I ignored it all because I was so . . . so . . . hungry for him. It was like a voice from the future telling me how our life would be, but I didn't want to hear. So I tuned it out, and here I am."

Her voice had dropped to a whisper, and she fingered her car keys that still hung from the ignition. Her key chain was a miniature globe, and she shook the world from side to side.

I was going to ask her about the tangled mess before my father that I assumed was code language for Truman, when outside the car a pigeon flapped its wings in a scurry of noise and feathers. The motion startled my mother, and I could tell by the look on her face that the sharing spell was broken. She wasn't going to tell me any more about following signs or Truman. "I'll find a way to make things better," she said, patting my knee and putting an end to our discussion. "You'll see."

Even with her hopeful words, I could tell she felt lost in her life as she put her gum back in the wrapper and stuck it in the ashtray again for later. We got out of the car and made our way up the stairs to our second-floor apartment. I thought of the sappy eight-tracks she sometimes played when she was down. The singers were nameless to me, but one of their rhymes drifted to mind now. *"I looked at my life today. I wish I was happy living this way."* The words were hopelessly melodramatic, enough to make me want to snap her out of it. "Which jail cell would I have slept in?"

"Well," she said, jumping right into the joke despite herself, "I would have taken the master cell. And you would have the one down the hall."

"Don't forget the guest cell," I said as she fumbled with the keys.

"Of course, we'd have to fingerprint any overnight visitors to protect ourselves."

By the time my mother got the door open, we were both laughing. The apartment smelled like the inside of a defrosted refrigerator. Cold metal and old food. "Maybe it was a little half-baked," she said. "But you can't blame me for trying."

"What was half-baked?" my father asked. He was sitting at the kitchen table with the *Holedo Herald* and a beer, his aviator glasses halfway down his nose, like he was too cool to bother taking them off.

Since he had been on the road during the week, my mother and I had developed new personalities for when he was and wasn't around. The two of us were downshifting, fast. "Oh, nothing," my mother said. Lately it took her longer to switch from my side to his when he showed. But she always made it there. "I thought you were away until Sunday."

Before he could answer, the phone rang. The noise mixed with the sound of the football game droning from the television. Rather than leaving the black-and-white on the shelf in the living room, my father had a habit of carrying the TV with him to the kitchen. Sunday mornings he liked to plug the thing in the bathroom and disappear in there with the newspapers. At the moment it was perched in the middle of the table, aluminum foil dangling from the bent-hanger antenna. His idea of good reception. On the second ring my father stood to answer the phone. "It's for you, Terry."

She took the receiver. After a pause she said, "Win some, lose some."

Probably the Bingo Lady herself, just off the set of her prime-time show. This was my chance to cut out. Headphones and The Who were waiting in my room. Leon and I always played "The Acid Queen" and "Pinball Wizard" at top volume.

"How you doing, son?" my father said.

I turned back, snagged into a conversation. The smell of his trip was all around him—rest stops and diesel fuel, too long behind the wheel of a truck. A voice in my head told me he was the visitor we needed to fingerprint.

"Fine," I said.

"School?"

"Okay," I said.

"Job yet?"

"I'm fifteen," I said. "Not old enough."

Since our little chat was going nowhere fast, he gave me a light punch in the arm, hoping for a wrestling match like we used to have. I thought of all those times when I was a kid and he'd let me pin him to the floor. When I least expected it, he'd break free and tickle me until I laughed and screamed in surrender. It seemed like years since we'd done that routine. But I was in no mood for a fake fight when so many real ones were happening beneath the surface.

"That was Officer Roget," my mother said when she hung up. She gave me a nervous look. Like her secret stash, her plan to buy the station had been hidden from my father as well. "He called to thank me for the volunteer work I did last month."

"Volunteer work," my father said. "What did you do for that crook?"

"You know," my mother said, her voice lilting the way it did when she lied. "This and that."

I could tell by the way she busied herself in the kitchen—wiping the circles of dried coffee from the stove top, untangling the crimson balls of fringe that dangled from the curtains—that she was still having trouble adjusting to his unexpected arrival.

"Well, then," my father said. "Since everybody is doing a lot of nothing around here, you'll both be glad to know the reason I'm home."

My mother tugged on the sleeves of her cardigan and made her way across the kitchen. She was forever moving cereal boxes and soup cans from one shelf to another, trying to find the best fit. Now she pulled down tomato soup and sank the sharp tooth of the can opener into the lid, twisting it open. She dumped the rust-colored blob into a pot on the stove.

"How come you're home?" I asked.

He looked at me and grinned. "I quit my job."

"Quit?" my mother said.

"What's the matter?" My father stretched his stomach out into a hard balloon and scratched, teasing her. "Can't I stay home and free-load, too?"

"Very funny," she said.

The thing was, it could have been funny. Not fall down, but a *Partridge*

Family sort of laugh. My father didn't understand, though, that his benders and trips away muffled things somehow. It was difficult for my mother and me to relax and act natural when neither of us knew when he'd vanish again.

"Let's just say that Kramer woman is one fucked-up broad."

At the mention of Edie, my mother turned toward the sink. She poured out the last of his beer and tossed it in the trash by the stove. I would have pulled the can out and stomped it flat the way I used to like to do, but I was dying for the Edie story.

"Please stop talking like that in front of Dominick," my mother said.

"He's heard it before. Right, son?"

I nodded yes to my father. But when my mother looked, I shook my head no.

She asked, "What about money?"

"I'll find something. Maybe one of those cross-country driving jobs."

I saw my mother's face wilt, and I knew she must have been thinking about all those signs she had ignored so many years ago. But there was nothing I could do. Their conversation would loop round and round for hours. My mother would keep asking her tentative, worried questions but never get the real deal. In a week or so he'd be on to some better-than-ever dream job. There would be no news about Edie. I was ready to retreat to my room when I spotted an envelope among the empty fruit bowl, the newspaper, and the television set. My name written in block letters across the seal. "What's this?" I asked.

"In the mailbox when I got home," my father said. "It must have been hand-delivered, because there's no stamp. Maybe you've got an admirer."

I peeled it open, splitting my name in two.

> Dominick,
> I need to see you.
> E.

"Well," my father said. "Who's it from?"

I tried to fold the paper but nervously crumpled it instead. "Gritta," I said, shoving it into my pocket. "Gritta Alexander."

"Well, Terry," my father said, "it looks like our boy's got a girl."

I left my mother to deal with him and headed for my room. Door locked, I unfolded the paper—already creased from the short time in my pocket. "Dominick, I need to see you. E." No doubt that the "E." was Edie. I held her handwriting to my nose, hoping for that milk-and-skin smell, the jasmine of her house. Instead I breathed in the first day of school, homework. I puckered my lips against the *E* of her name. I stuck out my tongue and licked the tiny dot beside it. I couldn't believe she had finally made contact with me—actually driven over to my apartment and put a letter in the mailbox—after all the months I had spent swelling with thoughts of her and of our kiss, wondering if there could ever be more between us. Maybe she had been waiting for my father to be gone from her life before coming to me. Maybe now that he'd quit, things could begin with us.

All that mattered now was that she wanted—*needed*—to see me.

In my drawer I kept a tightly rolled joint I had sneaked from Leon months back. Most of the time we stuck to booze, mixing our own lethal concoction from his mother's black-lacquered liquor cabinet. A few weekends before, it was rum, vodka, whiskey, vermouth, a bit of Dr Pepper, and a splash of OJ. We called it the Holedo Hell-Raiser and promptly puked our guts out after chugging the whole thing from an old milk carton. Whenever we wanted to raise hell but thought our stomachs needed some R&R, Leon scored a dime bag of pot. I had been saving some for just this occasion, in hopes that if I ever got the chance to be alone with Edie, a few puffs of a joint would help open her up again. Before closing the drawer, I caught a glimpse of a stack of baseball cards I used to collect with my father. Something made me pick them up, flip through the stack. Once upon a time I was pretty good at remembering the players and their stats. Wilbur Wood: relief pitcher for the Chicago White Sox, 22 wins, 13 losses, 1.91 ERA. Brooks Robinson: third baseman for the Baltimore Orioles, 2 homers in the '70 Series, .429 batting average, .810 slugging percentage. Billy Williams of the Chicago Cubs, lead player in the National League a few seasons back, 42 homers, 129 RBIs. When I used to whip out those names and numbers, I knew it made my father proud. But remembering all those stats was as pointless and dull to me as doing math homework. And somewhere along the way I stopped bothering to keep up. The players and their numbers became a blur in my head, just some faces on a bunch of cards that still smelled like bubblegum. I tossed them back into my drawer and was about to close it again when I spotted the return address I had copied from Uncle Donald's last letter to my mother.

DONALD F. BIADOGIANO

97 BLEECKER STREET, APT. 3B

NEW YORK, NEW YORK 10014

Every time I saw it behind my gray sweat socks and blue-banded underwear, I thought of Truman. He was part of me, really. A half brother living almost two hundred miles away, and I had made up my mind to find out more. For the moment, though, I wanted to focus on Edie. I closed the drawer and went back to the kitchen.

"Shoes," my father was saying. "I'll give that lady shoes. She's lucky she doesn't get my size ten right in her teeth."

He wrapped his arms around my mother's waist as she stood at the stove, filling a bowl with soup. She was still trying to pry out the details of his job, not realizing I was closer to the answer. "Where's my girl?" he asked her, kissing the back of her neck. "Where's my girl who used to like to have fun?"

"Later," I said and headed down the stairs to my ten-speed.

My mother opened the kitchen window and called to me like I was a little kid. "Do you want something to eat?"

I stared up at her soft face, a burst of white against the brown, BB-punctured aluminum siding. This was the choice my father must have faced all the time. My mother and her warm food, quiet voice, and careful movements. Or Edie and her big house, big tits, and big money.

"I'll grab something later," I said, climbing on my bike and pedaling away in the damp air.

As I rode toward Edie's, I wondered if it would be as easy to kiss her this time as it was the first. The pot would help. I looked down at the black shoes she had given me. Day after day I slipped my warm feet into their soft leather. Now they were scuffed from so much wear. Part of me wanted to turn back and give the shoes a quick polish before showing up at Edie's. But my heart was beating too hard to turn back. I pushed the shoes out of my mind and thought of licking the teeth my father wanted to kick. The image of my wet tongue against Edie's hard white smile kept me pedaling up and down side streets until I reached the top of the hill near her house.

In daylight the Victorian looked even more decrepit than last time. Leaves from the red maple had dried, curled, and fallen to where they lay unraked on the dead hairs of grass. The once-white rocks of the drive-way were speckled with black, like hundreds of cavitied teeth crunching beneath my bicycle tires. I stopped pedaling and caught my breath. When I took a step toward her porch, I felt choked with nervousness. I wondered if I should have rushed over here like this, if crossing enemy lines like my mother always did with my father was a mistake. After all, Edie had lied to me that night about my father not being in her bed. Every time I thought of that, I told myself I should be pissed at her.

But she *needs* to see me, I reminded myself. With those words in mind I walked to the door, kicking at the shavings of yellow paint that lit-tered the porch. Against the dreariness of everything else, it looked as if pieces of sun had fallen and landed at Edie's doorstep for her to sweep away. A lion's-face knocker had turned red with rust and blank in the eyes. I gave the sorry-looking guy a clank or two, then waited.

"Edie," I called when no one answered. "It's me, Dominick Pindle."

A bird squawked in the sky, but no noise came from the house. The place had the feeling of people coming and going. Wandering in and out, like I had last summer. A rest area off the highway. A cheap motel.

Finally I put my hand on the knob and turned. It wouldn't move, so I walked around back to where my father's truck had been parked that night. This time there was Edie's Cadillac. Edie was turned away from me, loading a tiny red Chiclet of a suitcase into the trunk. After all these months apart, I couldn't believe the sight of her. She wore a long-sleeved T-shirt that hung down to her knees. Under the blue material she could have been naked, since all I could see were her bare legs and flip-flopped feet.

"Hello, Edie," I said, using a voice I had been practicing. It was the well-honed deep echo of a cave. The sound of a solemn male soldier.

"Dominick," she said, turning around. She reached out and hugged me. I felt her arms slip under my arms, wrap around my back, and pull me to her. Her tits and stomach pressed against me. "You're here sooner than I expected," she said, and I could feel the heat of her breath against my neck.

My body went into overload—my chest burned, my mouth felt sticky, my dick went hard. I had hoped and hoped that Edie would want to be near me again but was never really sure how she would act when we met a second time. In that moment I knew our kiss had changed her, too. And this is what I told myself: Edie had come to her senses and realized my father was a fuck-up.

When she let go of me, I could see a purple puff of skin under her left eye, like the bruises Leon got after a fight. The flash of color seemed to belong on him. But on Edie the look was like smeared makeup, messy and all wrong. I heard my father say *Size ten right in her teeth.*

"What happened?"

"Do I have to tell you?" she said, closing the trunk. "I'm sure you can put two and two together."

The bruise was split in the middle by a sharp line of blood. I thought of the painted lips of a doll, deep red dried into a smile. Edie smelled of hampers and used clothing. Her hair was wormy and unwashed.

"Are you going somewhere?" I asked, keeping my voice low.

"Yeah," she said in her raspy, rock-band voice. "Fucking crazy."

I laughed, unsure whether she meant it to be funny.

"I'm going away for a few days," she said. "But I needed to see you first. Do you want to come inside for a while?"

I followed her up the short stack of stairs to the house. A seashell wind chime hung by the door, clanking out hollow noises in the breeze. The kitchen had fallen apart since my last visit. The stove, cluttered with dirty pots. The windows, fingerprinted and cloudy. The table looked as if it had been interrupted during a meal—two plates, half emptied of fish sticks and french fries.

Edie brushed her fingers through her mess of hair. Every one of her long nails was gone. All of them bitten down to nothing, like her pinkie nail that first night. "Do you mind if I take a minute to freshen up? Last time you found me in my nightgown. And this time I look like a rag doll. I should at least clean myself up."

"I'm just glad to see you," I said, grateful that she gave me an opening to compliment her. "Take your time."

When she was safely down the hall, I looked for some sign of my father. The desk in the corner was piled with pink and yellow bills the color of baby clothes: $5,614.10 owed to D.T.E. Manufacturers in New Jersey; $2,952.72 owed to Galepsy Dye Incorporated in Alabama; $3,982.19 owed to Marathon Truck Rental right here in Holedo. FINAL NOTICE. FINAL NOTICE. FINAL NOTICE. Underneath all that, a blue doctor's bill asked Edie for $350 even, the "Services Rendered" column neatly torn from the page. The bills of a rich lady, I thought. But why hadn't she paid?

My stomach grumbled, and I made my way to the fridge. Empty except for club soda, salad dressing, jelly, and assorted crap. If my father had been spending a lot of time here, there would have been Schlitz or Bud. Maybe Edie dumped it all out the way my mother sometimes did. I wandered to the hallway to check out the shoes and to see about that old sneaker I had left behind. But there was just a matted carpet, the color of a brown egg, which led to the door. No high heels. No cleats. No slippers.

Edie's footsteps shuffled about the other side of the house. A drawer opened and closed. I went back to the kitchen and picked up the phone to dial, carefully muffling the rotary as it wheeled its way back to zero.

"Hello." It was Leon. I pictured him in his basement bedroom, doing flies on his bed to build his chest muscles, stopping to grab the phone.

I whispered, "You will never guess where I am."

"In a fucking jail cell," he said.

"No. I talked the old lady out of buying the station. So guess where I am."

"Home, popping the pimples on your ass," Leon said.

"Try Edie fucking Kramer's, nipplehead." Even if the bruise on her face had distracted me from wanting her at the moment, I could still act like I did.

"Pindle. You're not starting this little fantasy again, are you?"

"It's the truth."

"I'd love to hear more, but I'm on my way to fuck Mrs. Lint."

Lint was the blond algebra teacher who had flunked Leon last year. He was always saying he'd love to give her an F right back. I pictured Leon at home with his mother and her tall skinny glass of vodka tonic clinking with ice cubes as she smoked her mentholated Salems. I hated when Mrs. Diesel's bitchy personality completely rubbed off on him. He barely believed me the first time I told him about kissing Edie. No way would he believe again, unless I had proof. "Wait fifteen minutes and call here. When Edie answers, ask for me. Then you'll see."

I heard her padding down the hallway so I settled the plan with Leon and hung up. Edie must have made a pit stop, though, because the house was quiet again. When she didn't show, I made my way over to the back of the kitchen. Through a narrow door I could see a sunroom I hadn't noticed before. The mattress from the basement covered the center of the white wooden floor. On top lay a zigzagged blanket, some pointy high heels, and a scattering of pillows. I felt the heat of the room press against my skin when I stepped inside.

"The light's nice in here," Edie said from behind me. "I put the mattress in this room so I could nap in the afternoon."

When I turned around, she looked more like the Edie that Leon and I always talked about. Brushed blond hair that curled at the ends. Barn-red lipstick. A cloud of sweet perfume. She still wore the loose shirt, only now there were black pants beneath.

"Have a seat," Edie said.

I sat on the edge of the mattress, and she did the same. Between us there was a single unstrapped shoe, red as a cooked lobster. I wanted to ask what she needed but decided to go with the flow the way Leon always said to. This was my chance to be cool.

"Do you get high?" I asked, trying to sound casual.

"I used to," she said. "But I've decided to cut back on my vices. You know, clean up my act."

Just my luck. Everything was all wrong—Edie's bruises, her messy house, and her clean act. Still, I kept trying. "Too bad," I said, tempting her. "I have some good stuff."

"Well, by all means light up. Just because I'm turning into a nun doesn't mean you have to."

"Really?" I said. My voice sounded more stretched and thin than I would have liked. It felt stupid to light up and smoke in front of her, but I couldn't back out. Besides, once she saw all the fun I was having, she was bound to change her mind. I took the joint and the Doghouse matchbook from my pocket. Edie pulled an ashtray from the shelf. A blue-scaled ceramic fish with a wide-open mouth. Edie and the fish watched as I lit the tip and toked. "Monster," I said when I exhaled. I had heard someone call it that in a movie once. It sounded pretty cool, so I said it again. "Monster."

"I bet," Edie said. She kept switching her position on the mattress, folding her legs beneath her on one side, then another. I wanted her to get comfortable so she could concentrate on us.

Thinking of Leon, I looked at the clock in the kitchen. Almost one. The whole day seemed like a blur now—the ridiculous auction, my mother and her secret stash, my father quitting his job. "I wonder what Officer Roget wanted when he called," I said out loud without meaning to.

"Who?" Edie said.

"Oh," I said. My tongue had grown an inch, gained a pound. My head felt spongy. "Never mind."

I took a couple more hits and shook my head, trying to focus on Edie's lips. Good old Mr. Bruise below her eye kept getting my attention instead. It seemed strange my father had let loose on her like that. For all the talking he did, I had never seen him hit anybody. Not me. Not my mother. Still, Edie's eye was proof enough. "I'm sorry about your face," I said.

"Don't be. You didn't do it."

In the reflection of the window I caught a glimpse of myself. My face was the wide-eyed, scrappy kid's face in the Boys' Club commercial. Only it was stretched like a caricature of myself around the end of the joint. T-shirts and sweaters never looked right on me, so I covered up with the same gray sweatshirt, the hood carried on my back like an empty, useless pouch. I decided I should anchor myself in a conversation before my mind drifted off into that reflection. "So what do you need me for?" I asked.

Edie tilted her head and looked at me. She was beautiful despite her beat-up face. "I wouldn't have snuck that note in your mailbox if I had someone else to talk to," she said.

"*Yo comprendo,*" I said and laughed at my Spanish. Edie didn't seem to think it was funny, though, so I pulled my lips together. Something in my head was shrinking, fading away. I watched the thin line of smoke twist its way through the air between us until Edie spoke again. "Do you love your parents?" she said finally.

That was not the type of question I had expected her to ask. "Yeah," I said. "I guess."

"Both of them?" she asked.

"Yes," I said. Then I thought about it. "I guess I love one more."

"Your mom?" she said.

No matter how stoned I was, I wouldn't let Edie trash my mom. I could confuse the old lady with opposites. I could take off when she was making lunch. But that was me. "Yes," I said, defensive.

"I don't blame you," she said. "Mothers are usually easier to deal with. And your father can be a real prick."

Trashing him didn't bug me so much. In fact, it made me feel like I had pulled something over on him. "Yeah," I said. "A fucking prick."

"Do you think he and your mom will stay married?" she asked.

I thought of the conversation in the car with my mother. "Yes," I told her. "They have big plans. They want to buy a house. Drive around on his motorcycle. Make breakfasts together."

"Breakfasts?" Edie said. "Motorcycle? I didn't know he had one."

"Yup," I said, sounding smug because I knew more about him than she did, even though I'd just found out about the motorcycle an hour ago, and even though he didn't own it anymore.

"Well, I guess there's a lot about him I never knew," Edie said. "That's no surprise."

"Don't feel bad," I told her, taking another hit of the joint. The smoke in my lungs left me with a confused confidence. I decided to say whatever came to mind. "I'm here now."

"I'm glad for that," Edie said, leaning toward me. "Dominick, can I show you something?"

This was it. We were going to kiss again. Maybe even fuck. "Show me," I said. "Show me anything."

Edie knelt in front of me and put her hands on the bottom of her shirt. I swallowed hard. The pot had left my head feeling cinder-blocked and messy. For months I had waited for this moment, but I still didn't feel ready. She needed to look more like the women Leon and I checked out in *Hustler* and *Penthouse*. Splayed and nipple-pinched, gazing off into nowhere like the eyes of that fish ashtray. Instead Edie stared at me intently, her face marked by that bruise. Signs of my father's love all over her. "Are you ready?" she asked.

No more pot, I thought. "I'm ready," I said.

Slowly she lifted her shirt. Her skin was creamy and white beneath. Her stomach fatter than I had imagined. I thought of the hard belly my father had made in the kitchen a few hours ago. Now the gesture seemed funny after all, and I laughed. Edie ignored the sound and kept pulling the material up, stopping before her breasts. "Why are you stopping?" I asked.

"What do you mean?" she said. "This is what I wanted to show you."

"Your stomach," I said, trying to sound appreciative. "It's beautiful."

"Dominick," she said and pulled my hand toward her. Sparks ran between us. She pressed my palm and fingers against her belly. "I'm pregnant."

The sponge in my brain squeezed itself out and left me suddenly sober. My hand yanked back on its own. That SHARON TATE MURDERED headline popped into my head for a split second, then vanished. "Pregnant?" I said.

"Pregnant," she repeated.

All at once it came to me in one of those "boy meets girl" kind of stories. Only mine went like this: Woman has affair with man and gets knocked up. Man already has a wife, and a kid to boot. Man beats the shit out of her. Woman picks herself up and contacts man's kid. Here the story fell apart. Woman wants kid to . . . to what exactly?

"Why are you telling me this?" I asked, not caring how my voice came out. Shallow and quivering. Young and confused. Fucked up all the way.

"I told you. I don't have anyone else."

"So get a shrink," I said.

Edie rolled the shirt back over her belly. Five months, I guessed. Maybe a hundred. I had no fucking clue when it came to this baby shit. "Why don't you get rid of it?" I said.

"I'm keeping the baby," she told me. "People in this town think I'm a whore anyway. So now they'll have their proof. But I'll have my child."

I snuffed the joint out in the fish's mouth. I thought the sucker looked happy. "So why do you need me?"

"Forget it," Edie said. Her eyes were moist and mapped with tiny red veins. The smoke. Or maybe tears.

I let out a huff. "This just isn't what I expected."

"I understand," Edie said, rubbing her stomach.

But I don't think she truly did. She had no idea I wanted to kiss her again. Maybe even more. There was no use bringing that up now. My father had won after all. "So what can I do for you?"

"I need you to talk to your father for me," she said.

"And tell him what?"

"Tell him I need his help," she said. "Financial support."

I laughed. "If you remember, he quit his job working for you. He doesn't have a dime. And you've got this big house. Your business."

"The business is dead," she said. "He helped piss away every last penny."

I thought of those bills the color of baby clothes. FINAL NOTICE. FINAL NOTICE. FINAL NOTICE. "You've got your house," I said.

"I can't pay the mortgage anymore, and my ex-husband refuses to lend me money. Listen, if you could just talk to him. Explain my situation. I need some help getting back on my feet. Believe me, I'd rather get a bank loan than beg from that bastard. But the bank would laugh me right out of the building."

I thought of my mother's money, hidden somewhere in case of an emergency. No doubt she would keep her fifties and hundreds at the bottom of one of her music boxes—a plastic ballerina twirling every time my mother made her deposit. I thought of the half brother I already had living on Bleecker Street. If I helped Edie, I would know this brother or sister. I wouldn't have to wonder. My mind flip-flopped like that fish come to life on dry land: I could lend her some dough for a bit and she could pay me back down the road without my mother knowing.

No, I couldn't.

Yes, I could.

I couldn't. I could.

I couldn't.

Just then Edie reached her hand up and touched the dried slit of her wound. She rubbed gently with her pinkie and naked ring finger. I pictured all five of my father's fingers curled into a tight fist, swinging into her soft face. I hated him for doing that to her.

"I could—" I blurted as the "couldn't" faded to black.

"Talk to your dad?" Edie said.

"No. I could lend you some money."

"Dominick," she said. "That's very sweet. But I need real help. A lot of money."

I wondered how much I could get away with. After all, my mother would never really use it. "Listen," I said, figuring the math would come later. "We both know my father won't give you anything. So let me loan you some cash for a while. You'll be surprised at what I can come up with."

The phone rang—sharp and unfamiliar. Leon. Suddenly our plan seemed as crazy as one of my mother's. I didn't want him to know about this part of my life anymore. Edie wasn't a *Penthouse* girl or *Hustler* whore. She was choiceless and sad, like so many other real-life women seemed to be. I wanted to let the phone ring and ring. But Edie went to the kitchen where I could see her and answered. "Dominick Pindle?" she said like a question, eyeing me from the doorway. Her free hand pressed to her cheek.

A faraway voice in my head said, *He's not here. He is riding his bike in the parking lot behind the Doghouse. He is home eating canned tomato soup in front of the tube with his mother.* I looked at Edie and shook my head no. I slid my index and middle fingers across my throat in the way that means "cut." It looked like I was slashing the skin there, the breathing tube beneath. Again and again I slashed. Shook my head no.

"You must have the wrong number," Edie said. "There's no one here by that name."

When she hung up, I looked at her—bruises, belly, and all. "If I get you the money," I told her, my voice angled and serious, "it's just between you and me."

Three

Four hundred fifty dollars and twelve cents from her music box.

*Two thousand nine hundred twenty-five dollars from between
her mattress and box spring.*

*Three thousand from a Thom McAn shoe box in the
back of her closet.*

*A steady stream of hundreds from under the two-tone
beige carpet in her bedroom.*

The radiator broke in our apartment, and my mother took to wearing her coat all day and night—sometimes even to bed. Walking around the kitchen, covered up in an ankle-length black wool number, she looked like the angel of death. Chalky white face. Hard, chapped lips that peeled and shed layers like two miniature snakes. The soles of her white socks gone gray because she'd been wearing them so long. "You're giving me the creeps," I told her as she steadied a teakettle over her mug and poured. Water funneled down in a great steamy release. I thought of that kids' rhyme:

This is my handle.
This is my spout.
Tip me over and pour me out.

I wondered if someday soon I would sing that song to Edie's baby.

"It's freezing in here," my mother said. "I need to cover up."

She was right about the cold. Outside our kitchen window, crooked fingers of ice reflected the blue light of the moon, frozen right down to the sill like igloo prison bars. I made an O with my mouth and forced a burst of air from my lungs. My breath was a tissuey cloud before me, and then it vanished. As dishonest as I had been since I made the money deal with Edie two months ago, I half expected to breathe fire. Horns and a pitchfork—that was me. "Why don't you call the landlord for once, instead of Marnie?"

"I did call," she said quietly. "He's coming next Monday."

"He told you that weeks ago."

"Dominick," my mother said, gathering her mug and plate of jelly-covered Ritz crackers. "I'll get it fixed."

I decided to lay off for a while, since she seemed on the brink of a nervous breakdown. My father's new job shipping Christmas trees south had kept him away from home all through the holidays. Now that it was January, he claimed to be delivering the nonsalables to a lumberyard outside Chicago. You'd think my mother would've been happy for the break. I was. But his long absence had practically totaled her. Watery-eyed and runny-nosed, she moved around the frigid, metallic air of our apartment almost looking for a reason to cry. The brown scabs of grease that couldn't be scoured from the stovetop. The clogged toilet that gasped and burped as she plunged away. Instead of surrendering the scouring pad or plunger, my mother absently carried her failed weapons around the apartment after her battles. Her eyes poured tears down her face until eventually she fled to her room to call Marnie.

"We should move to Acapulco or someplace warm," I said into the frozen air, hoping it would ease things between us. After all, I needed to make nice if I hoped to get into her bedroom tonight and pull off one of my financial transactions before sneaking over to Edie's.

"Funny you should mention faraway places," my mother told me. "Because I'm thinking about taking a little trip."

That same old she's-going-to-leave-you feeling blistered inside me and spread like poison. Here I was taking care of her while she went to pieces over my father, and she was secretly planning a trip without me. I had my own secret, I reminded myself. I had Edie. "Good for you," I said. "Are you going to visit Truman?"

My mother shook her head no at his name. "Somewhere different this time. If your father can disappear, why can't I take off for a week or two?"

I felt a last bit of blistering but fought it off. Her words were bold, but the way she spoke—tight-lipped, gazing at me through the genie-smoke of steam that rose from her mug—left me feeling like she wanted my approval. "Let me guess," I said. "New Mexico?"

"Nothing's definite. But I've already talked to Marnie about moving in while I'm gone."

No. Fucking. Way. I wasn't going to blow this vacation eating Kraft Macaroni and Cheese and watching monster movies every night the way Marnie liked to do. Whenever any of her pets died—which was often because she lived near Route 67 but couldn't stand the thought of keeping an animal trapped inside or tied to a chain—Marnie holed up at our place, since her apartment felt lonely after the loss. Last year she was dealt what she called a "double blow" when a truck hit her two dogs, Fred and Ginger. She spent a whole week on our couch, hogging the television and eating cheese noodles to ease her pain. The year before that, her cat Milky had been nailed on the highway, too, and we had to go through the same pathetic routine.

"I don't need her to change my diapers," I said. "Just tell the old gal to stop by once in a while to make sure I haven't frozen to death."

My mother stared at me with that vacant, dam-about-to-burst look she sported all the time since my father had hit the road. Her lips pinched and twisted up tight, like the knot of a balloon. I made a rigor mortis face, tightening the skin on my neck and making giant moons out of my eyes, trying to get her to laugh. No such luck.

"We'll talk about it later," she said, her bruise-colored jelly wiggling atop her crackers. "I'm going to my room to call Marnie."

"Wait." This was my last chance. I hopped up from the chair where I sat at the table. "Your room is the coldest one in the whole apartment. Why don't you call from the kitchen?"

"Don't you want the kitchen?" she asked.

"I'm going to hang out in my room, then head down to Leon's to warm up later."

My mother considered the plan a moment, picked up the phone, and settled in at the table. "It sure is drafty in there," she said, dialing.

On my way down the hall I listened to the steady click-click-click of the rotary wheeling its way back to zero. I wondered how anyone could possibly have that much to say to Marnie and why it was always so urgent. That's what bothered me most about my mother: Marnie and my father always came first. "I'm bleeding to death," I might say. And my mother would tell me, "Hold on until I call Marnie." Or "That's how I feel whenever your father disappears." I let those scenarios bounce around my brain until a pissed-off feeling took hold. A fat dose of anger always made these cash withdrawals easier. Even though I knew Edie was going to pay me back, I felt guilty sometimes. But the way I saw it, Edie had been fucked over by my father even worse than my mother had been.

I waited around the corner for the right moment, listening to scraps of her conversation.

"I told Dominick I'm going away," she said. "I've got to call about the ticket and make this final."

Her voice was firm and serious, not the anticipating squeal of someone leaving for vacation. It made me wonder if Truman was involved in this after all. I told myself to forget it. To think of Edie instead. She wasn't going anywhere. With a stretch of my neck I could see my mother at the kitchen table. She chewed an orange cracker and wrapped the phone wire around her shoulders and arms.

Tighter and tighter.

"You tried your best," my mother told Marnie after a long silence.

I was about to walk across the hall when she turned my way. I stepped back and waited.

"It's a hospital," she said. "Trust me. People have asked that question before."

I peeked again. This time she was facing the kitchen window.

All those icicles.

Figuring she was deep into another segment of Marnie's bingo hell, I made my move. The door opened in a quiet hush, and I closed it right behind me.

"She's not going to tell anyone. Don't worry," my mother said, carrying on.

A thin sliver of light from a streetlamp outside made its way through a crack in the shade, casting a dark shadow on the wall. The red-flowered sheets on her bed were twisted and tangled, her pillows were two dead lumps in the middle of her mattress. A draft of cold air rushed through the room, practically numbing my skin. Proof it really was cold in here, something I hadn't been quite sure of when I said it.

I peeled back the rug where I had been skimming money for the last two months. Ever since the radiator broke, most of the usual smells of our apartment—canned food, cooked beef, furniture polish—had been muted. But beneath the rug the musty earth scent was as strong as ever. I grabbed three stiff hundred-dollar bills and shoved them into the pocket of my sweatshirt. "Just a few Bennies," I said under my breath, thinking it sounded cool.

Here's how it worked: I always left the top bills in the stack untouched. In place of what I took, I stuck one-dollar bills or clipped coupons—an outlaw trick I had seen on *Adam-12*. I kept track of how much I had taken but never counted what was left. Knowing how close I was to zero would have been a total brain fuck. Besides, Edie had caught up on most of her bills and was making money stuffing envelopes and selling off her old furniture. She promised to start paying back the whole shebang in a few more weeks.

My mother would never even know it was gone.

I let the rug flap back into place like a lip pulled and let go. Even though I should have snuck out right away, I couldn't help reaching under the bed and taking out that picture of the man I knew was Truman's father. I didn't know what I expected to see there in the shot I had looked at a thousand times before. I stared down at the dark eyes, the tuft of black hair hanging over his forehead. I wondered if he looked anything like Truman. Someday soon, I kept telling myself, I was going to meet my brother. For the time being, I tucked the picture back into the box beneath my mother's bed and hightailed it out of there.

In the kitchen my mother had absently twisted the cord up to her neck. "I'll be at Leon's," I said, throwing on my bulky winter coat.

She kept talking to Marnie but waved good-bye.

Outside, it was practically tundra weather. One of those cold, cold nights that made my shoulders automatically scrunch to my neck in a way that would leave me stiff and sore later. "Colder than a witch's tit," my father would say. Whatever that meant. The ride to Edie's would be a bitch on my bicycle, but I kicked back the kickstand anyway. I was about to break into a fast pedal onto Dwight Avenue when I spotted Leon's mother across the parking lot. She fidgeted with her cigarette lighter and car keys at the same time—back and forth, not getting her cigarette lit or the door to her flinty Datsun unlocked.

"Hey, Leila," I called out over the wind. She liked it when people referred to her by her first name. Even Leon.

"How you doing, Dominick?" she said, finally getting her cigarette to burn. The red eye flashed at me when she puffed. "Where you off to?"

"Cumby's Mart to pick up food," I said. "Then to a friend's."

"You'll freeze on that shitty little bike. Get in the car and I'll drop you."

It turned out Leila was headed to the store anyway—and probably then to the packy, though she didn't mention that part. Riding in the car alongside her, glancing at her big-jawed face and don't-fuck-with-me stare, made me think of Leon. I hadn't been down to see him in at least a month. Ever since I had been hanging out with Edie, Leon's stories seemed predictable. A girl who blew him at the quarry. Some lady's bush he spied through a window. The cashier at Svelletski's who wanted him to lick her crotch clean. Who needed to listen to that crap when I had Edie all to myself? Maybe she wasn't my girlfriend, but the way I took care of her made me feel like we had something.

The first time I went to Edie's house with the money, I was smothered by my own nervousness. It felt like a date, or not a date exactly but like something official and adult was happening between us. Edie made dinner—two chicken pot pies from a box because she said she had no clue how to cook anything real. I loved the burning-hot crusts and mushy insides, so her lack of culinary talent was fine with me. As we sat in the silence of her house, I tried my best to make real conversation, like something you might hear on a TV date. I asked her where she was born and she told me, "Santa Monica, California." I asked her what she did for fun and she said, "I have dinner with you." Finally, when I asked what her sign was, Edie reached across the table and stroked my forearm. My sweatshirt sleeves were pulled up and my arms were the one place on my body where I had a lot of hair besides my head, so I didn't feel shy. "Dominick," she said, "you don't have to be so formal. It's me, remember. I feel like we've been through a whole lifetime together already." Technically it was only our third time together, but I knew exactly what she meant. Our history already seemed to add up to something solid: the night we met, the kiss in her basement, her letter in my mailbox, the hug she gave me when we saw each other again, her bruised face, the baby, the money. The details of our relationship left me feeling like our lives had always been webbed together. So I stopped asking my TV-date questions and settled into normal conversation.

We talked about a lot of things, but what I remembered most was this: She told me that for as long as she could remember, she had been a lonely person. She was an only child, but her mother had miscarried a baby boy the year before Edie was born. Sometimes she thought that if that boy was alive, if he weren't missing from her life, she wouldn't feel so alone. I opened my mouth to tell her about Truman, about the way I felt when my mother talked about starting a new life, but something made me stop. I decided not to work my parents into the discussion, since that could lead down roads I wasn't interested in traveling. I told Edie I understood how she felt, since I was an only child, too. We both stayed silent for a moment after that, and I wondered if she was thinking what I was: We had each other now.

After dinner Edie walked me to the door, stroked my hair with her hand, and wrapped her arms around me. A part of me wanted to turn my lips to her, to kiss her again, but her swelled belly and the baby inside came between us. "Thank you for the money," she said. "Will you be back next week?"

"Yes," I told her. "I will."

And I came back until we were up to a three-night-a-week routine. I lent her the cash in dribs and drabs so I had a reason to keep visiting. Edie didn't seem to mind the setup. On my way over I'd stop and pick up a bag of groceries that I pedaled on my bike. Eggos. Frozen dinners. Fish sticks. After a while we skipped the dinner table and shared our meals on her pillowy peach bed, watching *Marcus Welby* or *The Flip Wilson Show*. During commercials she told me about her doctor's visits, her plan to sell Stanley's dusty furniture and maybe rent out some of the rooms in the place when she was back on her feet. Leon had his dog-in-heat life, my mother had Marnie and her mystery vacation, and my father no doubt had a new girlfriend somewhere, but I had my nights with Edie.

"So," I said to Leila, the smoke from her cigarette warming my insides. "What's Leon up to?"

She was too busy exhaling an endless stream of smoke through her nostrils to answer. It had to be one of the ugliest sights I'd ever seen. Then she said, "Flunking school. Messing up his life as much as possible. He wants to guarantee a future as pathetic as that deadbeat father of his."

Believe it or not, her answer surprised me. The last time I had been down to see Leon, I found him in his room surrounded by books instead of motorcycle and stroke mags for once. "Check it out," he said, pointing to the wood-paneled wall beside his bed. I stared at a bunch of notes taped up there, all of them in Leon's crooked handwriting.

This is where I get off.
Absolutely no reason except I had a toothache.
I can't struggle anymore. Good-bye.
Do not notify my mother. She has a heart condition.

"I don't get it," I said. "What are they?"

"Suicide notes," he told me. He lay back on his bed and clasped his hands behind his neck. He wore gray cords the color of a battleship, tight and faded in the crotch. Not only had his mustache fully grown in, but the sides of his face and chin were sprouting hair, too. He obviously didn't plan on shaving anytime soon. I imagined that dark, coarse hair growing and growing until all I could see were his squinty brown eyes, thick nose, and fat red lips.

I stared back at the wall and wondered about someone ending his life with nothing to say but *The survival of the fittest. Adios, Unfit.* "For real?" I said.

"I'm doing a term paper on suicide. I found those in a chapter on the shortest notes ever written. Imagine," he said as we gazed up at his collection, "scribbling some bullshit like that on a piece of paper, then blowing your fucking head off."

"Weird," I said, glancing at a note that read *I've had enough. See you on the dark side.*

"After that, Pindle, there's nothing. You're dead. No more."

"Okay," I said to him. "I get the point."

Leila wrestled with the steering wheel and managed to score a bonus spot right in front of Cumberland Farms. When we got out of the car, she had a coughing fit outside by the ice machine. For a moment I thought she was going to blow a lung. "Are you all right?" I asked.

She hawked up a wad the size of an egg yolk and spit through the cloud of breath that surrounded her head. Make *that* the ugliest thing I had ever seen. "It's just this piss-ass cold," she said.

Did she mean *her* cold or *the* cold? Either way, she finally swung open the door, and Cumby's heater blew out air hotter than a Bunsen burner. Compared to my subzero apartment, this place felt tropical. I ditched Leila and made my way up and down the aisles, grabbing a six-pack of Dr Pepper and two TV dinners. One chicken. One turkey. Both with mashed potatoes and chocolate cake.

In front of me at the counter was that skinny girl who had been picketing the sale of the police station last fall. She was carrying a kid in a snowsuit, and there were two boys at her legs, pushing each other and grabbing at the candy. "Stop it, you cretins," she said. "Or I'll burn you at the stake."

She looked at me and smiled, rolling her brown eyes. I smiled back, even though something about her seemed a little odd. The kids must have been her siblings, I figured, since she looked only about my age. But why hadn't I ever seen her in school? She took one of them by the hand and said, "Okay, midgets. We're finished here. Let's go."

"Do you have anything smaller?" the pock-faced guy behind the register wanted to know once she split and I stepped up and handed him a Benny.

I shook my head no. He bent down to break the bill in a drawer beneath the counter, and my hands went for a pack of Juicy Fruit, shoving it in my pocket to help my mother through the international gum shortage. Welcome to the wonderful world of shoplifting, I thought. It was my first time stealing anything outside of my mother's money, which technically I was only borrowing. But more and more I realized that if you acted like you owned the world, you got away with whatever you wanted.

Look at Leon.

Look at my father.

Mr. Cumberland Farms popped his head up and counted out my

change with a lick-lick of his thumb between bills. Leila was still in the back by the soda. Probably choosing between Tab for her rum or tonic for her vodka. I grabbed a pen off the register and wrote a note on the back of my receipt: *I had to split. Thanks for the ride. Dominick.*

"Can you give this to that lady when she pays for her stuff?" I asked. He barely nodded, but I figured he'd follow through once Leila started bugging out and asking for me.

Outside, I rolled up the top of the bag with my gloveless fingers, tossed it over my shoulder, and clomped off down the road. I was within walking distance of Edie's now and didn't want Leila to find out where I was headed. I was smart enough to know about secrets and the way things got around. Once you let one person know what you're up to, you might as well tell the whole fucking world. Say I let Leila drop me. Once she got tanked up, she'd mouth off about it to Leon, and Leon, after getting over his shock that I wasn't bullshitting all those times when I told him about Edie, might run off about the whole thing to some chick he was trying to lay, and that chick might mention it to her mother who worked at the hospital with a bigmouth named Marnie Garboni, and she would definitely blab to Marnie because they had nothing better to do than talk about other people's lives, and before I could say "Bingo!" Marnie would practically climb through the telephone wire and spill the dirty beans to my mother. Basically, I'd be in a lot of hot shit.

So no thank you, I'd walk the rest of the way.

I reached the Holedo Motel, only a mile or so from Edie's. Old Man Fowler, the guy who owned the place, had his office light off for the night. Officer Roget's car was parked in the lot, probably waiting for a speeder to whip around the curve so he could write a whopping ticket. I crossed over the solid yellow line and walked along the edge of the woods, away from the buzzing streetlight where he couldn't see me. In the summer, stock-car races at Hogway's Racetrack drew a major crowd, and the dilapidated motel was packed every weekend. Fowler dragged out a two-dimensional wooden race car and set it up on the front lawn every year along with a sign: HOLEDO GOES HOGWILD! Summer after summer, tourists bunched up in front of that race car like it was the real thing, like it could take them somewhere fast. During the winter the place stayed empty, except for maybe the occasional truck driver like my father, who pulled in, paid for a room, slept, shaved, took a shit, maybe jerked off, then hit the road. Other than that, just Roget's car waited silently under the streetlight.

At the top of the hill I spotted Edie's house. When I arrived at night, the silhouetted roof and bare branches always made me think of Norman Bates's house on the hill. A gust of wind lifted my overgrown bangs off my forehead and played with the arrangement, leaving me shivering. I couldn't wait to get inside.

My feet crunched across the snow-covered lawn and up the porch steps. I turned the doorknob. Locked, so I banged the lion clanker and waited. A plastic bird—Edie's or maybe her ex-husband's lawn decoration stuck in the grass and long forgotten—swung one broken wing round and round. The sound made me think of creaking bedsprings.

Old parts. Plastic and metal.

Still no Edie.

I knocked again, this time harder. More silence. More wind. More shivers. Finally, from the deep belly of the house, I heard footsteps. A moment later the outside light clicked on, and Edie swung open the door. "Sorry," she said. Her stomach between us like a basketball-under-the-shirt type of deal.

Edie had managed to stay beautiful during the course of her belly-busting pregnancy. No puffed-up face. No flabby arms. Right now, though, her eyes looked heavy, her shoulders slumped. Usually I got a "Hey, handsome" at the door. "Is something wrong?" I asked.

"Just tired of carrying this load," she said, straightening up in the doorway. "But I'm better now that you're here."

I stepped inside, squeezing the grocery bag to my side and smiling despite my numb fingers.

"You must be freezing," Edie said. "I would have picked you up somewhere."

I had never come clean about being the ripe old age of fifteen, though sometimes I got the feeling Edie suspected. Just in case, I reminded her again and again that the only reason I never drove was that my mother needed the car every second of every day. I didn't mention my father's truck, but I'm sure she knew that would be off-limits. Since I didn't want to settle for some hippie machine like a VW Bug or a lousy Pinto, I told her I was holding out for just the right '70 'Cuda. One with mag wheels and a supercharged Hemi. I didn't have a clue what a Hemi was, but Leon always mentioned it when he spotted a hot car. A Barracuda was his dream machine. Tonight, since it was freezing and I was without my bike, I might have to let Edie drive me home. We could work it out later.

"This is nothing," I said, sounding rugged and durable, like one of those baseball players from my old collection might sound. Wilbur Wood. Brooks Robinson. Billy Williams. "A little cold never hurt anyone."

Edie smiled and gave me a peck, not really on my lips but not on my cheek either. I loved when she did that. It seemed to make my wind-whipped face warm. She took the food to the kitchen, and I went to the bedroom and stripped off my coat, sweatshirt, the same black shoes she had given me months ago, and lay back on her bed. All part of our routine.

One more thing.

I picked my sweatshirt off the floor and pulled out the money, including the change from Cumby's, and set it on her nightstand where I always left it. It felt a little like paying a hooker, only without the good stuff. Whenever I slapped down the bills, I wondered about the sex thing with Edie. Strange the way those I-want-to-fuck-you feelings for her surfaced only when I pictured the woman I used to see at the Doghouse, back before I really knew her. When I thought about the Edie I knew now—pregnant, poor, my fish-stick-and-TV-dinner buddy—all I wanted was to take care of her.

While the food cooked, Edie popped in and out of the room making small talk. She liked to get going about newsy things some nights. And this was one of those times. "I can't believe Nixon today," she huffed, her oven-mitted hands on her round waist. A few minutes later she was back with "They still haven't found out who killed those two women in Boston last week." Since Edie and I had been together, I had taken to reading the newspaper to keep up. I didn't admit this to her, but the more I read, the more botched-up and confusing the world became for me. Whenever I put the paper down, headlines like that one about Sharon Tate swirled in my head for the rest of the day.

MAO'S HEIR APPARENT LIN PIAO DIES

IN MYSTERIOUS PLANE CRASH

U.S. AND U.S.S.R. SIGN TREATY BANNING NUCLEAR WEAPONS

ON THE OCEAN FLOOR

CYCLONE AND TIDAL WAVE KILL 10,000 IN BENGAL

I didn't even know where the hell Bengal was. I did my best to keep up anyway and acted like I cared about people like Lin Piao. Later I'd try repeating some of Edie's opinions about the world to my mother as if they were thoughts all my own.

Me: "Lin Piao's death must have had something to do with his unsuccessful coup attempt."

My mother: "Lin who?"

Obviously she knew as much about world news as I did.

When Edie was gone for a while, I flipped channels and left it on *Here's Lucy* for lack of a better choice. It was such a raging bore that I stared over at the stack of children's books on Edie's bedside table. She had picked up a pile of old fairy tales from a tag sale for only thirty-five cents apiece. *Jack and the Beanstalk. Cinderella. Thumbelina.* Some nights while she fussed with dinner in the kitchen, I read a story. My favorite thing about fairy tales—or at least the ones I had read so far at Edie's—was that no matter how shitty these people's lives got, things always seemed to work out. Cyclones never wiped out ten thousand people on the last page. Fathers didn't disappear in the end. Mothers didn't leave.

I slid *Sleeping Beauty* out from the bottom of the pile and flipped pages. The book practically had museum paintings for illustrations. Loads of bright colors. Tiny wrinkles drawn around the characters' eyes. Dark forests that were more frightening and haunted than the real thing. On the first page Sleeping Beauty was set out in a sparkling glass coffin in the middle of the forest between two thick willow trees. I flipped some more and stopped on the page where the Prince awakens her with a kiss. When I looked up, Edie was standing with our TV dinners on a tray.

"Do you want to watch *Here's Lucy?*" I asked, closing the book. "There's nothing else on."

Edie put the tray on the bed and waved her hand at the television. "She was only funny in black and white. The color makes her seem crazy instead of cute."

I got up and clicked off the TV, then sat with my back at the headboard to eat my turkey dinner. I forked out my string beans and put them on Edie's tray. "They're good for the little guy."

"Little girl," she said and smirked.

Edie had all sorts of reasons for her it's-a-girl hunch—a needle and string that swung in a circle over her stomach, a dream about an old woman holding a pink basket. But something told me it wasn't a girl.

"If it is a boy, maybe I'll name him after you," she said.

I acted surprised, but really the thought had occurred to me more than once. After all, I wanted proof that I meant more to Edie than a loan and some company. "Dominick Kramer sounds pretty good to me," I said.

Edie gulped down half a glass of Dr Pepper, took a pill off her tray, and swallowed. I couldn't tell if it was a vitamin or an aspirin. Probably a baby thing. She took them all the time. "So," she said, "your dad called me today."

I had skipped over the rectangle of white turkey and was already chowing on my chocolate cake. A ball of it stuck in my throat when she mentioned my father. We had what I thought was an unspoken, don't-talk-about-*him* rule ever since that afternoon when Edie peeled back her shirt to show me her pregnant stomach. I had imagined that we both felt the same way: Bringing up my father made her pregnancy seem sad instead of exciting.

Ditto for our relationship.

I liked it better when Edie talked about the baby, filling me in on the position of the head, the extra pounds she had gained, the weird kicks, somersaults, and flutters. Some nights she'd stop me midconversation and press my hand to her stomach. "Feel her?" she'd say. Beneath my fingers the baby would make a sudden, watery motion that made me think of a fish swishing its tail. I'd smile wide like an expectant father who had just felt his child move for the very first time.

"What did he want?" I managed, though I should have asked his whereabouts for my mother's sake.

"He wanted to make sure I 'took care of things' was the way he put it." Edie stopped to eat a string bean with her fingers, then continued. "I told him the same thing I said months ago. I am keeping this baby. I mean, it's a little late now anyway. I'm due in February."

I pushed my potatoes around, then set the fork on the tray, my appetite gone. "And then what happened?"

"He got pissed off and said he'd like to run me over with his truck."

We were quiet. I thought of Marnie's dogs looking up at a set of headlights coming at them as they cut across 67. Her cat Milky, too.

Edie chewed and swallowed.

The wind rattled the glass of the bedroom window. The sound made me think of change jingling in someone's pocket. A box of nails dropped on a cement floor. I waited for more.

"I really think he wants to kill me," she said.

"People say things like that all the time when they're ripped. He doesn't mean it."

"Your father's dumb enough to pull something stupid."

The more she talked about him, the more my mind retreated back to reality: My father *was* the baby's father. I was just keeping Edie company until the pregnancy was over and she moved on. Our friendship meant a loan to her. Since she knew that the baby would be a girl, it was no big deal to talk about naming the baby after me. Questions I shooed away months ago formed in my mind: How could Edie expect something different from my father when she knew the way he treated his own family? Why wasn't she more careful in the first place? What if she didn't give me the money back? That last thought made me swallow. Hard. "Just forget about it."

Edie reached across the bed and laced her fingers between mine. Sometimes at night she held my hand when we lay in bed. She said it made her feel less lonely, that my hands were soft but strong. The feeling of her skin against mine made my heart beat fast every time. "Dominick," she said, "if something should happen to me, I want you to know that I appreciate all you've done."

If something should happen to me. She sounded just like my mother.

"He's not going to kill you," I said and let out a nervous laugh. The prospect of my father as a murderer seemed ridiculous. He was a major pain in the ass. But a killer he was not.

"You don't understand the way he gets," Edie said. "You haven't seen it."

I didn't know what to say to that, because she was right. I had never seen my father get violent before.

"And it's more than just him," she said finally. "Sometimes I get scared thinking about labor."

"Stop it," I said. "You'll be fine."

"All right. But I want you to know that I couldn't have gotten this far without you."

Edie let go. She stretched back on a pillow and let her hair fan out behind her. Her jaw tightened, and I could see the slightest bit of movement under her cheek from her teeth pressing against each other. Her blue eyes traveled up to the ceiling fan above the bed. The fan spun constantly, since Edie liked the air to circulate even in the winter. The constant whirring, like a helicopter's blades, always reminded me of a story my mother once told me. She had been in a pottery shop when a man came in with his baby daughter on his shoulders. He simply walked toward the register, and the baby got caught in the metal blades of the fan. The thing pulled the girl right off her father's shoulders, sliced the tender white skin of her neck, her face, her ears, and sent her sailing across the store, where she crashed into a bin of ceramic pots. Dead.

The bloody image made me reach out and put my arms around Edie, around the baby that was growing inside her. "There are so many things that can happen in life," I said, sounding older and wiser than I really was. "But we'll just be careful. We'll pay attention to the signs around us. We'll watch what we do."

"Thanks," Edie said. "You know, it's hard to believe a nice guy like you could have such a prick for a father. If I was younger and things were different, I might have married you by now."

I shook my head, still trying to get rid of the image of that ruined baby, the tortured look I imagined on her father's face, on my mother's as she stood in the shop. "I wish other girls felt that way," I said, then instantly regretted it. I wanted to seem tough. As hard and unbendable as Leon's back-pocket comb. Roget's stiff pistol in his holster.

"Still no luck with girls?" she asked.

Embarrassed, I wanted to lie. I could have whipped out a big one, too: *Oh, there's this one chick who wants me to lick her crotch clean.* But it seemed stupid and pointless. "You're the only person I ever kissed. And that doesn't count, because it wasn't real."

"Why wasn't it real?" she asked.

I was testing, measuring her feelings for me. "It wasn't mutual, I guess. And besides, our mouths were closed."

"Oh, Dominick," she said and let out a sigh as heavy and weighted as one of my mother's. "This whole thing has been so complicated. I mean, I should have—" She stopped, then started again. "I mean, you—" She was quiet a moment, biting her lip, thinking. Then she turned to me. "Let me give you a real kiss. It will be my thank-you present to you."

I didn't know what to say. I had grown pretty comfortable with our routine. Her pregnancy made kissing seem off-limits somehow. "Really?" I said.

"Sure. I can spare one kiss. And it will make you feel in control the next time you're test-driving a new girlfriend. It's the least I can do."

How could I tell her that I didn't want to be with another girl, that all I wanted was to be with her, to stay as we were? Talking about the kiss first made the whole thing seem rehearsed. It didn't matter, though, because this time Edie did all the work. She leaned toward me, curled her hair over her ear, and pressed her mouth to mine. Instantly her lips parted, and I could feel wet air from the back of her mouth. Edie's fingery tongue pushed its way into me, against my lips, warm inside my mouth. I wanted to lean back, to enjoy it. I thought of Sleeping Beauty being brought to life with a kiss. Edie pressed her mouth harder against mine and touched her fingers to my chest.

She wanted me to remember this.

It worked, because the *Sleeping Beauty* watercolors blurred and my mind filled with centerfolds. A thin strip of hair between every girl's legs. Pink folds of skin. Empty and waiting. And then that image of the slutty Edie at the Doghouse mixed with the woman who was kissing me now. My hips moved to press against her, against something, but her body was too far away. I rolled toward her and pressed myself against the mattress while I slid my tongue between her lips. Before I could help it, I felt myself let go in my pants. Breath from my mouth poured into her. My hand moved to her breast but brushed her belly.

Her baby.

My father's baby.

My brother. My sister.

I pulled away.

"How was it?" she asked, pulling a strand of hair from her eyes and smiling. The ceiling fan cut crooked shadows across her face.

"Great," I said, though it wasn't great at all. I could feel the dampness in my underwear. The chocolate cake and one or two bites of white turkey pushed their way to the surface through the tunnel from my stomach. I held my breath to stop it.

"Do you want another one?" Edie asked. Her mouth, ready and waiting.

My mind felt foggy. My body, drained. I prayed she didn't catch on that I had come from just her kiss alone. "Maybe later," I whispered, too tired and embarrassed to really talk. "Can we just rest awhile?"

"Sure," she said, patting the spot where her breast, arm, and shoulder met. I put my head in the warmth and coziness of that spot and closed my eyes. In a moment my stomach felt calm.

This was what I wanted from her, after all.

My mind closed door after door down a long, dark hallway, and before I knew it, I fell asleep.

When I opened my eyes, Edie was gone and I was stretched out on my stomach. I must have pulled off my shirt and pants the way I always did when I slept, because I was dressed only in my underwear. I hoped the sight of my body and come-stained drawers hadn't scared Edie off. On the nightstand the money was gone. The bedside clock read one-thirty and I almost shit my Fruit of the Looms. My mother was probably freaking out, wondering where I was.

I sat up and reached for the floor in search of my pants and shoes.

Nothing.

I felt under the bed, and here's the weird part: I pulled out that old sneaker I had left behind last summer, dust-balled and curled from no use. I stared at the thing like it was a museum relic. A body part I had amputated and left behind. In my misty afterbirth of sleep, I put the thing on and laced it up. My foot must have grown, because the fit was almost too tight to wear. I shoved one of Edie's oversize pink furry slippers onto my other foot to keep warm on the cold floor. Then I grabbed a thick blue wool blanket off the chair and draped it around my shoulders, and made my way down the hall in pursuit of her.

After all this time the hallways and wooden doors in the old place still puzzled me. The sunny room with ivy wallpaper was over there? No, over here. The back staircase led to the pantry? No, the main hallway. It didn't help that Edie had emptied most of the rooms of furniture, so each vacant room looked the same. I was about to call out to Edie and ask her why she hadn't woken me, when I heard her voice. I followed the soft murmur until I was outside the kitchen door. I opened it just a crack and could see her reflection in the picture window, broken and fractured in the six different panes at each side. Her back was to me as she talked on the telephone. From behind, no one would have ever guessed she was pregnant. It seemed weird to me that she'd be on the phone in the middle of the night, so I stood there longer than I should have, without going in. I listened as she talked about selling a bunch of her ex-husband's shitty furniture to a woman from Buford. Then she went on about some sort of shipment that had never been delivered. Finally, she was silent for a moment and I worried she had spotted me. I realized, though, that she was just listening to the person on the other end of the line.

"We'll leave in the morning," she said quietly after a moment. "Then we'll check in to the room together."

Something told me to interrupt her, that I wasn't going to want to hear the rest of this call.

"Thank God for that," she said.

"I've got the money," she said.

"Of course," she said.

Then she said this: "I started off not caring. But now I feel bad."

Silently I tugged in a breath and felt my heart drum.

Move your legs, I thought.

Too late.

"Stop bugging me about it," Edie said. "He's just a kid. A harmless boy."

Me.

My breathing seemed to stop. Her words raced around my brain. Before I could move, she giggled, and I heard her say, "I just want to be nice about it. Don't worry, I'll find a way to get rid of him."

From somewhere inside me another voice came with a message that had been waiting there all along: *She has been tricking you.* For a flash I considered storming my way into the kitchen and raging. But that was something other men would have done. I found myself stepping back. I felt not the whole of myself but the parts. My feet—one sneakered, one slippered—moved to the foyer. My hand gripped the diamond-shaped knob of the front door. My back, covered only by the blue wool blanket, stiffened as I stepped onto the crooked porch and into the night. That plastic bird was still spinning its broken wing, though the sound seemed to come from inside my head now. A dull creaking, then a steady scrape of metal and old parts.

In my mind I heard a car crash.

Screech of brakes.

Ambulance sirens.

A woman's shrill scream without inhalation.

Then silence.

I was walking across the snowy lawn, away from Edie's house. When I was far enough away, my brain returned. Given what I had just overheard, it was funny that my first thought was numb and practical: *You will never make it home without freezing.* I kept walking because I couldn't turn back. Edie's voice came and went, came and went.

He's just a kid.

A harmless boy.

I'll find a way to get rid of him.

Her giggle jumped around my head and worked itself into a cackle. As evil as one of those green-faced witches from one of Edie's fairy tales.

"You have been so fucking stupid," I said, my voice croaking into the blue-black darkness. My eyes weighed heavy at the corners, and tears slipped out. Their warmth on my wind-burned cheeks made me cry harder. "So motherfucking goddamn stupid."

I stared down at the steady white line on the side of the road. My slippered foot slapping and stinging against the salt and chunky scraps of ice on the pavement.

My teeth chattered. My ears felt numb. The only thing not frozen now was my mind. It burned and whipped. A wild comet landing on the same thought again and again: eight thousand some-odd dollars that I had stolen from my mother and would never get back. "What the fuck is wrong with you?" I shouted in a voice that came out weak and broken.

The only answer came in a wind that blew its way between my lips, past my teeth and down the dark hole of my throat, chilling me more. I have to get indoors fast, I thought. Wasn't there a path through the woods that would save me a few miles? Then I remembered that it involved crossing Pegluso's swamp on a log and some rocks. With one shoe and a slipper and all the ice, I'd never make it. If I could get to Cumby's and hitch a ride home. But the place was long closed by now.

As I trudged along in the frosty darkness, I thought of my note to Leila: *I had to split. Thanks for the ride.* If I froze to death tonight, Leila and Leon might hold those words up as my farewell message, a suicide note. The thought of it made me laugh despite myself.

When I looked up, the Holedo Motel loomed before me, all those dark windows like dead eyes. Roget's car was gone for once. Maybe he was actually doing some real police work instead of whacking off in the parking lot of this dumpy shithole. I could get a room, I thought as I stared at the even row of doors on the first and second floors of the place, if only I had shoved one of those Ben Franklins up my ass in case I'd be walking home half naked.

In the distance I could hear the faint gurgle of a stream bubbling from somewhere in the woods. Movement kept the water from freezing completely. I decided to do the same and lifted my legs in a sort of march. Only my slippered foot felt like it was being electrocuted whenever it hit the ground, so my march was more like a limp.

"Almost home," I said, lying to myself.

From behind me a car moved in a fast whoosh around the corner. I could hitch a ride, I thought. But no one would pick me up dressed like this. I hopped off the road into the dark woods. The headlights moved past, and I held my breath.

Gone.

I stepped out onto the pavement, and another car came from the opposite direction, surprising me. When I moved back into the woods, my blanket snagged on a branch. I should have ditched the thing, but I panicked and crouched foolishly by the side of the road instead.

A squeak of brakes. The hum of a car stopping. Then a flash of bright lights on me. Keep on trucking, I thought. It's just a half-naked kid on the side of the road in the middle of the night. Don't mess with me. But the car didn't budge, and the light was far too bright to be a headlight. I noticed red and blue shimmering against the trees when I lifted my head. My body shivered uncontrollably now.

"Stand up," a voice said.

I turned to look. Mustache. Pouchy face. Roget. The thought of him escorting me home in nothing but my underwear and a sneaker and a slipper to face my mother made me run. I took off into the woods, leaving my blanket behind. Snow crunched. Sticks jutted up and poked at my numb foot. Branches snapped against my chest with a rhythmic slap-slap-slap followed by a sharp burning sting. But I kept on hauling ass. I would have made it away from him if it hadn't been for a low-to-the-ground barbed-wire fence that sent me sailing.

"Dominick Pindle?" Roget called, catching up to me. He said it like a question. I was a shaking heap in the icy snow. "What the hell are you up to, kid?"

My tongue felt blue and frozen in my mouth. A stream of blood moved down my leg like the crooked red line of the interstate on a road map.

I didn't say a word. This is Edie's fault, I thought.

Roget must have realized he wouldn't get an answer from me until I was warm. In one fell swoop he bent down and picked my body up from the cold floor of the woods. He carried me to the backseat of his car, cranked the heat, pulled a scratchy wool blanket out of the trunk, and poured me some coffee from his thermos. After he dabbed peroxide on my slashed leg and taped on two big Band-Aids, he sat up front in silence, shuffling papers for what seemed like an hour. Ten hours. Once in a while he looked in the mirror and fingered that mustache of his. Shifty or vain, I thought just as I did that day at the auction. A little of both. When I saw him looking down at his chest, straightening his badge like an impenetrable, golden heart pinned there, I decided he was probably one of those men who loved nothing more than being in charge. He had carried me out of the woods not because he cared but because it made him feel like a hero. And taking that badge from him would be just like taking his heart, the thing that gave him power. He would be left almost lifeless, weakened without it. Like my gym teacher without his whistle. My father without his muscles.

The blue and red lights on top of the car were a rubbernecker's dream. I must have been the most exciting thing to happen to Holedo in ages, because in no time a parade of cars was slowing down to check me out in the backseat. At first I gave every single one of them the finger behind Roget's head. But when I couldn't stand one more bug-eyed freak staring at me, I said, "Are you going to take me home?"

"Oh, so the little shit does speak," Roget said from the front seat, turning to look at me. "I'll drive you home when you answer me one question: What were you doing out there, running around almost naked in the middle of the night?"

I took in a long breath of the hot, dry car air, a sip of his bitter black coffee. I hated coffee, but it felt like a pool of warmth in my shaking hand, and I couldn't stop drinking. "It was a dare," I said.

He cocked his head at me. I thought maybe he'd get into some boys-will-be-boys type of story and probably want to share some of his own, so I came up with this: "There's a guys' club at school. To get in you have to do a dare. Mine was to run by the motel naked. My buddies took off when they saw you. They're probably home asleep by now."

Roget fingered his mustache. "Did it occur to you and your idiotic friends that you could cause a major accident? Or that walking around like that is what we call indecent exposure? I could arrest you."

I wanted to tell him to cuff Edie Kramer instead. Then I thought, Arrest me. A jail cell was meant to be my bedroom after all. I wiped out a big chunk of my mother's savings, not to mention shoplifting a pack of Juicy Fruit. But the thought of actually being arrested scared me so much that all I could manage was "Please don't" in my weakest voice.

Roget clicked off the carnival lights and put the car in gear. I was as good as home now. I prayed he wouldn't want to talk to my mother.

"I'll make you a deal," he said. "I'll drop you off at home, no more questions asked, if you go easy on your mother for the next few weeks."

"Deal," I said without even thinking. The part about my mother must have been his hero routine—looking out for the ladies.

"You don't sound like you mean it," he said. "Your mother's got a lot on her plate right now, so I want you to go easy on her."

"How do you know what's on her plate?" I asked.

He signaled and turned down Dwight Avenue, almost to my house. Finally he said, "I'm the sheriff. I know everything."

At the corner of the lot to my apartment, Roget stopped the car. "You can keep the blanket," he told me.

"Thanks," I said, and he came around to open my door.

The cold air felt like pinpricks of torture all over again. I thought of my mother holding hamburger meat under a warm-running faucet, watching it break into fleshy pink chunks in her hands as it thawed. I stepped away from the car.

"Remember," he said. "Take care of her."

"You bet," I said, waiting for him to drive away.

He stood there, though, and I got the point that he wasn't going to move until he saw me walk up the stairs and into my house. So I limped up the steps and saluted to him from the top. He still didn't leave. I turned the knob and stepped inside, closing the door behind me. When I peeked through the curtains, I saw his car door close. A moment later his taillights disappeared down the street.

"Dominick," my mother said from behind me.

I turned around and noticed for the first time that the apartment was ablaze with lights. After what I'd been through tonight, the place actually felt warm. Marnie stood beside my red-faced mother in a tight tangerine sweater with a cat-whisker design by the neck. What the hell was she doing here in the middle of the night?

My mind raced with excuses. I fell asleep at Leon's. I was playing strip poker.

"It's gone," my mother said before I could even speak.

"What's gone?" I asked, pulling Roget's blanket around me to cover up.

Tears rolled down my mother's face when she opened her mouth again. "The money is gone."

Part of me must have still been frozen, because I didn't react. Statued and silent, I realized that I appeared confused, not at all suspicious. "What money?" I said.

"All my savings except for some coupons and a measly six hundred dollars." She put her head in her palms and cried. Every choked and ragged sob left me drained.

"Calm down," I said.

"Don't tell me to calm down!" she screamed, whipping her head up to face me. Her hair was wild and matted. Her eyes opened wider than I'd ever seen. A vein bulged in her wrinkled forehead. "That's our emergency money! And let me tell you, an emergency has come up!"

"What?" I said, confused. "Who?"

"Never you mind," Marnie said. "Your mama's just upset. Did you see your father take it?"

My father. It had never occurred to me that if she found the money missing, she'd automatically blame him. It was as simple as this: My father was the one who had gotten me into this mess in the first place. So fuck him.

"I didn't know what he was looking for," I said, taking a long, deep breath. It felt like my lungs were filling up with something, a thick and weighty substance that was barely breathable. "But I saw him fishing through your music box, then searching under your bed."

Four

I woke up early and snaked seventy bucks from the last of my mother's stash. The money would get me to New York City, where I planned to dump the whole story on Uncle Donald. My hope was that he would loan me the cash if I promised to repay him with the income from whatever crappy job I landed on my sixteenth birthday. When I got back to Holedo, I'd slip the bills into my mother's hiding places—only under the left side of her mattress instead of the right, in her pink plastic music box instead of her wooden one, and so on.

"You see," I would say, "Dad didn't steal your savings after all. You just forgot where you put it."

Okay, so the plan had its kinks, but blaming my father would last only so long. And once my mother saw the money, I knew she'd be too relieved to get hung up on the details. Besides, the trip would buy me time to figure out what to do about Edie, to deal with the shredded, butchered feeling in me that wouldn't leave. More than that, I would finally come face-to-face with my brother, Truman.

I pulled a duffel bag from my closet, smacked it around a couple of times to shake off the dust, and unpacked the contents from my sixth-grade hiking trip three years ago. Out with the baby binoculars and crumb-filled plastic Baggies. In with the socks, underwear, jeans. I threw in a flannel shirt, since my hooded sweatshirt had been abandoned at Edie's. I didn't plan on staying overnight, but I wanted to be prepared for just about anything.

Last night had taught me something.

The bus schedule I nabbed from the bottom of my mother's stuffed purse said my ship sailed at 8:00 A.M., so I had to move fast. I scribbled a quick note to my mother: *Gone for the day with Leon. Don't worry. Things will be okay.* Another mini–suicide note. I dropped it on the kitchen table and stuffed a banana and two Ring Dings into the pocket of my father's orange hunting coat, the only thing I could find to keep me warm, since my winter coat had also been abandoned at Edie's.

On my way out the door I stopped to look at my mother, asleep on the living room couch. Eyes closed shut. Lips puckered and tight. Hair frizzed around her face in a branchy black web. Her black coat pulled to her chin with a clasped hand. A folded silver gum wrapper on the coffee table in front of her. Lying there with the tweedy couch arms raised above her small frame, she reminded me of a somber Sleeping Beauty in her glass coffin. I couldn't look at her without hating myself for what I had done.

Last night after Marnie had said her kissy-face good-byes, my mother left a long, pissed-off message with my father's dispatcher. I took the opportunity to bow out and drew a steaming bath in our midget-size tub. While my feet thawed under the hot faucet, I listened to my mother crying on the couch. The sound made me think of a kitten being squeezed too hard. A baby struggling for air. It killed me to know I had fucked everything up so miserably, and more than anything I wanted to get out of the tub and say something stupid to make her laugh. But I was too worried she'd pick up some sort of guilty signal flashing above my head, and that would blow the lie about my father. So she cried herself to sleep while I soaked in the warm water, mentally rehearsing my plan to make things better.

Even as she slept on the couch, my mother wore that black wool coat—her body shivering anyway. I wanted to go to her, to pull a blanket up to her chin the way loving parents do to their sleeping children on *The Wonderful World of Disney*. But I was afraid she'd wake up. Instead I quietly walked over to the radiator in the kitchen to check on the heat myself. From deep inside its rusted rib-cage body, I could hear a steady ping and knock. The landlord obviously wasn't going to get his ass up here anytime soon. For the hell of it, I twisted the knob by the cracked linoleum floor. Steam spit into the air like a miniature geyser. Heat pricked my face. Then silence. Again I twisted the knob and waited.

Ping.

Knock.

Ping.

A long, steady breath of steam sprayed into the room and kept coming. The piece of shit wasn't broken after all—someone must have turned it off. Why hadn't my mother tried giving it a good, hard twist like I just did? It didn't make any sense. But with only twenty-six minutes to get to the station, I had no time to play detective.

I left the soon-to-be toasty apartment and hiked it downstairs to my bike. The chilly morning air smelled like a tire fire. Even though it had warmed up a bit, my body shivered—probably remembering what I had been through six short hours ago. Pedaling like crazy, I retraced part of my route from last night. Past Cumby's. Past the motel. This time no Leila. No Roget. No Edie.

I made it to the bus station with five minutes to spare, dumped my bike behind a fence, and bought myself a ticket. It was my first time ever taking off to such a faraway place, and my stomach felt cramped and twisted when I thought about the crowded city streets of New York. A million faces as strange and scary as those newspaper stories.

NIXON ORDERS 90-DAY PRICE FREEZE TO CURB
DOMESTIC INFLATION
BENGAL REBUILDS AFTER CYCLONE
POLICE STILL SEARCHING FOR SUSPECT ACCUSED
OF SLAYING TWO BOSTON WOMEN

I repeated the plan in my head to calm myself: find Uncle Donald's apartment, explain the whole dirty deal, get the money, and head back home. With every passing minute my scheme sounded more far-fetched. But what choice did I have? The thought of going back to Edie's made my hands shake and my breathing speed up. I was afraid that if I walked through her door, if I caught sight of her face, if I heard the sound of her raspy voice, then the dark tangle of feelings inside me would well up and overtake me. I was afraid I might hit her like my father did and that maybe I wouldn't be able to stop there. I thought of the knife plunged into Sharon Tate's pregnant stomach, and this is what came into my mind: *If a person could get that swept up in their anger and commit such an unthinkable evil, then maybe I could, too, simply because I'm human.* The thought came and went in a flash, leaving me feeling sick. I looked around the station, as if to make sure that no one had heard what I was thinking.

At two minutes to eight I spotted a walking skeleton of a man across the parking lot. He boarded one of the buses and drove it around to my gate. "All aboard," he said when he swung open the door.

I climbed the rubbery black steps, and he ripped my ticket in half.

"Looks like it's just the two of us until Hartford. Why don't you sit up here with me?" he said when I took my seat three-quarters of the way back.

I could have told him to bug off, but I decided just to go with it. I dragged my duffel bag to the first seat and sat right in front of a sign that read PLEASE DO NOT TALK TO THE DRIVER WHILE THE BUS IS IN MOTION. Obviously my gummy-mouthed chauffeur didn't give a dirty nipple about that rule.

We were about to shove off when someone outside screamed, "Wait! Hold the bus!"

The driver slammed on the brakes and opened the door. I looked up to see that skinny girl from the police auction and last night at Cumby's. Again. This time she was carrying a sign that said EQUAL PAY FOR EQUAL WORK. She was dressed in a St. Bartholomew outfit—plaid skirt, dark sweater, and tights—which explained why I never saw her in my school. Leon always said that Bartholomew girls were starved for action, so he hit on them every chance he got. I didn't think he'd go for this one, though. Not that she wasn't pretty, because she was. Sort of. But her signs were a bit much.

"Thank you for stopping," she said to the driver, breathless. "You saved me from Saturday services."

The old guy must have thought she was a bit weird, too, because he didn't invite her to join our party. She moseyed on down the aisle to the very back of the bus, clumsily balancing her sign, a duffel bag, and a giant black guitar case in her arms. No kids today. When she passed me, she smiled. This time I looked away, because I had too much to think about and didn't want her chatting me up as well. When we started moving again, I turned to look out the window but couldn't help stretching my neck a bit to see what she was up to.

"Damn it!" she said to herself as she stood by the bus bathroom emptying her duffel bag. "I forgot my boots."

With that she took a bunch of clothes and went into the bathroom and shut the door.

"So," the driver said after a long, long silence in which he steered the rickety bus out of Holedo and down the highway, "what's your name?"

I had been staring out the window, thinking of my father out there, somewhere on a similar highway. A series of solid yellow lines connecting us in a complicated route. A stretched umbilical cord from my seat in this bus to him. "Leon," I said, wanting just for this ride to be someone else.

"I'm Claude. What're you going to do in the city, Leon?" Claude spoke in a too-loud, over-the-shoulder voice that he must have cultivated through years of trapping passengers in this seat as he drove with their lives in his withered, hairy-knuckled hands. The high volume probably did the trick when the bus was jam-packed. But at that moment, in the empty belly of the beast, Claude's voice sounded louder than necessary. Adult to child.

I glanced behind me to make sure the picket girl was still in her dressing room. She was. "I'm going to meet a girl who wants me to lick her crotch clean," I said, giving him my best Leon. Served the guy right for not leaving me alone. After all, I had a mess of shit to sort out. Talking to him was a waste of time.

"Well, there's nothing like some good pussy," Claude shouted back.

Obviously my Leon tactic didn't give him the leave-me-the-fuck-alone shock I had expected. We switched lanes, and a tractor-trailer passed. I thought of my father again. Driving. All those connections between us. I didn't know why I was thinking about him, almost missing him right now. Maybe because we had both been burned so badly by Edie. And even though we'd never swap war stories, it might feel good to have him around as a silent partner in all this.

"Listen," I said, wishing I had ignored Claude's invitation to sit up front in the first place, "I need to take a snooze. So if you don't mind, I'm going to close my eyes."

"Sure thing," he said. "May as well rest up. The city's a tough place for a young fella like you."

"I can handle it," I said.

"I hope so," he shouted back. "All those muggers, beggars, murderers."

A flapping feeling swept through me. In my stomach I imagined an invisible embryo somersaulting and leaving me unsettled, the way Edie always described. But I wasn't going to let this no-brain bus driver get to me. "I said I can handle it," I told him.

"Good thing," he said, taking his eyes off the road and looking at me in his big mother of a mirror longer than I liked. His eyes were set deep in his face, with barely any lashes. His cheeks were jowly. "Police are always finding young kids like you dead in some fleabag Harlem motel room."

"I'm just going to visit my uncle," I said, wanting to shut him up once and for all.

"What about the girl?"

"Girl?" I asked, then remembered. "Oh, I'm going to visit my uncle after I lick her crotch."

"Right," he said.

The picket girl emerged from her dressing room wearing flared denim jeans bleached blue and white like the sky and a long-sleeved tight black shirt with buttons down the front. No more schoolgirl.

I closed my eyes to put an end to all the distractions. In the darkness behind my lids I saw a blizzard of Edie images: Edie writing the Dominick-I-need-to-see-you note last fall when her face was black-and-blue. Edie tilting her head and lacing her fingers between mine as we lay in her bed. Edie tucking her stray hair behind her ear and leaning forward to kiss me. Edie walking into her bedroom and finding me gone last night.

As much as I hated to admit it, and as pissed off as I felt, I was going to miss my nights with her. Over and over I wished there were some sort of explanation. Maybe I had heard her wrong, I tried to tell myself. After all, she hadn't said my name. For all I knew, she could have been talking about the paperboy. But I knew what she had done. What I didn't get was how she could go through with it. How could Edie have faked all those nights at her house? Laughing with me? Holding my hand? Kissing me? It was a lot of effort just to get her claws on some cash. And there had to be an easier way to get back at my father.

To stop myself from thinking about Edie, I tried to conjure up everything I knew about my Uncle Donald. A few hours earlier, when I sneaked into my mother's room to grab the bus fare, I dug up Uncle Donald's number and gave him a wake-up call. When he answered—his fat-man's voice, crackly with sleep—I hung up. Just a test to make sure he wasn't off globe-trotting to get funding for one of his engineering projects. I wanted to be sure he would be present for my visit, since it wasn't the type of thing I could blurt out over the phone. After all, since he traveled so often, and since my mother usually went to visit him instead of the other way around, I had only met my uncle a handful of times. From what I knew, he seemed like a cool enough guy—big and burly, always cracking some over-my-head joke and making himself laugh. I used to ask my mother why he didn't invent something useful, like a remote control that would start her car in the morning so it would be warm when we got in, or a radio battery that didn't die after a couple of days. But my mother said his inventions were not that gimmicky. He focused more on doodads for disease-research laboratories, more interested in curing cancer than warming my ass. And for that he made a bundle.

As far as I knew—which was not much—Uncle Donald didn't have a girlfriend. Probably because his Santa Claus belly and gray beard weren't exactly the type of thing chicks got hot for. Besides, between traveling and raising Truman, how could he have time for a love life?

Truman.

The thought that I was actually going to meet my half brother face-to-face after all this time was too much to think about. I could have let my mind hunker down on a million different questions: What if he wanted to come back to Holedo with me? What if he was retarded or crippled and that's why my mother didn't like to talk about him? Instead of sailing off into one of those scenarios, I told myself not to focus on it too much in order to avoid jinxing anything.

I peeled my banana and practiced my conversation with Donald in my head. I decided I would tell him exactly what had happened.

Direct. Honest for a change.

In Hartford a gaggle of giggling girls boarded, all of them dressed in University of Connecticut sweatshirts. Ponytails. Twisted braids. Fruity perfume. Mint gum. Without any coaxing from Claude, they bunched up front and whipped up a conversation with him in no time. He played Mr. Innocent pretty damn well, too. All flattery and laughter. Little did they know one of the last things he had said before they boarded was "Nothing like some good pussy."

I kept waiting for him to warn them about dead people in motel rooms, but he never said a word on the subject. They were traveling in a pack. I guess he thought I needed to be warned.

"Cool!" one of the girls said to Claude, and the whole crew shrieked with laughter.

I had missed the punch line but was really sick of their flirt-with-the-bus-driver routine anyway. Out my window the miles of forest gave way to clusters of neighborhoods. An aboveground pool left uncovered in somebody's backyard. A lawn with patches of frozen mud and snow. As the scenery flashed by, I made promises to myself. The first had to do with my mother. Before I went into the bath last night, the final thing she had said to me was "Dominick, I'm just so tired. Things have got to get easier for me." I didn't have an answer for her then, but when I got home tonight, I was going to make sure she got the rest she needed. I had been a bigger prick than my father, and I was going to make it up to her. First with the money. Then by being the kind of son she wanted. Like one of those changed people in a fairy tale.

Poof.

Clean bedroom.

Grade-A student.

No girlfriends over the age of seventeen.

That would be me.

The second promise I made was about Edie. I vowed to myself that I would get even with her, squared away. Somewhere, somehow, she was going to pay. I didn't have a specific plan, but I knew one would come to me.

By the time the bus pulled into Port Authority, I had pretty much stitched up my entire life, complete with Edie begging my forgiveness, a tropical vacation with my mother, every last penny paid back to Donald from a part-time job, and even a girlfriend my own age. In my head it was perfect.

Now I just had to make it come true.

Claude slapped me five, and I hopped off the bus behind the girls, trying to look like I knew how to get where I was headed. The truth was,

I didn't have a fucking clue. On the way here, the bus had driven through a stretch of burned-out brick buildings and sidewalks crowded with scowling faces. We almost sideswiped two taxis, and the bus stalled at an intersection, instigating a honking chorus from the parade of cars behind us. The whole experience left me feeling more than unstrung about my New York adventure.

Thank God for the I-for-Information sign at the top of an escalator. I waited in a line that looked more like one at a soup kitchen than a bus station, folding and refolding Uncle Donald's address in my hands. Around me the dirty station was a hive of activity. People darted past one another, racing out to the street or down to the buses. Whenever I breathed in, I got a good whiff of a pissy, ammonia smell, so I tried to hold out for as long as possible before taking in more air.

In. Out. In. Out. I felt like a woman in labor.

"What's the best way to get to Ninety-seven Bleecker Street?" I asked the lipsticked black woman on the other side of the glass when it was my turn. She hooked me up with two sets of directions. One for the subway and one for the bus. But when she saw the lost look on my face, she told me my best bet was to take a cab.

I made my way out of the station into the silvery winter daylight. The air felt cold and windy, but nothing compared to the arctic freeze I had survived last night. I had seen enough New York movies that making my way along the sidewalk felt pretty much like I had imagined. Gritty. Massive. Holedo times a thousand. It reminded me of a carnival ride or a movie that ran endlessly. All anyone had to do was take a breath and jump on in, which is exactly what I did.

A pink neon sign flashed WET! HOT! NASTY! Another buzzed LIVE GIRLS! If I were here for any other reason, I might have walked by those buildings, maybe tried to sneak inside even though I was underage. But I had to keep my mind on my mission.

The money.

My brother.

A taxi zoomed down the street. I waved my hand in the air, but the driver whizzed on by. Another taxi was right behind. Again I waved, and again the driver blew past me. I stood on the street a moment, wondering what the hell I was doing wrong. Looking lost was a direct invite for a wacko to brush up against me. "Plan A: You give me a quarter," he said. His breath pure decay. "Plan B: You give me fifty cents."

I clutched my duffel bag against my chest like I was protecting something precious in there. A baby. A bundle of money. In my head I heard Claude's warning: *muggers, beggars, murderers . . . kids like you dead in some fleabag Harlem motel room.* I made my way down the sidewalk away from the creep. And when a cab wheeled down the block, I waved both my arms in the air like someone drowning, calling for help.

"They're full!" another man who looked enough like Claude to be his brother shouted from a slumped position on the sidewalk. "Look for one with the roof light on."

I couldn't even hail a cab without a how-to lesson from a bum. I thought about thanking him but heard Claude's warning again, so I scoped out an available taxi and threw my hand in the air. When the driver actually stopped, I leaped inside and told him to take me to 97 Bleecker Street, Apartment 3B.

"Should I drop you in the living room or the kitchen?" he asked.

I knew he was making a joke, but I didn't get it. I was too busy rationing breaths again, since the cab smelled worse than the bus station. In. Hold. Out. Hold. Repeat. "Huh?" I managed on an exhale.

"I don't need the apartment," he said in a tongue-clucking accent. "Just the building number or the cross street."

Taxi lesson number two. "Oh," I said, cranking the window open to make breathing a bit easier, only to find exhaust blowing back at me. "Sorry."

As we drove downtown, the tall steel buildings and straight-arrow streets slowly vanished. Before I knew it, we were bumping along a crooked road lined with trees and brick houses only five or six stories tall. It was a part of the city I had never seen in movies, like something straight out of a storybook, one of Edie's fairy tales.

The driver stopped in front of 97. I gave him five bucks and hopped out. My uncle's building was a wide, brick-faced job with only six floors and dead ivy vines stretching across its face. I couldn't bring myself to buzz right away, so I stood there a moment looking up and down the block. Not far down the street a playground was deserted, probably too cold out for little kids. One of the swings—left twisted and tangled into a noose by some long-gone brat—moved back and forth in the wind. A man with a braid walked the perimeter of the park, a bouncy white poodle on his leash. I watched his ropy knot of hair drum against his back as he moved. I watched his dog press its gummy nose to the ground.

When I gazed up at the building again, I thought about my uncle and brother inside, living their lives. Making lunch. Watching television. Reading books. Whatever an abandoned brother and a kooky uncle do on a cold Saturday afternoon in January.

"It's just one little visit," I said out loud, trying to unjumble my insides, to stop the somersaulting feeling. I unfolded the address one final time and checked the apartment number. Before I lifted my finger to the buzzer, I thought about turning around, getting back on the bus to Holedo. But what was waiting for me there?

My sad, angry mother who thought my father had ripped her off.

Edie, who had fucked me over.

I couldn't go back now. And it seemed too late anyway.

My hand was reaching up.

My finger was pressing the button.

My shoulders were tightening against the cold as I waited for Uncle Donald's thick voice to answer. Or Truman's.

"Who is it?" a woman asked instead.

So my uncle had a girlfriend after all. The sound of her singsong voice made me feel better. Maybe she would take a liking to me and help Donald understand my need for the money. Maybe she would understand how nervous I was about meeting Truman. "I'm looking for Donald Biadogiano," I told her, trying my best to sound calm, mature. "I'm his nephew, Dominick."

The intercom went shhhhhhh, then chirped. "Dominick?" She said my name like a question. Obviously my uncle had never mentioned his dear old nephew from Massachusetts before. "Sorry. Donald's not at home."

"Will he be back soon?" I asked, praying for a yes. What had I been thinking? Just because he answered the phone at the crack of dawn did not mean he would be here in the middle of the day.

"I don't know when he'll be home. Try back later."

"Wait," I said.

"Yes?"

I took a deep breath. My throat tightened. "Is Truman here?"

This is it, a voice said. *You are going to find out about your brother.*

Shhhhh. Chirp. "Truman?" the woman said after what felt like forever. "Truman who?"

I had never really thought about my brother's last name before. It certainly wasn't Pindle. But did he use Biadogiano? Or the last name of the man in the photo beneath my mother's bed? "I don't know his last name exactly, but he lives here with Donald."

"Donald lives alone," the woman said. "And that's more information than I should be giving out over the intercom. Like I said, you'll have to stop back later."

The speaker went lifeless, and I stood on the street staring at the playground. The man and his poodle were gone. The noose was swaying in the breeze. The New York sky was the same dismal gray as the feathers of the pigeons on the sidewalk. A shitload of wet winter snow was bound to drop sometime soon. The thought of wandering the streets, waiting, hoping for Donald to show, made me lay my finger on the buzzer again.

"Who is it?" the woman asked as if she really expected it to be someone else.

This time her singsong had a little less song to it. The wishful image of her as my accomplice went splat in my brain. "Me again. Listen. I came all the way from Massachusetts to see my uncle. Can you at least let me up so I can leave him a note?"

A long pause that I took as a no. Then the door buzzed. Before she could change her mind, I pushed myself into the cramped lobby. The place had the flat, chalky smell of chemicals. Rife with powdery poison, like our apartment back in Holedo after the exterminator sprayed for roaches and set traps for mice and rats. For the third time that day I found myself rationing breaths. I was becoming an expert at barely breathing. I treaded up the ancient wooden staircase in the winter work boots my mother had given me Christmas morning. I hadn't worn them before today, and they were heavier than my sneakers, heavier than Edie's black shoes. I hated all that weight on my feet. It made walking work, especially upstairs.

Before I could knock, the woman called from inside the apartment, "Leave your message on the landing and I'll get it later."

She had an Irish accent, a squeaky leprechaun sort of deal that I had thought was merely singsonginess through the intercom. I wondered if my uncle had met her on one of his trips overseas.

"I don't have a pen and paper," I told her. "Besides, I'm his nephew. Can't I at least come inside? Who are you anyway?"

"I clean for Mr. B," she said.

The friggin' cleaning lady. No wonder she didn't know anything about me or my brother. "Well, I'm sure Mr. B told you to expect me," I said.

"He told me nothing."

Plan A: You open the fucking door. Plan B: I trick you into opening it. "Could you slide a piece of paper and a pen under the door?" I asked, staring down at the fluffy hallway carpet, flush against the door. I knew it would never fit and she'd have to open up. After that, I wasn't sure what I had in mind.

My Irish enemy shuffled around on the other side of the door. After a couple of tries she actually managed to slide out a piece of paper, crinkled and torn. Lucky for me, the pen wouldn't fit. Right on schedule, two locks twisted and clicked. The door creaked open. The woman behind the voice was too tall, with a white, papery face and white hair pulled back in a kerchief. A ghost with big ears, a ringed neck, and a billboard forehead.

"Thanks for opening up," I said, trying to put her at ease. "I really appreciate it."

She smiled—her teeth yellow against the rest of her backdrop—and handed me the pen. She kept guarding the door, though, like I was going to make a break for it. "Sorry I can't let you inside. But this is New York."

"I understand," I told her, still waiting for step two of my plan to come to me.

"I'll clean while you write," she said. "Knock when you're ready."

Before I could stop her, the door was closed again. I stood in the hallway a moment, clenching the pen and paper. Part of me wanted to slam my fists against the door until she let me in. But I doubted that would work, and not knowing what else to do, I wrote:

Uncle Donald,
Surprise! I'm in the city! But don't tell my mother. I'll walk
around your neighborhood for a while, then stop back. If you
come home, please stay put. I really need to see you.
Remember, <u>please</u> don't tell my mother I'm here.

Love, Dominick

If I'd had another piece of paper, I would have written the thing again, getting rid of those overly cheerful exclamation marks and making myself sound a little less worried about him blabbing to my mom. Erasable ink. That was another invention Donald could make billions on. People like me would pay big bucks to fix their mistakes. I was just about to fold the paper and knock when the door opened. The white lady was holding a framed picture. "It's you, right?" she said.

In the photo I was a kid—only about two or three years old—with a bowl haircut at a lake beach with Uncle Donald. Must have been taken before my memory kicked in, because I couldn't remember a single day like that with Donald. Still, I knew where this was leading.

"That's me all right. Donald and I go to the lake every summer."

"I'm Rosaleen. I dust your face whenever I'm here. I didn't recognize you because you're so big now." The door opened all the way, and Rosaleen ushered me inside. Finally.

The apartment had red-painted walls that made the place feel closed in, slippery, and bloody. The inside of a clot. The clutter of dusty furniture made me think of those overpriced tag sales that Marnie loved to raid, filling her trunk with junk, junk, and more junk. Donald had piles of paper and boxes everywhere, like he was either moving in or moving out. Black-inked labels read DO NOT THROW AWAY! IMPORTANT! RESEARCH MATERIALS!

"Sorry again," Rosaleen said. "But it's New York. Killers are everywhere. Nobody's safe. Do you want some tea?"

I wondered if she was reading from the same script as the bus driver Claude. After all, there was a playground practically across the street. How dangerous could this place really be? "Tea would be great," I told her, figuring a drink would guarantee me at least ten minutes in the apartment.

When she disappeared into the kitchen, I scoped around for clues about my brother. Good thing Donald hired a housecleaner, because the place was filthy. A disaster area, my mother would say, like she sometimes did about my bedroom. The wooden floors scuffed with skid marks from someone's boots. The frosty windows smudged and fingerprinted with swirling lines. Shelves crammed with books — *Discoveries in Turbo Physics*, *Nuclear Cooling Systems*, *Biomedical Engineering in the Twentieth Century*. A regular *Fun with Dick and Jane* collection.

I wandered over to a three-legged table next to a rocker with a frayed, woven seat. The tabletop was covered with framed pictures. Donald and a group of smart-looking guys in glasses and tuxes. Donald and another man with a beard and mustache, both in lab coats, holding up certificates with sunny golden seals. Donald wearing a dark sweater with a molten blue sky behind him and a smoldering sun.

None of anyone who could have been my brother.

On the mantel above the fireplace there were more photos. Still none of Truman, but I spotted one of my mother—a black-and-white shot I had seen before at home. It was taken when she was pregnant, and her stomach jutted out in front of her. Bigger than Edie's and impossible to hide. She wore a loose patterned shirt that made me think of Indians and powwows. Around her neck hung a string of beads. Her hair was longer than I'd ever seen it and looked windblown. Her smile was nothing like the lips-together one I knew. She was actually grinning, showing her two overlapped teeth.

I'm just so tired, I heard her say. *Things have got to get easier for me.*

At least the heat was working now. She wouldn't have to keep warm in that awful black coat. And I was going to replace the money somehow. I put down the picture and spotted one of Donald with the man from the photo under my mother's bed.

Same bushy hair. Same tight mummy skin.

Bingo.

When Rosaleen came back into the room with my cup of tea and a plateful of miniature sandwiches, I showed her the photo. "Do you know who this is?"

"I haven't the foggiest. But I dust him, too."

She was a regular information bank. At the very least I hoped she could give me an estimate—give or take an hour or two—of when my uncle would return. But when I asked again, she shrugged her shoulders, whipped out a dirty dust rag, and started cleaning. Defeated, I put down the picture and took a sip of tea. The taste was a flower petal on my tongue, not at all like my mother's Lipton's. The tea bag bobbed up and down inside my mug, a tadpole in a murky pond. I was dying to press her about Truman some more, but I didn't want to seem so unknowledge-able about my family that Rosaleen became suspicious and hurled me back out onto the street. I held in my questions and rode the wave of her mindless chatter as she moved around the apartment swiping random objects with her rag.

She talked about her cousin's hip surgery.

She talked about her part-time job as a nurses' aide.

She talked about the killer snowstorm that was headed our way.

She talked and talked and talked about everything, except my uncle and my brother. I wolfed down her eggy sandwiches and let my tea grow cold. When I couldn't take one more second of her babbling, I asked, "Are you sure nobody lives here with Donald?"

Rosaleen put her hands on her hips and shook her head. A loose white curl of hair bounced against her huge brow, and she blew it out of the way. "I told you, your uncle lives alone."

"Then where does Truman live?"

"I've never even heard of Truman," she said. "Whoever he is, he doesn't live here. I would charge more money if there was another mess-maker in this place."

I thought of all those mornings my father and I drove my mother to the bus station so she could travel to New York. All those carefully wrapped presents in her dainty hands that I used to wish were for me.

I decided Rosaleen-the-cleaning-machine had to be wrong. Maybe my uncle lied to her about Truman for the exact reason she had said: He didn't want her to charge more money for her services, which, judging from the looks of the place, weren't very good anyway. But that scenario smacked of bullshit. While Rosaleen straightened up the apartment—or at least went through the motions—I ducked out of the living room and poked around some more.

In the bathroom: a single, worn red toothbrush, one flannel robe complete with crusty tissues in the pockets, and one comb with dandruff in the teeth. In the first bedroom: a queen-size bed made up like one in a motel with two pillows tucked under the top sheet, a baby-chopper fan above the bed just like Edie's, which made my heart sink, a dresser filled with balled gray socks like dozens of dead mice, a closet filled with XL suits as somber and dark as an undertaker's. In the second bedroom: no bed, just a desk bigger than a casket and cluttered with crap, doodles of something that looked like a car without wheels or a piece of compli-cated hospital equipment, formulas and equations with numbers and let-ters and symbols that looked like an algebra nightmare.

All of it Donald's.

I was beginning to realize that Rosaleen was right, and the thought made me clench my teeth, squeeze my fists. There was no Truman. At least not in this apartment. Of all the scenarios I had imagined, it never occurred to me that Truman would simply not be here. First Edie had fucked me over. Now my own mother had lied to me. Not for days or weeks or months but for years.

My whole fucking life. She had lied to me.

Without planning it, I picked up the phone on Donald's desk. As I spun the rotary, my mind raced with all the things I would say to her.

It's time you told me about Truman.

Where the hell is my brother?

Why have you been lying?

Tell me. Tell me. Tell me.

The phone clicked through, and my heart felt like it might explode in my chest, the red chunks of it splattering against the wall for Rosaleen to clean like the flesh of that baby sliced to bits by the ceiling fan in my mother's story. A recorded voice crackled, "I'm sorry, the number you have reached is temporarily out of service. Please check the number and try your call again." I hung up, dialed again, slower this time. "I'm sorry, the number you have reached—" Again I hung up and redialed. Same recording.

What the hell was going on?

Outside the window, snow had started to fall. Wind pressed the flakes against the glass, where they melted and drooled down the pane. I glanced at the pile of papers on Donald's desk. Between the doodles and nightmare formulas was a desk calendar. Under January 23, 1972, I recognized my uncle's handwriting from the envelopes he addressed to my mother. It read: Pan Am Flight 237 to Cleveland, 1:00 P.M.

He wasn't coming back in a few hours.

He was halfway to goddamned Ohio.

I wasn't sure what to do next.

No Truman. No Donald. No money. The entire trip had been one big bust.

Down the hall Rosaleen was humming something hopelessly happy, and I closed the door to block out the sound of her. I picked up the phone and dialed Leon's number. Maybe he could clue me in on my mother's whereabouts, the reason for her disconnected phone. He answered on the first ring. "Man, you are just the person I wanted to see," he said. "Where the hell are you?"

"New York. But don't tell anyone."

"What the hell are you doing there?"

"It's a long story. I'll explain later. Have you seen my mother around today?"

"Nope. But your imaginary friend Edie was upstairs banging on your door."

I felt punctured at the sound of her name. Edie was at my apartment, and I could have been there to make her pay me back. I could have been there to listen to what she had to say. Only I had come up with a brilliant plan to go to New York, which so far was a complete and total waste. "Tell me what happened."

"Not much to tell. Edie Kramer was knocking away. When no one answered, she just stood there. Then she turned to me at the bottom of the stairs and said, 'Are you Leon?' "

Shit. I never should have mentioned Leon to her those nights at her house. Who knew what was coming next? "What happened?"

"I told her it was me in the flesh, and she handed me a letter in an envelope. Said to give it to you."

"Do you have the letter?"

"Yeah. Do you want me to read it?"

"No. I'll wait until I get home tonight."

"Too late," Leon said. "I ripped it open the second she waddled off."

"You fucker. That's my private letter."

"What are you, the postmaster general? Do you want me to read it to you or what?"

I huffed. "Fine."

Leo crinkled the paper a moment, then cleared his throat. "Are you ready?"

"Yes."

"Are you sure?"

"Read it!" I yelled, not caring if Rosaleen heard me.

"Okay, okay. It says, 'Dominick, I don't know why you left without saying good-bye last night. But I want you to know that I'm sorry if what's about to happen will hurt you. I needed a friend during this lonely time, and you were an angel. Someday I hope you'll forgive me. Someday I hope you'll understand. Love, Edie.' "

I walked to the bedroom window, stretching the phone cord as tight as it could go. Up close I could see that the snow was mixed with rain. Wind whipped the flakes and drops around into a blur of white and gray. Down the street the swing had twisted itself out of the noose and was moving back and forth. I imagined a child out there, swinging. "That's it?" I asked.

"The end," Leon said. "What the hell is all that about? Man, you weren't shitting me about knowing her. Did you get the bitch pregnant, angel?"

I wished I could have bragged about Edie like I did after that first night. Back then if this had happened, I would have gone on and on about it to Leon, flaunting that letter like it was some kind of trophy. But what Edie had done to me was nothing to brag about. And even though the Dominick who would have carried on like that was inside me somewhere, he seemed invisible. There but not there, like the child I imagined on the swing in the storm.

"Did she say anything else?" I asked, unsure of what I was hoping to hear.

"Sorry, angel. Just got in the car with some dude and left."

If he called me "angel" one more time, I was going to head straight back to Holedo and pummel him. I didn't care if he was twice my strength. "There was a guy in the car?"

"Yeah. A black guy."

"Who was he?"

"Flip Wilson. How the fuck should I know, Pindle? You're really annoying the shit out of me. See if I ever open your mail again."

"Dominick," Rosaleen called from the living room. "I finished cleaning."

"I gotta go," I said. "I'll see you when I get home."

I hung up the phone while Leon was still in the middle of another crack. When I returned to the living room, Rosaleen was fussing with her coat, a way-out green cape that she tied around her neck. The place seemed as if the storm had moved inside, dust floating in the air like snowflakes from Rosaleen's cleaning frenzy. Other than that, the apartment looked the same as when I had arrived. Fingerprints still smudged the windows. Papers still unfiled.

"I suppose I could let you stay until Donald gets home," Rosaleen said, pushing her arms through two slits in the cape. "But I have no idea what time that could be."

A week from Tuesday, I wanted to say. "He's expecting me, so he should be here soon." Silently I thanked God that she was leaving, that she hadn't asked who I was talking to in the bedroom.

"It was nice to meet you," she said at the door. "Try to keep things neat."

Good thing I wasn't in a better mood, because I would have busted out laughing. "I'll do my best," I told her.

The moment she was gone, I bolted the door and came up with a new plan: one last look around for signs of Truman, then head home to Holedo on the three o'clock bus before the storm shut down service. I would pedal my ass straight to Edie's and find out what she meant by "what happens next." I would demand my money back, then go home and nail my mother down about my brother's whereabouts once and for all.

I walked back to the bedroom and got down on my hands and knees to look under Donald's bed. Torn blanket. Old shoes. New shoes. More textbooks. I opened his nightstand drawer and dug around. Nasal spray. Antacid. Tissues. Take-out menus. I went to his desk again and pulled open those drawers. Scraps of scribbled notes—*Pick up samples before noon. Mail grant material by September 1. Prepare lecture on cell duplication*. A checkless checkbook with a balance of $10,422.89.

A lot of good that did me.

Just as I was about to give up, I hit pay dirt in a shoe box in the back of my uncle's closet. Nothing about Truman, but I found some cold hard cash instead. Fifteen hundred to be exact. Either it was a family thing or most of America was hiding their money in the same place and I could get pretty damn rich robbing houses. I hadn't planned on getting the money this way, and it wasn't enough to replace what I had stolen from my mother, but I would take what I could get. Donald could blame his batty cleaning lady when he found it missing—*if* he found it missing in this dump.

Inside the shoe box with the money was a Bible. It threw me for a loop, since Donald didn't seem like the type who would own anything religious, never mind keeping the good book in a special hiding place. I flipped the thin pages, hoping he had crammed more money inside. No green stuff, but a scrap of newspaper fell to the floor, fluttering like a fat gray moth.

DAY 3: BOY STILL MISSING

It didn't make any sense that he would save a headline but not the article, yet that's all there was. The words gave me the same nervous feelings I got from all those headlines I'd read with Edie about murder, cyclones, and fucked-up things in the world. I had enough to think about at the moment, though, so I shoved the slip of paper back into the Bible, tossed it in the box, and headed for the living room.

Before walking out the door, I picked up that picture of the man beneath my mother's bed. Carefully I slid out the frame, looking for a name or date on the reverse side. There was nothing. I shoved the photo back behind the glass, put on my dad's hunting coat, and stuffed the money into the duffel bag. I walked to the kitchen window to check on the weather. Outside it had grown dark.

Wind still whipping.

Nobody on the sidewalk.

Rosaleen had left the picture of me at the beach with Donald on the stove. Clearly not where it belonged. I carried it back to the living room and was about to put it with all the others when something made me stop. I flipped back the frame and slid the photo out like I had the other. I guess I was wondering about the date, since I really couldn't remember a single beach excursion with Donald. On the back of the photo my mother's even, careful script made me hold my breath.

Donald and Truman, Laguna del Perro, 1955

It wasn't me in the picture after all.

It was my brother.

I turned the photo around and looked at Truman's face. After all this time, there he was smiling back at me, erecting a bucket-shaped castle with the rocky sand. Even with different fathers, he looked so much like me that it was scary. Same stringy hair. Same wide eyes. Same wimpy white skin that would be burned at the end of a too-sunny day like that one. He was my brother for sure. A part of me.

I could have stood there staring at the picture for hours. But the thought of getting back to Holedo, where I would sort out this shit for good, instead of playing my lifelong guessing game, made me carefully place the picture in my duffel bag and head toward the door. Before leaving, I took a set of spare keys off a nail by the coatrack, tried them in the dead bolt to be sure they worked in case I ever needed to get back in the place and didn't want to deal with Rosaleen, then headed downstairs.

Even with the storm, my uptown trip was easier than downtown.

An available taxi. An odorless driver who moved swiftly through the slippery streets.

Five bucks later I was back at Port Authority. This time I didn't have that lost look on my face and nobody bugged me as I rushed through the station, careful not to slip on the wet floor, down the escalator to my bus. I climbed on board, and instead of Claude, my driver was a sloppy-looking, red-faced man who tore my ticket without even looking me in the eye.

The bus was mobbed, and I found the only empty seat near the back, next to a sleeping nun.

The driver made an announcement that because of the weather, we would be traveling slowly and the trip would be longer than usual. More good news. I settled in as best I could without getting too comfy with the nun, since the *last* thing I wanted was to wake her. As the bus chugged out of the station and moved through the snow and rain onto the highway, I caught my breath, tried to clear my mind.

Across the aisle a porky girl with a freckle overdose was chowing down on Good & Plenty. Smack. Smack. Gulp. "Please don't eat me! I don't want to be dead," her older brother said in the squeaky voice kids use to animate almost everything. Once he got his sister to feel guilty, she set a few of her pink or white beans on the armrest and stroked them with her pudgy fingers like pets. Then her brother said, "I waited my whole life for someone to eat me, and now I'm just going to waste away on this dumb bus." After that the girl happily mashed the candy to bits in her mouth, only to find it calling to her from the depths of her stomach. "Why did you kill me? Why? Why? Why? I hate being dead." When the girl was near tears because of her brother's brain fuck, their mother cranked her fat neck around from the seat in front of them and told them to knock it off. They shut up for a few minutes, but then the routine started all over again.

The whole game made my head pound. While they carried on, I kept staring at the picture of my brother. I flipped the photo over and read my mother's handwriting, then flipped it back and looked in Truman's brown eyes. I wondered what he was thinking that day at the beach. I wondered what he was thinking now. Most of all I wondered how my mother was going to explain all this. I must have flipped that picture back and forth a hundred times and asked those questions about a thousand more as the bus moved north toward Holedo.

The Good & Plenty gang got off in Hartford. The girl left a row of candies stashed on her seat like the colorful eggs of a bug waiting to hatch. "I saved their lives," she said quietly to me so her brother couldn't hear. He was too glad to be getting off the bus to notice anyway. "Take care of them," she whispered.

The second she stepped off the bus, I brushed the candies to the floor and stretched out on the empty seats. Across the aisle the nun stirred and let her mouth drop open like a ghoul in a black cape, but she kept sleeping. In her hands she clutched a Bible. In mine I clutched Truman. In between staring at his picture and piecing together all I had or hadn't learned today, I poked my head up to check on the bus's progress through the storm. Over the even domino row of seats I could see the driver's dark, shadowy figure like death at the wheel, the green road signs slipping by, one after another. Other than the occasional dull murmur of people's conversations, the only sounds were the ratchety squeak of the seats, the hum of the tires beneath us, the wind blowing through the rubber of the folding bus door. We were moving pretty fast, considering. I decided to give some shut-eye a shot, and by the time we got to Holedo, my neck and shoulders were stiff from sleeping in my cramped and twisted position.

"It's eight P.M. local time here in sunny Holedo," the driver announced over the loudspeaker when we finally pulled into the station after what felt like a decade on the road. "Our flight is landing only one hour behind schedule."

Everyone on board was too dead from the trip to react to his joke. The nun, in particular, was still out cold, and I was beginning to wonder if she had missed her stop. But I decided to let God take care of her.

I put the picture of my brother back in my duffel bag and hopped off the bus. The air had that muffled hush of a winter storm. The snow falling full throttle. A plow rumbling in the distance. I could see its yellow flashing lights reflected on the weighed-down white branches of the trees. Buried in a thick layer of slushy snow, my bike looked like a crooked skeleton behind the fence where I had dumped it that morning. I picked it up, wiped the seat with the sleeve of my father's hunting coat, and started pedaling. I may as well have been pedaling on the moon, as desolate, dark, and cold as everything was. I usually did a decent job of maneuvering my bike in snow. But the stiffness in my neck and the duffel bag over my shoulder made steering near impossible. Twice I lost my balance and fell against the curb. After the second fall I stayed off the bike and walked it toward Edie's instead.

The colder I got and the heavier my feet felt, the more I wanted to abort the mission. But Edie's letter kept ringing in my ears.

I'm sorry if what's about to happen will hurt you.

I needed a friend during this lonely time, and you were an angel.

Someday I hope you'll forgive me.

Someday I hope you'll understand.

When I wasn't thinking about the letter, I found myself thinking of my mother's handwriting on the back of that picture, wondering about the disconnected phone at our apartment. At the corner where I would have to turn either toward home or toward Edie's, I stopped in the middle of the empty, snow-covered street. Breathless and cold, I thought about simply going home. My direction depended on whose answers I wanted more. My mother's or Edie's. I knew that the truth about Truman mattered to me the most, but when my feet started to move, I was walking toward Edie's.

At the top of the hill I could see that her house was completely dark, not even the porch light lit. Near the end of her driveway a sign had been pitched by the mailbox. FOR SALE. MOOREHEAD REAL ESTATE. CONTACT AGENT: VICKI SPRING. The sight of it made my face wrinkle and wince as if I had been slapped. So that's what she had meant by what happens next. Edie was moving. Selling off her old furniture and now the house. Skipping town with my mother's money.

Not if I stopped her first.

I dumped my bike and trudged through the snow to the front porch. The door was locked, so I started banging. "Edie!" I yelled in a white fog of air. "Edie! Open up now!"

I waited for her to answer, pacing the porch and punching the door when I walked by. The wind let out a lonely-sounding whistle, like someone far away calling for help. In the distance I could hear another plow scraping and moaning. No noise came from inside the house.

Finally I peeked in a window.

The living room was empty.

I walked around to the back of the house and looked in the kitchen window.

Empty as well.

The seashell wind chime still hung by the back door; I ripped it down and hurled the piece of shit at the picture window. It clanked against the glass and fell to the snow in a soft, silent hush. Nothing broke. In my throb of anger I found myself digging around for a rock or a brick. I got my hands on an empty planter, lifted it up out of the snow, and hurled that, too. This time the glass shattered in an explosion of noise. It looked like a million stars or icicles coming undone. The second the shattering was over, the air seemed even quieter than before. Just the patter of snow and rain hitting the ground. I made my way up the stairs, stretched my arms to the window, and climbed inside.

What was I looking for? Clearly, if Edie had been home, she would have come running by now. I suppose I wanted proof that she had taken everything, left nothing behind, and was gone for good. And that's exactly what I got. All that remained was the ivy and flowered wallpapers, the matted brown carpet in the hallway, scattered dust balls blowing through the place like tiny tumbleweeds. The house felt like a giant clammy mouth that had finally been stretched open and forced to breathe with the breaking of the window. Air blew in through the rooms and seemed to snake around every corner, wiping out even the faintest smell that might have been left of Edie's perfume.

I walked through the echoing, hollow hallway to her bedroom and stood in the doorway. She had left the ceiling fan going, and the blades kept moving above the empty space where her bed used to be, as menacing and evil-looking as ever, circulating the air the way she liked even though she was gone. I remembered the first time I saw my father in this room, bare-chested and sleeping in Edie's bed. I remembered the last time I woke here in my underwear and went to find her.

I should have known that between that starting point and now, something was seriously wrong. A woman like Edie didn't go after a kid like me unless she wanted something. She had used me. No matter how she tried to soften things in her letter, that was the only truth about our relationship. And even if I missed her as much as I hated her, even if I worried about her out there somewhere with that baby in her belly, with that man who I never met behind the wheel of her car, I had to swallow that truth and move on. She was gone, and I needed to walk out of this place and stop thinking about her forever, no matter how hard that would be.

I decided that I would go home and tell my mother everything. Then I would make her tell me everything, too, beginning with the truth about my brother. After that, we would start fresh with our lives.

I walked outside and found my bike, blown over by the wind and twisted in the driveway. I climbed on and pedaled away from Edie's house, listening to the gravel crunch beneath the snow and my bicycle tires one last time, feeling the wind from the top of the hill blow against my forehead and muss my hair. I coasted down the hill faster than I should have considering the trouble I had steering. I wanted to make a plan for my mother and me, to stop thinking about Edie like I promised myself when I walked out her door. But she was still with me. As I rounded the corner toward the Holedo Motel, I heard her words in my head.

We'll check in to the room together.

When I looked up, there were dozens of cop cars in front of the motel. No sirens. Just the buzz and murmur of a police radio. I heard the words "Body. APB. Pregnant female." I heard the numbness of radio static, then the same words repeated: "Body. APB. Pregnant female." I wheeled my bike through the snow-covered parking lot, which had been flattened into a slick white rug by so many tire tracks, and got off between two empty cop cars. I spotted Marnie's yellow Dart parked in the far corner of the lot. Roget was nowhere.

We'll leave in the morning. Then check in to the room together.

Edie had to be here. But something was wrong.

I'm sorry if what's about to happen will hurt you.

I left my bike and made my way up the cement stairs to the crowd of policemen on the second floor, outside room 5B.

"Hey, kid," someone called from the parking lot. "You can't go up there."

"Who's in there?" I asked when I got closer to the mob of policemen.

Two of the cops turned and looked at me. Marnie was standing behind them, and they opened up to her like two double doors. She screamed at the sight of me. Not a word, but a sound. "Oeopllejjjj! Ooopllejjjj!" One of the officers held her by the arm. She looked ancient. Broken. Black, inky tears smeared down her cheeks.

"Marnie. Who's in there?" I said, but it was no use. She just kept screaming.

"Is Officer Roget here?" I asked.

Both policemen eyed each other. "We're looking for him," one said finally.

"Is Edie Kramer in that room?" I asked, loud and trembling.

With that, Marnie let out a yelp louder than all the others and fell to her knees. And I knew that it was true. Edie was in there, and something was very wrong.

If something should happen to me, she whispered.

I broke past both cops who tried to hold me back. They got tangled up in Marnie's flailing arms instead. I busted by an ambulance man in a white uniform, shoved myself into the motel room, and slammed the door behind me. Locked it. Closed my eyes. "When I turn around, Edie will be here and she will be okay," I said.

Slowly I turned.

I felt my body lift from the ground.

I was looking down on the room like a camera on the ceiling. The scene came in flashes: On the floor was a woman. Facedown. Hair matted. Neck twisted. Hand holding the telephone. Towels between her legs. Blood running wild along the carpet. A pregnant woman trying to get rid of her baby. Only she had killed herself instead. The woman was my mother.

FIVE

She met him one night last spring when she set out on her own in search of her husband. After spying out all the usual places, she parked on the side of Hanover Street, wondering where to go next. That's when he pulled up behind her, got out of his car, and tap-tap-tapped his sleek black flashlight against her window. She had failed to signal, he explained, and her brake lights weren't working either. He could have written her a ticket. But if she promised to have her husband fix those lights first thing in the morning and to remember to signal the next time she pulled to the side of the road, he would skip all that and simply follow her home to make sure she got there safe and sound.

She sat behind the wheel of her car and made that promise.

She actually crossed her heart.

He wasn't at all the type of man she usually found attractive. Her first husband, before he died, had been a dreamer, always working odd jobs while coming up with a new way to hit it big. And her present husband was *a free spirit, a trait she had been drawn to until it wreaked havoc on her life. But this man—a police officer—seemed solid and strong, despite what her husband always said. Like his squad car steadily trailing her home— secure, capable, watchful.*

She told herself that none of those feelings mattered. After all, she was a married woman. Given the way her last family had fallen apart, along with all the other lives she had traded in, she was determined to make this one work. If not for her sake, then for her younger son's. But then she saw the officer again in the market on a Sunday afternoon in June. Her husband had been on a bender for days, and the sheriff walked alongside her, up and down the aisles of the grocery store, past the rainbow of cans and boxes, until they had both filled their carts.

Not long after, she began meeting him at the motel.

July. August. September.

To be kissed.

To be held.

To close her eyes and listen to his deep voice.

He left her with a sense of calm that wasn't quite love but something almost more indelible, because there was none of the turmoil she had known in her other relationships. With him she still had the pieces of herself intact even when they were apart, whereas those other men had left her feeling shattered. Unglued.

Then she missed her period.

At first she lied to herself. She was nervous, and that had thrown off her body clock before. But her belly began to show, and she simply wanted to will it all away.

October. November. December.

She twisted the knob on the radiator until it stuck. The heat's broken, she explained to her son, I'll wear this coat until it's fixed.

Until I'm fixed, she kept saying to her best friend. Then it dawned on her: Couldn't her friend use her hospital connections to ask someone for help? Couldn't she sneak into a supply room and steal some ergot? But the nurses threatened to report her friend, and now she was worried for her job.

It's a hospital, she told her friend again and again with a false sense of calm. Trust me, people have asked that question before.

Her husband called from the road and said he would be home in one week. He acted as if it were perfectly normal for a man with a wife and kid to be gone through the holidays. More than anything she wanted to shake off these last months the way he had. But when it came time to face him, her pregnancy would be impossible to deny. And since there was not a chance that it could be his child, she was afraid of what he might do.

She made plans to go away.

The officer had no money of his own, but he knew a friend who knew someone who could arrange for her to have a late-term abortion. She planned to use a few thousand dollars of the emergency money she had saved from her brother. She would fly to Mexico City. An expatriate doctor would take her to a house where he did this sort of thing all the time. It was safe. It was clean.

She opened her jewelry box, and almost all of the money was gone.

She peeled back her bedroom rug and pulled out coupons and singles tucked between two hundred-dollar bills.

She lifted the top to an old shoe box and found only a handful of small bills inside.

She was four and a half months pregnant and could not wait another day. The officer said a doctor friend had told him exactly how to do it. This doctor friend had given him the instruments. Her best friend came up with the latex gloves and sterilization kit. She unplugged the phone so people would think there was trouble with the line instead of wondering where she was if they called and didn't get an answer. She met the officer in the parking lot of the motel where the child inside her had been conceived.

It was a bitter, snowy night, and she wanted to say good-bye to her younger son just in case something went wrong. Things had been tense between them, and she wanted to make amends. When this was over, she might even tell him about the nightmare with her first husband and son. He was old enough now to know. But he had gone off for the day with his friend.

A speculum. A smooth slim probe of steel.

Her stomach convulsed. Her vagina bled. The officer kept trying to stop the blood, but it gushed, faster and faster. The towels became drenched, and the more he tried to help, the more the blood pooled around her. She looked up in a blur and saw that his face had gone ghost-white with panic. He had been trained for emergencies but never for an emergency like this one. He could be arrested for his involvement here. He could lose everything he had ever worked for. In a court of law, he would be treated no different than a murderer. She knew. He knew. They both knew. Be right back, the officer said, gripping the gold badge on his chest as if his heart ached beneath it, broken and hardened by fear.

He left the room.

She thought of her husband calling him a coward—a lazy, crooked coward—and something told her he would never be back. That's when the unglued feeling overtook her. There on the floor, she felt as if a pack of wild dogs had been let loose inside her, trampling her insides, shredding her to nothing. She rolled her body over. In one last effort, she stretched her hand to the phone.

Her best friend answered.

Something's wrong, she told her between breaths. I'm bleeding and it hurts. He said he would be right back. But I know he's gone for good. How quickly can you come?

MARNIE TOLD me again and again the story of how my mother died. As we drove inside the dry cockpit of her car on our way to the memorial service, she found it necessary to go over the details one more time. My mother's first meeting with Roget, their secret rendezvous at the motel, her pregnancy hidden beneath that coat, and, of course, the missing money. Each time my mind bubbled with questions but only grasped them for a few fleeting seconds before letting go. The answers didn't matter, because the end result was the same: My mother was gone, and I was to blame.

When I looked over at Marnie, she was crying again, her face crinkled into a distorted blob. One hand held the steering wheel while the other dabbed a clump of baby-blue tissues at her cheeks. "How dare those policemen cover for that chicken bastard. If he had just stayed with her, called for help . . ." Her hand smacked the steering wheel. Her tears kept coming.

Your mother might still be alive, I thought, finishing her sentence.

The more Marnie repeated that story, the more numb I became. My eyes bulged. My voice whispered. I spoke in one-word sentences, if at all. I stared out at the road, the double yellow line stretching before us and leading the way. Tree branches leaned over both sides of the street, tunneling us as we drove beneath. The sky had been full of glaring, after-the-storm sunlight for the last couple of days, but it had yet to melt the bulk of the snow. My mother couldn't be dead, I kept telling myself as I stared out at all that whiteness. I had just seen her two days before, asleep on the couch while I cranked on the radiator. But then my mind flashed on that image of her body in the motel. After I found her like that, I had blacked out, fallen to the floor. Right smack in the middle of my forehead I sported a plum-colored bruise the shape of South America. Not from the fall but from the door hitting me when the officers busted back inside. I reached up and touched that bruise as we drove. I winced at the sting, then finger-combed my hair forward to cover it.

"How's your head, Dominick?" Marnie asked, turning her red eyes away from the road toward me. No more "honey cake" or "sweet lips"— just plain old Dominick. She had ditched the Southern act the night my mother died.

Whenever I tried to speak, it felt as if a giant metal fishhook were lodged deep in my throat. Yes. No. Okay. Maybe. That was all anyone got from me when it came to conversation. "Okay," I said and looked down at the worn floor mats of her car. Another thing I couldn't do: make eye contact.

Even though her dogs, Fred and Ginger, had died over a year ago, I could still smell them from where I sat, dressed in the stiff blue suit

Marnie had brought to me that morning. At my feet were scattered pennies, torn coupons, and newspaper clippings. When I was a kid, I used to collect that crap off her floor. Marnie would make like her tape deck was a candy machine and pull out red and white pinwheel mints for me to buy. A penny apiece. She accepted coupons, too.

My mother was dead, and here I was thinking about Marnie and our stupid baby games. What kind of son was I? I didn't let myself answer that question. Instead I thought of what Marnie had told me about my mother turning off the radiator so she had an excuse to wear that coat. If only I hadn't been so caught up with Edie, I might have suspected. I thought of all the clues that I had let fly right over my head. The way my mother carried on about Roget at the auction. His phone call afterward. That night he had driven me home in my underwear. What was it he had said? She has a lot on her plate, so go easy on her, or something like that. Yeah, well, maybe he should have listened to his own advice and gone easy on her instead of leaving her alone to die. I wanted to kill him, to grab the pistol from his holster and shoot it into his stomach, to let him suffer a bloody death the way my mother had. But I told myself that as guilty as Roget was for abandoning my mother in that motel room, I was far guiltier for betraying her long before that.

She needed that money. She needed me.

We pulled up in front of the funeral parlor—a one-story white building that looked like an ordinary house, something a little old lady might own, if you took away the RINETTE FUNERAL HOME sign above the door. I saw my father standing beneath that sign shaking hands with everyone who entered. Ever since he showed up the day after my mother's death, he had been acting as if we had all been one big happy family until tragedy struck. He had yet to address the fact—at least to me—that my mother had died from a botched abortion, never mind mentioning that the baby couldn't have been his. He simply played his part as the brokenhearted husband. He made all the arrangements: memorial service today, a few words at the cemetery afterward, burial when the ground thawed. He had even gotten here early this morning to have "some time alone with my wife." His perfect-father routine made me hate him more than ever.

Inside, there were more people than I expected. Leon and Mrs. Diesel. Mr. and Mrs. Ramillo, the egg-shaped older couple from next door. A few of Marnie's friends from the hospital, all gussied up in frumpy Sunday dresses. My father's drinking buddies and Mac Maloney, the owner and bartender of Maloney's Pub. The place smelled moth-bally and used, like a library, only without the books. A bald-headed priest made a beeline for me the moment I stepped through the door-way. His name was Father Conroy, he told me. He was new to the parish in Holedo and deeply sorry for my loss. As he launched into a speech about God's great plan for all of us, I looked away from his eyes, down at his hand shaking mine. The guy was missing a thumb, just like my wood-shop teacher last year who had accidentally cut his off with a radial saw. I found myself imagining the far-fetched occupational hazards of a priest that could have led to losing a finger. Maybe he had sliced it off while cutting up a batch of holy bread. Maybe some hungry church lady had sunk her teeth into it as he lay a communion wafer on her tongue.

"She's with the Good Lord now," he said and gave me the kind of watery-eyed, dull expression that made me think of a fish tank. Steady bubble. Zero surprise.

That hook was still lodged in my throat, so I simply nodded. He couldn't possibly believe what he was saying anyway. Ask every Catholic on the planet and they would tell you abortion was a sin. Never mind a priest, who was bound to believe that my mother had bought herself a one-way ticket to hell the night she checked into that motel room. I knew better. If there was a heaven, my mother would be there, the child inside her grown full-term.

I'd be the one in hell.

Father No Thumb led me to a chair at the front of the room, where I was bookended by my father and Marnie. My mother's closed wooden coffin was buried beneath dozens of tight red roses like animal hearts, baby's breath all around. I imagined the hushed silence inside, the thin breathless air, the stillness. There was a framed picture of her on top of the casket, smiling in that closed-lip way. Seeing it made my head feel thick and cloudy, used up. "How you doing, son?" my father said, clasping his hand on my shoulder and squeezing.

I shrugged. Across the room a line was forming, and I kept my eyes on the crowd in hopes that my father would look away, too, and not say anything else to me. One by one, people began filing past my mother's casket, doing a kneel-and-pray routine before moving on to my father, then me, then Marnie. Before I knew it, I was caught up in a blur of faces and whispered apologies.

"I'm so sorry . . ."

"If there's anything I can do . . ."

"Please call if you need help . . ."

Marnie got right down to wailing and carrying on. But I stayed stone-faced with each and every handshake. I told myself that I didn't deserve their condolences, seeing as I was the one who had put my mother in that casket. I had led her straight to death's door with all my lying and underhanded schemes, so I was the one who should have been saying how sorry I felt.

As I sat, blank and stiff, letting their words slide right off me, my father sponged up every last bit of their attention. He kept saying the same thing over and over: "I loved that woman . . . God, how I loved that woman."

If you loved her so much, I thought, then why didn't you bother to come home for the last month of her life? And why were you in Edie Kramer's bed last June? That's what got this doomsday ball rolling in the first place. But I didn't bother saying anything, because I had a funny way of showing love to my mother as well. I just let him play his part and kept nodding and looking down at the red rug of the funeral home with each passing person.

No tears, I promised myself.

When I looked up, Leon was kneeling before me. Hair grown almost down to his shoulders. New sand-colored cords and a blue button-down shirt with metal snaps left unsnapped over his chest. A guy from school named Ed Dreary stood behind him. I hadn't hung out with Ed since the fifth grade. He was so dopey and pathetic, with his dandruff-flecked hair, rhino nose, and Nixon cheeks, that guys in school had started calling him Special Ed a few years back, and the name stuck. Weird that he and Leon were together.

"Hey," Leon said.

"Hey," Special Ed said, too.

"Hey," I said back to both of them.

"You okay?" Leon asked.

I nodded yes. I was fine. I wasn't crying, was I?

"About that letter," Leon said. He stopped and glanced at my father, who was busy professing his undying love for my mother to a stubby woman with windshields for glasses. Leon lowered his voice still more and said, "From your friend."

I cocked my head at him, confused. Sniffled because my nose was running. Must have been that library odor. All those roses that looked like animal hearts.

"Edie Kramer," he whispered, close enough that I could smell the last cigarette on his breath.

I felt that fishhook shift and dislodge itself in my throat, choking me as I tried to speak. "I don't ever want to talk about her again. Ever!"

My first full sentence in days, and it came out louder than I had expected. The woman with the Bozo glasses looked over, then turned back toward my father. "I loved her more than anything," he told her.

Leon cleared his throat and stood, let his hands fall near his crotch the way he always did. Like he was pointing to his package, or something perverted. "Okay," he said. "Sure thing. Forget about it. I'm sorry."

I wanted to say something more to make sure he got the point, but I was afraid I might start bawling, so I held back. Leon and Special Ed walked off, and I let myself get swept up in the sea of long faces and condolences. The woman with the glasses was gone, but a pack of Marnie's friends made their way over.

Jeanette. Lois. Ruth. Carol.

"I'm so sorry for you . . ."

"I lost my mother recently, and I know it's hard . . ."

"All we can do is pray for her soul now . . ."

"She's looking down on you . . ."

After they blew off, I sat there kicking at my seat and wondering how long this torture would last. I couldn't stand people feeling sorry for me when I was the reason we were all here. I was the reason my mother was gone. "Hey, kid," someone said, and I looked up.

Uncle Donald. He had trimmed his beard back so it was just a thin shadow around the edges of his fat jaw, a dark line over his lip. He could have penciled the thing on. I had been so busy missing my mother and blaming myself that I hadn't even planned on seeing him here today. I scanned the room in search of my brother, anyone who looked remotely like that boy at Laguna del Perro in 1955. Nothing. I stared back at my uncle, his large brown eyes behind wire-rimmed glasses. He wore a wrinkled black suit with a white shirt and a long thin tie. A folded yellow envelope stuck out of his pocket. This is my mother's brother, I thought. If he's alive, then how can she be dead?

"How you doing?" he asked me.

I shrugged. "Okay," I told him. My voice cracked, but I didn't feel that fishhook in my throat any longer.

"Come here," he said and wrapped his bear arms around me.

Caught off guard by his hug, I felt myself begin to slip. The tears started even as I tried to hold them back. My mouth opened and let out a shapeless sound I had never heard myself make before. I don't know why it took him to break the dam inside me, but it did. I cried, and I couldn't stop. Everyone was probably staring at me, thinking what a pathetic mess I was or feeling sorry for me without realizing that it was all my fault. But I couldn't help it. I missed my mother and wanted her back. I was never going to see her again.

"It's going to be okay, kid," Donald said. "Let it out. You loved her and it hurts, I know. Just let yourself cry."

The more he said those things, the more I bawled. My nose was running all over the place, and whenever I tried to gulp in more air, I let out that shapeless sound that embarrassed me. I must have carried on like that for five minutes. Ten. Finally I loosened my grip on Donald and caught my breath. The funeral line was backed up like a traffic jam on Route 67. The crowd must have taken my cue, because most of the room had their waterworks going full blast. Even the priest was shedding a few tears, and he probably did a funeral or two a week.

I looked at my uncle, opened my mouth, and said, "Truman."

His face was expressionless. He blinked, took a breath, blinked again.

"My brother should be at our mother's funeral," I said.

My uncle was quiet a moment. He rested his hand on mine. "I'm sorry."

I started to say something else, but Marnie stood and pulled Donald away. She led him over to the priest and made the introductions. The father launched into his spiel about God's great plan, and I resumed my staring contest with the rug.

Where was my brother?

If this event didn't drag him out of the woodwork, nothing would. I decided that maybe he was dead, too. He had drowned that day at Laguna del Perro in 1955 after the picture was taken. My mother had been one of those women who couldn't accept the loss of her child, so she still fantasized that her son was alive, simply living with her brother in Manhattan.

"Dominick," a woman said, "it's me, Mrs. Tanenbaum. I'm so sorry."

It was the woman with the too-big glasses who had been listening to my father's sob story a few minutes ago. I shook her hand and nodded, letting the name Tanenbaum bounce around my brain in hopes of recognition. I came up empty until she finished what she was saying and walked away. From behind I recognized her squat body and chunky rear from seeing her up at the chalkboard. Mrs. T. My kindergarten art teacher. Something about the sight of her—remembering the pasty smell of her skin as she had helped me make macaroni montages and cut scraps of construction paper into refrigerator art for my mother—caused my stomach to bend and coil. An invisible hand pushed on my chest and made it hard for me to breathe. I bolted for the glowing red EXIT sign, left the I'm-so-sorry parade behind.

Outside, I retched by the Dumpster. I'm not sure what my body was churning up, because I hadn't really eaten since the bus ride two days before. But out it came, all soft and yellow whatever it was. When I couldn't heave anymore, I stood there leaning against the cold blue metal of the Dumpster, wondering why a funeral home needed such a big garbage-disposal system. What could they possibly have to throw away? Dead flowers. Body parts.

When I turned around, I noticed Leon and Special Ed standing across the lot. They were dragging on cigarettes and flipping pages of *The Discount Car News*, circling ads. Leon raised his chin up at me as a way of saying hello. He had seen me puke my guts out plenty of times on our Holedo Hell-Raiser drinking nights, but this was different. "Sorry," I said, feeling pathetic.

"It's cool," Leon said. "Do what you need to do."

Special Ed nodded, and something about that nod—like he knew what the fuck I was feeling, like he knew what it was like to be responsible for your mother's death—made me want to rail him. But I just turned and walked away. Special fucking Ed. What the hell did he know?

I stayed numb for the rest of the service and for the whole trip out to the cemetery, where Thumbless gave a speech about death being the beginning or some such line of bull. In my head I listened to the entire *Tommy* album to block it all out.

What about the boy?
What about the boy?
What about the boy?
He saw it all.

When the priest finished, Marnie promptly collapsed by the pile of flowers that covered the ground where my mother would be buried come spring. Jeanette, Ruth, Lois, and Carol fussed over her like a stew they were taste-testing.

"She needs air."

"She needs water."

"She needs to walk around."

More salt, I thought. Less pepper. Let her boil down.

"Let's walk her to the car," they all concurred and escorted her to the Dart. Her meltdown would give me an excuse to keep riding with her instead of my father, who was side-saddling with the priest. As people plucked roses from the pile for keepsakes, I ran those Who lyrics in my head to keep from crying again. When I couldn't stand it anymore, I switched to those lines from my mother's sad songs. *"I looked at my life today. I wish I was happy living this way."* That brought me closer to the brink, so I turned off the DJ in my head and started thinking about those fairy tales. That mother who gave her son the last of her money and he blew it on some beans. A giant stalk.

When it was all over, I got back into Marnie's car and let out a sigh. My plan: to head straight home, lock my bedroom door, and cry alone. After that my life was as black as a blank chalkboard to me.

Once we were on the road I realized the whole gang was following us to the apartment for a reception. "Is this a bon voyage party?" I asked Marnie. "Enough is enough."

"Dominick," she said, her voice still shaky, on the edge of tears, "there are always receptions after funerals. It gives people a chance to reminisce about the person who's left us. Besides, everyone needs to eat."

"That's right," I said. "Now that we've all worked up an appetite standing around my mother's grave, let's go back and rustle up some grub. I bet my kindergarten art teacher and Mrs. Diesel will have a grand old time discussing their millions of memories of my mother. We can all talk about her affair with the sheriff. Or about her plans for an abortion. Or about her son who didn't show at his mother's funeral!"

Without realizing it, I had seriously raised the volume and was out-and-out screaming. Marnie looked at me with an open-mouthed,

Halloween-horror expression on her face. She seemed to me like someone with no bones inside her anymore. Flimsy. Collapsible. We pulled
to the side of the road, and she stretched her wobbly arms toward me to
give me a hug. I knew that would only lead to one of her crying jags, and
I'd end up having to console her, straighten her back up.

No thank you.

"I don't want a hug!" I screamed, pushing her weak arms away.

"I'm sorry," she said, recoiling. "It's all my fault. I should have talked
your mother out of it. Should have gone with her or something. I understand why you're blaming me."

If I traced back the blame, it landed on one person: yours truly. Sure,
I could hang some of it on my father for meeting Edie in the first place,
my mother for carrying on with Roget and getting pregnant, and Edie for
fucking me over. But the biggest onus fell on me. If that money had been
there, none of this would have happened.

"I'm not blaming you, Marnie," I said, calmer than before. "You
were the only real friend she had. Believe me, it wasn't your fault." I saw
myself as a black-robed judge, slamming down his gavel. Marnie
Garboni is found not guilty by reason of insanity.

Marnie pulled that same clump of stiff blue tissues from her pocket
and blew her nose. "I was?"

"Yes," I said and meant it. "Out of all the people at that service who
told me how much they would miss my mother, I know you're the one
who will miss her the most. You talked to her more than I did. Listened
to all her worries." To myself I added, And you never lied to her like my
father and me.

"Thank you for saying that, Dominick. It means so much to me."

Even without the hug, I had wound up consoling her again. But
there didn't seem to be any other way out of this. I wanted to get back on
the road, get through the dog-and-pony show at my house, then get rid of the
whole clan so I could be alone. "She loved you so much," I said.

A moment later we were moving again. We stayed quiet the rest of
the ride home, where the party was already hopping. Jeanette, Ruth,

Lois, and Carol were carrying on like they entertained here all the time. They had pulled back the sheer curtains my mother always kept over the closed windows, and the sun poured into our apartment, sprinkling shafts of light in unfamiliar places. Someone had clicked on the radio, and a flute was tittering in the background. On the kitchen table they had set out platters of food. Eggs with yolks whipped fluffy, sprinkled with a blood-colored spice. Lunch meats curled into finger-size slices, fleshy and damp. Hard squares of cheese, orange as the sun. Mrs. Ramillo brewed a vat of coffee, and everyone was getting tanked up on caffeine. She shoved a foam cup in my hand, filled to the rim. Holding that cup made me think of sitting in the back of Roget's car, sipping from his thermos.

Your mother's got a lot on her plate right now, so I want you to go easy on her.

I drank the coffee down despite the bad taste, then bumped around the kitchen with the empty cup in my hand. I thought of Ed Dreary, who used to eat a whole Styrofoam cup in the cafeteria if you gave him a quarter.

Some party trick.

My father was in the living room pinballing from person to person, sucking up more of their condolences, reminiscing about his "beloved wife." I heard him say, "It's just me and Dominick now. The two of us."

Yeah, I thought. Until you disappear. Then it will be just the one of us.

I wandered out of the kitchen and ended up in my parents' bedroom, where the bed was perfectly made, my mother's nubby cardigan folded neatly on top of her dresser, her hairbrush full of black strands nearby. It looked as if she had only stepped out of the room for a moment. A piece of Juicy Fruit gum was folded in its foil wrapper on the nightstand. I picked it up and put it in my pocket, saving that weird habit of hers, though I wasn't sure why.

"Knock, knock," my uncle said, even though the door was wide open. "Anybody home?"

I had flipped open my mother's music box, and that plastic ballerina was twirling away. He looked around her room at the threadbare white curtains, the oversize bedroom set she had picked up at a tag sale, the oak dented and nicked. "So this is where my sister was living," he said, emphasizing the word "this" in a way that sounded condescending.

What the hell was he acting so self-righteous about? I'd seen his pad, and it wasn't exactly the Taj Mahal. But I kept my mouth shut on that subject. I reached under the bed and pulled out the picture of the man I believed was Truman's father. I held it in front of Donald's face without saying a word.

He let out a sigh, took the photo from my hands, and stared at it. "This is your mother's first husband," he told me. "His name was Peter, and he drowned in a boating accident."

Laguna del Perro, I thought. 1955. Had my brother drowned, too? I wanted to whip out that picture of my uncle and Truman but held back because I didn't want him to know I had taken it from his apartment. My guess was he still hadn't run into Rosaleen, so he had no clue I had even been there. "Did my brother drown, too?" I asked.

Donald handed the picture back to me, reached over and closed the music box. "You are dealing with a lot right now. I don't think it's a good idea to fill your head with more worries." He picked up one of my mother's pillows, then put it down, sat on the edge of the bed. "Listen. I have to leave tonight for a conference in Germany. It's a series of presentations and a research seminar that I can't get out of. Even for this. I'm sorry. But I'm going to give you my number at the hotel and some money in case you need anything. When I get back next month, we'll figure things out together. I promise. Okay, kid?"

No, it wasn't okay, but he didn't seem to be giving me a choice. He pulled a yellow envelope out of the pocket of his blazer. Just a few days before, I had been counting on him to bail me out with some cash, and here he was forking it over. A little too late, I thought as he shoved the envelope into my suit pocket. He told me I should take a few days off from school, then force myself to go back. It would take my mind off things, he said. He gave me another hug, told me again that we would work it out when he got home.

After he left the room, I walked down the hall to the bathroom and splashed cold water on my face. I stood there staring in the mirror and trying to imagine sitting in a classroom as if nothing had changed. Could anyone tell by looking at me what a mess I had made out of my life? I imagined people gawking at me, whispering that I was the kid whose mother died from an abortion in the Holedo Motel.

Outside the door I heard snippets of chitchat from my mother's farewell bash.

"I think Dominick is still in shock," my father said. "It hasn't really hit him yet that she's gone."

"He's just a boy," a woman's voice said in response. "The poor thing."

"Roget hasn't heard the last from me," Marnie said in a stage whisper right outside in the hallway. I didn't know who she was talking to. Lois? Jeanette? "I'm not going to drop this. For Dominick's sake."

I looked in the mirror and decided I had a choice: I could stand around being pitied by this pack of losers or I could find a way to make things up to my mother. I didn't have a plan, but I knew I needed to get out of here and clear my head. I waited until Marnie's voice floated back down the hall, then went into my parents' bedroom, where Marnie's pocketbook sat on the chair under the pile of people's coats. I had learned my lesson about stealing money, but this time I was only borrowing something: her car. With the keys in my pocket, I made my way through the living room and told my father I was going for a walk.

"Want some company?" he asked, doing the concerned parent routine in front of his audience.

"No thanks," I answered and headed out the door before anyone else snagged me.

When I reached Marnie's Dart, I took a breath and climbed inside. I looked around to make sure no one was watching, then adjusted the seat, stuck my key in the ignition. The piece of shit started right away, and I put it in reverse, backed out of the lot. Without knowing exactly where to go, I headed slowly down Dwight Avenue. I had watched my mother drive enough to know when to gun it and when to brake. Marnie's boat swayed back and forth on the road, and I felt like I was sailing. A cop car was stopped in the parking lot of the Doghouse. My heart lurched for a second, but the officer didn't even look at me. Let him pull me over. I'd tell him to spend his energy nailing that no-good sheriff instead of picking on an orphan like me. The way Marnie had explained it, she told the police right away that Roget had been with my mother in the motel. They put out an APB, but when he turned up, their take on things suddenly changed. Roget had been with two other officers in a meeting at the new station, the police explained. He couldn't have been there. It was impossible. Marnie was flabbergasted. She kept telling me she was going to find a way to nail Roget, but I couldn't imagine the Bingo Lady taking on the Holedo Police Department and winning. And even though it tore me up to imagine him walking away from this whole thing, I didn't know what I could do about it.

When I passed the motel, I slowed the car down. The place was still blocked off with DO NOT CROSS — POLICE INVESTIGATION yellow tape. No cars in the lot. A NO VACANCY sign out front. I glanced up at room 5B and a cold tingle moved through me like ice in my veins at the sight of that door.

You will never see your mother again, a voice said.

I bit my lip.

Imagined her in a glass coffin instead of that heavy wooden one at the funeral parlor. Imagined that someone could kiss her and bring her back to life. But who would that be? Not Roget. Not my father. Maybe Peter, her first husband. I wondered if she loved him. I wondered if she was with him now.

To keep myself from crying, I stepped on the gas. Without planning it, I made the turn toward Edie's. I wasn't sure why I was going there, seeing as she was long gone. But I guess I didn't know where else to go or what to do next. And when I came over the top of the hill, there it was in front of me. The slanted roof. The lemonade paint, peeling. The lion-faced knocker. I stopped the car dead in the street the way my mother had the night we came looking for my father. I had reamed out Leon just for mentioning Edie's name, only to leave my mother's reception and park in front of her house. Add the word "hypocrite" to my list of personality flaws.

As I sat there in the bright afternoon sunlight, staring at the place, the only sound was the whining of a chain saw, someone somewhere must have been doing away with a tree that had fallen in the storm. I listened to the revving and putt-putting of that hungry saw as it sliced and tore through wood. A breeze blew over the hill and sent Marnie's antenna clacking back and forth.

"I hate you, Edie Kramer," I whispered into the air. I said it once, twice, three times. Then again, louder, "I fucking hate you!"

I took my mother's silver gum wrapper from my pocket and held it in my palm like some sort of magic charm. I felt myself tearing up, losing my grip the way I had when Donald hugged me. I snorted and sniffled. Hammered my hand against the dashboard until it hurt so much I had to stop. A lot of good it did me to talk to an empty house. I had really avenged my mother's death, telling that Victorian how I felt. I needed to do something. I needed to show my mother that I loved her. I wiped my eyes and looked at the FOR SALE sign half covered with snow and knocked crooked from the plows.

CONTACT VICKI SPRING.

Follow the signs, I heard my mother's voice say. *Life lays them right in front of you.*

One. Two. Three.

All you have to do is look.

That's when it came to me: If anyone might know where Edie had moved to, it would be her. Vicki Spring.

Maybe my mother had led me to this spot, given me this sign because she wanted me to find Edie. There was nothing I could do about Roget at the moment, but maybe this was the way she wanted me to make things right. Once again I saw my life as that blank black chalk-board, and I thought of the choices before me. I could go home and lie on my bed, stare at the ceiling, and miss my mother. In a few days I could go back to school as if nothing had ever happened, even though I knew different. And then what? I just didn't know. Or I could follow the signs like my mother told me to do. I could follow them to Edie, get that money back, and keep all those promises I had made to my mother on the bus a few days before. Even though they were promises I had made to my living, breathing mother, I told myself that if she was looking down on me, then she would see how much I loved her despite the mess I had made. She would know that I was trying to fix what I had done.

Then I saw something glittering beneath the surface of those thoughts. An urge that was far more powerful and determined. A desire that rose up in me, fast and quick, like something from the bottom of a lake rushing toward the surface, breaking out of the dark, still water and letting its ugliness be glimpsed in the light of day. And this is what that desire said:

Get back at Edie.

Make her pay for what she did.

She should suffer.

She should ache.

She should feel the way you feel.

Then those words disappeared, submerged back into the dark waters of my mind. I found myself chilled, shaking, afraid of what evil I was capable of committing. Just as I had a few days before, I wondered again if a hungry darkness could possess me the way those Manson followers had been possessed the night with Sharon Tate.

I shook my head to get rid of the thought.

As much as that feeling scared me, everything seemed to pull me toward Edie. All the things I wanted, or thought I wanted—the money, proof to my mother that I was sorry, and something else that I wasn't quite sure of yet—swirled together in my mind. And I knew I had to find her.

At that moment I felt my old self shriveling and a new self being born. This me was harder and more determined. He wouldn't be tricked. He wouldn't be scared. He wouldn't show anyone his sadness. "Bury it," I said out loud. "Bury it and do what you can to make up for your mistakes."

The car windows had fogged up a bit and I wrote BURY IT in crooked letters on the driver's side. I put the car in drive and made a U-turn. The Moorehead Real Estate office was located over in the next town of Buford. It took me fifteen minutes to get there. Already I was a pro at driving, and I still had just over a month to go before being legal. My only behind-the-wheel crime so far was braking too hard a couple of times, which sent the junk on Marnie's floor scuttling forward. Other than that it was smooth sailing.

I parked the Dart out front and made a plan in my head. If I flat-out asked this Vicki woman if she knew where the owner of the Victorian in Holedo had moved to, I doubted she would divulge that information. But if I pretended to be interested in the house, then casually dropped in a question about the former owner, she might spill. I knew I didn't look like their typical customer, but I was banking on my suit and tie to win Vicki over. The old me would have been nervous, but I refused to give in to that feeling. My mother had sent me into bars. She had sent me into Edie's. It was as if in some strange way she was sending me into this office right now. And I didn't intend to disappoint her.

"Is Miss Spring here?" I said over the jangle of bells on the door.

An apple-cheeked woman sat at the front desk looking totally bored despite the ringing phones. "She's behind you," she said, flipping through the pages of a *Cosmopolitan*. The cover lines read "Complete Guide to Encounter Groups" and "Confessions of a (Formerly) Fat Girl."

I turned around, but the second desk was empty. Then the door opened with another jangle of bells, and I got what Apple Cheeks meant: Vicki was just coming in herself. She was a pert-faced woman with narrow shoulders and a slim waist. Thirty, I guessed. Thirty-five. Dyed blond hair, cut super short like a man's. Soft pink lipstick.

"This boy is here to see you, Vicki," the secretary—or whoever she was—said, putting away her magazine.

Boy. That wasn't going to help in my effort to convince her I was legit.

I thought about bagging the plan and straight-out asking Vicki if she knew where Edie had moved. But something still told me she wouldn't give that information to a perfect stranger. Act casual, I reminded myself. Like I don't really need to know where the previous owner had gone—I'm simply wondering.

Vicki smiled, which crimped the skin around her eyes and aged her. Forty, I thought. Forty-five. She had the thickest eyelashes I'd ever seen. Only six or seven spider legs to a lid. "What can I do for you, young fella?"

First it was "boy," now it was "young fella." This rickety little scheme was never going to fly. Still, I did my best to get the thing in the air. "I'm here about the house in Holedo that's for sale. The yellow Victorian on Barn Hill Road." I talked in a low voice, buttoning my blazer and standing up straight.

"What about it?" she asked. Vicki took off her scarf and hat, hung them on the knotty wooden coatrack by the door. "Do you know something about the vandals?"

"Vandals?" I said, then remembered. The window. "Oh, no. Nothing about that. I'm here because I'm interested in buying the place."

"You!" that secretary said over the ringing of another phone. "Call us when you've finished high school."

"Would you mind answering the phone, Lydia?" Vicki said.

"Actually, my mother would be the one buying the place," I told her as Lydia picked up one of the lines and gave an overly cheerful "Good afternoon, Moorehead Real Estate." Just saying the words "my mother" put a hole in me and left me feeling deflated. But I struggled to keep afloat. "I'm just here to look."

"If your mother is interested in the place, then why isn't she here?"

Because she's dead, that's why. Stay cool, I told myself. You can swing this. "She sent me to scout out places for her. I was wondering if you could tell me about the house so I could fill her in."

Vicki made her way to the desk and began flipping through messages. She picked up her phone and started to dial. "I'm a very busy woman. If your mother is interested, she will have to get in touch with me herself."

Fuck you, too, Vicki Spring. "Fine," I said, pissed that my plan was doing a crash and burn right before my eyes. It was all that secretary's fault. If she'd just stuck to answering the phone and minded her own business, I might have been able to play this thing my way. It's not over yet, I reminded myself. You'll get what you want somehow. "Will you still be here in a few minutes? I'll pick up my mother and come back."

Vicki put down the phone, taking me seriously once again. "I have an appointment. But I'll be done at four-thirty. If your mother wants to see the place, I can meet her at the house then."

"Great," I said, not knowing what I would do to make this happen. "We'll see you at four-thirty. Barn Hill Road. Holedo."

I left the office and headed back toward home, wondering how I was going to pull this one off. I could just skip the four-thirty appointment, but then I'd never have another shot at finding out where Edie had gone. I could show up alone and tell Vicki that my mother couldn't make it after all. Maybe she'd give me a quick tour and I'd fish out the answer to the $64,000 question. But I knew she was too no-bull for that. The moment she saw me alone, she'd probably get in her car and drive back to Buford.

By the time I reached Dwight Avenue, I was wishing I had just gone for broke and asked her what I wanted to know right up front. So much for following the signs, I thought as I parked Marnie's car in the same spot where I found it. Just skip the appointment and let Vicki Spring wait in the cold for you and your mother. Serves her right for giving you the runaround.

Upstairs, the party had cleared out except for Marnie. She sat at the kitchen table, picking at the leftover baloney and staring off into space. Her puffy eyes and red nose let me know she had just finished up another one of her sob sessions. "There you are," she said. "Your father went to look for you."

I pulled off my blazer, loosened my itchy tie. "For me? Why?"

"He said he was worried." Marnie tore a fleshy baloney scrap in half and dropped it in her mouth.

"Spare me," I said.

"He seems to have mistaken himself for Mr. Cleaver all of a sudden. It's all I can do not to smack the man across the face. If your poor mother only knew the way he was carrying on after what he put her through." At the mention of my mother, Marnie looked down at her almost-empty platter of lunch meats. "I don't know why I'm grazing on this stuff. I'm too upset to eat. But you should get something in your stomach, Dominick. I want to make sure you stay healthy."

My mind flashed on an image of my mother calling from the window to ask if I wanted lunch when I first got that note from Edie. Marnie was beginning to sound just like her. "Marnie, could I ask you a favor?"

"Whatever you need. Just name it."

Here goes. "I want you to help me find out where Edie Kramer moved to."

Marnie made a sour face. She stuck her fingernail in one of the eggs and scooped out a mouse's portion of the yellow stuff. She held it in the air when she spoke. "How do you know that woman moved? And why in the world do you want to find her?"

"It's a long story."

She sat there staring at me, not eating a bit of that yolk on her finger. I got the feeling she was in the mood for a long story, that she wasn't going to budge until I gave her more. But I couldn't trust her with the truth. No way could I confess to anyone what I had done to my mother. So this is what I came up with: "I think my father gave the money he stole to Edie. I hitched a ride with Leon's friend Ed over to her house to see about getting it back, but she's gone. There's a 'For Sale' sign out front."

"Hold your horses. Why don't you just ask your father—" Marnie said, then stopped herself, finally licked her finger. "Never mind. That dog wouldn't admit a thing."

We were both quiet a moment. I sat down next to Marnie. Up close, her skin looked papery and blotched. God had cheated her out of a chin and given her that beak nose as some sort of sick joke to keep men away. Anyone else might have given up, but Marnie kept on dyeing her hair all these years, wearing her wild colors and acting like a celebrity with her bingo show. I wondered what she would do with herself now that my mother was gone. Maybe she would finally land some dream man like she had always wanted.

"Marnie, I never told you this before. But do you remember that night last summer when we drove over to Edie's house?"

"Of course," she said. "Your mother was really fired up that evening."

"Yeah, well, I told you guys that my father wasn't inside. But I lied. He was there, asleep in Edie's bed. I didn't tell the truth because I hated to see her cry. And Edie, well, she sort of conned me, too. But I am really sorry for it." I decided to rein myself in before I said too much. "I know my father was having an affair with her. I even know that Edie needed money because she's pregnant. That's why I think he gave it to her."

Marnie rested her cheek in her palm, digesting what I had just told her. Normally she would have puffed right up at the first hint of gossip. Something this juicy would have had her bloated. But she just sat there. She looked wiped out from all that had happened the last few days, and here I was dropping more news in her lap. After a moment she took my hand. "Dominick, finding that money isn't ever going to bring your mother back. You know that, don't you?"

"I know," I told her. "But I feel like I have to do something."

"Me, too. That's why I want to find a way to get Roget. You know, your father doesn't even realize it wasn't his baby. Your mother was sure he would figure it out. All I know is that he and Roget should burn in hell together."

I sat there waiting for something more than Marnie's usual line of tough talk that would land us nowhere. Finally she said, "Okay."

"Okay what?"

"I'll help you," she said. "What do you need me to do?"

I explained the whole plan on the way to Edie's house. I told her that Ed Dreary had given me a ride to the real-estate office and that Vicki had treated me like a criminal. "Say no more," Marnie said when we pulled up front. "I know her type, and I'll take it from here."

Vicki was waiting outside, her face masked behind a pink scarf, hands stuffed in her pockets. She was doing a little bounce number on her heels in an effort to stay warm. The moment we stepped onto the porch, Marnie became my mother—or not exactly *my* mother but some warped version of one. "Pleased to meet you, Miss Spring. I'm Dominick's mother, and I understand you have a problem giving out information to my son when he is perfectly capable of scouting out locales for us to take up residence."

Locales? Take up residence? Jesus, she made it sound like we were house-hunting in the South of France. Thankfully, Vicki had left her wise-ass sidekick back at the office to *not* answer phones, so we were spared her commentary.

"Nice to meet you," Vicki said, completely ignoring Marnie's opening diatribe. "Before we go inside, I just want to warn you that I have four other buyers who are close to signing."

"Let's skip the broker routine," Marnie told her. "I'm freezing out here, and I want to see the place."

Oof. I wished Marnie would lighten up a bit, or she was going to blow this whole scheme. The idea was to get chummy with Vicki so she would give us the dirt. Not piss her off so she'd send us packing.

Vicki had trouble getting the front door unlocked, and we stood there a moment longer. I kept feeling as if Edie were going to open up any second. "Hey, handsome," she would say and give me a kiss as if the last few days hadn't happened. Then for some reason I imagined my mother opening the door. She was pregnant and happy. She hadn't died after all; she had moved to this house, and we were coming to visit.

"There we go," Vicki said when the lock finally turned. She stepped back and let Marnie and me enter before she did.

It felt strange to walk through Edie's front door without her around. I thought of that first night when I made my way down the hall in search of my father. But there was not much time to reflect on any of what had happened here because Vicki stayed on our backs, moving us from room to room with only a few seconds in each one. There were rooms in the house I had never even seen. A whole third floor with three bedrooms, one with a bookshelf that opened up and led to a narrow twisting staircase like something out of a mystery movie. Marnie kept making a tsk-tsk sound with her tongue and pointing out the features she didn't like, hamming up the prospective-buyer routine more than she needed to. I kept my hands in my pockets, fingering that silver gum wrapper of my mother's like a good-luck charm.

When we made our way back down the stairs and landed in Edie's bedroom, Marnie started in. "Look at these hardwood floors. They're a mess. And that ivy wallpaper in the dining room is the ugliest thing I've ever seen. I can't begin to imagine the heating bills. Do you feel the draft, Dominick?"

Just ask the fucking question already. "It sure is cold in here," I said, crossing my arms. Someone had taped a sheet of plastic over the broken kitchen window, but it didn't help, because the place was colder than ever.

"Like I told your son this afternoon, the window was smashed the other night," Vicki said, eyeing me. "Vandals. That explains the draft."

I was getting the distinct feeling that Vicki suspected me as the window smasher. She was right, of course, but God knows how she picked up on it. Just let her try to prove it. Vicki Spring and her broken window were the least of my problems.

Finally Marnie said, "Tell me about the previous owners."

Bingo.

"Well, they were divorced, and the wife lived here alone for a few years." Vicki held her hand to the side of her mouth and dropped her voice to a whisper as if there were someone in the next room who she didn't want to hear. "Between you and me, she's pregnant with an illegitimate child. She was planning on renting out some of the rooms originally. But then she called me up and said to put the place on the market. She was leaving town."

"Really. Where did she go?" Marnie said.

"New York City," Vicki answered. "Manhattan." And then she snapped back into business mode. "So are you interested? Because I have another buyer with an offer breathing down my back. But I like you people, so I want to give you a fair shot."

Marnie looked at her deadpan. "I wouldn't live in this dump if you gave it to me for free. Let's go, Dominick."

With that, we were out the door. Part of me wished Marnie had taken the time to fish for more information, but I was glad for what we got.

New York City. What in the world was Edie doing there?

On the ride home Marnie was busy making plans. "Okay," she said, "I'll call my Aunt Gladys who lives in Queens to see if she has any leads that will help us find Edie."

"Marnie, it's a big place. I doubt she'll know."

"Gotta start somewhere," she said.

The truth was, I didn't want Detective Marnie Garboni investigating this case with me any longer. Just being with her made me think of my mother. I kept feeling as if I were going to turn around and see her in the car with us, that she was going to interrupt Marnie any second. And when she wasn't there I felt my insides drop. Still, I let Marnie make her plans. She made it sound as if we were going to be the Caped Crusaders, righting the wrongs of the world. All we needed was our superhero costumes and a couple pairs of tights.

We reached the apartment, and Marnie stopped the car. It had grown dark, and we both stared up at the dim blue light of the television flickering in the living room window. My father was home again.

"Do you want me to come in with you?" she asked.

"That's okay," I said. "I can handle him."

"I want you to take this." Marnie handed me a yellow pill smaller than a baby aspirin, lighter than Styrofoam. "My doctor gave them to me. Just take it tonight if your mind is racing. It will help you sleep. And if things get ugly, you can always stay at my place. Just give a holler." She reached over to hug me, and this time I let her. She felt smaller than I remembered, but I probably hadn't hugged her in years. I didn't know why, but I felt like I wasn't going to see Marnie again for a long time. Maybe what had happened with my mother would always make me feel that way when I said good-bye. I would never know when I left someone if it would be forever, because who knew what the world could deliver? Charlie Manson's gang could walk in and butcher Sharon Tate when she never expected a thing. My mother's first husband could drown in a boating accident and change her life for good. I could leave one morning for New York City and find my mother dead when I returned that night.

"Thanks for your help," I told Marnie as I got out of her car.

"No need to thank me," she said. "I'll call you tomorrow."

I knew she was trying to be nice, but the thought of Marnie calling me seemed strange. She was my mother's friend, after all. I nodded and smiled anyway, closed the door, and headed up the stairs to my apartment. Welcome to your new life with your father, I thought as I stood at the door.

I found him at the kitchen sink when I stepped inside. A soldier's line of Schlitz cans and a bottle of vodka on the counter. Great, I thought. Now it's time to get drunk.

"Hi, son. I was waiting for you."

I didn't say a word.

"I want you to witness something." He took each and every can, snapped off the top, and dumped the shit down the sink the way my mother used to do. The vodka, too.

I watched him without saying a thing.

"Aren't you going to ask why I'm doing this?"

My voice had shut down again. I nodded. Shrugged.

"That's it," he said. "No more. I swore to your mother today when I stood at her grave that I would take care of you. No more drinking. No more disappearing. I quit my job, too. I'll find something close to home. I'll be here every night."

I stood there staring at him, felt that icy tingle in my veins. He could have just tossed the cans and bottle in the trash. I didn't need the circus act, watching it wash away like liquid gold down the drain.

Big. Fucking. Deal.

"Well, don't you have anything to say?" he asked when he was done.

I took a breath. Tried to find my voice, but it was still gone. I shook my head no. Buried my feelings. Gave him that bug-eyed expression. The new me.

For a moment he actually looked disappointed.

Good. He should be hurt. Like I needed his big-deal promises. He should have sworn off booze and other women while my mother was still alive. Then none of this would have ever happened.

You stole the money, a voice in my head said.

"That's okay. You don't have to say a thing," my father said. "So do you want to watch TV or something?"

"No thanks," I told him, finding my voice again. With that I turned and went to my room. Left him standing with all those empty beer cans and the vodka bottle.

I waited a moment to see if he would follow me, but he didn't. I closed my door and popped Marnie's pill without any water to slug it down. All day I had wanted to be by myself, and I was finally able to stretch out on my bed and let my mind wander. I thought about my mother, dredged up all kinds of memories. Christmas morning when I unwrapped the boots she had given me. The sad look on her face as the two of us sat by our tree with its blur of blinking lights like a traffic accident. Our final Christmas together, and that was the image that stuck with me. One memory I kept replaying happened when I was younger and my father was working at a machine shop. She let me stay home from school to keep her company, and when he came home for lunch unexpectedly, she hid me in their closet. I remembered being terrified as I stood in the dark pressed between his flannels and her blouses. I remembered her hysterical laughter when he left and she came to my rescue. "It's our little secret," she had said, hugging me.

I fell asleep.

When I woke, it was just after midnight. My father was at the foot of my bed. "That baby wasn't mine," he was saying. "I did the math, and it couldn't have been mine."

I rolled over and looked at him, his bulky shoulders silhouetted in the moonlight from my window. I could tell by his smell and by his slurred words that he had been drinking. So much for his promises. What did he do, stick a straw down the drain and suck all his booze back up through the pipes?

"I thought you were through with that stuff," I said, shifting the pillow under my head and letting my eyes adjust to the dim light. He had his shirt off, and I could make out my mother's name tattooed in small letters on his chest. When I was younger, I used to wonder what he would do about that tattoo if they ever split up for good. I guess I would find out soon enough.

"I *am* through with it. But I came across a flask in my truck when I went for cigarettes. I thought I'd have one last farewell toast to your mother. You know, I kept wondering why she would do such a thing. I mean, we were on the skids, but to do that to our baby. Then I realized it wasn't our baby. Couldn't have been."

I kept quiet. It wasn't my job to help him piece his pathetic life together.

"I still love that woman, though. Even if she did get herself in trouble with some other guy, I still love her."

Maybe it was Marnie's pill, or maybe I had finally had enough, because I felt a hard pellet of anger taking shape in the back of my mouth, and out it came. "If you loved her so much, then why were you such a shitty husband? You want to know what she was like when you weren't here? She cried all the time. We drove around looking for you constantly. Maybe if she wasn't married to such an asshole, she wouldn't have found someone else to fuck."

My father dropped his chin and gave me a stunned look. He clocked his hand back to hit me, but his fist froze in the air.

You don't understand the way he gets, Edie said. *You haven't seen it.*

His eyes ballooned. His jaw locked itself in a snarl. He growled, then punched the wall instead. Put a good-size hole in it, too. He lifted his fist again and jackhammered three more craters in the wall. Then he grabbed the chair by my desk and hurled it at my closet door, knocking over my record player in the process.

Well, now I had seen the way he gets. And I didn't give a shit. Let him tear up the whole apartment if it made him feel better.

"Fuck you!" he shouted. "Don't you dare judge me. Who do you think you're talking to?"

He raged on and on, first yelling, then talking to himself, then finally blubbering away. Good. He deserved his misery. When he finally got the hint that I wasn't going to feed into his psycho scene anymore, he left the room. I could hear him bawling in their bedroom. I listened until his cries became whimpers and then the whimpers became snores.

That's when I got out of bed. Something made me go to my window and look outside. Leon was out there in the parking lot. I watched him in the bright moonlight as he climbed into a red Thunderbird with a bunch of guys. They were all laughing and smoking. Special Ed was there, too. I stared down at them until they drove off to who-knew-where, and then I picked up that picture of Truman and my uncle at Laguna del Perro.

You are dealing with a lot right now, I heard my uncle say. *When I get back next month, we'll figure things out together.*

I didn't think I could wait that long. I put the picture down and stood in my dark bedroom, looking at the damage my father had done. The holes in my smooth blue bedroom wall looked like craters on the moon. I reached into the pocket of my pants and pulled out my mother's silver wrapper of Juicy Fruit. I don't know why I did what I did next, but I unwrapped the gum and held it in my hand. It looked like a miniature clump of Silly Putty, wrinkled and gray as an old woman's skin. I lifted it to my mouth, slipped it between my lips. The flavor was gone, but I kept it there anyway, let it rest on my tongue, then moved it around my mouth.

I walked to the kitchen and grabbed a garbage bag to pack some things. But when I looked around, there didn't seem to be anything in this place I really wanted. The picture of my brother. The money from my uncle. Other than that, my mother had been the only important thing here, and she was gone. She was never coming back. I found a scrap of paper. This is what I wrote:

Dad—
    I don't want to live here anymore.
            Dominick

I dropped the note onto the kitchen table and put on my coat. Opened the front door, closed it behind me. And just like that, I left home.

Six

If you tilt your head back and look up at the ceiling in St. Patrick's Cathedral, you'll see a line of round red hats floating above the altar, suspended in the air by strings as invisible and strong as fishing wire. These are the ceremonial hats of all the cardinals who have passed on. Galeros, they're called. The church has an old joke that when a hat finally disintegrates and falls to the floor of the cathedral, the cardinal is released into heaven. Until then he waits in purgatory.

Not very funny, but like I said, it's a church joke.

I learned about the hats during one of my twenty-nine days in New York City before I found Edie. Since the idea of shacking up with Marnie didn't exactly appeal to me, I made my way to Manhattan on a bus the night I left home. After helping myself to my uncle's vacant apartment with the keys I took on my last visit, I bought a map and spent my days wandering the streets, getting the lay of the land, and figuring out what to do next. The Village. Murray Hill. Hell's Kitchen. Wall Street. I walked so much my feet ached and my mind took on an aimless, empty quality that might have resembled the alleyways I passed.

This time around I came face-to-face with New York's nastier side, the reasons Claude and Rosaleen seemed to dislike the place. Piles of black and green garbage bags cluttered the sidewalks. The subway rumbled, restless and angry, beneath my feet, blowing hot stinky air up through the grates on the sidewalk. Sirens howled endlessly. Sometimes I stopped to study the graffiti that covered so many of the buildings and seemed to contain secret messages—Taki 183 and Marto 125. Letters and numbers that were like a foreign language to me. Other days I wandered along the murky gray river, where men kissed each other out on the dilapidated piers. In my daze I walked down dangerous, deserted streets all alone. Twice I was followed by a pack of kids who couldn't have been much older than me but seemed deadlier and more evil than anyone in Holedo. The worst had already happened, I figured as I ducked around a corner to shake them, so what did it matter?

I buried my fear and loneliness, the same way I did my sadness.

And I kept walking.

It was during one of my many wandering days that I stepped into St. Patrick's Cathedral. Not to pray or confess, though I probably should have done both, but simply to rest my feet. When an old woman with lipstick on her teeth and a black net over her church-lady face saw me staring up at the red things above the altar, she explained what they were, told me that old church joke.

"Farley, McCloskey, Spellman, and Hayes," she said, pointing her wrinkled finger at each hat and rattling off the names of the dead cardinals they once belonged to, like some sort of ancient prayer. "From here they remind me of balloons let loose into the air, don't you think?"

I just nodded, because for the most part I never really talked to anyone during my wandering days. When homeless people stalked after me for change, I just plowed on by. When businessmen bumped into me on the crowded streets, I kept going without so much as an "Excuse me." Besides, those galeros made me think of my mother, not balloons. I pictured her soul as something red and tender as a heart, suspended between this world and the next. Waiting for someone—something—to set her free.

That someone was me.

That something had to do with finding Edie.

And there was something else I needed to do for her, but I still wasn't sure what that was yet, so it remained just a feeling that pawed eternally at my insides. A mangy dog at a thick white door.

At night I sat in my uncle's filthy apartment—chain link on the door in case Rosaleen showed—wasting away in the armchair I had pushed right up in front of the Colorvision. Amazing how much death figured into every program on the air. If an anchorman wasn't blathering on about somebody who had been stabbed or gunned down or left for dead, then someone on *Laugh-In* was joking about inheriting her dying grandmother's pet anteater.

The end was all around us, and no one seemed to care.

Whenever I came across a reference to death on TV, I wound up staring right through the screen, retracing the steps that had led to my mother's last night in that motel. I replayed the moments, wishing I could have done something to stop what had happened. I longed for even the smallest note from her, like the ones in Leon's term paper, telling me good-bye. When it became too much to think about, I reached up and turned the channel, tried to lose myself in another show. Sooner or later there it was: a strung-out prostitute on *Hawaii Five-O* holding a roomful of men at gunpoint and threatening to blow their heads off; an ABC Movie of the Week about a man who murdered his wife and buried her in the backyard.

That was all it took for me to start thinking about the end again.

You need a plan, I told myself when I woke up to day twenty-nine in the apartment. Down on the street I heard a car honking, a truck banging and rattling. A pigeon perched on the windowsill and let out a muffled wheezing sound that made me think of a chest cold. Your uncle will be home any day, and you need to figure out what to do. I knew I should hunt for Edie the way McGarrett would on *Hawaii Five-O*. Search for clues. Track her down. Every night I called the patient-information line at each of the city hospitals to see if a woman named Edie Kramer had checked into the maternity ward. I even dialed 411 on a daily basis to check for a new listing. For McGarrett those schemes would have worked; for me they didn't turn up a single lead. And the more I tried to come up with my next move, the more helpless I felt. I kept holding out for some sign from my mother, like the one that told me to go to Vicki Spring. But after so many aimless days without the slightest hint about what to do, I was beginning to believe that my mother had given up leading me anywhere. My life seemed to have frozen up on me like the icy face of a steep mountain, until after so much cold and quiet, the wind hits the snow just so and everything shifts and slides, causing an avalanche.

That's the way it was for me.

Almost a whole month of nothing. Then a wind blew and something shifted, causing another thing to shift, then another. A rumbling began and gained so much momentum that it couldn't be stopped. And in a few short hours my life was in motion again. Faster and more dangerous than ever.

I got out of bed and dressed in the stiff blue jeans and hooded gray sweatshirt I picked up when I stumbled upon an army-navy on Mac-Dougal Street during my first week in the city. Between the fifteen hundred dollars I'd found in my uncle's closet on my last visit and the couple hundred he'd given me the day of my mother' service, I had plenty of cash, and I'd barely spent any of it so far. In the kitchen I filled a pot with water and struck a match to get the burner going on the gas stove. As I stood there waiting for the water to boil, wondering how many brain cells I knocked off smelling that gas each morning, I looked around at the dusty tile floor, the windowsill cluttered with weary cactus plants, the worn Oriental carpet in the living room. When I had arrived at the apartment, I ransacked the place again, searching for some sign of my brother I might have overlooked the first time around. I came up empty-handed and decided that it was time for me to give up thinking about Truman, since it had led to so much trouble in the first place. Whatever it was about my brother that no one wanted me to know was fine, because I was forcing myself to forget about him.

As far as I was concerned, I was an only child.

My brother was a thing of the past.

I poured oatmeal from my uncle's military-size container into the bubbling water and mixed it for a minute. Outside the window a woman in a long blue coat led a duck line of elementary-school kids down the block. I dumped my breakfast into a bowl and watched them turn the corner on West Eleventh Street as I ate. Since something wouldn't let me take my mother's gum out of my mouth, I had gotten into the habit of tucking it up behind my back molar when I ate, slept, and brushed my teeth ever since I'd left home. Mornings always felt a little funny in my new life away from Holedo. I supposed I was missing the place despite myself. The odd thing was that I didn't long for the recent times. What I found myself missing was the old days with my mother, and even my father. When I was as little as one of those kids in that duck line, standing at the bus stop with Leon and both our moms or collecting baseball cards and wrestling with my dad. I imagined someone telling that childhood me what was to come in only a handful of years. A loud-speaker voice announcing, *Your mother will die, and you will leave home.* I pictured my childhood face twisting in terror at the sound of those words.

If I listened, I wondered, could I hear my mother's voice warning me of what would come next? One of the signs she told me to watch for. I tried. I actually closed my eyes and listened. The kitchen was silent except for the hum of the refrigerator and the chest-cold sound of pigeons outside. Nothing came to me.

No whispers. No warnings.

Without any signs to steer me, I could only keep plodding along into the uncertainty of my future. I was a hiker in the woods after sundown without a flashlight or a map. A pilot in a small metal plane over the stormy ocean without instruments to navigate. All I could do was move forward, put my empty bowl in the sink, slip on my coat, and head out the door aimlessly in search of Edie.

A few blocks from my uncle's place, across the street from St. Vincent's Hospital, was a Chock Full O' Nuts where I made a pit stop each morning for hot chocolate. The waitresses behind the big U of a counter were all weary-looking women with disappointed eyes and dyed hair, dressed in white uniforms. They never paid much attention to me, too busy complaining about their sore feet, the filthy city, or the latest obnoxious customer to sit in their section. But there was a Chinese mom-and-pop couple who treated me as if I had been a regular for years. Mom worked the register, and Pop ran the coffee and cocoa machine. With the exception of a few phrases, they didn't speak English. But Mom always got a big smile on her face when she saw me, made motions for me to button my coat when it was windy outside. Pop always fussed over extra napkins, managed a mangled compliment that sounded vaguely like "American boy much too healthy."

When I stepped into the place that morning, we all went through our routine—Mom squeezed her arms and flapped her lips in a mock shiver, Pop made a production out of preparing my hot chocolate, grabbing the marshmallows and winking as he dropped them into my cup. I stood smiling and nodding like the "American boy much too healthy" they thought I was. Through the front window I caught a glimpse of a pregnant woman getting out of a taxi. She looked nothing like Edie. But she resembled my mother so much that my throat tightened at the sight of her. The same height. Same small frame. A puffed-up stomach like the one my mother had kept hidden from me. Coal-colored hair held back in a headband, too. A familiar, wilted-flower expression on her face. I couldn't take my eyes off her as she crossed the street and walked through the double doors of St. Vincent's. Then, a moment later, I saw another pregnant woman trotting down the sidewalk. Again not Edie. But this one looked like my mother, too.

And that's when I heard her voice for the first time since I left Holedo. Her message blew in my ears like a gust of warm wind thawing my frozen life.

Follow the signs, she whispered.

Life lays them right in front of you.

One. Two. Three.

All you have to do is look.

"Now can pay you," Chinese Mom was saying.

Distracted, I grabbed a quarter from my pocket and set it in her soft hand. She mock-shivered again, made the button-your-coat motion. I bundled up to make her happy, then stepped out onto the sidewalk. A few doors down I took the lid off my hot chocolate and blew on it. Three lumps of marshmallow floated on top. A drowning snowman. I pushed him around with my tongue and began taking slow sips as I watched the doors of the hospital. In five minutes I counted two more pregnant women—one coming, one going. These two didn't look as much like my mother, but they were both wearing dark wool coats like hers. One even wore a see-through plastic kerchief on her head with a funny-looking lump from a hair bun in the back.

Follow the signs.

I had called St. Vincent's every night along with all the other hospitals, and no Edie Kramer was ever listed. Still, I finished the last of my drink and tossed the empty cup into a trash can. When the WALK sign gave the signal, I crossed the street and let myself get swallowed up by the same double doors as all those pregnant women. Inside, the hospital had a flat antiseptic smell that made me think of the times my mother and I had stopped to see Marnie at Griffith Hospital in Holedo. Just like that dump, there were women at St. Vincent's dressed in chipper pink smocks holding clipboards and gabbing in the corner. Slumped in the waiting-room chairs were visitors who looked depleted and pale enough to be patients themselves. Most of them were coughing or sneezing or honking their noses into handkerchiefs.

Maybe, I told myself, maybe Edie had checked in this morning or in the middle of the night, and my mother had led me in here to find her. I walked toward the front desk and forced an I-know-where-I-am-going look on my face. Just beyond I could see the group of elevators, their metal doors opening and closing, spitting out a half dozen people at a time. I figured I'd head up to the maternity ward and snoop around. An amazon security guard in a burgundy blazer and a dandelion puff of gray hair stopped me. "Show me your pass," she said, army style. The walkie-talkie clipped to her belt made a steady chh-chh-chh sound.

"I'm just going to visit my friend who had a baby," I told her, hoping she'd see me as an "American boy much too healthy," too, and simply let me go.

"What's the patient's name?" she asked.

"Kramer," I answered, figuring if there were even a chance Edie was up there, at least I'd find out.

The guard flipped through the clutter of papers on her clipboard, smacked her lips, and tapped her long nails on the desk. "No Kramer registered here," she said. "And you can't go up without a pass."

"How about Elshki?" I said, since I always checked under her married name as well whenever I called the hospitals, just in case.

"Nope," the guard said, flipping through her papers again. Then she rubbed it in: "And you can't go up without a pass."

I glanced at all the crossed-out names on her list, the initials C.O. written next to a slew of them. I assumed it meant checked out. "Oh, I thought she was here," I said because I didn't know what else to say. Disappointment settled over me like something damp on an already damp day. Those signs hadn't been signs at all. Just a bunch of pregnant women walking into the double doors of a hospital. The voice I'd heard had been only in my mind.

I was about to turn and leave when the guard said, "If she had a baby in this hospital anytime in the last week, it would be listed over on that board."

Across the waiting room a giant bulletin board read WELCOME TO THE WORLD! Smiling suns and war-torn pink and blue ribbons made up a border. I had no other leads in my search for Edie, so I walked over and read the thing up close. THE STAFF AT ST. V'S PROUDLY WELCOMES THE FOLLOWING BABIES INTO THE WORLD . . . Below were two columns: boys blue, girls pink.

William Samuel Glazier, born February 24, 1972, at 3:36 P.M.

David Richard Rusiek, born February 25, 1972, at 12:13 P.M.

Arnold Jefferson Hyatt, born February 25, 1972, at 4:56 A.M.

Stanley Dale Hudson, born February 25, 1972, at 6:00 P.M.

The list went on and on, but none of them were Kramers. Next up I scanned the girls: *Maria Ann Rizzoli . . . Stacy Ann Davis . . . Gillian Margaret Halls . . . Mary Beth Rusells . . . Janice Elizabeth Kovach . . .* Again no Kramers.

I stood there reading the names, over and over, wondering what McGarrett would do in a situation like this. I supposed he'd have some sort of solution, but I didn't. He'd keep digging, I thought, as I stared at the board. I was about to head back to the front desk so I could push that guard some more, when I noticed last week's baby list tacked beneath the current one. Even though I had called patient information the week before, I flipped the page. Read another bundle of names. Still no luck. I flipped back further and found the list from three weeks ago. No Kramers, so I kept flipping until I was staring at the list from the week *before* I came to New York. *Before* I'd ever called any of the hospitals.

And that's where I found it.

At the very top of the girls' list from a month ago was the name: *Sophie Dominick Kramer, born January 23, 1972, at 11:53 P.M.*

The same day my mother died.

Follow the signs, her voice whispered once more. A wind picking up speed, blowing hard against my life.

I read that name and date a dozen times as my heart kicked into overdrive. Edie had been due in February, so she would have gone into labor early for it to be her baby. If it was her, she had already given birth before I even left Holedo. That's why her name was never listed when I called patient information. Still, I couldn't be certain it was her baby. I mean, Kramer was a pretty common name—then again, not Dominick for a girl. I tried to remember if Edie had ever mentioned Sophie in one of our name-the-baby conversations. Donna. Cynthia. Those names I remembered. But Sophie I couldn't recall.

"I think that might be my friend's baby on one of those leftover lists," I said to the guard when I walked back to her desk. "But can you tell me if the mother's name is Edie?"

"No can do," she said, tapping her talons like a musical instrument on her desk. Tippity-tap-tap-tap. "I only have current patient information."

I looked down at the wad of papers on her clipboard again, knew that if she really wanted to help me, she could find a way. "But I see all those crossed-out names and dates right there. You could just look it up on an old list or something."

Her walkie-talkie kept on chh-chh-chh-ing away, and she kept tapping. She was a regular marching band. "Are you telling me how to do my job?"

"No. I just need to find out if the mother of that baby on the board is my friend Edie. That's all."

Chh-chh-chh. Tap-tap-tap. She ignored me, looked over my shoulder at a visitor who held up his green plastic pass as he walked by. "Welcome to St. Vincent's," she told him, smiling. When he was gone, her frown returned and she looked down at her desk as if I weren't even there.

"Fine. Up yours," I said barely under my breath as I turned on my heels to leave the hospital.

I bundled up and made my way across Seventh Avenue and down Bank Street. It was too cold and blustery, and I was far too frustrated to do my daily walkathon, so I decided to head back to my uncle's place. I knew I shouldn't have let loose back there like that, but I was so sick of all the Vicki Springs and burgundy-blazered guards in the world. Give them an inch of power and they acted like they ruled the world. All I wanted was a name, for Christ's sake.

Sophie Dominick Kramer, born January 23, 1972, at 11:53 P.M.

If it was Edie's baby, I thought, then she had probably gone into labor the same time my mother was hemorrhaging in the Holedo Motel. That synchronicity hit me like a giant fuck-you from the universe and left my skin stinging.

I could kill Edie.

I could wrap my hands around her neck and stop her breath.

That's how angry I was.

I reached the doorway to my uncle's building. At my feet was a bundle of new phone books that had been plopped by the garbage cans, still untouched by anyone in the building. I kicked the stack with my foot to release some of my rage toward Edie—toward the world—then unlocked the door. Before stepping inside, though, I reached down and untied the knotted twine around the White Pages and took a copy. I knew Edie wouldn't be listed, seeing as she had just moved to New York. But when I got upstairs, I flipped open to the K section anyway. There was a whole page of Kramers. Three Edwards, one Ethel, two Ernests. No Edies or Ediths. Not even the initial *E*. I closed the book and decided to try calling information again.

"City, please?" a woman's voice said.

"Manhattan," I told her. "It's a new listing. Edie Kramer."

She paused. I heard a clicking sound in the background. I prepared myself for the usual "Sorry, there's no listing by that name." And right on schedule she said, "Sorry, there's no listing by that name."

"There's no number?" I said.

"No number."

"Are you sure?"

"I'm sure," she said, sounding annoyed.

Another one of these people with too much power over me, but this time I let it go. "Thanks anyway," I said, feeling guilty about my outburst at the hospital.

I hung up and reviewed what I had found so far: Vicki Spring telling me Edie had moved to Manhattan and a baby born the night my mother died, with the name Sophie Dominick Kramer. It could have been the beginnings of a trail leading me toward Edie, or it could have been a bunch of bull. If only that guard had let me upstairs. Maybe I could have gotten more information.

With that thought I picked up the phone again and dialed 411, got the number for the maternity ward at St. Vincent's. If I skipped over the patient-information line and that puffy-haired guard, I might find some-one else who could help me.

"Fifth floor. Maternity," a woman's voice answered.

"Um. Hi. My aunt had a baby at St. Vincent's recently. I want to send her flowers, but I'm not sure if she's still there."

"What's her name?" the woman said.

"Edie Kramer," I told her.

I waited for her to put me on hold, but the woman said, "Oh, Miss Kramer checked out ages ago. Sorry, but she's long gone. Not to worry, though, she left with a very healthy baby girl. I was one of her nurses."

"Great," I said, thinking fast. It *was* her. "Do you happen to have her new address? I have these flowers, and I don't know where to send them."

"You're a little late," she said and laughed. "But hold on a sec. Let me see."

I waited. My heart beating. My hand clenching and unclenching. I heard nothing but dead air, the same hushed silence I imagined inside my mother's casket, and then she came back on the line. "Four sixteen West Forty-seventh Street. Apartment One-B."

I stretched the phone cord, grabbed a pad and pen off the coffee table. "Let me write that down," I said, trying to sound composed as I scribbled, which was just about impossible.

She waited, then repeated the address. I thanked her a little too much and hung up. West Forty-seventh Street. Hell's Kitchen. No-man's-land. I had been in that neighborhood, just north of the bus station, last week, and that's where I'd been followed. Hookers on the street in broad daylight. Porn shops and strip bars all over the place. The build-ings burned out and boarded up. Nothing there seemed safe. I had to hand it to Edie, she picked a great neighborhood to bring up a baby.

I paced the apartment, waiting for a what-to-do-next lightbulb to click on in my head. I thought about going straight to her place and pressing her buzzer. But what would I say when she came to the door? My breaths were fast and frantic just standing in my uncle's living room;

I couldn't imagine how I'd act face-to-face with her. The way I felt, I might very well wrap my hands around her neck. Stop her from breathing. From living, like my mother. I had to calm down first so those dark feelings didn't surface and possess me. Get a grip, I told myself. Figure out exactly how to play this. I saw the things I wanted from Edie print out in my mind like a grocery list.

Remember to pick up:

An explanation

The money

Proof to my mother that I was sorry

I heard Marnie's voice interrupting, telling me, *Dominick, finding that money isn't ever going to bring your mother back. You know that, don't you?*

Yeah, I knew that. But there was something more I wanted and needed — something unnameable and blank at the bottom of that list. A clutter of words in white ink on white paper. I knew that something would remain invisible until I got closer to Edie. In the meantime I decided to hike up to her neighborhood and stake out her building while waiting for those white words to become clear.

I put on my coat and was about to walk out the door when the phone rang, startling me. During the last month the phone had barely rung, and when it did, I let it go unanswered. No one buzzed the door either. And I hadn't seen or heard from Rosaleen.

I counted. Five, six, seven rings.

What if it was my father on the other end of that line? I pictured him standing in my damaged bedroom, even though there wasn't a phone in there. Breathing hard like a bull. Nostrils steaming. Chest puffing and unpuffing. My knocked-over record player and moon-cratered wall were his backdrop. That good-bye note open and flat in his hand. A paper airplane waiting to be folded into flight.

Eight. Nine. Ten.

Silence. The ringing stopped. I buttoned my coat and grabbed my uncle's black Russian hat with the earflaps that made me just about deaf. A semi-disguise wouldn't hurt if Edie spotted me before I was ready to reveal myself to her. When I opened the door, the ringing started again.

One. Two. Three.

I knew I shouldn't have, but I lifted the earflap on my hat and grabbed the receiver. "Hello." It came out like a question: Hello?

"Is Mr. Donald Biadogiano at home?" a man asked.

"Who's calling?" I said as that image of my father faded away.

"This is Joshua Fuller from *Newsweek* magazine."

"No thanks," I told him. "We don't subscribe."

He laughed. "I'm sorry to hear that. But I'm actually calling about a story I'm writing. Is Mr. Biadogiano at home?"

I muffled the receiver, thinking this had to do with one of his inventions. For the hell of it, I said, "He wants to know what the story is about."

"About his sister, who I was sorry to hear recently passed on."

Newsweek was doing a story about Donald's sister. My mother. "Hold on. I'll ask him." I put my hand over the phone and scrambled for something to say, a way to get more information. "He wants to know exactly what the story is about."

"I'm connecting the Burdan trial to her recent death. And I just found out that her youngest son from Massachusetts is missing. I'd like to chat with Mr. Biadogiano for a bit. Ask a few questions. I've been trying to reach him all week."

That headline I found in my uncle's Bible flashed in my mind:

DAY 3: BOY STILL MISSING

I hadn't really thought of myself as missing until now. But I supposed to my father and Marnie I was. I wondered if that's what had happened to Truman. If, like me, he had vanished. Maybe that headline in my uncle's Bible was about him. "What's the Burdan trial?" I said, skipping the hold-on-while-I-ask-him routine. "And what's it have to do with my . . . his sister?"

The man on the other end was silent a moment. I could hear the dull murmur of what I assumed was a newsroom in the background. People pushing words around all day long. "May I ask who I am speaking with?" he said.

I took a breath, cupped my hand over the receiver, and said quietly, "This is Terry Pindle's son, Dominick."

"Well," he said. "Aren't you supposed to be MIA?"

"How do you know anything about me?" I asked.

"You're news, kid," he told me. "A lot of people know about you. At least in the state of Massachusetts."

My Russian hat felt heavy on my head, and I started sweating in my coat, not knowing what to say next. Finally Joshua Fuller asked, "Would you like to meet? Maybe I could chat with you instead of your uncle."

Newsweek wanted to meet. I thought of that headline again, this time twisting it my way—DAY 29: BOY STILL MISSING. What if he told my father where I was living? What if I was forced to go back to Holedo?

My mind spun with questions until I heard a voice in my head. It was the one I had been listening for that morning in the kitchen. The one I had heard when I saw those pregnant women walking into the hospital, when I found that name on the list. My mother. Stronger now than before, she whispered, *Joshua Fuller will tell you everything you want to know. He will lead you to your brother.*

"I'll meet you," I said, pushing my mother's gum around the inside of my mouth with my tongue. "But only if you don't tell anyone I'm here."

Joshua Fuller agreed without taking a moment to debate the deal. We set it all up. Nine the next morning. A diner on University Place, not far from Washington Square Park.

When I put down the phone, I stood in the silence of my uncle's apartment listening for that voice to tell me more about what was to come next. But it was quiet again. The refrigerator hummed. Footsteps creaked in the apartment upstairs. I waited a while longer, feeling pressed to the floor in my coat and hat. Sweating. Listening. Finally I gave up and headed out the door, down the stairs, and uptown toward Edie's.

The whole way I kept thinking of Joshua Fuller's words.

About his sister, who I was sorry to hear recently passed on.

The Burdan trial.

A lot of people know about you.

I could have hailed a cab or grabbed a bus, but the instant replay of that conversation kept me walking straight up Eighth Avenue. I kept trying to connect the dots in my head but came up with only a scribbled mess. Eventually I started thinking about my mother again. The frigid air against my cheeks reminded me of those last weeks with her in our apartment. I wondered if she had any idea when she turned off that radiator how cold it would get for her. I thought of her body waiting in a chilled, dark compartment at the morgue until the ground thawed. No one had told me exactly how her body was being kept, but I had seen a TV movie the other night where a detective hid in the morgue during a chase scene. He slipped right into an empty steel drawer where bodies were stored as simple as socks in a drawer. Human Popsicles. That's how I imagined my mother: stiff and frozen in the darkness. Something retrievable with a single tug of a handle. Irretrievable, too.

When I landed in Hell's Kitchen, I did my best to shake off those thoughts about my mother and my conversation with Joshua Fuller while keeping an eye out for that pack of kids who had followed me the last time I was here. I didn't see them, but I felt their eyes watching me from those windows with rags for curtains.

There he is, I imagined them saying. *Let's get him this time.*

A siren blared somewhere in the distance, and I pulled out Edie's address from my pocket, crossed over a few blocks, and ticked off the numbers: 388, 402, 410, 412. Edie's building, 416, turned out to be a five-story town house like the ones in the Village. A brick job with a cement slab for a stoop and a wide window on each side. Except this place was more run-down than Village buildings. Random windows were covered with boards. The painted brick was peeling—actually peeling— just like Edie's place in Holedo. Only here it was the red-pink color of sunburned skin instead of lemonade. The siren had faded, and the neighborhood—if you could call it that—seemed eerily quiet for New York.

Down the block a group of old guys in bulky winter coats were standing on the corner shooting the shit despite the cold weather. One of them was pushing the other, and I couldn't tell if they were horsing around or about to go at it for real. Either way they were too busy to notice me, so I climbed the steps.

Edie's name wasn't on the buzzer. Just a blank space beneath Rodriguez in 2F and Clancy 2B. As I stared at that empty slot, I glimpsed the whiteness of what I wanted from her again. I still couldn't name what it was, but I knew something was there. I had come this far for a reason, and when I saw her, I would know what that reason was.

The apartments all had an F or B next to them, which must have meant front and back. Since Edie was a B, I walked down the stairs to the street again and checked out an alleyway to the left of the building. It was jam-packed with trash cans and a stripped Oldsmobile. I stepped into the shadowy darkness and squeezed past the skeleton of a car. A bony tuxedo cat sat in the backseat. Blinking and licking. The car's trunk was open and full of rusted plumbing pipes, curving this way and that like intestines. I made my way through a tear in the fence and found a spot where I had a perfect view of the windows to the two first-floor apartments.

One was boarded up, vacant.

The other had a light on even though it was two o'clock in the afternoon. Thin rusted bars guarded the curtainless window, which was open an inch or two. The glass was smudged like a librarian's spectacles, or a glass in a sink. I stared through those bars and smudges right into a bedroom. Edie wasn't inside, but I recognized her peach bed instantly. Although she had ditched the canopy, the pillows and cover were the same ones she'd had in Holedo.

I guessed I hadn't quite believed that I'd found her until I laid eyes on that bed. On that cracked-open window, which made me think of her need for fresh air. A surge of emotions swept over me in waves: first a "gotcha" kind of feeling, then anger, then a steady uneasiness that didn't leave. The list of things I wanted from her took shape in my mind once again.

An explanation

The money

Proof to my mother that I was sorry

Then those white words at the bottom.

What were they? I still didn't know. But I saw that there were three of them. And I knew that whatever they spelled out, that's what I had really come for.

Behind me a metal contraption that looked like a giant's missing shirt button blew out hot air, courtesy of the Puerto Rican bodega on Ninth Avenue. It left the alley smelling of grease. The residue from somebody's heartburning last meal. I stood in that fusty back lot for over two hours, waiting for some sign of life in Edie's bedroom. But nothing happened. The only thing that kept me from going crazy or freezing was the thought of that phone call from *Newsweek*. That voice telling me Joshua Fuller was going to lead me to Truman. I imagined myself as one those Christmas decorations dangling from a wire back in Holedo as the seasons passed. Or one of those galeros, suspended above the cathedral, waiting and waiting and waiting to finally drop. To be released.

After hanging there for what seemed like forever, my nervousness turned to hunger. That greasy bodega air actually started to smell good to me. My stomach made a loud churning noise that might have sounded like the engine to that Oldsmobile if somebody had managed to turn it over. I left my post and walked to Ninth Avenue, where I grabbed a take-out sandwich—a pork and cheese creation I'd never had before—and a Coke from the bodega. I pushed my mother's gum to the back of my mouth and wolfed down half the meal right on the street before I even got back to the alley. Once I slipped past the Olds with its resident cat and trunkful of pipes, then through the tear in the fence, I lost my appetite.

Edie was in the window.

She looked like a faded version of her former self. A woman washed ashore after a shipwreck. Shocked and exhausted. Still alive, but not the same. Hair greasy and twisted into a knot behind her head. Gray circles under her eyes. Swollen white cheeks. Not unlike the way my mother looked in the days before her death. Edie was holding her baby in her arms, swaddled in a yellow blanket. I stepped as close to that smudged glass as I could without her seeing me and listened.

"You are my precious child," she said in a baby voice that sounded shaky even through the glass. "You are my sweet darling. You are my perfect little angel. You are my life."

I dropped the rest of my food on the ground, and that cat wasted no time claiming it. I wanted to hear more of what Edie was saying to her baby—my sister, if she really was my father's child—but the radiator beneath the window clicked on. It hissed steadily, drowning out her words and blowing puffs of steam into the air, right out the window. Two pink balloons were tied to the radiator and they struggled against the blow of heat, thumping the glass. I tried not to think about my mother's silent radiator during the last month of her life. But it kept on hissing, taunting me. I watched Edie through that window like a television with the sound off.

She cradled the baby.

She made mushy faces at her.

She looked as spent and troubled as that gun-toting prostitute on *Hawaii Five-O* last night. The woman who was ready and willing to blow the heads off all those men.

It didn't matter that I couldn't hear her anymore because I knew what she was saying. *You are my sweet darling. You are my precious little girl. You are my life.* But what kind of life was this for a baby? And if Edie had paid off all her debts with my mother's money, then why was she living here?

As I waited for that white want to finally come clear, two men entered the room. One was tall and thin, with skin so smooth and black he looked wet. The other was stockier, with a head as bald and black as the dark lightbulb Leon sometimes screwed into his bedroom lamp. Both wore flared jeans and shiny shirts—one rust-colored, one blue. Gold necklaces poured down their chests and made me think of the flashy drug dealers on TV, the way they tried to fast-talk everybody. I wondered if the apartment belonged to one of them and if that's why her name wasn't listed with 411. They fussed over the baby, twiddling their fingers in front of her face, which I couldn't see because of the blanket. After a moment the tall guy took the baby from Edie. He held Sophie in one arm and hugged Edie with the other. I watched her kiss him the way she used to kiss me at her front door. Not on the cheek exactly, but not on the lips either. Somewhere in between.

In the back of my throat I tasted an acidy trickle. I made a fist and pushed my knuckles to my mouth. Every one of those kisses she had given me had been a lie. I should have been numb to it, but the sight of her—pressing her lips to that drug dealer or whoever he was—made me sick. I wondered if he was Sophie's father. If the whole story about my father getting her pregnant had been a lie. No doubt I was looking at one of the men who had been on the other end of the phone the night I'd overheard her. She must have planned to move here all along, not giving a shit that it was no place for a child.

Edie took the baby back from him and set her sweet darling, her precious little girl, her life, down in the bassinet by the window. It looked like a white wicker boat. Something Edie could set afloat down a river, sending the baby on her way like Moses or Jesus or whatever biblical infant had drifted on water in a basket.

In that moment I knew I wasn't going to kill her. I wasn't going to do anything at all. My anger had transformed into something sad and empty at the sight of her with her baby and those two men. Before I could stop myself, I sank down to the hard cold earth and started to cry, unable to bury my feelings this time around. What did I really expect would happen when I found Edie? I had thought those white words in my head would guide me. But they were still invisible, a nameless something I wanted from her. Edie was living her new life in the shoddy coziness of that bedroom. And I was living mine in the darkness of the alley. Those white words in my head were still just that: an empty blankness, nothing more than my desire to make everything better. But that was impossible. I couldn't help but think of how simple my life had been before, though I hadn't realized it at the time. Driving around with my mother and Marnie, dragging my father out of bars.

It all seemed so harmless now.

When I finally got hold of myself, I stood up and wiped my eyes with the earflaps of that ridiculous Russian hat. I looked one last time into Edie's apartment. But she was gone, and so were the men. Sophie, I suspected, was napping in that wicker bassinet. I made my way out of the alley and caught the first taxicab downtown, back to my uncle's apartment.

Inside, I clicked on the TV and let myself listen for all the references to death. In four hours I counted twenty of them. Instead of turning the channel or drifting off into thoughts about my mother's last night, I forced myself to pay attention to the screen. I wanted to get used to people talking about the end without always losing myself in a mess of thoughts about my mother and what I had done to her. Then I came across one of those panel shows on PBS. A bunch of old farts sitting around a table yapping. Normally I would have ripped right by this type of thing, but the subject had everything to do with my life.

Abortion.

A woman on the panel had short gray hair and tight lips. She spoke with the certainty of a schoolteacher who knew her subject. "I find that most women are drawn to the movement because of something that's happened to them," she said. "They can't get an abortion or they can't get the job they wanted." She went on to say that she believed abortion should be legalized so women could choose whether or not they wanted to give birth in certain situations. But there was a priest on the panel, who—no surprise—disagreed. Abortion was baby-killing, he said. That was that. But the teacher woman didn't let up. What about rapes that resulted in unwanted pregnancies? she asked. What about the hundreds of unwanted children who are raised without proper parenting? What about all the women who die each year from kitchen-table abortions?

To each question the priest's refrain was "It's God's will."

It's not that I didn't believe in God, because I did, but I couldn't help thinking that he needed to come up with a better argument. I mean, if that was the case, then why didn't we simply let sick people die without trying to help them? Or throw up our hands when people broke their legs or arms, let their limbs heal bent and wobbly without casts? The more the priest spoke, the more I pictured God as a big silvery eye in the sky among puffs of white clouds, looking down on the women who suffered from His will and refusing to stop it.

I listened for a while longer, until their discussion looped back in on itself, clearly going nowhere. They both believed what they wanted, and neither of them was budging. Finally I turned off the TV and sprawled on the couch. The streetlight outside cast stretches of square black shadows on the wall. I stared up at those shadows and counted the hours until my meeting with Joshua Fuller the next day. As tired as I felt from all the emotion of the day, sleep never came to me completely. I dozed on and off on the couch for hours. Woke to think of Edie holding her new baby and whispering those words. Woke again to imagine that I was her baby and she was whispering to me.

You are my life, she cooed in her shaky voice again and again. *You are my life.*

When the faint light of dawn made the shadows disappear, I got up and showered. Dressed in the same jeans and sweatshirt I had worn the day before. I waited by the window, watching the street until eight-thirty rolled around. Then I put on my coat and headed out to meet Joshua Fuller.

The diner he suggested was not really a diner at all, or at least not like the one in Holedo. This place had wood-paneled walls and tables instead of booths. No mini-jukeboxes to play. The waitress who seated me wore jeans instead of a drab uniform. She flipped over the upside-down cup on my table and asked if I wanted coffee. I don't know why I kept drinking the stuff lately, even though I didn't like the taste, but I pushed my mother's gum to the back of my mouth and gave her the green light to pour. The menu was a mix of regular diner food—burgers, omelets, turkey clubs—and weird Polish dishes, too—pierogi, borscht soup, beet salad. They also had some Chinese and Italian stuff. I scanned all that food as I waited for Joshua Fuller to show. On the phone he had described himself as six feet tall with curly brown hair and glasses. Each time the door opened, I looked up expecting to see someone who fit that description. At exactly nine o'clock he walked through the door. He had described himself accurately enough, minus the fact that his hair was more gray than brown and there was a purple birthmark above his eye. It looked like an eye patch he had lifted to his forehead so he could peek out for a moment. His turtleneck and black blazer made him seem slick and smart to me. Like one of the guys from a Ballantine's scotch ad, swirling his drink and looking nonchalant.

This is him, I thought. The man who is going to deliver me to my brother.

"Dominick?" he said when he got to the table. He carried a smooth leather bag, stuffed and heavy on his lanky arm. "It's you, right?"

"It's me." I shook his hand when he put it forward, which made me feel older than I was. A scotch-drinking sophisticate, too.

"Nice to meet you," he told me, sitting down.

The waitress came by with the coffeepot. She flipped his cup, poured, refilled mine while she was at it. After she left, we fell into a moment of awkward silence.

"You know," he said, breaking it, "I realized after we hung up that I could get in serious trouble for not letting anyone know where you are. I mean, you're fifteen. A minor."

"Are you going back on our deal?" I asked, thinking I'd bolt for the door if that were the case.

"No," he told me. "I decided that you're not really missing if you're staying at your uncle's place. All your father has to do is pick up the phone like I did."

Maybe he doesn't want to, I thought, sipping my coffee. And that's okay with me.

"So let me ask you a few questions," Joshua said. He took a tape recorder out of his tan bag and set it on the table.

I braced myself for whatever he was going to ask me, then thought that it would be smarter if I got my dirt up front. "How about I ask you some questions first?"

"Sounds fair," he said, holding a finger in the air over the red "record" button, not yet pressing it. "What do you want to know?"

No more wasting time. "The Burdan trial. What is it?"

I watched his bushy eyebrows cinch together. That purple patch crinkle like the skin on a rotten eggplant. "Let me get this straight. You don't know anything about your mother's first son?"

"Just that she was married to a man named Peter and that they had a kid named Truman. My brother."

"Okay, then. Here goes." He stopped and seemed to be mulling something over. Maybe he was wondering whether or not it was right to spill my mother's secrets just to get his interview. I tried to fix my face so that it looked like I could take or leave both him and his information. Finally he breathed in and said, "Your mother's first husband was Peter Tierney. When she was pregnant with their child, he died in an accident. She had the baby five months later."

I leaned forward for more but decided I didn't want to seem too anxious, so I leaned back again.

"Peter Tierney didn't have any money to leave her. No insurance. So she took a job as a waitress to try to support your brother. But she was young herself, and it was never enough to make ends meet. And she still couldn't quite pull herself together after Peter's death."

I stopped him there. "How do you know any of this?"

Joshua reached into his bag and pulled out a manila folder, handed it to me. The thing was stuffed with pages of clipped newspaper and magazine stories. I scanned the headlines. BIOLOGICAL MOM WANTS BABY BACK. BURDAN FAMILY CHALLENGES CASE IN COURT. EXCLUSIVE INTERVIEW WITH TERRY TIERNEY.

I was about to dig into the articles—not for the words right away but for the pictures of my mother and brother that must have been there—but Joshua started talking again. "Your mother's doctor kept pressuring her to give up the baby in a private adoption. He said he knew a family who could give him a better life than a single mother with no money could. Finally she decided to go through with it."

So that was the secret. My brother had been given up for adoption. But why did my mother claim to be visiting Truman when she came to New York?

"According to what she said in those interviews, when your mother's grieving for her husband let up, it was like coming out of a fog. She couldn't believe what she had done. She missed her child and wanted him back. At the same time your uncle had come into some money. He helped her get a lawyer who built a case that claimed Terry had made the adoption decision under duress. During the grieving period after her husband's death. They went after that doctor first, and it turned out he had made a big chunk of change finding that baby for another family. The courts ordered that the adoption records be unsealed."

My curiosity gave way, and I started flipping through the articles, looking for a picture of Truman. I didn't find one of him but I came across a few of a stuffy-looking couple. Bald guy in a business suit. Woman with straight shoulders and pearls, glasses on a chain. Mr. and Mrs. Burdan. "So the Burdans are my brother's adoptive parents?"

"Yes," he said. "And they're a wealthy family. Your biological brother is one rich young man. Also, you should know that his name isn't Truman anymore. It's Randolph."

I gripped the articles in my hands and tried to wrap my mind around what he was saying. My brother was rich. But he wasn't my brother at all. He was someone named Randolph Burdan. My mind flashed on one of my afternoons spent wandering the city. Last week I'd been on the Upper East Side when I passed a school where a flock of boys in blue blazers were streaming out the front door. Something about their neatly parted hair and unblemished faces had made them appear flawless, extraordinary to me. A bunch of rich kids who seemed incapable of being harmed. As I sat there listening to Joshua, my mind put Truman in that picture, made him one of those flawless kids.

"Your mother didn't stand a chance in hell against their family lawyers," Joshua was saying. "Courts ruled that the adoption was final. But by then the story had made national news. I covered the case for the paper I worked for back then. And the Burdans weren't happy with the publicity. When your mother's lawyers tried to get her visiting rights, they shot that down, too."

"End of story?" I said.

"Not quite. A year after the ruling Randolph Burdan was missing."

So that headline in my uncle's Bible was about Truman . . . Randolph. "Did anyone find him?"

"He turned up on the playground five days later. He was all by himself, pushing an empty swing on a Sunday morning. Of course, the family suspected that your mother had taken him. But she had an alibi, so no one could prove a thing."

I tried to picture my mother as a kidnapper but came up only with the image of her in that black wool coat, her lips chapped and peeling, plunging our clogged toilet and crying. She wouldn't have taken my brother only to abandon him at the playground. "So where is he today? I mean, he must be eighteen by now."

"Twenty, actually. A sophomore at Columbia. And he goes by the name Rand, not Randolph."

The waitress appeared, pad in hand. "What can I get you?"

I had zip for an appetite and told her that coffee was all I wanted. Joshua said the same, so she refilled us both.

"My mother used to come to the city and tell me that she was visiting him," I said when the waitress was gone. "Was she? I mean, were they in touch? Because he didn't come to her funeral."

"I highly doubt your mother was visiting him. The family shunned her, and so did Rand. He didn't want anything to do with her. They thought she was just after money."

I flipped through the articles again. No pictures of my brother. But I saw a bunch of my mother being interviewed by reporters. She looked shaky and nervous with those microphones in front of her face. I bet she hated all that attention. I thought of the way she used to talk about him, calling him Truman even though that was no longer his name. Why couldn't she just let go?

"So now that I've brought you up to date," Joshua said, taking out a notepad and carefully pressing that red button, "I want to ask you a few questions. The story I'm doing is about the way your mother's life exemplifies the choices women face with unwanted pregnancies. She tried both paths—adoption and an illegal abortion—and neither was a solution. I thought I'd begin by writing about her attempt to start a new life and why it all went wrong in January."

Question: Why did it all go wrong?

Answer: Edie and me.

My mother had been cheated out of her first child and her last. The one in the middle had cheated her out of her life. Meanwhile, I was a runaway. And Edie was living happily ever after in a run-down apartment in Hell's Kitchen.

Something was happening in my head.

I felt the electric hum of a railroad track when you put your hand to it, telling you the train is around the bend. I saw that blank white space at the bottom of the list of things I wanted from Edie. It grew bigger and whiter as that electric hum grew stronger. Louder. Those three white words were finally turning blue, then black. They weren't just three words; they were a name:

Sophie Dominick Kramer.

That's what I wanted from Edie. The sibling I never had. The one who was given to another family before my birth. The one whose life had been stopped in that motel. I couldn't get my mother back, and my brother was someone else now. But if that baby was my sister, then I wanted her. I was going to save her from whatever life on the edge Edie had in store. And I was going to take something from Edie in the process, the way she had taken something from me.

Joshua Fuller was still talking. "I have an interview set up next week with your mother's best friend as well. A Marnie Garboni."

I stood up from the table, clutching the folder with all those stories about my mother's life. Her bad decisions. "Marnie will tell you everything you need to know. I have to leave."

"But we had a deal," he said, jerking his head up from his notepad. His face looked tough suddenly. The Ballantine's scotch man losing his cool. "You can't go."

I ignored him, walked toward the door of the diner.

"We had a deal!" he called.

I stepped out onto the street and started across town. My plan was to make a pit stop at my uncle's place, gather up what money I had left, then find a way to get that baby. I passed a long line of people on the street waiting to see a movie I'd never heard of called *The Go-Between.* I passed a ratty-haired woman hanging out of a phone booth with one hand down the front of her cranberry-colored pants. A prostitute. A drug addict. Maybe both. "I got to get some sleep," she was saying into the black mouth of the phone. "I just got to get some sleep, man." Something about her tangled hair and drawn eyes made me think of Edie. I imagined that she was a vision of the woman Edie would become. And I refused to let her drag my sister along for the ride.

When I reached the apartment building, there was a dark sedan parked out front. The driver was removing a suitcase from the trunk, and my uncle was digging in his pockets for his keys.

Welcome the fuck home.

"I'll let you in," I told him, knowing he'd be shocked to see me.

"Dominick," he said, surprised. "What are you doing here?"

"I left Holedo and stayed at your place for a while. But don't worry, I'm just grabbing something, and then I'll be on my way."

"Does your father know where you are?"

"I don't think he gives a shit," I said and stepped forward, unlocking the door for both of us.

My uncle dillydallied with the driver, signing a receipt, then tipping him, before coming inside. I marched up the stairs ahead of him, and he trailed behind, clunking his suitcase the whole way and spitting out half sentences. "But you— I thought— How did you—"

I let him keep babbling until we were in the apartment. After he took off his coat and collapsed into the armchair by the TV, I told him that I knew about the Burdan trial, my brother, all of it. Figured I might as well get his end of the story before leaving.

"So now you know," he said, calmer than I suspected. His voice was tinged with something. Maybe sadness; definitely confusion. And in that moment I saw him for the first time as a person separate from my uncle, maybe the way the rest of the world saw him, too. A lonely man who buried himself in his work. Something told me that the sadness of his sister's life left his heart feeling saddled, because he had wanted to help her over the years but didn't know what to do. All those checks he had sent her were Band-Aids to cover up her Truman wound. "Your mother never told you the truth because she was trying to make a fresh start," he said. "She wanted you to know you had a brother in case somehow things worked out with him. But she didn't want you to know about all that business of the past. If you ask me, Dominick, I think she wanted to believe he was living here with me. It was like some kind of fantasy of hers. The only thing she had left of her first son."

I had so many questions, but what came out was this: "Who were those presents for?" My childhood jealousy bubbling up one final time. Those presents I always wished were for me.

"What presents?" Donald said.

"The ones she brought with her on the bus here when I was a kid."

"Oh. She used to leave stuff with the doorman at the Burdans' building at first. Little letters to them, pleading. But when the doorman stopped taking them, those gifts just piled up around here."

"Didn't you try to talk some sense into her?"

"Yes. I used to tell her she had to let him go. To just be happy knowing he was taken care of. That he had opportunities she could never give him. And she did let it go for a while. She met your father. She had you, which made her incredibly happy. But I guess she always felt like something was missing."

"Tell me one more thing," I asked, reaching into the drawer where I had stashed my cash. "Did she take him? Was she the reason he was missing for those five days?"

My uncle sighed. "I have never told anyone this. But yes. She took him."

"Why did she give him back?"

"Your mother used to watch his nanny and him in the park. It was her only way to see him. One morning, as your mother sat there watching, and probably weeping, she just strolled over and picked the kid out of the sandbox while the nanny was busy gabbing. She walked right out of the park and called me a day later from New Mexico."

As my uncle went on, my mind painted details into the story he told, letting the whole scene take shape before me. My mother was desperate and beautiful, a woman who had done the unthinkable. On the plane to Albuquerque she kept Truman at her side, playing peekaboo with him like any other mother and child. Right away she found out the words he knew and kept asking him to say them. "What goes woof-woof?" she asked. "Doggy go woof," he answered proudly. "What goes meow?" "Kitty go meow," he said and giggled. He also said "Dada," and it broke her heart, because Peter was gone. But her son never said "Mama." She thought that meant he knew the truth. That somewhere in his toddler heart he sensed that the rich woman who had paid a doctor to get him was not his mama after all. And as the plane soared through the clouds, across the country, to somewhere safe, Terry tried to get him to call her Mama. "Can you say it?" she kept asking. "Mama. Can you say it?" By the time they landed, he still hadn't said it to her. But that was okay, she told herself, because someday soon he would.

"I flew out there as soon as I could to meet her," my uncle was saying. "She had checked into a little hotel in Santa Fe with Truman. I mean, Rand. I told her right off the bat that she couldn't go through with it. She had to give the baby back."

The more he spoke, the more the story unfurled in my mind, vivid and clear, as if I had been there, too. The moment my mother saw her brother step off the plane, she regretted her decision to let him in on what she had done. "You can't keep him," he told her when they got into a rented car and drove under the open, blue sky of New Mexico. His words were like a heavy weight pressing on her shoulders. She told him that the child belonged to her. That she had been tricked by that doctor and the Burdan family. That she wasn't going to let them keep her baby and ruin her life simply because they had more money and a fancy lawyer. But Donald didn't let up. He wanted to know what kind of life she hoped to lead, hiding out like a fugitive. He wanted to know how she was going to feel if they found her and sent her to jail. "And then where will either of you be?" he kept asking. "Truman will have a good life in New York. That's what you told yourself when you gave him up. That's what you have to tell yourself again."

"It wasn't easy. But eventually I convinced her," my uncle said to me. "We made a plan. Truman and I would fly to New York. I would bring him back to the playground first thing in the morning before anyone was there. Make a call informing the police as to where he was. The whole while I would watch from a distance to make sure they found him. Your mother agreed, but she asked me for one thing first."

"What was that?" I said.

"She wanted one last day with her child. So I agreed. The next day we woke up before sunrise. Drove south to a little town called Estancia and had breakfast there. We spent the day at—"

"Laguna del Perro," I said.

My uncle looked at me, momentarily puzzled, then went on. "Yes. We walked through the trails. Swam in the water. Truman was only about three years old at the time."

I thought back to all those stories about New Mexico that my mother used to tell me. Now I pictured Donald by her side, walking through the dry, open landscape as she carried Truman. My mother memorizing every detail of that day so she could take it with her for the rest of her life.

"I have a picture of Truman and me by the lake somewhere around here," my uncle told me.

I've seen it, I thought. "And at the end of that day?"

"I took the child back to New York. The next morning I did everything just as we planned. I bought him a balloon and an ice cream, then took him to the park. Your mother spent one more day in Santa Fe. Out in the open, so she had an alibi in case anyone tried to prove she'd taken him. And it worked, because no one ever could."

"So my mother never lived in New Mexico?"

"No," he said, then told me that she kept saying how she wished she could. Instead my mother had her perfect day with her son, and the Burdans got their baby back. It had been one canyon walk, one breakfast, one single day that she stretched into a lifetime with Truman. That was all she had of him.

I didn't want to hear any more. The only thing I could think about was getting the hell out of here and finding Sophie. My maybe sister. A baby with my middle name. I felt the way my mother must have just before she picked what was rightfully hers out of the sandbox.

"Where are you going?" Donald said when I walked toward the door.

"I have to run an errand."

"Now?" he said. "What could you possibly have to do?"

I didn't answer him. Just walked out the door and down the stairs. I knew what I had to do. And I had to do it for my mother.

When a cab drove by, I flagged it down and told the driver to take me to the corner of Forty-seventh and Ninth. Five minutes later I was standing in front of Edie's building. I slid through the alley, passed the gutted and left-for-dead Oldsmobile. I kept as quiet as that tuxedo cat, barely making a sound as I pawed through the tear in the fence. The bodega fan was blowing, and I could smell the greasy residue from other people's breakfasts. Eggs and bacon. Sausage links. A rat scurried beneath my legs—right between them—like I was something inanimate and non-threatening to scurry beneath on its way to find food. Or green poison pellets that would leave it foaming at the mouth. Or a sturdy wooden trap that would snap its neck just as it was about to eat. I didn't even flinch. Just watched its gray body move under the Olds and toward the bodega.

I turned and saw Edie again through the bars and smudges, still looking wiped out and holding the baby in her arms. To me it was not just a baby. It was the one my mother couldn't keep. The one she aborted.

The radiator was off, and I could hear her again.

"You are my life," she kept saying in the high voice of a cartoon princess, a little less weary than the day before. "You are my life."

After a long, anxious half hour, I watched her set her life down in that boat bassinet. And I thought once again of that biblical baby floating down a river. Edie bent to kiss the baby, then left the room. I walked right up to the window and peered inside, knowing she would see me if she came back. I pictured the surprised O of her mouth, her hand slapping her heart, startled. With my face so close to that dishwater-dirty window, I could hear the shower running and Edie humming. I didn't recognize the tune, but it had as many peaks and dips as a roller-coaster ride. Up and down she hummed, as the sound of spraying water accompanied her.

I reached my hand under the open wedge of the window and pulled. I had expected the thing to be as stuck and glued as it looked, but the frame slid right up. The wood on wood made a loud scraping sound, and I froze. Waited to see if Edie had heard, but she hummed still. And the water sprayed. I had a clear view of the bedroom but no way to get in because of the bars. In that moment I made a plan in my head: grab one of the curved pipes out of the trunk of that car, hook the hood of the bassinet and drag it toward the window, gently lift my sister through the bars.

Difficult. Not impossible.

But I had only so much time before Edie would be done with her shower. I was about to put my plan into action when I looked at the edge of those bars over the window and saw that they were hinged. I tugged on the other end, and they opened with a rusty creak. There was no lock, or if there was, it had long since rusted away or been removed like everything else in this dilapidated building. I took it as a sign that I was meant to get inside.

One hand pushed the pink balloons out of the way. Legs first, then body, and I was standing in the bedroom. The very spot where I had watched Edie kiss that man. It was as if I had stepped into the television set, a room I had been watching for years. The dimensions were different than I imagined from outside. Smaller. Brighter.

Sophie made a gentle cooing sound, and I carefully picked her up. She was as light as a kite, something airborne and gravityless. I felt that if I let go of her, she would float up toward the ceiling instead of falling to the floor. She looked less like a baby and more like an alien, an embryo still. Too unformed and fragile to be out of the womb. Her face was round and pink. A baby with light-colored skin who could definitely be my sister. She made an uncomfortable little peep, and that was all. My arms were fine, she must have thought, better than that rickety bassinet, because she kept on sleeping.

I took her bottle, her blanket.

Quietly scooped all the baby stuff into a bag that hung on the door-knob.

Edie hummed. Shower water sprayed.

I walked toward the window, then thought better of it.

The front door opened easily, and I didn't have a reason to hide.

I was taking what was mine.

My mother's.

Even my father's.

A moment later I was out on the street, and Sophie was beginning to cry. A long, breathless shriek in the cold New York afternoon that made me shake. I reached the end of Forty-seventh and turned down Ninth Avenue. My heart beating fast and frantic like Edie's would be when she stepped from the shower, her wet feet making impermanent patterns on the floor as she walked to the bedroom and found the bassinet empty. For the moment, though, she was simply humming, probably staring up at the giant silver eye of a shower nozzle as the hot water poured all over and steam rose like clouds. I imagined that eye to be God. A great being who already knew what suffering awaited the woman below but refused to stop it.

This was His will:

The woman was humming.

And I was walking away with her life in my hands.

Seven

Sophie shrieked louder and louder as I moved along the dirty gray sheet of sidewalk. A deafening rattle of a sound that seemed too wild coming from the small pink hole of her mouth. She sounded like she was choking, gagging, struggling for air. I envisioned her throat as a black tunnel filling itself with phlegm until there was nothing left for a newborn baby like her to breathe. Clogged like a sink or a sewer, she would end up dead and lifeless in my arms. A punctured balloon, deflated and impossible to patch.

The sheer terror of something like that going wrong now that I had her sent my heart ramming beneath my rib cage. I tried to shift Sophie around so she'd stop. Her head wobbled in a way that chilled me, loose and liquidy, like it might slide right off her body. I thought of my father's drinking buddies, the way their heads swiveled and swayed, sloppy just like the boozy wet tongues in their mouths. Somewhere in a distant memory I heard Marnie's voice say, *Her head's not screwed on too tight.* But she had been talking about one of the dippy nurses at the hospital. Not a baby. Just a turn of phrase, I knew, but it rang in my head regardless. I wondered if there was something wrong with Sophie. Something I wasn't aware of, something I couldn't have known watching from her the window. Or were all babies' heads loose until their spines grew strong like the trunk of a tree to support the weight? Screwed them on good and tight. I simply didn't know. But I didn't want to take the chance that her head would roll off down the sidewalk—a fleshy bowling ball knocking at the bright stabbing heels of three hookers making a daytime appearance on the corner—so I cupped my palm at the back of her skull and held her body tight to my chest. Kept walking as she cried.

A homeless man looked up at me and winked one of his glazed eyes. For a brief second I wondered what it was he saw when he stared at me. A boy with his baby sister. A young father with his child. It could have been anything given his perspective, slumped and delirious against the hard beige brick of a city building. An empty McCormick's vodka bottle in his unclean hand.

I walked past his gaze and put my mind on Sophie. She felt so fragile inside her blanket that I worried her fingers might freeze like icicles. Just in case, I decided to get her out of the cold ASAP. There wasn't a cab in sight, so I walked one block over to Forty-fourth and Eighth, feeling the eyes of those evil kids who had followed me upon me still, watching from the shadowy windows above my head. On the corner I hailed one of those Checker cabs and climbed carefully inside.

"Where to?" the driver asked over the crying the second I settled in with Sophie in my arms. He was a gray-haired Italian man with thick black glasses and an unlit cigar dangling from his mouth.

"Can we just drive around?" I asked him, not knowing where to go next. I had to calm the baby down but still wasn't sure how to do that.

"I need a destination," he said. "So I can record it for my boss."

Leave it to me to find the only cabbie in New York who played by the rules. "Then take me to the Statue of Liberty," I said, spitting out the first location I thought of.

When he picked up his clipboard and started to write, I looked down at Sophie, who—for no apparent reason—decided to stop crying as I rocked her in my arms. I said a silent prayer of thanks and kept watching her. She had a strange V-shaped indent on her head beneath the soft blond fuzz. Again I thought she seemed more like an alien than a child. I counted her ten fingers the way new mothers always do, just to be sure. She was zipped up in one of those soft infant outfits that covered her feet; otherwise I would have counted her toes, too. I reached beneath the blanket and held one of her feet in my hand. It was the smallest foot, and she was the smallest baby, I had ever seen. My mind flashed on that PBS show from the other night, and just for a moment I found myself on the priest's side. I couldn't imagine yanking this poor little life before her birth.

But would Sophie have been Sophie eight months ago?

I wasn't sure.

"You mean the Liberty Island ferry?" the driver was saying, still holding his clipboard.

"Huh?" I said without turning my gaze from the baby. I was trying to spot some resemblance in the miniature landscape of her face. Truthfully, she looked too small and unformed to gauge a thing like that. But I kept searching.

"Lady Liberty is on an island," the driver told me. "If you want to get to her, you have to take the ferry. Is that where you want to go?"

No, it wasn't. I had just suggested it to stall for time. But taking a boat ride with a baby in such cold weather didn't seem like a good idea. In fact, New York City itself didn't seem like such a good idea anymore—especially since Edie, and no doubt the police, would come looking for Sophie the second she found her missing. I stared straight ahead, out the driver's window, and racked my brain for a place to go. Heading back to my uncle's was a definite dead end. But where else was there? That's when I thought of the bus station only two blocks away.

"Would you like me to take you someplace," the driver said, "or are we just going to sit here all day and meditate?"

I glanced down at Sophie, and she blinked open her eyes. They were a watery blue color, and she looked not at me but through me. Inside me in a way I couldn't explain. They made me think of the liquid window in the slick black Magic 8 Ball that Marnie kept on her coffee table. To me Sophie's eyes were like one of those underwater messages.

It is decidedly so . . .

Without a doubt . . .

Outlook good . . .

I let that be my sign that the bus station was the place to go. "Take us to Port Authority," I told the driver.

"Jeez Louise," he said. "Another schizo in the big city. Imagine my surprise."

A minute later Sophie and I were dropped off in front of Port Authority. I held her close to my chest as I walked inside. Carrying a baby seemed like dangerous work, and I watched my feet as I moved to be sure I didn't stumble.

The place was relatively deserted compared to my other trips in and out. People darted for their gates. A voice announced departing buses on a hollow-sounding speaker: "Chicago, Gate Nineteen . . . Baltimore, Gate Eleven . . . Washington, D.C., Gate Twenty-four . . ." When the list was finished, the speaker switched to the Fifth Dimension singing, "Up, up and away in my beautiful balloon . . ." A maintenance worker mopped the floor where someone had spilled a strawberry shake. I stood there watching him slosh that pink goo around, soaking it up in the stringy gray noodles of his mop, as I wondered where to go with Sophie. The board above the ticket counter listed all the buses leaving in the next few hours. I could have caught one to Chicago, Baltimore, Washington, or even Miami. But all those places seemed random and pointless. A cross-country bus was leaving for Santa Fe at five o'clock, and for a moment I thought that maybe I should get on it as some sort of tribute to my mother. When I tried to picture Sophie and me among the cacti, eating one of those New Mexican breakfasts my mother always talked about, I came up with an empty, lonely feeling. It wasn't as if that place had worked out for her either, so I decided against it.

The maintenance worker finished wiping up the spill and walked off with his mop dripping behind him, leaving a trail of pink dots. I closed my eyes and listened for that voice again, hoping it would tell me what was to come next. The only thing I heard was the speaker still playing that balloon song. Up, up, and away until the balloon burst and the music stopped abruptly. A muffled voice announced, "Boston-bound bus number Thirty-three will depart from Gate Seventeen in ten minutes. The bus will make stops in Bridgeport, Hartford, and Holedo. Passengers wishing to travel aboard this bus must purchase their tickets at the counter by the northeast entrance of the terminal." The message repeated, and when it was done, I looked down at Sophie. Her eyes were open once again. Watery and blue. Looking into nowhere. I wondered if I should take that announcement and her open eyes as another sign. Until that moment I hadn't considered going home, but it started to make sense to me. At least in Holedo I could enlist some help. If not from Marnie, then definitely from Leon. I could ask him to help find me a place to stay with the baby until I figured out my next move.

Holedo it was, I decided.

I was taking what was mine and going home.

With nine minutes to spare, I stepped around that line of pink dots and bought my ticket at the counter. Before heading down to the gate, I stopped at the newsstand, where I scoped around for anything Sophie might need. Next to the paperbacks and newspapers I noticed a pile of children's books. Probably there for parents who wanted to occupy their kids on the bus ride. Sophie was way too young to appreciate any of the stories, but I grabbed two for her anyway—*The Little Engine That Could* and *Hansel and Gretel*—remembering the stack I used to flip through on Edie's nightstand.

After paying up, I caught the escalator to Gate 17 and boarded the bus. I found two empty seats near the middle and sat by the window. I put my bag on the seat next to me so no one would park their ass there, and then I took to staring down at Sophie's unformed face. Occasionally I looked out at the darkness of the station, smelling that dieselly bus smell and the dirty air from the bathroom as I tried to calm down. Out there in the darkness there were all kinds of faceless voices that called to me.

Now you've done it.

Now you've really done it.

You've saved this baby.

You've put this child in danger.

You've proved something to your dead mother.

You've taken something from Edie the way she took something from you.

You're about to ruin your life.

I shivered at it all and looked at Sophie, who seemed peaceful again in the comfort of my arms. I already knew what a ticking time bomb she was when it came to crying, so I made every effort to keep still so she wouldn't start screeching. This is my sister, I said in my head. I didn't know if it was some sort of prayer or if I was just plain trying to convince myself. But that's all I kept thinking: This is my sister who I am holding in my arms.

"Excuse me," a soft voice said. "Is this seat taken?"

I looked up to see that skinny girl I always ran into. The one who had protested the police auction and ridden into the city on the bus with me the day my mother died. Her bulky black guitar case was strapped on her back like a heavy shadow. Bumper stickers on the thing read WOMEN'S LIB, EQUAL PAY FOR EQUAL WORK, ABORTION ON DEMAND. I thought of what my father would say at the sight of this girl and her opinions: *Of all the seats on the bus, this lesbian has to sit next to me.*

"Sorry," I said. "That seat's for the baby."

"But the baby is in your arms," she said, tilting her head and dropping her mouth open, exasperated.

"Why don't you just take another one?" I told her, not caring how rude I sounded. "Clearly I need the space."

She shifted her guitar case, and it accidentally clunked against another passenger's bald head. "Watch it!" he said.

"Sorry," she told him, then flashed her brown eyes at me. "Look around and point to an empty seat, and I'll be glad to take it."

I craned my neck back and noticed that all the seats were full. I had been so distracted by the baby and those voices that I hadn't been paying attention to all the people getting on. "Have a seat," I said, moving the bag of baby stuff aside.

"Why, thank you," she said, plunking down with her mammoth guitar case next to Sophie and me. "How nice of you to offer."

I shifted toward the window so she wouldn't bother us anymore. Under my shirt I felt Joshua Fuller's manila folder press against my stomach. With Sophie in my arms I couldn't figure out how to get to those articles, so I decided to wait. Besides, I knew what they said, more or less. As I held Sophie's tiny hand in mine—no bigger than a petal plucked from one of my mother's funeral flowers—I tried to figure out exactly what I was going to do when I arrived in Holedo. Call Leon. Swear him to secrecy. Ask him to help me find a place to stay. Then what? A big part of me knew that I should get off this bus and undo what I had done before taking it any further. But holding this baby, just looking at her miniature face and soft bump of a nose, knowing that she was possibly—probably—my sister, made me feel like I had salvaged something from my mother's tragedy. In a weird way I was making things up to her by taking Sophie. Keeping this baby the way she wanted to keep Truman.

I couldn't turn back.

And besides, it was too late.

The bus was starting.

The wheels were moving.

Little Miss Big Guitar emptied her bag as I held Sophie close and careful in my arms. I watched her reflection in the window as she pulled out a sandwich made with stuff that looked like it was picked from a field. Stringy, weedy browns and greens. No meat that I could see.

A vegetarian lesbian, I heard my father say. *The worst kind.*

When she finished nibbling her sandwich down to nothing, she took out a box of perfume called Tigress. The label asked, "Are you wild enough to wear it?" I guessed the answer was yes, because she squirted a dab of it on her slender wrist, stinking up the air around us. Next she pulled out a silver cigarette case. If she lit up, it would probably send

Sophie into another crying jag. That was all I needed. But when she snapped open the case, there were nothing but colored guitar picks inside, all lined up like a woman's painted fingernails. The girl slipped a pink pick back in place, then proceeded to snap and unsnap the case for no apparent reason. Maybe she liked the sound. Maybe she just wanted to bust my balls.

Sophie had been quiet up until this point, but she burst out again with a giant "Waaaaaaaaaa! Waaaaaaaa! Waaaaaaaa!" At first I figured the perfume and snapping had bugged her. But when she wouldn't stop crying even after the smell had faded and the snapping had ceased, I worried I was hurting her somehow. I moved her this way and that in my arms, but her head kept doing that eerie wobble and she kept on wailing. The shrill pitch made me panic. What if something was really wrong with her? I was hardly prepared to handle it. The more she cried, the more nervous I became. I decided she might be hungry, so I grabbed her bottle and tried to pop it into her small, open mouth. That seemed only to make her more upset. She screamed louder than before. Her pink face turned red, highlighting the tiny veins under the soft blond fuzz and wrinkled skin on her head.

The man who had been clunked by the guitar glared at me. "Great," he said to the woman sitting next to him even as he looked my way. "I can tell what kind of ride this is going to be."

"Shhhh," I said to Sophie, praying that she didn't cry herself to death. "It's okay. Shhhh. Shhhh."

"Can I give you some advice?" the Vegetarian Lesbian Tigress said.

At first I didn't realize she was talking to me. But when she repeated herself, I turned to her. The last thing I needed was lip from this girl. "What?" I said over Sophie's screaming.

"Baby-sitting 101. You're holding him wrong. Don't squeeze him to your chest so tight. Just keep your hand behind the baby's head for support and let him lie in the crook of your other arm. Rock him a bit, and I bet he'll stop crying."

"It's a she," I said, indignant. And if Sophie weren't screaming so loud, I would have let the VLT know that her perfume and snapping were probably to blame for the outburst. But Sophie's face was so red, and I was so terrified that she'd explode in my arms, that I had no choice but to listen to the advice. I moved my hands just as she said and— voilà!—it worked. Sophie was quiet. Slowly her red skin faded to pink. She was going to live after all. "Thanks," I said, despite myself.

"Sure thing," she said, flashing her brown eyes again. "And if you don't mind one more piece of advice, I'll let you in on a secret."

"I don't mind," I said, equal parts begrudging and grateful.

"Lesson number two. When you want her to take the bottle, don't shove it in her mouth. Rub the nipple by her lip, and if she wants it, she'll start sucking."

"Okay." I looked at her again as if for the first time, trying to shush my father's assumptions about her in my mind. She was pretty, all right, but on Leon's one-to-ten girl-rating scale she would only have been a seven and a half. Just below his eight-point cutoff. She lost points for her almost-flat chest, skinny body, and mousy hair. But she gained points for everything else. Her smooth, clear skin. Her sugary-brown eyes. She had a nose that narrowed at the top and widened in a press-me sort of way at the bottom. Her lips made me think of a kiss mark she could leave on a piece of paper, if only she were wearing lipstick. Her eyebrows arched big and wide over her eyes, like she was surprised or holding back a joke. I didn't know whether to add, subtract, or divide for her clothes, though, because her head was sticking out of a crocheted shawl made from a patchwork of squares. Blue, yellow, pink, and green. I guess Leon would tick off a point there, but I didn't bother. That rating system seemed sort of dumb now that I thought about it. "How old are you?" I asked without really intending to.

"Sixteen." She put her cigarette case in her bag and took out a party pack of peanut M&M's and Neccos candy. Enough to feed the entire bus. "How old are you?"

"Same," I told her. "In another few days." I couldn't believe that my birthday was coming and I'd barely thought about it. Each year my mother baked me a chocolate cake and gathered up Leon, Marnie, and my father to sing an excruciatingly off-key rendition of "Happy Birthday." Leon and my father always kept the song going longer than necessary with the "how old are you now?" shtick and a list of all the zoo animals that I looked and smelled like. The routine came complete with sound effects, courtesy of Leon's armpit.

So much for that tradition.

"Want some?" she asked, holding the bags of candy out to me.

"No thanks," I told her, pushing my mother's flavorless gum around inside my mouth. I hadn't eaten a thing all day, but the emptiness in my stomach didn't seem to matter. Hunger was the least of my concerns.

"More for me," she said and gulped down a handful of M&M's. "So we're both going to the Hole."

"The Hole?"

She pointed to my ticket, which I was still holding in one hand, squeezing it between my thumb and forefinger because I hadn't wanted to stick it in my pocket and risk dropping Sophie. All that was left of the word Holedo after the bus driver had torn it in half was "Hole." How appropriate.

"I always notice that when they rip the bus ticket. One of those weird things." She grabbed another handful of M&M's and dropped them into her mouth.

"I guess you have a sweet tooth," I said.

"I'm trying to be a vegetarian. But nothing ever fills me up, so I end up eating junk. Last night I finished a plate of steamed veggies, then inhaled half a cake and three Diet Shastas. I was healthier before I gave up meat."

"So why are you doing it?" I asked. She was skinny enough that she didn't need to worry about dieting.

"I feel bad for the animals," she told me, waving a red M&M in the air as she spoke. Her fingernails were short and unpainted, unlike her guitar picks. "Think of it this way: If you saw a cow in a field, you'd never walk up and take a bite out of it. But basically that's what you do every time you eat a hamburger."

"I do?"

"Sort of." She pooched her lips and looked a little perplexed by her logic. "I read something like that in my vegetarian handbook anyway. But maybe I said it wrong. Don't listen to me. I'm the world's worst vegetarian. Do you eat meat?"

"Yeah," I said, feeling as if that was some sort of sin. I thought of my mother excavating a frozen red pot roast from the back of the freezer on Saturday nights so we could eat it with boiled carrots and mashed potatoes on Sunday afternoons. I pictured a bulgy-eyed cow in a field of tall grass but couldn't imagine the steps between its standing there mooing and becoming my meal. Sophie let out a peep that made me worry she might start crying again. I rubbed the bottle gently against her lip, and she started sucking.

"You're a fast learner," the girl said.

My mind flashed on that night she had been standing in front of me at Cumby's Mart holding a baby and trying to rein in the two boys at the candy counter. I had been so wrapped up in Edie that I had barely noticed her. "Were you baby-sitting that night I saw you in the store?" I asked.

"Oh, so you admit to seeing me," she said.

"What do you mean?"

"People in Holedo have this weird thing where they see each other all the time but pretend they don't. I never understand it."

I thought of how I had turned away from her when she smiled at me on the bus to New York with Claude last month. So I got what she meant, I guess. But she still hadn't answered my question. "Were you baby-sitting?"

"I have five younger brothers. Baby-sitting is in my blood."

"Well, can I ask you a question?"

"Sure," she said.

"Do you think this baby looks okay?"

"What do you mean?"

"Her size. She's so small. And her head wobbles when I move her."

She looked down at Sophie's little face, then turned to me. "My professional opinion is that she is a hundred-percent normal. Infants are more durable than they look. And they're always a little weird when they're this young. She'll get cute in a few months. Not to worry."

Okay, so she wasn't Dr. Spock, but her analysis made me breathe a little easier. The loose neck was normal. Sophie was tiny because she was an infant. That was all. But then Sophie spit the bottle out of her mouth and started crying again just as loud as before.

"Now what?" I said.

She reached over and felt Sophie's bottom. "When was the last time you changed her?"

Never, I wanted to say.

The blank look on my face must have told her all she needed to know. "Don't you have any diapers with you?"

I held Sophie in one arm and reached down with the other to pick up the bag of stuff I'd taken from Edie's. Only one diaper was inside, and I had no idea how many I'd need. Did babies get changed every hour or every ten hours? I scolded myself for picking up those two useless books instead of a package of Pampers before boarding the bus. In the bag I also found a pacifier, a tube of white gunk, and a container of something marked Enfamil. I pulled out the diaper like I knew what I was doing. As I set Sophie down on my lap and tried to figure how to get her outfit off her, she shrieked uncontrollably.

"Let me help before she blows my eardrums," the girl said. "But you better watch and learn."

I was glad she was willing to do the job for me, but at the same time I felt like crying along with Sophie. As I watched the girl expertly unsnap the buttons around the baby's legs, pull off the old diaper, wipe her clean, and put on the new one, I kept thinking that I had no idea how unprepared I was to handle an infant. And how was I going to manage back in Holedo with a baby? Leon would help me somehow, I reminded myself. Maybe Marnie, too.

The girl got Sophie changed and quieted down again, then placed her back in my arms. "That's much better," she said.

"Thanks." I sighed with relief as Sophie nestled into my chest. I knew I should spend this ride figuring out what to do when I got to Holedo—the Hole—but I couldn't help talking to this girl. There was something about her—her soft voice, her "before" picture hair, her plain and pretty face—that made me feel better. "This is my sister, Sophie," I said, making the introductions. It felt funny to say "my sister" out loud. But I decided to stop wondering whether Edie had been lying to me about my father getting her pregnant. I wanted Sophie to be my sister. And until further notice, that's what I was going to believe.

"Nice to meet you," the girl said in a baby's voice not unlike the one Edie used to talk to her. She shook Sophie's miniature hand. "I'm Jeanny."

"I'm Dominick," I told her when she looked up at me.

I thought I saw something in those eyes of hers. Some flicker of recognition in the way her brows narrowed, then rose again. "Pindle?" she said.

I was right. "Yeah. How do you know?" In my head I heard Joshua Fuller telling me I was news in the state of Massachusetts. I figured she had read about my mother's death in the paper just like everyone else in Holedo. Then I wondered if she had read about me.

"We used to go to school together," Jeanny said, not mentioning my mother or me in the newspaper. "My last name is Garvey." She looked as if she were going to say something more but stopped herself. "Jeanny Garvey" was all she said.

"I thought you went to Catholic school."

"Well, we used to go to school together. Back in elementary. Now I go to St. Bartholomew. When I go, that is."

"Why don't you go?" I asked her.

"I'm in New York a lot," she said.

"And your parents let you miss school? I mean, you just take off to New York whenever you want?"

Jeanny looked out toward the aisle, then back at me. "Let's just say my mom is not like most mothers. She checked out a few years ago."

"You mean she left?" I asked.

"Mentally, not physically. And she's always preoccupied with my younger brothers. It's all she can do to get them dressed and fed in the morning, so she hardly has the time to pay attention to what I do." Jeanny laughed, even though what she was saying wasn't funny. "I think as far as she's concerned, I'm fully grown and through with my need for parenting."

Since she didn't mention her father, I didn't want to bring him up. Maybe he had checked out, too. "Well, what do you go to the city for?"

"Auditions," she said. "Protests."

None of the girls I knew in Holedo ever seemed to care about anything outside the bubble of our town. Their goals were the flip side of Leon's. Guys wanted to get drunk, get laid, and get a car the second they got their driver's license. Girls wanted to get a boyfriend, get their makeup on perfectly, and get asked to the prom when the time came. No one ever auditioned or protested except in the movies and the newspaper. "What are you trying to get?" I asked her. "And what are you trying to get rid of?"

"I was trying out for a backup part in a band. And I picketed in a protest for equal pay for women."

I heard my father's voice begin to say something about lesbians, but I squashed him in my mind. "You sing?" I asked, since that interested me more than the protest.

"Yes," she said. "And I yodel, too."

"Yodel?"

"Yeah," she said. "Want to hear?"

I didn't think she'd really let loose right there on the bus, but I nodded anyway. She took a deep breath and a moment later out it came: "Yodeleheeeyodeleheeeeyodeleheeeeyodelheehooooooooo!"

All over the bus people were craning their necks to see where the noise was coming from, and Jeanny kept right on going. "Yodeleyodeleyodeleyodelheehooooooooo!"

"Keep it down, Heidi!" someone shouted.

That stopped her mid-yodel, and we both busted out laughing. "How did you learn to do that?" I asked.

"When you grow up in the mountains making moonshine, you've got nothing better to do."

I didn't exactly believe her but wasn't sure what to say to that. Finally I said, "I thought you grew up in Holedo?"

"I'm kidding," she said and jabbed my side with her elbow. I felt Joshua Fuller's folder pinch my skin, all those stories about my mother that had led me to this bus with my baby sister in my arms. "You're too serious, Mr. Pindle. We've got to loosen you up."

I knew that she was right. But feeling that folder beneath my sweatshirt reminded me of how tangled my life had become. The prospect of loosening up, as she put it, seemed as impossible as bringing my mother back from the dead. "Well, how did you really learn to yodel?" I asked, skipping right over the topic of Dominick Pindle's multitude of personality flaws.

"When I was little, my dad took me to see a show in New York at Radio City. They had all kinds of singers and dancers. It was like a performance pupu platter or something. Anyway, there was this one yodeler and she was far out. She stepped onstage, and as soon as the spotlight hit her, she let it rip. After that I was obsessed with yodeling for a year or so. I basically taught myself."

"So do you yodel at auditions?"

"No way," she said. "I sing regular there. I only yodel for cute guys who I meet on the bus."

At that I felt a lump in my throat. I was the cute guy she met on the bus. For me she yodeled. Made a fool of herself without so much as blushing. Leon would have thought she was a seven-and-a-half. But to me she was better than that. I glanced down at Sophie in my arms, though, and told myself it was no time for me to be picking up girls when I had a baby to take care of. As much as I wanted to tell her that I thought she was beautiful, I didn't say a thing. I let the silence hang between us as a sign that I wasn't taking the bait. All that quiet must have left her feeling stupid, because she smiled at me, beaming those eyes for a moment more, then turned away.

"Don't get nervous," she said. "I have a lot of boys in my life."

"You mean your brothers?" I asked.

"Maybe," she told me.

"And your dad, too?"

"No," she said. "He's gone."

I asked her if her parents had split up and she told me no, that her father had died two years ago. He fell on the train tracks during a snowstorm. Freak accident. "After that is when my mom checked out," she said.

I studied her face to be sure she wasn't messing around again. She must have known what I was thinking, because she said, "No kidding this time."

If I opened my mouth to tell her about my mother, it would have been my first time explaining her death to a stranger. She must have known about it from the paper, but since I didn't quite know how I would fill in the details of what had happened, all I said was "Sorry. That must have really sucked."

"It did suck," she said. "It still does suck. Present tense."

She seemed to be waiting for me to say something more. And I wrestled with a way to get it out, to tell her that I knew how she felt. My mouth actually opened, and I searched for the words. But nothing came, so I pressed my lips together, clenched my teeth with my mother's gum in between.

After that we rode for a while without saying anything. Finally Jeanny let out a big yawn. She pulled off her poncho and draped it over herself like a blanket. "I'm beat. Excuse me while I take a nap."

I wanted her to stay awake so I could enjoy the rest of the ride with her, because after that I had to start thinking about the mess I was in again. But the moment she closed her eyes, I realized I'd be able to watch her, to study her face so I could conjure up the memory of her later on my own. The way my mother must have done that day in New

Mexico, recording the details of a life she couldn't lead. Jeanny shifted her head toward the aisle and tilted her neck against the seat in an effort to get comfortable. When that didn't work, she shifted her head forward, chin to chest.

I knew the way Leon and my father would have handled the situation. They would have put their arm around her and pulled her into them without saying a word. But that seemed wrong for me. "If you want," I said, taking a deep, nervous breath, "you could put your head on my shoulder. I mean, only if you want to."

Jeanny didn't even answer. She kept her eyes closed and leaned her head toward me, resting it there as if she'd been doing it for years. She yawned one more time. And just like that, fell asleep.

For the rest of the ride I took turns watching Sophie and Jeanny. Sophie was nestled up inside her blanket with only her little bug of a face showing. It looked more like the face of an old woman than of someone just born. I noticed, too, that she had a cluster of white bumps around her nose. Under the skin like whiteheads, only she was too young for acne, so who knew what it was? Every once in a while she let a saliva bubble pop from her mouth. A line of drool managed to leak onto my sweatshirt, but I didn't care. Jeanny, meanwhile, kept her lips parted ever so slightly, like she was ready to leap into conversation or start yodeling even in her sleep. She had long lashes. Not clumped together like Vicki Spring's. Hers were soft black brooms that swept the skin beneath her eyes.

With the two of them sleeping near me, I felt the way a man must feel with his wife and child. Not a father like mine. One who cared about the people around him. Loyal to his wife. Loving toward his children. I wondered if that was the type of man Mr. Burdan was. If he had been home every evening of my brother's childhood, waiting to hug and kiss the boy he refused to return to my mother. I wondered, too, if I would ever have a child of my own who I loved that much.

When the bus arrived in Holedo, the baby started fussing and crying the second we pulled into the station. The reality of what I had gotten myself into came back with her every shriek.

I had taken a baby.

I had no place to go.

"I'll carry her off the bus for you and get her settled down if you like," Jeanny said when she stretched and stood. "Just grab my guitar for me."

I handed Sophie over and picked up Jeanny's guitar case. When I looked back to make sure we'd left nothing behind, I caught sight of a few of Jeanny's scattered M&M's in the crack between our two seats. I thought of that freckled girl on the ride home the night my mother died. *I saved their lives,* she had whispered to me. *Take care of them.* This time I left the candy on the seat as I walked off behind Jeanny and the baby.

The sky was the steely blue color of dusk. It wasn't snowing, but random snowflakes lingered in the air, blown from the rooftop of the bus station. One landed on Jeanny's nose, and she blew it away. "I'll trade you one baby for one guitar," she said, smiling.

"Go fish," I told her.

We had a hard time switching Sophie for the guitar, and our hands got tangled for just a moment.

"Got her?"

"Got her."

When I was holding Sophie again and she had her guitar, we stood there not talking. Jeanny kicked at the frozen fossil of a tire track in the snow with her black boot. Across the lot a metallic blue Barracuda like the one Leon always wanted was spinning doughnuts in the unplowed area. The engine revved and revved.

"Well, I guess I'll see you around," I said, even though I probably wouldn't.

"See you," she said, and another snowflake landed on her nose. This time she let it melt before touching her face with her oversize mitten.

I had the urge to lean toward her and press my lips to hers. With Sophie in my arms, though, I didn't think I could manage it. There were questions I wanted to ask Jeanny, but I couldn't marshal the energy in my tongue to get them out. "I'm glad we met," I said.

"Me, too," she told me.

Still we stood there. "Okay," I said. "I really have to get the baby out of the cold."

"Okay," she said. "Bye, Sophie. Bye, Dominick."

With that she turned and clomped off across the parking lot, her guitar case banging against her back. I tried to memorize the details of this moment, this other life I might have led, walking away from me. And then, before I knew it, Jeanny turned the corner and was gone.

To stop the funny feeling in my chest, I rocked Sophie in my arms and stared down at her. "Okay," I said, trying to sound sure of myself. "Let's find us a place to stay."

I made my way to the pay phone and dialed Leon's number. Mrs. Diesel answered, her cigarette-rattled voice blasting into the phone. Cheap Trick played on the stereo in the background. "Is Leon there?" I asked, dropping my voice and mumbling in hopes that she wouldn't recognize me.

"He's out joyriding in his new machine," she told me.

"What new machine?" I said, switching Sophie from one arm to the other and rocking her.

"He got his license last week, and now he's got a car," she explained.

I squinted my eyes at the driver of the Barracuda doing doughnuts across the lot. Leon. Right in front of my face. But where the hell did he get that car?

"Is this Dominick?" Leila asked over a guitar riff.

"It's Ed," I said and hung up the phone. I walked across the lot, cradling the baby in my arms. As Leon twisted the car in circles, I stood by a snowbank and watched him. Snow sprayed and cascaded all around his dream machine. Finally, when he fishtailed to a stop, I called out to him.

"Well, if it isn't Dominick Pindle," he said, getting out of the car. He was wearing a burgundy ski jacket and aviator sunglasses like my father's. All new duds. "You've been in the paper all month. Your dad reported you missing."

"Where'd you get the wheels?" I asked, ignoring his spiel.

He crossed his arms, leaned against the car. Looked at the hood, looked back at me. "Let's just say that Ed and I came up with a money-making scheme."

"Why are you and Ed like bosom buddies all of a sudden?"

He took off his leather driving gloves. I guess he thought he was driving on Hogway's racetrack. "What's the matter? You jealous or something?"

"Hardly," I said. "It's just that he's such a loaf."

"You're entitled to your opinion," Leon said. "So what's with the bambino? Oh, wait. Don't tell me. I knew it. You *did* get Edie pregnant. You know, at first I was jealous. But she was too old for me anyway. You're a father. Congratulations, man. Who knew you'd beat me to the punch?"

I stood there staring at him, trying to figure how I was going to unload all my shit. Sophie started to cry again, and I rocked her until she shushed. I was beginning to realize that she was happiest in motion. The second I stopped moving, she got fussy.

"You and the bambino want a ride?" Leon asked.

"That's a start," I said. "But I need more than just a ride."

"Get in," he said, pulling open the passenger door and holding out his arm chauffeur style. "We'll talk."

I climbed carefully into the car with the baby on my lap. The bucket seats still had that new-car smell. Like a pool liner and new carpeting mixed together. On the dashboard Leon had stuck one of those silhouettes of a big-breasted naked woman that usually showed up on mud flaps of eighteen-wheelers. "Where's the fuzzy dice?" I asked, still rocking Sophie.

"What do you think I am, Pindle? Low class?"

"No comment," I said.

Leon turned on the stereo and pushed in an eight-track. Daltrey was singing, "*Give us room and close the door. Your boy won't be a boy no more.*" He put the car in gear, and we fishtailed out of the unplowed part of the lot.

"Easy," I said. "No car games. We've got a baby in here."

"I hear you, Pops. You're concerned for your kid. I understand."

"She's not my kid," I told him.

"Whose is it then?" he said.

I blinked, sucked in a breath, looked down at Sophie's pink face. Her squeezed-together eyelids. I knew she liked the wheels beneath us, all that motion. "She belongs to Edie. But I'm not the father."

We pulled out onto the main street and drove toward the center of town. Surprisingly, Leon seemed cautious out on the real roads, like the new driver he was. He kept both hands on the wheel. He braked early for lights. He didn't even mouth off or say anything until we got to Hanover Street. "Then who's the father?"

We were passing Maloney's Pub, the Dew Drop Inn. I thought of that night last summer when I cruised this strip with my mother and Marnie before driving over to Edie's house. Hadn't it been my suggestion to go there in the first place? No surprise that I was to blame from the get-go. "She's my father's baby," I said. "Edie doesn't know I have her."

"Whoa. Whoa. Whoa," Leon said. "Did you just say that she doesn't know you have the baby?"

"Correct," I said. "Ten points."

"And I take it, since your father reported you missing, that he doesn't know either."

"Ten more points," I said.

We stopped at a light in the center of town. A truck pulled up next to us, and I glanced over, momentarily panicked that it might be my father. Thankfully, it wasn't. I tried to hold Sophie low on my lap, because I didn't want anybody wondering what two teenage guys were doing joyriding with an infant. Sophie didn't seem to like that, though, because she made one of her unhappy squeaks. After the light turned green, I lifted her up against my chest. I could feel the surge of the engine as we started moving again.

"In other words, you're a kidnapper," Leon said.

"You could put it that way," I told him. "But since the baby is my father's, that makes her my sister. She kind of belongs to me. I have every right to take her after what Edie did to my mother."

At the mention of my mother, Leon was quiet. My mind flashed on the way I had chewed him out at her memorial service. *About that letter. From your friend,* he'd said, and I'd let him have it, told him never to mention Edie again. And here I was unloading all this crap on him. "Remember at my mother's service when you said you wanted to tell me something about Edie? What was it?"

Leon shrugged his shoulders and stepped on the gas. "Who knows? I guess I was going to ask if you wanted that letter from her."

"Burn it," I told him.

We drove through a series of turns, and Leon snapped back into concentration mode. When we were on a straightaway again, he said, "Well, you're just lucky there's not a reward for you. Otherwise I'd be driving to the police station to turn your ass in."

"Thanks," I said. "I knew I could count on you."

Leon reached one arm around to the backseat and produced a copy of the *Holedo Herald.* My picture was on the front page, a yearbook shot from the seventh grade that looked like somebody else now. A little kid with a crooked collar and an awkward smile. Hair parted unevenly with choppy bangs hanging over the forehead. Beneath the photo was that same headline from Truman's disappearance. BOY STILL MISSING. The article gave all the details: "Dominick Pindle, 15, of 88 Dwight Avenue, was reported missing by his father, Roy Pindle, 42, of 88 Dwight Avenue. The report of his disappearance comes just weeks after the death of Theresa Pindle, 38, of 88 Dwight Avenue."

"Do you think people will get the point that we live at 88 Dwight Avenue?" I said to Leon, thinking that the *Holedo Herald* really knew how to knock out some Pulitzer Prize–winning journalism. "I mean, it's a little vague."

"Huh?" he said, not paying any attention to me.

"Never mind," I said, wanting to simply keep driving.

And that's exactly what we did. We drove and drove and drove while

Leon rattled on about his car, which he referred to as a she. She had a dual exhaust system. She had a pistol grip four-speed. She had a four-ten Dana rear end. She could do zero to sixty in 5.8 seconds. The whole time he spoke, I stared out the window at our scenic tour of moonlit Holedo—"the Hole," as Jeanny had called it. I found myself wondering if one of the houses we passed might be hers and how she had gotten home on foot from the bus station. I imagined her inside one of the windows we breezed by, dreaming of her singing career or her next protest. I imagined—hoped was more like it—that she was thinking of me, too.

We passed the Doghouse.

We drove by the new police station.

We drove by the old police station, still closed, awaiting renovations from Vito Maletti.

When Leon finished yammering about his new set of wheels, I let him in on the entire Edie story. My kiss with her. The money. The baby. I gave him a blow-by-blow right up to the moment I called out to him in the parking lot of the bus station.

He didn't say anything at first, because he seemed to be thinking. All that silence and brainpower produced, though, was "Whoa, man. That is a lot of heavy shit. What are you going to do now?"

"I need a place to stay until I figure that out. Any suggestions?"

"I'd let you stay at my place. But my mom would have a shit fit about the bambino. She hates kids. Happiest day of her life was when I turned sixteen."

"That's okay," I said. "It's a little too close to home anyway."

"Ed's grandparents have a cabin in the Poconos."

"Forget it," I said. "I don't want him involved with my life." Marnie was out, too, I realized once I gave it some serious thought. She wouldn't be able to deal with my taking the baby. I had a desperate, sinking feeling in my stomach. When I looked out the window, we were passing the Holedo Motel. The yellow police tape was gone. Still no cars in the lot. A NO VACANCY sign hung out front. The place was empty. I stared at the two sets of cement stairs on each side of the motel, the crooked shutters on the row of windows. When I caught sight of room 5B, my stomach dropped still more. "Why is the motel closed?" I asked.

"After what happened to your mom, Old Man Fowler freaked. That night he got in his car and took off to Florida for the winter. The cops had everything cleaned up, and they took down the yellow tape a few days after you left. I hear the guy might sell the place."

"I can stay there with Sophie," I said, the second the idea occurred to me. It seemed strange and fitting at the same time.

Leon slowed the car down and did a 180. We headed back to the motel, pulled around to the rear of the building so no one would see us from the street. As soon as Leon cut the engine, Sophie began fussing. I rocked her in my arms. "How am I going to get in?"

"Leave that to the pro," Leon said.

He got out of the car and opened his trunk. I watched him carry a crowbar toward the back office window. It occurred to me that the crowbar might have something to do with his and Ed's moneymaking scheme. Breaking and entering. Robbing houses. I had my own life of crime to worry about, though, so I decided to mind my own business. Leon examined the window, and my guess was that he was looking for a place to jimmy the thing open. But then he stepped back and held the crowbar in the air like a baseball bat. A second later he swung and gave the window a whack. Glass came crashing down like Edie's kitchen window had the night I threw that planter at it. Shattering, then silent.

"Open for business!" Leon announced, turning back to me and smiling.

"Jesus Christ, Leon. Couldn't you have jimmied the lock or something?"

"Do I hear a complaint? Because you and the bambino are going to be mighty cold on the street tonight."

"I just meant— Forget it. No complaints here."

"Good," Leon said. "I like a satisfied customer." He took a blanket out of his trunk and threw it over the broken glass on the window ledge, then climbed inside. A moment later he came around and opened the back door. "Welcome to the Holedo Motel," he said.

I stepped through the doorway carrying Sophie and thought of my mother checking in to this place. The newspaper article that ran after she died had quoted Fowler, who was working the desk: "A woman came in and said she needed a room. I didn't notice anything unusual about her at the time."

Nothing unusual except that she was about to die.

The office was cold and dark. The walls were covered with pictures of race cars as well as paintings of goldfish that looked like they'd been done with a paint-by-numbers kit. On the desk there was a meatball grinder, three stale brown lumps covered with dried red sauce, a single bite taken out of one end. I guessed Leon hadn't been exaggerating when he said Fowler freaked out and left in a rush the night my mother died. I imagined him standing up from his meal, shaken and changed by what had happened here, and walking outside to his car. Driving south without so much as packing a suitcase. Leon flicked on a lamp and surveyed the office. Keys to each room hung on a rack by the desk, marked in descending order: 10A, 10B, 9A, 9B, 8A, 8B, and so on. "Would you and your sister like a suite with an ocean view, sir?" Leon said. "Or an economy room overlooking the septic tank?"

"I want to stay in Five-B," I told him. "My mother's room."

Leon stopped for a moment, then scanned the row of hooks, grabbed the one I was asking for. "Are you sure?"

I knew it was a strange request. But I had come this far, and I wanted somehow to be close to my mother. The only way I knew how was to stay in the room where she had breathed her last breath. Maybe part of her—a spirit, a ghost—was still up there, waiting for me to return with the baby. Maybe she'd been leading me here all along. "I'm sure," I told Leon.

"Okay," he said and looked down at a sort of switchboard near the desk that reminded me of one an old-fashioned operator might use. Plugging pegs into holes, connecting people all over the world. Leon fiddled with the wires, then flicked a switch at the top of the board. "I believe your phone works now, sir. But there will be a five-dollar surcharge for every minute."

"Thanks," I said, trying to smile. We unlocked the front door of the office and peeked outside to be sure no cars were driving past. When there was a break in the traffic, we made our way up the stairs to 5B. The second Leon opened the door, it all came back to me. Marnie moaning and making that indecipherable sound, the police clustered around the stairwell, the way I made a break for the door and shoved myself inside, only to find my mother lying there. That night I had expected it to be Edie inside the room. And I wondered if there had been one brief second of relief that it wasn't her on the floor, before I realized it was my mother.

The thought made me dizzy.

I sat with Sophie on the bed and looked around. A gold bedspread. Beige lamps on the two wooden nightstands, each with a tattered white shade. The curtains by the window were beige, too, and Leon pulled them shut, draped two blankets over the rod so no one would see the light on up here. A picture of a red stock car at Hogway's was screwed into the wood-paneled wall. The number "5" painted yellow on the driver's-side door.

A pretty typical motel room.

No one would ever have guessed what had happened on the floor beside the bed. The blood had all been cleaned up. The stained rug taken away, a flat beige rug put down in its place. I didn't know why, but I found myself imagining a second accident that would replace that stain with more blood. I could almost see it there. Round, red, and horrifying. Even more permanent than the last. The image sent a shiver loose inside me.

I actually shook.

"You okay?" Leon asked.

"Yeah. It's freezing in here. That's all."

"Got that right," he said and found the register by the back window, cranked the dial so that the heat started to sputter through the vent.

"I met a girl on the bus today," I told him, shutting out the image of another bloodstain. Jeanny was the one part of the story I had left out when I filled him in on my life during our cruise around town.

"Who is she?" he asked.

"Her name is Jeanny. I had this feeling about her. Like I knew her already. Or not that exactly, but just that I liked her more than most girls from around here."

"Big tits?" he said.

"Shut up," I told him, not wanting to rate Jeanny on his stupid scale. "Why do you and—" I stopped myself from saying "my father," from saying every other guy out there who had always made me think that being a man meant sizing up a woman like she was a car. I was sick of it. And that wasn't the type of man I wanted to be anymore. "Why do you always have to act like that?"

"I'm a red-blooded American male, that's why."

"So am I. But I don't want to talk that way about this girl."

"Sounds like love," Leon said. "Did you get her number?"

I thought of her walking away, my tongue heavy with words I couldn't muster. "No. But that's okay. I don't need to get her caught up in my bullshit."

Leon was surveying the room, pushing open the bathroom door, flicking on the light. I could see the pink tiles from where I sat on the bed. He closed the door partway, and I could hear the splashing in the toilet as he took a piss. "You know," Leon called out, "if this Edie chick is keeping company with dealers from New York, you could be in a lot of danger."

I didn't say anything to that. The last thing I needed was another worry. But Leon kept going. "I mean, they could come after you," he said over what had to be the longest piss I'd ever had the honor of listening to. "They could find you here and kill you. Slit your throat or something."

"All right already!" I called to him. "I get the point."

"I'm just trying to warn you," he said, finishing up in there.

I pulled Joshua's folder out from under my sweatshirt and set it on the nightstand to read once Leon split. Then I looked at Sophie's bottle, which was just about empty. I pulled that Enfamil container out of the bag and read the label. It was formula. Almost empty, too.

"Listen," I said, raising my voice again so Leon could hear me. "I

need another favor. Can you go out and get some baby formula and diapers? Plus some food for me." I still wasn't hungry but knew I would be
sooner or later. There was a half-size refrigerator in the corner of the room,
and I could put things on the window ledge to keep them cool as well.

Leon flushed and stepped out of the bathroom, still zipping himself.
"What kind of formula?"

I held up the container for him to see. "Get some of this stuff.
Enfamil. Just look in the aisle with the baby supplies, I guess."

"I'll hit the store and be right back," Leon said, looking happy that
he had an excuse to leave.

I tried to put Sophie down on the mattress, but she didn't like the
idea, so I picked her up again. "Let me give you some money."

"Forget it," Leon told me. "It's on me."

"Thanks," I said, thinking I might as well take him up on his new-
found generosity while it lasted. "But go to the grocery store over in
Buford. I don't want anyone around here to see you buying baby supplies. They might get suspicious."

"Yes, sir," he said, spinning his keys around his middle finger.

After Leon walked out the door, I turned the lock and slid the chain
link in place. I pushed aside the curtain and blankets just enough to
watch from the window as his car zipped out of the parking lot and onto
the street. When he was gone, I went to the heat register, because the
room still felt cold. Leon had set the thing on medium; I turned it up to
high. Then I unplugged one of the lamps. With my free hand I picked it
up off the nightstand and carried it to the corner of the room away from
the front window. I plugged it in there and tilted the shade so the light
was dim. Even though Leon had hung those blankets over the window, I
didn't want to take any chances that someone would spot the light from
outside.

"Okay, little alien," I said to Sophie. "Let's get you settled in."

I rearranged the four thin pillows on the bed in an attempt to make a
border so she wouldn't roll off when I placed her there. But was she too
young to roll over? And did babies sleep on their stomachs or backs?
There were so many things about this kid-care business that I didn't

know. And she was just so small. So breakable. Jeanny's positive prognosis was already receding in my mind, and I felt afraid that if I even put Sophie down the wrong way, I might hurt her.

Just be careful, I kept saying to myself.

None of my efforts at making a bed for Sophie seemed to matter anyway, because the second I put her down, she started to whine. I had to keep rocking her in my arms, which was starting to feel like exercise. Unfortunately, I had to take a piss, too. But I figured I'd hold it until Leon got back, because I wasn't sure how I'd manage that one. With Sophie gaining weight in my arms by the second, I made my way around the room, peeking out the window, looking in the bathroom and the closet. In one of the dresser drawers was a phone book and a black Bible like my uncle's. I flipped the Bible open to a passage:

As the soldiers were about to take Paul into the barracks, he asked the commander, "May I say something to you?"

"Do you speak Greek?" he replied.

"Aren't you the Egyptian who started a revolt and led four thousand terrorists out into the desert some time ago?"

Paul answered, "I am a Jew, from Tarsus in Cilicia, a citizen of no ordinary city. Please let me speak to the people."

I didn't know how that PBS priest and the rest of the holy-rollers found all their opinions about the world in the Bible, because every time I cracked open the good book, I came upon some yawn of a passage like the one I just read. It seemed more like a history book than a set of rules. I tossed the thing back into the drawer, sat on the edge of the bed, and picked up the phone. The long, steady hum of the dial tone made me think of my mother's last call to Marnie. I imagined her frightened and alone in this room. I imagined her moments before, unlocking the door, nervously collecting the towels from the bathroom and laying them around her. Roget carrying the equipment his doctor friend had given him.

A long, sleek piece of metal he would use to make her bleed.

It killed me that he had gotten away with leaving her here, and I wished more than anything I could do something to nail him for my mother's sake. Someday, I promised myself.

I put down the phone and tried to think of something else. Anything else. When I closed my eyes, I pictured Jeanny. That snowflake landing on her nose, that guitar case clunking against her back as she walked away from me. I opened the drawer and pulled out the phone book. Thought of Leon asking me if I'd gotten Jeanny's number. I flipped to the G page. Only one Garvey listed in Holedo. On Little Street, which was just that, a little street, a few blocks from the bus station behind Peaceful Pizza. One of those downtown houses smooshed together like crowded teeth on a narrow street that no one ever drove down. My father used to call it Hippie Street, though I'd never seen any hippies the times I'd been there, so I didn't know why.

Sophie started to cry for no reason at all, and I picked up the phone again. Dialed the Garveys' number. This time I wasn't following any signs or voices. I was calling Jeanny because I wanted to. And despite Sophie's crying as I cradled her close to me in one arm, and despite the uneasiness I felt about my surroundings, there was a sliver of me that felt like any other guy my age dialing up the number of a girl he liked.

"Hello," her mother's sleepy voice answered. I could hear a television in the background. Kids playing.

Hang up, I thought.

Don't hang up.

"Is Jeanny there?" I said before I could back out. Sophie's crying was getting louder, and I was beginning to wonder about her timing.

The phone clicked, and someone answered on another extension. I heard, "Hello."

Jeanny.

"Hi, it's Dominick. I—"

"Hold on," she said to me. Then to her mother, "I got it." After the other extension clicked off, Jeanny said, "How the hell are you? It's been ages."

Sophie was out-and-out screaming again. My head pounded. This baby stuff was harder than I ever would have imagined. I told Jeanny to hold on, then I rocked Sophie, tried without much success to shush her one more time. "I've been better," I said when I came back to the phone.

"Baby trouble?"

"Well, yes." Tell her why you called, I thought. Here goes. "I was wondering if maybe—" I paused. What was it I was wondering exactly? I saw Jeanny as a narrow opportunity, a road as little as her Little Street that I could pass by and keep going. But I imagined myself stepping on the brake, signaling, turning the wheel, shining my lights on her house even though I knew it was selfish of me to be there. "I was wondering if you'd like to go on a date?" I blurted. That wasn't exactly what I imagined myself asking her, but it was close. And at least the words were out of my mouth.

"I'd like that a lot," Jeanny said. "When do you want to get together? I have a very busy social calendar."

"How about—" I knew I should back away, pull out of her driveway and down her Little Street. But I couldn't stop myself. I wanted her with me. My voice was a horn calling her closer. "How about now?"

The line was silent, and I waited for Jeanny to turn me down. *I just got back from New York. I have to practice my singing. I've got a protest to plan.* Instead she said, "Now? I happen to have an opening on my calendar, so now sounds good to me. Where do you want to meet?"

I lowered my voice and said, "Promise not tell a single soul where you're going?"

Jeanny paused. "I promise."

I gripped the hard black handle of the phone, the same phone my mother had used to call Marnie for help. "I'm staying at the Holedo Motel," I whispered. "How quickly can you come?"

Eight

Jeanny and I made a plan. She would take a taxi from the bus station, get dropped off at Cumby's, and walk to the motel so no one would suspect where she was going. Twenty minutes and she'd be here. Thirty, tops. After we hung up, I worked at calming Sophie. She didn't want her bottle, so I pulled a pacifier from the bag. She didn't want that either. I walked her around the room. From the front window with the blankets draped over it to the back window where I'd hung two towels over the curtains to block the light. From the closet to the tiny bathroom. But that didn't make her happy. All she wanted to do was cry. Since I didn't know how else to help her, I took out one of those children's books I'd bought at the bus station and read it out loud as she shrieked and I moved her in my arms.

"'Hansel and Gretel walked deep into the forest...'" I read, remembering those nights I had flipped through those storybooks in

Edie's bed, marveling over the happy endings. Even though Sophie couldn't understand the words, something about the sound of my tired voice finally quieted her down. When I reached the end of the story, I turned back to the beginning and started again. On the second go-through, when Gretel suggests they toss bread crumbs behind them so they can find their way home, I decided to switch to the articles about my mother. I read each and every one of them aloud as I lulled Sophie to sleep. I read that Peter had taken a job on a lobster boat and slipped from the deck and drowned. I read that the Burdan family had paid my mother's doctor—a Dr. Horvath—twenty thousand dollars to get them a baby. I read that my mother had broken down in court when the judge announced the verdict. She had to be carried out of the room. Finally I stopped reading and lost myself in the pictures. None of my brother except a distant shot of him bundled in a blanket as Mrs. Burdan carried him down the steps of a fancy New York building. I stared at that image awhile, my mind oddly blank, then dug out the photo of my mother being interviewed in front of a courthouse. She looked hopelessly tired, anxious, and angry all at once. If I were a stranger opening the paper and seeing that photo, I might think she was a woman capable of snapping and going at you with her teeth, her bare hands, her words. But I knew that alarmed, lost expression on her face all too well, and it made me tear up even as I tried to bury my feelings.

Dominick, I'm just so tired, she had told me before I went into the bath that last night in our apartment. *Things have got to get easier for me.*

And then she died.

Jeanny will be here any minute, I reminded myself before I completely lost footing on my huge mountain of emotions and went tumbling to the bottom. I had to stay strong. Stay on top of all that was happening. I tucked the news clippings into the drawer of the nightstand and gently put Sophie on the bed so I could run into the bathroom and take a piss. The second I let go of her, she popped open her eyes and looked at me. "Just give me one second, little girl," I said, pleading with her not to cry. If she started up again, I felt like I'd begin wailing, too.

For once she didn't, and I went into the bathroom, where the pink rectangular tiles and lime-green sink gave the room a false cheer, like Marnie wearing her too-bright colors in the middle of winter. The floor smelled of Ajax over mildew. Sterile and public. The shower curtain was covered with schools of goldfish, and I was beginning to realize that Fowler must've had a thing for them. Above the toilet a painting of a log cabin in the woods was screwed to the wall. Smoky blue mountains in the background, a bed of rooster-red leaves up front. I found myself staring at the scene as I took a leak, wondering if I should talk to Leon about Ed's grandparents' cabin after all. Get Sophie out of here and find someplace like that to hide out.

After I finished, I turned on the water and stood in front of the mirror, wondering if my mother had washed her hands in this sink when she arrived at the motel.

That's when my breath stopped.

There, on the other side of the mirror, I imagined—or not so much as imagined but envisioned, saw—my mother staring back at me. She looked as if she had been dragged along the damp floor of the forest in that painting. Twigs and dead leaves in her snarled hair. Her skin gone gray, scraped, and bloody. Her breasts bruised blue and running with milk down her deflated stomach. Her eyes hollow and full of sadness. I wanted to look away from her but felt as suspended as one of those red cardinal's hats above the altar in St. Patrick's Cathedral, a balloon tied tight to a child's wrist so it couldn't escape. My mother's chapped lips began to whisper something I couldn't make sense out of.

Baby.

Maybe.

Manger.

Too.

Baby.

Maybe.

Manger.

Too.

"What?" I said out loud.

And that's when there was a knock at the door. I heard Jeanny's voice say "Dominick?" and my mother disappeared.

It was my face in the mirror. My hair grown past my ears and wispy in front of my forehead. My eyes wide and frightened by what I'd just seen, or thought I'd seen. I turned off the water, and the thought hit me hard that something in my mind was slipping. Perhaps all that had happened had broken my brain somehow, left me with haunted visions in the bathroom mirror and images of blood on the floor beside the bed. Or maybe what I had seen was another message, a sign from my mother that I should be following, if only I had understood.

Jeanny knocked again. "Dominick?"

I wiped my hands on a scratchy white washcloth and made my way to the door. When I opened up, Jeanny was standing there with her guitar case and a pizza. "If I'm not home by midnight, I'll turn into a pumpkin," she said.

"Midnight," I repeated, not really listening because I was still seeing that image in the mirror, hearing that strange message echoing in my mind.

Baby.

Maybe.

Manger.

Too.

What good was a sign if you didn't know what it meant?

"Are you okay?" Jeanny said. "You look horrible."

"Yeah," I told her, rubbing my eyes and trying to anchor myself in the conversation. "I'm just hungry. That's all. The pizza smells good. Come inside."

She stepped into the room and set the pizza box on the dresser, took off her coat and that poncho. Beneath all her layers she was wearing dark corduroys that flared at the legs, a crimson sweater with three snowflakes across her chest, a flurry of white dots on her flat stomach. Even though her breasts were small, I could tell by the way they filled her sweater—

loose and low—that she wasn't wearing a bra. My mouth went dry when I glanced down at them. The word "liberated" swam to the surface of my mind, and I pictured Jeanny burning a lacy white something on a fire, holding it out on a stick like you would a marshmallow. I knew what my father would say about bra-burners, but I didn't let myself think about it.

"I have to admit," Jeanny said, looking around the room, "I've never had a date quite like this one."

Distracted by her breasts and that image of my mother, I said, "I have."

Jeanny looked at me a little funny, and I realized my mistake.

"I mean, I haven't. Either." I shook my head and gave myself a mental kick. It had been so easy to talk with her on the bus, but now I felt tongue-tied, which left me thinking that this get-together had been a bad idea. Maybe we had clicked on the bus, but I should have left it at that. Having Jeanny in the motel room filled me with nervousness. She kept glancing around in a way that left me unsettled. It occurred to me once more that she must have known about what had happened to my mother in this room. But if that was true, would she have come?

"So how is our little angel?" Jeanny asked, looking down at the baby.

"I think she's happy to see you," I said, trying to smooth things out again, get rid of all that tension. "Almost as happy as me."

Jeanny was about to say something, but Sophie interrupted. She must have been bored on the bed alone, because she started making a commotion. Jeanny wasted no time scooping her up in her arms. "It's okay, little pea," she said. "You're having a bad day. I know."

I carried the pizza over to the bed where she had plopped down with the baby in her arms. As she coddled Sophie, I tried to think of something to talk about. But my brain felt muddled. I couldn't come up with a single thing to say. The room grew unnaturally quiet, and my mind drifted back to my mother in the mirror. I pushed the image away again and remembered Jeanny resting her head on my shoulder that afternoon. I found myself wishing we could just curl up together and go to sleep. But that wasn't exactly an option. I glanced down at a fat-faced cartoon chef who kissed the tips of his fingers on the lid of the pizza box. Over his puffy white hat were the words "You've tried the rest. Now try the best." How original, I thought and flipped the top open. The pizza: half plain, half covered with thick slices of pepperoni, lumpy sausages and meatballs, fatty bacon. I looked at Jeanny, wondering about her vegetarian diet and all the farm animals we were about to devour.

"That side's for you," she said, smirking. "Carnivore."

"I said I eat meat. I didn't say I was a caveman."

Jeanny laughed, and I felt like maybe things were beginning to ease up again. "Okay. I guess I got a little carried away. But I was thinking that I'd have one or two of those slices myself. I just don't think I can do the vegetarian thing anymore."

"Really?" I said.

"Really."

"Welcome back to the barbaric world of meat eaters," I told her, and that's when I did something to get rid of any stiffness once and for all. I leaned forward and kissed her. It was a short, simple kiss.

One. Two. Three.

Her lips were tender and the slightest bit moist. In my head I heard Edie's voice saying, *Let me give you a real kiss. It will be my thank-you present to you.*

Thank you for helping me rob your mother.

Thank you for letting me ruin your life.

I gave Jeanny one more softer, longer kiss and remembered the way Edie had pressed her mouth hard to mine. The way my fingers had brushed against her belly, feeling her baby—Sophie—inside her. It all seemed so strange and off-color; thinking back, I wondered how I hadn't known Edie was up to no good the entire time.

When our lips parted, I said, "Let me get something to wash down the feast." Instantly I realized that getting water for us entailed going into the bathroom and standing in front of that mirror. Since I had already opened my mouth, I forced my legs to move. I went into the bathroom and pulled the sanitary paper off the two glasses on the small sink.

Instead of filling them up right away, I stared at the picture of that cabin, putting off the moment of facing the mirror. Whoever had painted the thing played with the soft color that came from the cabin windows. Instead of yellow like you might expect, the light from inside cast a purple glow. It seemed warm in there. Safe. I pictured the dark windows of this room from outside, all covered up so they didn't cast any light at all.

"Hurry up," Jeanny called. "The pizza's going from cold to colder fast."

I cranked on the water and slowly turned my eyes up toward the mirror. Once again my breath stopped. I felt my heart thud. She was there, my mother, looking back at me again from the other side. This time her neck seemed loose, wobbly, like Sophie's. Her hair hung down in front of her face as brittle as dried seaweed. And her message had changed. Or maybe I had misunderstood earlier. She whispered,

Baby.

Maybe.

Stranger.

Too.

Baby.

Maybe.

Stranger.

Too.

"What are you saying?" I asked.

"I said the pizza is getting cold," Jeanny called to me.

And with that the image of my mother vanished once again.

It was me in the mirror. The water poured over the edge of the second glass, and I turned off the faucet.

Get a grip, I said to myself. Get a fucking grip.

Jeanny was with me, and I didn't want to scare her away.

"Did you drown in the toilet?" she called.

I took a breath and dipped the tips of my fingers in one of the water glasses and splashed my face. Baptism.

"Two glasses of our best champagne," I said, carrying the water back to the bed and trying to shake the image of my mother's mouth whispering that strange message. The horror of her harmed and helpless body.

"Why, thank you, sir," Jeanny said, taking a glass with her free hand and setting it on the nightstand. Sophie was fast asleep in the crook of her arm.

What little appetite I had finally worked up had been stolen by that vision in the mirror, but I forced myself to eat anyway. I picked off the bacon because it was overkill even for me, pushed my mother's gum behind one of my back teeth, and ate.

"You're done already?" Jeanny said when I called it quits halfway through my second piece.

"I feel bad for the farm animals," I said, kidding her.

Jeanny finished eating, too—one plain slice, one meat—and looked down at Sophie. "Hello, little cutie," she whispered in a baby voice.

"When can she start eating real food?" I asked, still trying to forget my mother in the mirror, to land myself in the reality of this room with Jeanny and Sophie.

"Don't hold your breath," she said. "It'll be a while."

I touched Sophie's shrunken hand, which she kept permanently closed in a loose fist. I wished she could say something, wished she could tell me what she thought about our adventure. If she liked being with her big brother and his new friend . . . girlfriend. "How long till she can talk?" I asked.

"She'll have 'mama' and 'dada' nailed down by the time she's one," Jeanny said. "But it'll be a bit before she's discussing politics."

"Is she going to do anything in the near future?"

"Probably dirty her diaper. Other than that, she'll cry a lot."

"You mean all she does is shit and cry?"

"And sleep. She's still an infant. It's in the job description."

Jeanny gave Sophie a peck on the forehead, then told me that I'd miss this stage once the baby started walking and talking. She said that her brothers were sweet when they were infants. She could always tell what they wanted when they cried. Bottle. Diaper. Crib. That was about the extent of their needs.

I thought of my mother—not the woman in the mirror but the young woman who had given birth to Truman after her first husband had died. She must have felt so hopeless and dazed to agree to hand over her baby like that. I thought of how blinded by happiness she must have been that day on the plane. Happy but scared, like I was now.

"Can I tell you something?" Jeanny said.

I nodded yes, lost in thought about my mother and brother. I still wanted to find Truman—Rand—just for her. Even though he was older now, I pictured him again as one of those flawless rich kids streaming out of that school on the Upper East Side. I wanted him to know how much our mother regretted what she had done, whether he wanted to hear it or not. How much she thought of him, right up until her death.

"I know about your mom," Jeanny said.

Her words were a pitcher of cold water poured over my head, snapping me to attention. She knew. Just as I suspected. I wanted to say so many things, explain why I was here, but the only thing I could manage was "How?"

"The paper."

"Oh," I said, feeling awkward once again. For the first time I noticed a thin slit of a scar beneath Jeanny's chin. It made me see her as a pig-tailed little girl falling off a bike, jumping too high from a swing and crashing to the ground. Bleeding and crying. "And you still came? I mean, it didn't freak you out?"

Jeanny put her hand on her chin, covering that scar, that image of her as a girl. She told me that after her father died, her mother used to load her and her brothers in the car and drive to the train tracks. "We'd sit there for hours. Crying or staring or thinking. I don't know. It was a way to be near him. I guessed that maybe it's the same for you."

The way she said it made it all sound so normal, uncomplicated.

"Does it feel weird for you to be here?" she asked.

I glanced around the room at the matching nightstands on each side of the bed, the long dresser along the far wall. All of it made from pressed board. Wood that was real but not real at the same time. "Mostly it seems like any other motel room. But I know what happened here." I kept quiet about my mother in the mirror, because I knew she would think I was crazy.

Then Jeanny asked, "Is Sophie really your sister?"

Another pitcher of water. More startling and cold this time.

I didn't say anything for a moment. I wanted to fess up to her about the whole story but was afraid of what she might say. In the silence I wondered if it would simply be better to tell her yes and leave it at that.

"It's just that they didn't mention her in any of the articles," Jeanny said. "It seems like they would have. And the way you acted on the bus, it was like you'd never seen the baby before. Plus the way your mom died . . ." She paused, must have gauged by the look on my face that this line of questioning was making me uncomfortable.

I took a drink and wiped my mouth with my sleeve. If she was going to be here, she had a right to know the truth. I was about to explain everything when there was a knock at the door. The sound made Jeanny jump; the jump made Sophie cry.

"Milkman," Leon said from outside.

"It's okay," I told Jeanny. "I'm expecting a delivery."

When I opened the door, Leon was standing there with a lifetime supply of Pampers in his arms. Behind him, Special Ed was carrying four bags of groceries.

"What's he doing here?" I said to Leon. "I told you not to let anyone know about this."

Leon ignored me. He and Ed made their way through the door and set down the boxes and bags. "Leon Diesel," he said, sticking his hand out to Jeanny. "I bet you're the girl from the bus. Dominick told me all about you."

I cringed. Jeanny shook his hand and said hello, but I got the feeling she was leery of them both. I probably should have warned her that Leon was going to come by. One of the many warnings on my list. "Nice to meet you," she said halfheartedly.

"I could ask you the same question about her," Leon said to me when he let go of her hand.

"But it's my room. I decide who comes and goes."

"Relax," Leon said. "Don't blow a gasket. I saw Ed hoofing it down the road, so I picked him up. He's just helping with the supplies. We bought out the baby aisle for you."

"As if that's not suspicious, too. You and Ed buying enough diapers to supply the Griffith Hospital nursery for the next decade."

"You know, Pindle, you're not sounding very grateful."

I didn't say a word to that, because there was no use arguing. Just reached into my pocket and pulled out some money to give him.

"I told you, it's on the house," Leon said, holding up his hands.

"Just take it."

"It's a gift. Keep the cash and buy yourself a few joints so you can relax."

I stuck the money in my pocket and walked to the window, peered out from behind the curtain and blankets to make sure he had parked around back. The front lot was empty, so at least he done something right.

"Would you guys like a slice of pizza?" Jeanny asked.

"No thanks," Leon said. "We've got errands to run."

"I'll take one for the road," Ed said, reaching into the box and grabbing a slice. He picked around for the loose bacon I had pulled off and shoved that in his fat face, too.

"What's rule number one in my new car?" Leon asked him.

Ed took a bite of the pizza and thought about the question. "No eating?" he said, mouth full.

"Wrong. Rule number one is no farting. Rule number *two* is no eating."

I glanced at Jeanny, who seemed to be ignoring their circus act. Busy opening a box of Pampers. Diaper duty. If Leon's and Ed's idiot zoo personalities didn't send her running, nothing would.

"I'll suck it down before we're even outside," Ed said. True to his word, the thing was gone in four bites.

"I'll swing by tomorrow to see if you need anything," Leon said.

I squinted my eyes and glared at him, which was my way of saying, *Not with Ed, you won't.*

"Don't worry," he said, getting my drift. "I'll come alone." He waved to Jeanny and told her he'd catch her later. And with that they were out the door.

"Is that guy a dealer?" Jeanny asked the moment the door closed.

"Car dealer?" I said, watching them from the window and playing dumb, though I wasn't quite sure why.

"Drugs," she said.

Sophie started to cry again, and I glanced at Jeanny. She had laid the baby down on the bed and was unsnapping her yellow outfit at the legs, getting ready to change her. "I know, little darling," she cooed to Sophie. "The world isn't fair. This will all be over in a minute, and you can go back to sleep."

I turned to the window again and watched Leon's car drive around front. "What makes you say he's a drug dealer?" I asked, figuring she was probably right.

"The car. The clothes. The groceries on the house. It doesn't take a detective to spot the clues."

As Jeanny spoke, I kept watching Leon's 'Cuda. Instead of pulling onto the street, he stopped out front and flicked on the inside light. I saw him reach over to the glove compartment and hand something to his new sidekick. Ed took whatever it was and got out of the car, walked back up the stairs toward our room.

"It's okay. It's okay," Jeanny was saying to Sophie, who was giving one of her big bad cries. "We're almost done."

I decided she had to be right. Leon was dealing drugs. I guess it wasn't so surprising. Still, it seemed funny to me, because I remembered how nervous he'd been the first time he scored a dime bag of pot. Now he was a dealer. Knowing him, he was sending Ed back upstairs with a joint.

I opened the door before he could knock.

"One more thing," Ed said, taking the package out of his coat and shoving it into my hand. Not drugs at all. But a slim, silver pistol wrapped in a McDonald's napkin. A box of bullets, too, tucked beneath the Golden Arches. In my head I heard Leon say,

They could come after you.

They could find you here and kill you.

Slit your throat or something.

"Protection," Ed told me. "Leon said you should have it just in case."

I had held a gun only once before. And the weight of it in my hand brought back the memory of when my father had come home with a Smith & Wesson he'd won in a card game. I was only nine or ten at the time, but he took me to the junkyard so I could fire it. Just like then, I felt nervous holding the thing. I worried that the piece of metal was something uncontrollable and wild that might fire unexpectedly at any moment. Or that perhaps *I* was something uncontrollable and wild and would have the impulse to pull the trigger at any moment. *Just hold her steady and aim*, my father kept saying that day. I did as he said, but all my targets—a beat-up dresser with missing drawers, a bent bed frame, a clump of dirt with an unidentifiable silver glint—went unscathed. I missed every time. *Because you're afraid of it*, my father had said. *It's okay. You'll learn.* Only he didn't take the gun out much after that, because my mom hated having it around. And I never learned.

"What is Leon doing with this?" I asked Ed.

"Confiscated it from his mother's new boyfriend. We've been shooting it down at the quarry. Oh, and he asked me to leave you one more bit of protection." Ed reached into his pocket and pulled out another package, put it in my free hand. Trojans. Ribbed. Lubricated. "Leon wanted me to tell you that we've got enough children in the family."

Behind me, Jeanny was busy with Sophie. I shoved the box into the pocket of my sweatshirt and prayed she hadn't seen it. The gun I held in my stiff hand along with the bullets. "Tell Leon that I appreciate his concern," I said and practically slammed the door in Ed's grinning face.

"Catch you later," Ed said from outside before clomping down the stairs.

"I hate guns," Jeanny said when I turned around. "I just want you to know that. I hate them."

"Me, too," I told her, wondering if she'd seen the condoms, since she didn't mention them. "Don't worry. I'm getting rid of it."

I looked around the room, holding the dead weight of it and feeling my body tense. I wanted to flush it down the toilet like a deceased pet fish. Toss it out the window. But what if it went off? I walked to the closet, where I planned to stick the pistol on the top shelf until tomorrow, when I would hand it back to Leon or get rid of it for good. That's when I noticed a door at the back of the closet. I turned the knob and gave it a push. It opened, and I stepped through the closet into another closet, pushed open that door and stepped into the dark of the neighboring motel room. Even in the dim light that came through the closets with me, I could see that the place looked almost identical to 5B, except that the cabin picture was above the bed in here and the paint job and rug weren't as new.

"Dominick?" Jeanny called, sounding farther away than she really was.

"There's a door," I shouted. "It opens to the next room. I'm in here."

I walked to the back window and looked outside. Directly below me, in the rear parking lot, was a Dumpster. From where I stood I could have pretty easily opened the window and dropped the pistol and bullets down inside of it. And that would be that. But as uncomfortable as I felt holding the gun, something told me I should keep it after all. Not a voice or a sign from my mother. Just my own instinct. After all, who knew what could happen or when I might need it? Just in case, as Leon had said.

I walked to the dresser and pulled open the top drawer. Inside was another phone book and a Bible, too. I opened the Bible to a random page and stuck the pistol and bullets inside.

"Just in case," I said out loud.

The Bible didn't close all the way, but I shoved it in the drawer, then walked back through the closets to my room, closing the doors behind me.

"Did you get rid of it?" Jeanny asked. She had finished changing Sophie and was holding her again.

"It's all gone," I told her because I didn't want her to worry. "I opened the window in the next room and dropped it in the Dumpster."

"Good riddance," she said.

I glanced at my watch. Ten-thirty already. I thought of Jeanny's words when I answered the door: *If I'm not home by midnight, I'll turn into a pumpkin.* The thought of her leaving made me feel lonely. I hated the idea of sleeping here tonight with just me and Sophie, that haunted vision of my mother calling to me.

When Jeanny turned to open her guitar case, I shoved the condoms under the bed. It wasn't that some part of me didn't dream of making it with her, because I did feel that way. I mean, she seemed prettier to me by the second. And those small, loose breasts of hers kept catching my eyes. Just being with her made me forget—if only a little—what had become of my life. But it seemed weird to think about sex in the room where my mother had died. And if I was going to be with Jeanny, I wanted it to be perfect. Not like that night with Edie when I had let go in my pants, felt my stomach twist and turn. Besides—not that it made a difference to guys like Leon and my father—but we had only really met that afternoon. As liberated as she was, I doubted Jeanny wanted to go all the way, or even part of the way, with me already.

"Do you take that thing with you everywhere you go?" I asked when Jeanny lifted her guitar out of the case. Beneath the strings the belly of the instrument was a gaping dark hole that opened in my direction. *Ooooooo,* I imagined it endlessly mewling. *Oooooooooooo.*

"As a matter of fact I do," she said. "It's like my best friend."

I asked her if she was going to play for me, and she said she already performed once for me on the bus that day. "Check with me another time. But I thought I could put a pillow in here and use my case as a little crib for Sophie. We'll keep it by the heater so she stays warm."

This is what I thought: If Sophie falls asleep, Jeanny might leave her guitar case behind and come back for it tomorrow. Or maybe she would just have to stay.

"You're the expert. Whatever you think is best." I waited for her to pick up the line of questioning she had begun before Leon and Ed arrived, but she kept quiet about it. We made the miniature crib for Sophie with towels from the room next door for blankets, then put her down to sleep. When Sophie stopped fussing, Jeanny went into the bathroom. I thought of her looking into that mirror and wondered how she would react if she saw what I had seen in there, heard that strange message.

A moment later she emerged holding her hair behind her head in a way that made me want to kiss her again, to touch her skin. She sat next to me on the bed, both our heads propped on pillows against the headboard. I stared at the whiteness of the ceiling and counted the smudges up there in an effort to keep my mind calm.

"So are you ready to tell me about Sophie?" Jeanny asked finally.

Ready as I'd ever be. I took a breath and began at the beginning. "Last summer my mother and I were out looking for my father. When we couldn't find him in any of the usual bars where he drinks on Hanover Street, I convinced my mother to drive to his girlfriend's house on Barn Hill . . ."

Jeanny listened quietly as I spoke. Unlike Leon, she stopped me from time to time to ask questions. "Did you have any clue that your mother was pregnant? . . . Did Edie ever mention moving to New York? . . . Do you think your father really hit her?"

No.

No.

I don't know.

I answered each question as best I could. And when I was done with the story, I found myself crying. Cursing Roget, who was out there walking around without any blame for leaving my mother to die. I wanted to get him, I told Jeanny, but I didn't know how. And the harder I tried to bury my feelings, the way I promised myself, the more it all came gushing out. It killed me to break down in front of her like that. To let her see me so messed up and weak.

Jeanny didn't seem to mind, though. She moved my head to her shoulder and stroked my hair. "It's okay," she said, the same way she had to Sophie. "It's going to be okay."

We stayed like that awhile. Her comforting me as I listened to the steady thump of her heart beneath her sweater. The room grew quiet, except for the occasional whiz of a car driving by outside. As tired and sad as I was, after a long time of lying close to her like that, I felt myself get hard in my pants. It wasn't the usual quick surge. This was something that came more slowly, but stronger, as we lay there. It seemed funny to be turned on at the same time as all those other emotions. But with my head so near the softness of her breasts, it was impossible not to be. I told myself to hold back, though. It wasn't right in this room. So I simply let myself float in the feeling of being next to her.

Her hand stroking my hair, touching my forehead.

My arm draped over her stomach, absently playing with the cuff of her sweater.

Slowly my mind began to drift off to sleep, until Jeanny said quietly into the dim light of the room, "Dominick, you have to give Sophie back."

I jerked my head up and looked at her, suddenly awake again. "What are you talking about? I thought you'd be on my side."

"I am," she said, keeping quiet so as not to wake Sophie. "But, Dominick, that baby is barely a month old. She needs her mother. She needs to go to the doctor. She needs a lot of things you can't give her."

"So I'll find a doctor. I'll figure it all out."

Jeanny sat up, crossed her arms in front of her, covering those snowflakes over her breasts.

"Didn't you understand what I just said? Edie used me. She tricked me into stealing that money. My poor mother was conned into giving away her first kid. Then I betrayed her. And her third baby . . . well, we know what happened. Besides, Edie is living in some drug den. Sophie deserves better."

"Like living in an abandoned motel. Now, there's a privileged life. From here she'll go off to boarding school, right?"

"This is just temporary," I told her, imagining that same purple glow from the windows of Ed's grandparents' cabin in the woods, wondering for the first time if somehow I could get money from the Burdan family and use it to start a new life. "I have plans for us. We're making a pit stop here, then splitting."

Jeanny's face changed. Flicker of surprise. Flicker of disappointment. She lowered her voice still more and asked, "Where are you going?"

"I can't tell you. Because you can't come."

"So you're going to ride off into the sunset with an infant in your arms," she huffed. "That's really going to solve your problems."

"I'm not saying I have it all figured out. But I know what I have to do. And that's make things up to my mother. Save this kid from Edie."

Jeanny stared over at the little dark lump that was Sophie in the gui-tar case–turned–bassinet. A truck zoomed by on the street, and when it was quiet again, I could hear the baby softly breathing. Maybe I shouldn't have told Jeanny everything. It was a lot for anyone to make sense of. What had I expected?

I looked at my watch. Quarter to twelve. Fifteen minutes and Jeanny would be a pumpkin. I thought of Hansel and Gretel again, dropping bread crumbs behind them. A dark, floppy-winged bird scooping that food up in its beak as they disappeared behind the trees. "Look, I'm sorry for involving you," I told Jeanny as we both watched Sophie. I hated her for not taking my side, but the truth was I needed her. Just the thought of being in this room without her made me lonely. I swallowed and said, "If you want to leave now and just forget about me, I understand. And I probably shouldn't be pulling you into this, but if you wanted to stay here with me tonight, I . . . I would like that."

Jeanny seemed to actually be turning the possibility over in her mind, not taking her eyes off Sophie. I wondered if she saw this whole situation as another crusade, something for her to fight for. I imagined the picket signs taking shape in her mind: RETURN SOPHIE TO HER RIGHTFUL OWNER. . . . BRING THE BABY HOME . . . She watched Sophie for a long while, then looked at me finally and said, "I'll stay only if you promise me this: that you'll think about giving her back. Just think about it. That's all."

"What about your mother?" I asked.

Jeanny laughed the way she had on the bus when she told me about her mom. Like there was something funny in the sad things she said about her. Something I didn't understand. "Maybe my absence will get her attention. She'll realize I didn't die when my father did. Besides, it's winter break. I don't have classes to go to. But will you think about what I said?"

I put my arm around her and pulled her close to me. Felt myself get hard again. She smelled like the motel soap she had used to wash her hands. Up close I could see that scar beneath her chin again. My mind filled one more time with the image of her as a little girl hurt on the playground. What she was saying made sense, the same way my uncle had made sense to my mother when he showed up in New Mexico. But I knew that the rational choice wasn't always the right choice. Look at the way it had wrecked my mother. If I gave this baby back, I would regret it the way she did, for the rest of my life. So no, I wouldn't think about it. "You have to understand. My mother's death was all my fault," I said, trying to make her see things my way.

"It's not your fault," Jeanny said.

"Then whose is it?" I asked her.

"Do you really want an answer to that?"

"Yes," I told her. "I do."

"I think it's the world's fault."

"The world's fault?" I said, feeling once more like she hadn't understood what I'd just told her at all. "That makes a lot of sense."

"Listen to me. It's the world's fault because of the way it's set up for women. Your mother didn't have any choices, so she got stuck in a lot of bad situations. If she could have just left your father and gotten a decent job, she might have had a chance. But it's practically impossible for a woman with a kid to survive on her own. As much as my mother drives me crazy, I see how hard it is for her without my dad. Women aren't paid the same. Women aren't given the same chances. And if abortion was legal, then your mother could have just gone to a doctor or a clinic and gotten a safe one on demand."

"But what about the baby?" I asked her, remembering that PBS priest.

"You mean, 'What about the fetus?' I'm not going to claim to know when life starts. But I know when it ends. It ends when a woman like your mother dies because she can't decide for herself."

I didn't say anything, because Jeanny seemed pretty worked up. I thought of all her picket signs and bumper stickers. Her war on the world. I replayed that moment when my mother and I first laid eyes on Jeanny at the policemen's auction. What was it my mother had said? *I like a woman who fights for what she believes in.* Something like that.

"Don't get so quiet," Jeanny said to me. "Guys always do when I talk about the world. I mean, don't you read the papers? Don't you think these things, too?"

I thought of the way I had started to read the paper when I got to know Edie. All those headlines about faraway places. The world seemed so immense and unpredictable. Too much to know. Too much to think about.

"I do think about it," I told her. "I just don't have all the answers."

"Neither do I," she said and turned to face me again.

"Just ninety-nine percent of them, right?"

"Ninety-nine point nine," she said and laughed just enough to soften things between us.

I didn't know what else to say, so I leaned over and put my lips to hers. We moved our mouths together for a long while. This time I thought of Edie telling me, *I can spare one kiss. And it will make you feel in control the next time you're test-driving a new girlfriend.* I had thought the day would never come, that Edie was the only woman I would feel this way about. But Jeanny's mouth was smaller, more tender, less pushy to kiss. My feelings for her were already the same but different.

When we separated, I felt around my mouth with my tongue for my mother's gum. I had forgotten to push it aside the way I did when I ate.

"What's wrong?" Jeanny said.

"My gum. It's gone."

She reached into her mouth and pulled out the piece, grinning. "Is this what you're looking for?"

"Yes," I told her. She had no idea what that stale, overchewed piece of gum meant to me.

"What flavor is this? Week-old rubber?"

"I've been chewing it for a while," I said, because there was no way to explain.

"Well, let's put it on the nightstand," she said and stuck it to my empty water glass. "Maybe next time your dealer friend stops by, you can ask him to buy you some more."

My mouth felt barren and empty without it, like I had lost a tooth or maybe my tongue. I wasn't getting rid of it, I told myself. But I decided to leave the piece where Jeanny had put it for the time being. I wrapped my arms around her and held her close and tight to me. We were both so tired from the day that we stayed quiet and were well on our way to sleep, holding each other on top of the covers. I found myself imagining all the families who must have stayed in the rooms of this motel in the summertime. Children unable to sleep, too charged with excitement thinking of the next day at the racetrack, the bright blur of stock cars zooming round and round their minds.

"So you never gave me an answer," Jeanny whispered in my ear as I drifted off to sleep thinking of those cars that I knew were made from junks. Gutted, then re-created into something stronger in their afterlife.

"About what?" I asked.

"About whether or not you'll consider giving Sophie back. Will you at least promise that you'll think about it?"

"Yes," I told her, as my mind stepped down a dark path in the forest. Jeanny's hand in mine as we made our way between the white birch trees that looked like bones. That dark, big-winged fairy-tale bird not far behind pecking away at our trail. "I will think about it."

"Promise me?" she whispered.

"I promise you." I meant it, then fell asleep.

NINE

That first night in the motel I dreamed about blood on the floor. Not the stain washed away after my mother's death but a glowing red pool that came from a second accident. One that hadn't yet happened. The red was radiant, phosphorescent, like the juice from those cherries that used to stain my hands and sweatshirt pockets when I stole them from the bars where I found my father. The shape began as a round cardinal's hat, as big or as little as Sophie herself. Soon it spread and transformed into a shining scarlet light that shimmered on the ceiling and coated the walls like the paint in my uncle's living room.

When I woke, it was still dark, and Sophie was crying. Jeanny wasn't moving, so I decided to get out of bed and figure out what was wrong with Sophie on my own. I remembered what Jeanny had said about her brothers' limited demands when they were this new to the world. Bottle. Diaper. Crib. Since I wasn't completely confident about tackling a diaper problem if there was one, I carefully picked up Sophie and tried giving her a bottle. Thankfully, that seemed to be the answer. She started sucking, and I pushed back the blankets and curtain from the window and stared outside. A branch had fallen in the spot where Roget usually parked his car to snag speeders. I watched the wind blow its crooked old woman's hand shape around until Sophie began to fuss again.

"What's the matter, little alien?" I whispered. "There's no need to cry. I've got you now."

With some coaxing she took to her bottle once more and quieted down. I felt like maybe I was starting to get the hang of this baby thing. If only I could get used to how delicate she felt in my arms. Every time I held her, my body went stiff with worry that I'd move her the wrong way and hurt her somehow. I knew that Jeanny had told me babies were more durable than they looked, but it was a hard idea to wrap my mind around when Sophie seemed like nothing more than a wrinkly lump of flesh. In my mind the heart that beat beneath her chest seemed too tiny. Her lungs couldn't have been any bigger than a kitten's. I nestled my nose into her soft yellow outfit. Breathed in her sweet, simple smell.

New skin, bones, and breath.

Saliva and tears.

Formula and powder.

When I looked into the dark of the room, Jeanny's eyes were open, watching me. I knew what she must have been thinking: *You have to give that baby back.* And maybe, I admitted to myself for the first time, maybe she was right. After all, I thought as I held Sophie close to me, what could I possibly do now that I had her? I couldn't take care of her, raise her, be a parent to her. But every time I thought of returning Sophie to Edie's arms, my mind burned.

I just couldn't bear to do it.

There had to be another option. Something I wasn't considering.

"Baby-sitting lesson number three," Jeanny said, yawning. "Infants never sleep through the night."

I went to her and rested Sophie in the crook of my arm as I sat back on the bed. She was really going at it with her bottle now, and the sucking sound made me think of Marnie's cat, Milky, the way she used to make the same noise as she lapped her milk. That cat would still be alive if Marnie hadn't been so stubborn about setting the thing free even though she lived close enough to the highway that freedom was a death sentence.

"Did you get any sleep?" Jeanny asked.

"Yeah," I said. "But I had a weird dream."

"About what?"

I watched Jeanny's eyes as she stared up at the blank vastness of the ceiling. It looked like outer space up there. Heaven or hell. A car passed, creating a grid of lights above us that changed shape and faded to black once more. I made a mental note to pull the blankets and curtain back over the window before falling asleep again. "There was more blood in this room," I told her. "A big spot on the floor at first. Then it washed over the whole place. Shimmering, sort of."

Jeanny put her hand on my shoulder. I don't think she knew what to say.

We were quiet a moment. I listened to Sophie making that Milky sound with her bottle as I tried to shake the red from that dream, that vision of my mother in the mirror.

Baby.

Maybe.

Stranger.

Too.

"Do you believe in signs?" I asked.

"What do you mean?" Jeanny said, rolling over onto her side to face me.

"Like there are things in your life — events or omens — that are meant to guide you to a certain place?"

"You mean, do I think things happen for a reason?"

That wasn't exactly what I was asking, but I told her yes anyway. As I waited for an answer, I watched Sophie breathing. Her body was a loaf of bread rising in the heat of an oven, falling when she exhaled.

"I guess I think some things are meant to be. Fate," Jeanny said after a while. "And other stuff is just up to chance. Who knows the reason behind it?"

My mind scrambled over the last month of my life—that FOR SALE sign pitched in Edie's front yard, those pregnant women walking into the hospital, that *Newsweek* reporter calling. All along I had believed that it was my mother guiding me. That I was meant to follow those signs. But something made me wonder if it was only me wanting to see it that way. After all, if she were going to lead me, wouldn't my mother make certain I understood her message in the mirror?

I found myself guessing how Jeanny would categorize all the things that had happened to me in the past year. Fate or chance?

Then I thought of Jeanny sitting next to me on the bus, and I asked, "Do you think when we met today, it was meant to be?"

Jeanny was quiet for a moment.

"Should I take that as a no?" I said, feeling stupid for asking.

She laughed. "It's not a no. I just have to think about it some more. I'm not sure yet."

Neither was I, I supposed. But I hoped that the answer might be yes for both of us down the road. I didn't say anything more about it though. Instead I kept quiet and rubbed my hand against Sophie's satiny baby skin. "My mother believed in signs," I said into the darkness after a while. "She told me once that if I watched carefully, life would always lay signs right out in front of me, telling me which way to go. And now that's she's gone, I keep looking for them."

"I used to think like that after my dad died. I thought that if he really loved me, he would find a way to contact me from the dead. I'd think, okay, if you can hear me, make the sun come out from behind that cloud, or make the phone ring. But it never happened."

More than ever I wanted to tell her about what I had seen in the mirror but felt afraid she'd think I was losing my mind. Hell, even I was afraid I was losing my mind. "Does that mean you don't look for him anymore?" I asked.

Jeanny stretched her arm over the side of the bed and grabbed her bag. She pulled out that silver cigarette case she had snapped open and closed on the bus. "See the letters?" she said, pointing to an engraved *M* and *G* on the top.

I nodded.

She told me that they were her father's initials. Michael Garvey. He used to keep his guitar picks in the case along with his cigarettes. Now Jeanny took it with her wherever she went as a reminder of him. "I guess I see him in the things he left behind and the things he taught me instead of looking for him in the clouds. Doing that helps me to let him go."

Sophie finished her bottle, and I got up to put her back in the makeshift crib. I thought of my mother, tried to imagine letting her go, but she felt too close. I pictured her spirit hovering above me like one of those galeros. What would it take for her to disintegrate and drop to the floor so she could be released from this world? I supposed I had thought it would happen when I took Sophie, when I proved somehow to my mother that I had made a mistake by stealing that money. But I wasn't so sure anymore. Maybe she would hang over me forever, an invisible weight on my back, like the angry eyes of those kids who had followed me on the street in Hell's Kitchen.

"Wait," Jeanny said as I was about to lay Sophie down. She had put her father's silver case on the nightstand next to the glass with my mother's gum. "You need to burp her first."

Jeanny told me what to do, and I gently bounced Sophie until she let loose a bunch of baby burps, which made us both laugh. She spit up a blob of creamy goo on my shoulder, too. Jeanny got up and grabbed a towel, cleaned us both up.

"There," she said. "My two babies are as good as new."

I put Sophie in her guitar-case crib and got back in bed next to Jeanny, wrapped my arms around her. Up close her sweater smelled faintly of that perfume she'd sprayed on back on the bus. Beneath that I breathed in something entirely different. It was the way I imagined her house might smell. Like hand-washed clothes and unvacuumed rugs. Meals stewed up in oversize pots to feed so many mouths for the week. I wondered if Jeanny sprayed that perfume on herself to cover the smell of her house. To help her become something other than a girl from Little Street. Thinking of that made me hold her closer. And when my mind filled with the image of Jeanny staring up at a cloudy sky, waiting for her father to make the sun come out, it broke my heart, because I knew how she felt. "What was your dad like?" I asked her.

"What do you want to know?"

"Anything," I said. "Just tell me about him."

"Well, he was a great musician. You name the instrument and he could play it. He loved any kind of art. Music. Painting. Dance. And he loved to talk about the world. My father always told me to speak up for what I believe in. A message I know most girls don't hear. He was pretty liberal like that. I guess you would call him a hippie."

I thought of my dad dubbing her street Hippie Street and wondered if he had ever come across Mr. Garvey around town. "I know your mom changed, but did anything go back to normal, or even close to normal, for you after he was gone?"

"Hardly," she said.

"What do you mean?" I wanted to know because I cared. I needed to know because I couldn't imagine my life ever going back to normal again.

"Well, for one thing, he wouldn't have put me in St. Bartholomew."

Not the answer I expected, though I wasn't sure exactly what I had in mind. "So why do you go there?"

"After a few years in elementary my parents decided to home-school me. But when my father died, it was too much for my mother to handle, so she wanted to put me in school again. Only the superintendent was not very happy about the" —she held up her index and middle fingers to put the next words in quotes— "hippie-dippy idea of home-schooling. The guy wanted me to stay back a few grades. So that's how I wound up at St. Bartholomew. I took a test, and they actually put me ahead one grade. My mother told me to ignore the religious stuff and absorb all the rest. Unfortunately, it's mostly religion. But it adds fuel to my fire, and it beats staying back."

"At least the uniform looks cute on you," I said, remembering that day on the bus when she had stepped on board wearing that wool sweater and plaid skirt. Transforming in the bathroom like Superman in a phone booth.

Jeanny groaned. "Oh, I hate that ridiculous outfit!"

"Really," I said, teasing her. "It suits you perfectly."

She seemed absolutely tortured by the thought of it. "If you ever say that again, I'll have no choice but to tape your mouth shut."

"It suits you perfectly," I repeated, deadpan.

"Stop it!" she said and grabbed a pillow, shoved it my face.

"Okay! Okay! I'm kidding!" I pushed her off. Poked a finger in her ribs. "We've got to loosen you up, Miss Garvey. You're so serious."

"Very funny," she said, rolling her eyes.

Something about her smile made me lean forward and kiss her again. Both our mouths opened to each other right away, and I slipped my tongue between her lips. Her breath was wet and warm, and I could feel my body getting hot as we moved together.

My chest against her chest.

Our legs touching on the bed.

I ran my fingers through her smooth hair. We kissed harder, and unable to hold myself back, I moved my hand to the front of her sweater. Slid my palm to her breast. She felt bigger there than I had imagined. I brushed her nipple with my fingers. When I pulled her closer, she stopped me.

"Wait."

I lifted my hands an inch or two from her body like someone caught in the middle of a crime. "Sorry."

"No. It's okay. But . . . it's just that . . . I'm, you know, I haven't—"

"Me neither," I confessed, wondering instantly if that was the type of thing I should admit. God knew Leon never would have.

"I like you, Dominick," Jeanny said. "But we shouldn't go too fast."

"I agree. I mean, whatever you want to do is all right."

"We can kiss some more. Okay?"

"Sounds perfect," I said and leaned my lips into hers again, because the truth was I didn't know if I was ready for more. As excited as I got being next to her, it still felt strange to think about sex in this room where my mother had died. It still felt strange to think of sex as an actuality at all.

We didn't go back to sleep completely that night. We kissed and talked for hours. From time to time Sophie woke, and we took care of her, got her settled back in. Then we spoke in whispers and made out some more. I told Jeanny that I remembered seeing her that morning at the auction last year, and she said she remembered seeing me there, too. I told her about my mother's plans to buy the station. I told her about that crazy cleaning lady at my uncle's, and we laughed. We laughed even more about our bus driver, Claude. We talked about Edie again. The way I used to feel Sophie move inside her belly as we lay on her bed. The shock I felt when I overheard that phone call. And Jeanny told me all about her mother and brothers, how her mom stayed numb with a steady supply of prescription pills, how sad they all felt since their father died. She told me that when he was alive he used to take her—just her— on the bus to New York to see shows or go to the museums. She missed those times more than anything. And when we were done talking, we put our arms around each other. Because I had forgotten to close the curtain, the sun soon streamed in through the window, bathing us in light.

We lived like that for three days.

Kissing.

Talking.

Sleeping.

Watching TV.

Taking care of Sophie.

Jeanny never left. Once when I was in the shower, she phoned her mother, and I could hear that they were arguing. I asked Jeanny about it later, and she shrugged it off, not wanting to get into it. I made up my mind not to ask anymore, because I didn't want her to give it too much thought and decide to leave. She knew what she was doing. And I got the feeling that staying in this motel was almost like another protest for her.

She was picketing the fact that her mother had checked out two years ago. That she'd stopped noticing Jeanny at all.

Leon swung by every afternoon to bring us whatever we needed. Clothes from my apartment that he snagged when my father wasn't around. More pizza. Chinese food. Soda. Pretzels. Toothbrushes. Toothpaste. All of it on the house. I asked him about Ed's cabin, and he said he would see what he could do, but I was going to have to be nicer to Ed if I wanted to use his grandparents' place. I promised, even though something told me that I wouldn't end up there. Not that I had seen any more signs from my mother telling me what was to come next. Whenever I looked into the bathroom mirror, only my expectant face stared back. I was beginning to believe that I had simply imagined her there. Imagined her voice all along, too.

At the end of each day Jeanny and I took turns going outside for air while one of us stayed behind with the baby. Taking walks was Jeanny's idea, since she thought we might go stir-crazy sealed in that dim room. In the woods behind the motel we found a narrow, snow-covered path that led to a pond. The surface looked more like some sort of galactic landscape than the slick, smooth white of a skating rink. All jagged bumps and craters left by the wind and snow. Whenever it was my turn to take a break, I walked along the path to the pond and stepped out onto the ice. All that black water seemed like death down there beneath my feet, waiting for me, waiting for all of us, even Sophie, who had only just been born. I always slid around on my boots, then sat down on a tree trunk near the edge of the pond. As the sun set and my breath fogged the air around me, I thought about all that had happened and wondered what to do next.

Beneath the ice a dozen or so goldfish the size of trout floated still in the cold water, which seemed weird to me because it was winter. But there they were—bright orange bursts of life under the frozen surface. Judging from the goldfish motif in the motel, I figured they must've belonged to Old Man Fowler. I had never seen goldfish so big, and I always stared down at them as I knocked those questions around my brain before walking back to the room. Even though I didn't come to a decision right away, I felt happy on those walks back to the room. It seemed odd to feel happy, considering my predicament. But knowing I was going to spend another night with Jeanny and Sophie filled me with a joy that I couldn't put into words. It was a little like the way a man must feel returning to a family he loved. And this is what I told myself: My mother had one perfect day with Truman; I had three with Sophie and Jeanny.

Three days, that was all.

As happy as I felt, the whole while I sensed that menacing fairy-tale bird pecking away behind us, getting closer and closer all the time. I knew it was the part of me that realized this life would end. That somewhere Edie was looking for her baby. That sometime soon I was going to have to make up my mind. So it was during my last afternoon trip to the pond that I finally decided what to do.

I had spent a big part of the day laughing with Jeanny because she was trying, unsuccessfully, to teach me how to yodel. She said I sounded like a dying goat. We watched *The Price Is Right* and guessed along with Bob Barker and the gang. Jeanny whipped my ass and walked away with a washer and dryer, plus a brand-new car. After we finished the sandwiches Leon had brought us the day before, we played with Sophie. If you put your finger in her hand, she squeezed it tight. Since that was her first major physical feat besides blowing our eardrums with her crying, Jeanny and I were pretty impressed. When Sophie had had enough, we put her down for a nap and went into the next room, through the closets, and fooled around on the bed in there. Something we started doing after I explained to Jeanny that it made me feel more relaxed to be with her in that room, away from my mother's tragedy. We both fell asleep in there, too, and when we woke, Jeanny suggested I go outside first.

I headed back to the ice and sat on that tree trunk. I was staring down at those meaty goldfish when I saw her.

My mother beneath the frozen surface.

She moved faceup, hair wet and snarled, watery and slow, drifting by me with that same message she had given me in the mirror the night I arrived in her room. Only this time I didn't let my fear distract me. I watched every move of her mouth. And that's when I finally understood her.

She wasn't saying, *Baby maybe stranger, too.*

She was telling me:

The

baby

may

be

in

danger

here

with

you.

The sign I had been waiting for. But what was the danger?

My heart pounded, and I scrambled along the ice to follow her, slipping and banging my elbow as she drifted off into the gray murkiness of the pond. I watched her blue legs vanish into a tangle of weeds.

"Are you okay?" another voice said.

I yanked my head up to see Jeanny standing at the edge of the ice. "Where's Sophie?" I asked, breathless.

"Leon came by. She's asleep, so I told him to stay with her for a few minutes while I came to see you. Outside of that room for a change."

"Is she okay? What if she wakes up?"

"I told Leon to shout out the window if he needs us. Don't worry. Nothing will happen."

"We should get back to her," I said, thinking of my mother's words.

"Relax. Leon will call us if she wakes up," Jeanny said. "What were you looking at down there?"

I took a breath and forced myself to trust Jeanny. Something in my gut told me that whatever danger my mother spoke of was far greater than Sophie waking up with only Leon in the room. I stared down at the ice, and just as I had come to expect, my mother was gone. But those fish were still there. A red one—not gold or orange but a flaming red— kept still beneath me. "I'm watching the fish," I said. "I wonder how they stay alive down there all winter long."

Jeanny stepped out onto the ice and slid her way over to me. She pretended to figure-skate. Twirling. Stretching her arms out before her. "Let's see," she said, kneeling next to me.

"There," I said. "See them."

We watched the red one. Its gills barely moving. Breathing in its own strange way. Jeanny said, "I guess their bodies adjust. They can take the cold."

We watched the fish a moment more, waiting for it to do something, I supposed. But it just sat there. Dormant.

"I've been thinking," I told Jeanny as we stared down at the ice, a blank mirror that wouldn't reflect our images. "Maybe you're right about giving Sophie back. Maybe she's not safe here." I hadn't quite realized my decision until the words came out. But it was my mother's message that had convinced me. I needed to reverse what I had done before anything else went wrong. And giving Sophie back to Edie seemed the only realistic thing to do, even if that felt like failure.

We stood up, and Jeanny put her arms around me, over my shoulders. I squeezed her low on the waist, locking us together. "I know it will be hard," she said into the air over my shoulder. "But it's the right thing to do."

You would have thought that settling on a plan would've caused a great weight to be lifted from me. But no, I actually felt more pressed down and flattened with hopelessness. I realized that giving Sophie back meant letting go of Jeanny, too, the temporary life we had been living in the Holedo Motel. I pulled away and took a good, long look at her. She was wearing a pair of my jeans that Leon had brought to us, so baggy the cuffs went down over her boots and touched the ice. Her cheeks were pink from the winter air. The thing that struck me as so cool about Jeanny was that she showed every part of herself to me. Most girls seemed to reveal only a glimpse of their personalities before reeling themselves back in. Jeanny was different. Real. Honest. She said what was on her mind, even if people—including me—didn't like it. But just because she had all her opinions about the world, that didn't mean she couldn't let loose and have a good time. Looking at her, I told myself that no matter what happened after I returned the baby—the same way my mother had Truman—I would always remember my time here with her.

"So do you want to go back?" Jeanny asked. "Unless you're part gold-fish, you must be freezing."

Leon wasn't exactly Mary Poppins, so I figured we'd better get back. I took Jeanny's hand, and we headed across the ice, shuffling our boots so we didn't lose our balance and fall. We were about to step off the ice and start down the path when Jeanny stopped. "Look," she said, pointing. "It's starting to snow."

The light flakes made the slightest patter as they fell onto the bare tree branches and the floor of the woods. More white to cover the white that was already there.

"I love when it snows," Jeanny said. "It slows everything down."

I couldn't help thinking of the storm the night I found my mother. Would there ever be a time that snowfall didn't make me think of seeing her body on the floor? We stood on the edge of the ice a moment longer. Listening to the patter. Letting the wet flakes land on our faces and melt with the heat of our skin. Then I tugged on Jeanny's hand, and she followed me back through the woods. Something made me think of Marnie as we stepped through the woods. I remembered her telling me that I could stay at her place, and I wondered if she had meant for good. In a weird way I actually kind of missed the Bingo Queen.

We stopped at the corner of the motel, made sure no cars were passing the place, then scooted up the cement stairs. When we got to the door, Jeanny stepped aside and told me to open it. "Why?" I asked.

"Open it," she said. "You'll see."

I turned the knob and pushed in the door. A dozen balloons floated up near the ceiling—pink, white, yellow, red, blue, green. On the dresser was a bowl of chips and dip. A six-pack of Dr Pepper. Two small presents wrapped in the paper from a brown shopping bag. A bow had been stuck to Sophie's guitar-case bed.

"Happy birthday!" Jeanny and Leon said in unison.

My birthday. Only it wasn't until tomorrow. I figured I didn't need to let them know they'd gotten the date wrong. We might as well start the party early. Jeanny picked up Sophie and brought her to me. There was a bow taped to one of her feet, too. I peeled it off and stuck it to Jeanny's head. Gave Sophie a kiss on her soft cheek. Then I heard my mother's voice telling me that Sophie was in danger here with me. As much as it killed me, I had to take her home.

"Here you go, birthday boy." Jeanny grabbed a present off the dresser and handed it to me, took Sophie again. "From the pea and me. Keep in mind, this is a low-budget birthday. I haven't exactly had a chance to go to Bloomingdale's."

I tore it open and found six twelve-packs of gum. Not Juicy Fruit, but Chiclets in every flavor. Along with that there was a doodly drawing of Sophie, Jeanny, and me. Jeanny had sketched herself in a pleated skirt and dark sweater. The bubbled caption read "World's Worst Outfit!" An arrow pointed to Sophie's hand with a bubble that read "Future Arm-Wrestling Champ!" Over my head it simply said "Birthday Boy."

I laughed, thinking I'd frame the drawing the way my uncle had that photo of him and Truman at Laguna del Perro. It would be my only tangible reminder of the last three days. Once again I saw my life stretching out before me. A blank chalkboard. An empty notebook. I felt the heavy weight of sadness I guessed I'd always feel without my mother. But it was my birthday—or almost anyway—so I tried to forget that for the time being and smile.

Jeanny tapped a yellow balloon in the air with her free hand. It bumped the red one, and I grabbed it, pulled it down to me, thinking of those hats at St. Patrick's. It was one of those balloons that had a smaller balloon inside. Like the kind Marnie used to bring me from the dingy gift shop at Griffith Hospital when I was a kid. She used to get the end-of-the-day no-sales on her way out of work, and they always sank to the floor in no time. I looked at the stretched rubber surface and saw a curved version of myself and the room behind me, tinted red just like my dream, only more disorienting because of the round reflection. I let go, and the balloon shot up to the ceiling, thumped against the flat white surface, and cocked its faceless face down at me. Watching. Staring. The balloon's string was more like a ribbon, and it hung like an upside-down question mark, curling in front of me. I thought of what it might be asking from up there:

Are you sure you want to give the baby back to Edie?

Before I had time to answer that in my mind, the balloon popped, making a gunshot of a noise, startling all of us. Jeanny let out a surprised sort of yelp. The baby began to wail. The shriveled bits of red skin dropped to the floor, and I thought of a cardinal released into heaven. My mother.

"Okay," Jeanny said. "No playing with the survivors. Let them float freely. Balloons have rights, too."

Jeanny worked at calming Sophie, and Leon took the second present from the dresser and handed it to me. I shook it near my ear. Not a sound. It weighed next to nothing. "Let me guess," I said, kidding him. "Another gun. More bullets."

"Just open it," he said, looking over my shoulder toward the door instead of at me. He kept tapping one hand on his leg in a way that seemed fidgety, not at all like him.

I tore off the paper and pulled out an office envelope. Peeled back the sticky, dried yellow lip he had sealed, then bent the wings of the metal clasp to find a wad of cash inside. When I pulled it out, my hand felt charged with energy, the way it did when I held that gun. Without even counting the bills, I said to Leon, "I can't take this."

"It's yours," he said.

"But it's too much. I can't accept it."

"No, man. I mean, it's yours." Leon looked toward the covered window then back at me. Fidgety still. "Well, the first installment anyway. There's more on the way."

"Installment? What do you mean?" I said, confused.

Leon's voice was shaky when he spoke next. He held both his hands out in front of him, palms up, as if there was something in them I was supposed to see. "I don't know how to say this, so I guess I'll just say it. Remember the envelope Edie gave me that day you were in New York? Well, there was a whole bunch of money in it, and I . . . well, I've been sort of holding on to it for you."

The floor shifted beneath my feet the way it had the night I found my mother in this room, the way it might feel if that ice cracked on the pond and I sank down into the freezing water, my boots sucked into the cold mud.

Leon was still talking. "I used it to get the car and then to make some more money with Ed. And now I'm going to start paying you back."

Everything around me seemed to shrink as Leon's face grew larger before me. His hands were still in front of him, empty with air. His eyes broad and blinking.

I let go of the drawing Jeanny had given me.

I dropped the bills, and they scattered at my feet.

"You fucking kept that money!" I screamed so loud I swore I felt something tear in the back of my throat. My skin was melting, on fire.

"I tried to tell you," Leon stammered. "But you told me not to bring it up."

I curled my fingers into a fist. Lunged at him. Swung at his lying sack-of-shit face.

"Dominick!" Jeanny shouted.

But her voice, and Sophie's crying, sounded far away. Above the ice when I was below. As muffled and distant as two sirens on the other side of town. My fists kept flying. He didn't swing back but grabbed my arms in an effort to hold me still. My anger was stronger, though, and I broke free, swung at him. Got in one, two, then three more solid punches before he pushed me off. I fell to the floor, slamming the back of my head against the hard wood of the dresser. When I looked up at him from where I lay among that drawing and those strewn bills, there were spots

in front of my eyes. Black, shapeless demons that floated in the air mingling with my dizziness. Taunting:

Edie paid you back.

Leon kept the money.

I screamed again, "You are a fucking asshole! How could you let me
keep thinking that Edie had cheated me when you had the money the
whole time?"

Leon's lip was bleeding, and he reached up and touched the blood,
wiped it on the back of his hand. "I *said* I was paying you back, you crazy
motherfucker."

I was about to say something more, to tell him to burn in hell, but
Jeanny interrupted. "Shhh," she said. "Did you hear that?"

Silence.

Leon and I looked at her. "What?"

"It sounded like a car door slamming." Jeanny walked to the window
and peeked out, holding Sophie and trying to massage the nipple of the
bottle into her mouth. As she stared down at the parking lot, her face
looked stricken. A girl in a horror movie who had finally met the monster. "Dominick. Come here."

I got up off the floor and clambered to the window. Outside in the
snowy, dusky air, Roget was getting out of his squad car. With him was
none other than Joshua Fuller. I felt a cold wave of fright wash over me.
Then my gut instinct kicked in. I told Jeanny to take Sophie into the
closet and quiet her down. I didn't giving a shit where Leon hid.

"What are you going to do?" Jeanny asked.

"I don't know," I told her, turning the bolt on the door, sliding the
chain into place. I supposed I was just going to watch them. See what
they were up to. Keep them from coming inside.

Leon slumped quietly into the bathroom. Jeanny took the baby and
settled in on the floor of the closet. She kept the door cracked open, and
I could see her nervously shushing Sophie. I turned and watched
through the peephole as Joshua Fuller pulled a camera out of his pocket
and snapped pictures of the motel.

Click. Flash. Click. Flash.

They walked toward the stairs.

I waited behind the door, and my heart throbbed in my chest. An unseeable claw—maybe the one that belonged to that Hansel-and-Gretel bird—scratched at my face, gripped my throat, and made me gulp for air. As they got closer, I heard Roget say, "Like I told you, the owner is in Florida for the rest of the winter."

The sound of his voice made those black demon spots dance in front of my eyes again. I hated Roget for what he had done to my mother. He could have helped her. Saved her life. It took all my strength not to open the door and go after him the way I had Leon. I shook my head to rid myself of that temptation, those dark spots, that claw. My neck felt stiff, and I reached up and touched my head where it had hit the dresser. When I pulled my hand away, there was blood on my fingertips.

"And like *I* told *you*," Joshua was saying, sarcastic, "I talked to him over the phone. But I just want to see the place while I'm here."

I heard nothing for a moment, then footsteps, and they were right outside the door. So close I thought I could hear them breathing. Inhale. Exhale. Inhale. Exhale. Through the hole I saw Joshua Fuller's purple birthmark, distorted and round, like the image in that balloon before it burst. I remembered the way he had called after me when I ditched him in the diner.

We had a deal!

We had a deal!

We had a deal!

"This is the room?" he asked.

"That's what the report said," Roget told him. "I wasn't here."

Joshua put his hand on the knob and turned. I watched it move one way, then the other, as my whole body shook. "Locked," he said.

"What did you think, the owner was going to leave the place wide open?"

"I was just trying for the hell of it. So would you mind giving me a lift to Marnie Garboni's place?"

"Sure thing," Roget said.

I heard their footsteps walk away, and I was about to let out a sigh when Joshua called to Roget, who must have already been ahead of him on the stairs. "The room next door is open."

Instantly I realized that the door was still unlocked from when I had gone out that way earlier. As a matter of fact, it had probably been unlocked for days. How could I have been so fucking careless? My whole body seemed to shake as I moved to the closet, crouched next to Jeanny. Her eyes big and wide as she rocked Sophie, who was busy with her bottle, making that milky sound.

Please, God, I prayed, don't let her cry.

"I don't know what you expect to find," I heard Roget's muffled voice say when the door opened in the next room.

"I don't expect to find anything. I'm a reporter. Reporters like to take everything in. That's all. Aren't police officers supposed to be curious, too?"

Roget didn't answer that.

"The bed's not made," Joshua said. "There's blankets on the window."

"I'll be sure to get the name of the chambermaid so I can arrest her for you."

"You're a funny guy," Joshua Fuller said.

Jeanny and I listened as they walked around the room. Hard, discordant footsteps on the floor, like two horses circling each other in a tight stable. Someone — I assumed it was Joshua Fuller — opened and closed a drawer. My mind filled with the image of that Bible stuffed with the pistol Leon had given me. Why hadn't I just thrown the thing away? I didn't have time enough to worry about them finding it, because something far worse happened.

I heard the closet door open on their side.

"Hey," Joshua Fuller said. "There's a door in the back of this closet. It must connect with Five-B."

Too late to turn the lock, because he would hear the sound. I reached up and put my hand on the knob. Held it as hard as I could. Joshua tried to turn it from the other side as I squeezed until my fingers hurt, pulled with all my weight. That's when Sophie spit her bottle out of her mouth. Jeanny and I watched her, willing her not to cry.

Please, God.

Please, God.

Please, God.

She moved her mouth but kept quiet.

"It's locked," Joshua said finally and let go.

I kept holding on anyway, in case one of them tried again.

"Oh, well," Roget told him, "I still don't know what you're expecting to find."

The closet door closed, and I heard more footsteps. "There's a car parked out back," Joshua said. "Is it the owner's?"

"Nah," Roget told him. "There's a pond on the property. Probably high-school kids playing a hockey game back there. Listen, if you don't mind, I'd like to take you to Miss Garboni's so I can get on with some business of my own."

"All right. I'm done here," Joshua said.

I heard their footsteps move to the door, and then they were outside again. My hand stayed gripped on the doorknob even as I told myself it was okay to let go. A moment later Roget's car started in the parking lot. I peeled my stiff fingers away and went to the window. Watched them drive off, my heart still racing.

Leon emerged from the bathroom. A piece of toilet paper stuck to his split lip like my father when he cut himself shaving. "I'm out of here," he said.

"Wait," I told him. "I want you to drive me and the baby back to New York right now."

"Now? I just can't drive to New York now. What would I tell Leila?"

"Since when are you so concerned with what you tell your mother? And I own that car of yours anyway. So if I want a ride, you don't have much of a choice."

"Dominick," Jeanny said. "We're all really worked up. And it's almost dark outside and snowing. You know how much I want you to take this baby back. But it would be smart if we all calmed down and left first thing in the morning. It'll give us time to figure out how we're going to get the baby to Edie."

I knew Jeanny was right, but I couldn't help thinking of my mother's message. If Sophie was in danger here with me, then one night could make all the difference.

"One more night," Jeanny said quietly.

And I could tell by the way she said it that despite her return-Sophie-to-her-rightful-owner campaign, she hated letting go of our life here, too. Just like me, she wanted us to sleep next to each other one last time. And I wanted to have my sister with me a little longer before our lives changed forever. "Fine," I told Leon. "Pick us up at seven. Don't be late. And don't bring that dope Ed with you."

Leon walked to the window, pushed the curtain and blankets aside, I guessed to make sure they were definitely gone. Before opening the door, he turned back to face me. "It wasn't like I set out to rob you," he said, his voice still shaky. "When Edie first handed me that envelope, she made me swear up and down that I would give it to you. And I planned on it. But then everything happened with your mom. And you didn't want to hear about it—"

"I was at her funeral, Leon. You could have tried to tell me another time."

"Okay, but then you were gone, and that money was just sitting in my drawer staring at me."

"I was only gone for a month."

"But I didn't know that. Christ, the way the paper made it sound, you were dead in a ditch or something. When you showed up at the bus station and I brought you here, I realized I fucked up. Why do you think I've been coming around like Santa Claus every friggin' day?" Leon stopped and touched his lip again. That piece of torn tissue. He sighed. "I'll drive you to New York in the morning. Then I'll sell the car. I'll pay you back every last dime."

"Just be here at seven," I said again, not ready to forgive him or to strike a deal.

After he was gone, Jeanny looked at the back of my head. "Are you all right?" she asked.

"Yeah, I'm fine."

"Dominick, no, you're not. You're bleeding." She took one of Sophie's diapers and pressed it to my head, then held it in front of my face. The thing had a spot of blood in the center as red as that fish in the pond. "It's actually not too big of a cut," she said once the blood was wiped away. She took one of those cold cans of Dr Pepper and pressed it to my head to stop the swelling.

"Some birthday party," I said and flopped back on the bed, feeling the weight of my head. A serious migraine coming on.

As I stared up at the eleven remaining balloons—the survivors, as Jeanny had called them—my mind filled with a picture of that day Edie left Holedo. I saw the scene unfold in my mind as if I were watching it like one of those balloons watching me. The way I imagined it, Edie pulled up in front of my apartment in her white Cadillac, that man I didn't know at the wheel, the trunk stuffed and heavy with her belongings. She looked around, nervous, checking to make sure my father's truck was nowhere in sight. When she felt sure he wasn't there, she got out of the car. The man who was with her offered to go up to my door for her, but she refused.

"I'll be right back," she said to him.

She walked up the stairs with her hands holding her swelled stomach and knocked. As she waited, she bit at her broken, once-beautiful nails. Kept watching to make sure my father didn't show. No one answered, of course. I was in New York. My mother was off with Roget. My father wasn't home yet from his extended trip. Edie knocked and knocked, then finally turned back toward the car. That's when she spotted Leon somewhere. Maybe right there at the bottom of the stairs.

"Hey, there," she said, piecing together who he was from the few things I'd told her about him. "You must be Dominick's friend Leon. Right?"

"That's me," Leon said, taking note of her pregnant stomach and wondering what in the world Edie Kramer was doing rapping at my door.

She walked down the stairs, one hand on the railing, the other on her belly again. At that very moment Sophie was probably preparing to be born. Kicking and squirming. Shifting into position. Edie may have even felt a cramp just then, before she said, "Can I ask you a huge favor?" uncertain of what else to do.

Leon shrugged. "Sure."

"It's very important that I get this envelope to Dominick. But he's not home, and I have to run. If I leave it with you, do you promise to give it to him the moment he comes home?"

"Okay," Leon said, already planning to rip open the envelope the second she left, for no other reason than to bust my balls. Only he had no idea what he was about to find. That envelope was like a prize from Bob Barker himself. A washer and dryer. A shiny blue car behind a shimmering gold curtain. The price was right.

I saw Edie's hand put the envelope in his. She squeezed his fingers closed around it, and Leon loved her touch, the way I had, even if she was pregnant. "Make sure," Edie said before walking off. "It's very important."

As my mind blurred around the image of Edie driving away toward New York City, I removed that can of Dr Pepper from the back of my head. The bleeding seemed to have stopped.

Jeanny had put Sophie to bed, and she stretched out next to me. It was our last night together. I didn't want to think about Edie or Leon anymore. As difficult as it was, I mustered up all my energy and forced myself to put that bullshit out of my mind so I could concentrate on her. The most important person in my life at the moment. When I turned toward Jeanny, though, her eyes looked heavy, weighed down by sadness.

"What's wrong?" I asked.

"Nothing."

"What?" I said.

"I guess as much as I'm glad that you've decided to take Sophie back, I'm also going to miss our time here."

I pulled her close to me and felt my body responding the way it always did next to hers. That heat. That tightening in my chest. I didn't kiss her, but my lips were close enough to hers that I could have. "Me, too," I told her.

We lay there looking into each other's eyes. My hand traced the curve of her hip up past her tickle of ribs to the soft skin of her neck. The feel of her body made the ache in my head fade away just enough for me to feel comfortable again. I thought back to that first night with Jeanny in the motel and remembered how uncertain I'd been about being ready for more with her. But I knew now that I was. And something told me she felt the same.

This was all I said: "Do you want to?"

Shy for once, Jeanny simply nodded.

Yes.

I took her hand, and we stood, walked through those closets into the next room. Any leftover shock that might have remained in the air from our unwanted visitors had gone, and it felt like our place again.

Nobody else's.

To be safe, I locked the front door before lying out on the bed beside Jeanny. We stayed there for a long while, just being with each other. Then I lifted Jeanny's hair and kissed the back of her neck. Made an invisible necklace of kisses all the way around her. Put my tongue against her ear and licked at the curves, down into the darkness of her, tasting her salty skin. In a way I felt grateful to Edie for that night she had let me kiss her, because I realized I had to keep control, not to let go before I could enjoy this and Jeanny could, too.

My body relaxed into the moment, and I held on.

I tugged Jeanny's shirt over her shoulders and unsnapped those baggy jeans she was wearing. Stood at the foot of the bed. Slid them off her. Started to undress myself, but she wanted to do it for me.

Slowly.

Carefully.

Unlike the way I felt with Edie, I wasn't embarrassed about my body. An easiness filled me as I stood there in front of Jeanny. And when I was completely naked, she kissed my bare chest, and my mouth went dry.

I let my body decide what to do next.

Gently my hands pushed Jeanny back onto the bed as she stared up at me. My knees knelt on the edge of the mattress. My palms pressed against her breasts. My mouth moved between them, kissing the hard bones of her chest. Jeanny arched herself, lifting her smooth stomach so that I could run my hands along the front of her, down past her belly button. My fingers slipped inside her. I found myself short of breath and wanting more air. The look on Jeanny's face was sweet and daring, her eyes glued to mine the whole while I touched her. Until finally I pulled my fingers away and put my lips and tongue between her legs. Kissed her there. Tasted her. I stopped to look at her face, and her eyes were still watching me, wanting more, so I kept going, and she made the slightest of sounds.

A breathy exhalation that sounded like relief.

A sudden high-pitched crinkle of her voice that came every few seconds.

I loved every moment of this, and I wanted Jeanny to love it, too.

Her hands stroked my hair, staying clear of that cut from the dresser, until I pulled my mouth away and moved up next to her on the pillow again. I whispered these words: "I think I'm in love with you."

Jeanny pressed her mouth to my ear and said, "I think I'm in love with you."

After a while of staying just like that, I told her about the pack of Trojans Ed had given me courtesy of Leon that first night. "So I have some in the other room," I said, a bit nervous about it still. "But I don't want you to think I've been planning this whole thing from the start."

"I know about them," Jeanny told me and smiled just a little. "I don't think I'll forget the look on your face when he put them in your hand."

"You knew?" I said.

She nodded yes. "I pretended to be busy with the baby to spare us both."

We laughed, and I kissed her. Kissed her again.

I went into the next room, those balloon ribbons brushing my shoulders as I walked. Knelt by the bed and dug out the box from underneath. Came back through the closets. It took me a minute, but I got the package open and managed to get one of them on me without too much fumbling. We kissed some more, and I lay on top of Jeanny. She helped me to put myself inside her.

"Are you okay?" I asked as she looked up at me.

"Yes," Jeanny said. "Are you?"

"Yeah." Since we were both new at this, our bodies took a while to find a rhythm. But soon it felt good. And once I got used to the sensation and the motion, it felt even better. It felt great. I tried my best to keep control as we moved. But it became more and more difficult. Jeanny's mouth was on my ear. Her hands were on my back. My tongue moved against the skin of her neck. And finally my body let go, and we both collapsed—sweaty and breathless on the bed.

A moment of nothing but our breathing.

Sweating.

One more kiss, and then Sophie started fussing in the next room as if she had been politely waiting for us to finish up in here.

"That baby has the world's worst timing," I said.

"If you'll excuse me," Jeanny said, nudging out from under me. "I can calm her down a lot faster than you. No offense."

"None taken," I said before rolling off her. "But you better come right back."

I hated the interruption, but I felt grateful for the chance to watch Jeanny's body from behind as she walked into the next room. Her hair was pulled around one shoulder. And the skin on her back was eggshell white with a dark mole down by her waist. Her legs were longer than I had realized before. She seemed so different to me from that girl I first spotted at the police station.

She was beautiful, I thought.

She was the girl I loved.

When Jeanny came back into the room with Sophie wearing only a diaper, she suggested we turn on the TV to catch the weather report for our morning mission. "Not to break the mood," she said. "But we better start thinking about tomorrow."

I knew she was right, so I turned on the TV and found the six o'clock news. We climbed under the covers with Sophie between us and held her tiny hands as we watched. The TV in this room had a serious sound problem. It shot up in volume, then down at random moments. One minute the anchorman sounded as if he were shouting his report about Nixon. And the next we could barely hear him. Kind of annoying, but Jeanny and I had gotten used to it.

As we lay there together—the three of us skin to skin, like some sort of natural-born creation, a family—I found myself thinking of that first night in the room again, the way I had been so nervous with Jeanny. I remembered all we had talked about, and one unanswered question came to mind. "So do you believe it was fate that we met?" I asked over the rise and fall of the anchorman's knowing voice.

Jeanny looked at me with those sugary-brown eyes of hers. "I've thought about it, and I believe that—" She stopped, looked through the tunnel of open closets into the next room. "Dominick. What's that?"

On the floor in there I could see the red shimmering light I had dreamed of. A rounded triangle. As big or as little as Sophie herself. We watched it for a moment, and then it began to spread, just like in my dream. I stood and wrapped a blanket around my waist. Jeanny did, too, carrying Sophie. We walked through the closets, and when we were inside the room, Jeanny said, "It's coming from the window."

I followed the glow and she was right. Leon had left the curtains open, and red shone in from outside. One step ahead of me, Jeanny went to the window. If her face had been stricken a few hours earlier when she looked out and saw Roget's car, now it was pure terror. "Oh, my God," she whispered in shock.

I walked to the window and looked outside.

Down in the parking lot were more cop cars than I could count. More than the night my mother died. Not a single siren, but all the racks on their roofs flashed red. The light bathed the room, drowning Jeanny, Sophie, and me in the glow the way I had dreamed.

That dream had been a sign, too.

The baby may be in danger here with you.

"What are we going to do?" Jeanny asked me, Sophie still quiet in her arms.

Desperate and numb, I walked to the bathroom and looked in the mirror for my mother. One final sign.

Not there.

Behind me I saw two of the survivor balloons. Yellow. Another red one. Their faceless faces looming over my shoulder. I looked away from the mirror, away from them, and stepped into the bedroom again. In the next room I could hear that anchorman still, his voice shooting up in volume. "After these brief messages," he said too loud into the emptiness, "we'll return with a look back on the Manson murders. Plus Penny Hatfield will fill us in on what to expect from the winter storm that's blanketing New England."

I put my arms around Jeanny and Sophie. Felt every part of me shaking. "It can't end this way," I found myself saying over and over. "It can't end this way. It can't end this way. It can't end this way."

The phone rang, and the two of us jumped.

"They're calling us," I said. "Don't answer it."

"Dominick," Jeanny said, her voice taut with nerves, "we have to give up and hand Sophie over. If you explain why you took her, they might not be too hard on you."

"They're going to put me in jail," I said, and my voice cracked the way it had when it finally changed last summer. I could feel tears rolling down my cheeks as I said those words again: "They're going to put me in jail."

"The police are out there anyway. If we don't answer this call, they'll just come knocking," she said over the phone, which rang and rang and rang. "Do we agree that we should answer it?"

I nodded yes, and my eyes poured out more tears.

"I love you," Jeanny said, crying, too. "Somehow this is going to be okay."

She walked across the room and picked up the phone. "Hello."

She waited, then said, "The baby is fine. Yes. Hold on."

Jeanny held the receiver out to me. "Dominick. It's for you. But it's not the police."

"Who is it?" I asked.

"Take it," she said. "You'll see."

I took the phone. Held it to my ear. Whispered, "Hello."

"Dominick," I heard a voice say, flat and cold. "It's Edie. And I want my baby."

Ten

My mother and Marnie always used to talk about thinking with their hearts versus thinking with their heads. But neither of them ever mentioned being led by their souls. That's what guided me the night that caravan of Holedo police officers and Massachusetts state troopers surrounded the motel. As I gripped the heavy black phone receiver, and snow spit fast and frantic from the sky outside the window, and the crimson cop-car lights splashed the walls of our room, I made a life-altering decision to try one final time to fix things for my mother so that her spirit could be set free.

But first the coming years of my life spilled before me. A messy gray puddle that reflected nothing but the most dismal future. I would be arrested, I would go to court, I would be sentenced and thrown into a juvenile prison for years. The strange thing was, once my mind settled on that scenario and released itself of the initial shock—handcuffs, court, prison—none of it sounded as unfair or even as scary as I had first thought. In my heart I felt certain that I deserved to be punished for ruining so many lives.

But that was my head and heart thinking.

Here's what happened in my soul.

I stood there, not speaking, as Edie rushed on, "Dominick? Dominick? I know you hear me. I asked the police to give you this chance to come out on your own. Just hang up the phone and step outside the door. Give me my baby back . . ." That's when the pitiful tragedy of my mother's life filled me up like the helium in one of those balloons above my head. A strange, invisible something that sent me floating over it all. My consciousness, my soul, blew backward through time, then back more, then forward, forward again. I heard a clacking sound and realized it was my mother fumbling with the phone so many nights before. Dialing Marnie in the storm. I could hear her voice, which was almost all breath. A rush of air and wind. Terror beneath.

Something's wrong, she said.

I'm bleeding, she said.

Then came an electric white flash like the fuzz of television static between channels, and I could see her standing in the lobby of a fancy New York building. A brittle, breakable expression on her face. A shiny silver present in her hands. Dozens of green plastic toy soldiers jumbled around in that box. Hard, pointy bodies with weapons forever attached to their skin. Pushed together in the darkness. Ready and waiting for war. Only those men would have to wait in there without air for too long. Unopened.

Again a blaze of white light and static, and I could feel myself being pushed down the long tunnel between her legs into the harsh brightness of the world. The gooey dew of new life on my skin. The tinny, metal sound of hospital instruments close by. My mother held my small body to her breast and cried. I was her hope, her fresh start. I was everything new to her. *Look at him,* she said to the nurses and doctors. *Oh, just look at him.*

A final white blur of heat and motion, and I was back where I started. Where it ended for my mother. I could see her body splayed on the floor beneath me. A slim silver probe snaked inside her. A river, a lake, an ocean of blood. Roget stood. He promised. He lied.

Be right back.

Be right back.

Be right back.

Nothing but her breath and blood after he left. She was a woman—like so many women—whose choices narrowed still more. A tunnel ahead of her grew smaller and smaller. Darker and darker. Then, after what seemed like too long for her to find any sort of strength, her hand moved toward the phone. Again I heard the clack and clatter of Marnie's number being dialed. Again I heard my mother's voice like a long, lonely wind cutting across the driest desert.

He said he would be right back.

But I know he's gone for good.

How quickly can you come?

After those words something in me burst. I felt dropped back down into the world of the here and now. Into the motel room, where my choices were narrowing, too. My soul felt gutted and hollowed. A carved pumpkin scraped of its stringy orange insides and filled with the hot, burning light of a white wax candle. That flame was anger, rage, resentment. The only thing left in the fast decay of my life. I saw a time lapse of two unlashed eyes collapsing in on themselves. A mouth rotted into a disfigured smile. A decomposed orange head tossed into the woods and forgotten.

Me.

My life.

And that's when I heard something deep inside me—not my head or my heart speaking, but some deeper part of myself that I decided was my soul—echoing these words:

After all of your mother's suffering, the only son she raised will be locked up. The man who left her alone to die will put him there, then walk away scot-free. One more sad fact of her life, her legacy, that you couldn't stop.

That feeling or message or premonition or whatever it was stoked the flame inside me, and my resolve flickered, burned hot and bright, then swept over me like a raging fire.

You have their attention.

Use it to prove Roget's guilt somehow.

For your mother's sake.

"Is my baby okay?" Edie was asking, her voice losing its flatness, turning wobbly, uneven. "Please tell me she's okay."

"The baby is fine," I heard myself say to her. Now I was the one who sounded flat, even. I could hear Edie crying on the other end of the line. Relief. Panic. Anger. All of it breaking her down. I let her weakness feed my flames, making me stronger, more steadfast in what I had to do. Jeanny was watching me with wide-open eyes as she cradled Sophie in her arms. I turned my back to her. "Where are you?" I asked.

"Down in the office. Dominick, please just come out."

Questions. There were so many I wanted answered, and they spewed from my mouth helter-skelter: "Who were those men in your apartment in New York? Why did you leave Holedo? Who is Sophie's father?"

Edie sniffled, took a breath. "What are you talking about? Your father is Sophie's father. I told you that."

"Why did you leave?" I asked, not letting up until I got the information I wanted.

"Your father kept threatening me. More than I ever told you." Edie's voice had grown exasperated, impatient, hysterical. I imagined her face flushed with anxiety, her hand tugging her hair, clutching, pulling as she spoke. "He beat the shit out of me once, and I was afraid of him. Of what else he might do to me. It wasn't fair to get you any more involved than you already were. So I couldn't tell you where I was going. I had to just leave you the money and get out."

My mind filled with the image of Edie's beaten face that day last fall. A puff of purple skin under her eye like smeared makeup. I remembered the way my father had clocked his fist in the air above me before I left home. The way he had growled, then punched the wall of my bedroom. Boom. Boom. Boom. I wasn't afraid of him, but Edie had been. Enough for her to leave town without telling me where she was going because she didn't want me to get hurt, too.

"I apologized in the letter I left you," Edie said. "But I don't understand why you've done all this. Why would you take my baby? Why? Why?"

The answer to that question was lodged inside me, tangled up like a wet ball of hair in the pink mouth of a cat. I could never get it out. The words to explain what I had done would only sound knotted and confused. The dots I had connected over the last month of my life wouldn't draw a picture clear enough for her to see. In my head I heard Leon's voice reading Edie's letter to me that day I had called him from my uncle's apartment.

> Dominick,
> I don't know why you left without saying good-bye last night.
> But I want you to know that I'm sorry if what's about to happen
> will hurt you. I needed a friend during this lonely time, and
> you were an angel. Someday I hope you'll forgive me. Someday
> I hope you'll understand.
>
> Love, Edie

Had Leon given me the cash, I might have forgiven her someday. I might have been able to understand just as she had written.

It was his fault.

It was her fault.

It was my fault.

"What about that phone call I overheard—" I started to ask, but Edie interrupted.

"Enough, Dominick! If you don't come outside in the next minute," she shouted, tired of our Q&A, launching threats, "I'm not going to be able to stop the police from coming in there after you."

I ignored her, kept digging. "I heard you on the phone that last night at your house. I heard you say that you would find a way to get rid of me."

"For Christ's sake, Dominick! Why are you bringing up all this bull-shit? I'm telling you that the police are going to come in there!"

"Why did you say it?" I asked her.

Edie was quiet a moment, then she sighed, surrendered to my ques-tion. "You were my boyfriend's son. I was in a bad situation, and I counted on you more than I should have. My friend kept telling me I had to stop it. I don't know what else you want to hear."

"Is your friend one of those guys who was at your apartment in Hell's Kitchen? Is one of them your boyfriend?"

"Hardly," she said. "They're each other's boyfriend. They helped me leave Holedo. I was supposed to stay at a hotel in the Village, but I went into labor on the drive down. They found me that apartment when I got out of the hospital. Christ. Why am I even fucking telling you any of this? I want my kid." Edie stopped herself, took a deep breath, tried one last time to reason with me. "Sophie's middle name is Dominick. Do you know that? I gave her your name because of all you did for me. Doesn't that prove anything?"

"I did a lot for you, Edie. But it cost me. It cost me my mother's life. I took that money from her. She needed it to go away and get an abor-tion. But it was gone. She died in this room because that money was missing. Because of what I did to help you."

Edie was quiet again. "Dominick. I am sorry. I am so, so sorry."

"Me, too," I said, holding back my tears.

"But there's been enough tragedies. Please end this and come out-side."

"You have to understand," I told her, feeling the heat of my resolve burning inside me. "I did something for you. Now you have to do some-thing for me. Me and my mother."

"What are you talking about?"

"You'll see," I told her and put down the phone.

It started ringing again almost instantly. Out in the parking lot car doors slammed. I slid the dresser in front of the door and walked through the closets into the next room. Jeanny kept calling to me, but I didn't answer her. The TV volume was doing a steady rise and fall, and I could hear bits and pieces of that anchorman recounting the brutal details of those Manson murders. *A house in California . . . A summer night . . . Sharon Tate . . . The last thing anyone ever expected . . .*

My next moves were mechanical:

Open the drawer by the bed.

Open the Bible.

Pull out the pistol.

The bullets, too.

"Dominick, what are you doing?" Jeanny stood in the doorway of the closet, holding Sophie. The blanket she had draped around her naked body was coming undone. Mine, too. "I thought you got rid of that thing."

"I kept it just in case," I told her over the blare of the television. "And I'm glad I did, because I'm not giving up. They're going to put me in jail. So I might as well right some of the wrongs of my mother's life while I'm at it." I pushed the cylinder open and slid a bullet into each of the holes the way my father had taught me so many years ago. I walked to the window as Jeanny stared at me, her mouth dropped in disbelief.

"Dominick, don't!" she yelled. "Stop it! Don't do this!"

The television eased down to normal volume again, and I could hear Penny Hatfield talking in a regretful voice about low-pressure zones, plowed roads, predictions of when we'd see the sun again. Outside, two troopers walked toward the stairs as the rest of the officers waited by their cars, backing them up.

Now or never, I told myself.

I reached my hand up to the window, pushed it open. Into the cold, hushed air of the storm, I screamed, "I've got a gun!" My voice didn't come out loud enough to be threatening, so I shouted again, "I've got a gun, and I will use it if you don't give me what I want!"

This time my words were unmistakable, sure and steady, as if I did this sort of thing all the time. The two troopers stopped, stared back toward the crowd of other officers, waiting for a sign as to whether or not they should proceed.

I decided to give them that sign.

I stuck the blunt nose of the pistol through the window. Aimed into the snowy gray sky above the woods across the street. The same woods where Roget had chased after me, scooped me up, and carried me back to his car as my leg bled. I pressed my finger to the trigger, and my hand shook. Then I heard my father say, *Just hold her steady. Don't be afraid of her.*

And I wasn't afraid anymore.

The shaking stopped. I fired.

The sound was a hundred balloons popping all at once, ringing in my ears.

Jeanny had carried Sophie into the other room, and I could hear them both crying in there. Other than that, in the moments after I shot the gun, the police in the parking lot were silent. I watched them stare up at the place in the red glow of their cop-car lights. Only their radios chirped out a staticky voice that said, "We have a ten-fifty-five at the Holedo Motel. We have a ten-fifty-five at the Holedo Motel."

Finally Roget said, "The kid's got a gun," loud enough for me to hear the dismay in his voice.

Something in the air changed after that. I believed it was because they realized that I was in control of this situation. Not them. Edie emerged from the office and walked across the parking lot, an officer's arm draped over her shoulders. She was crying, and despite everything, I felt torn apart by all the misunderstandings that the collision of our lives had caused. But I told myself that she would get her baby soon enough, and the tears would stop.

With the police held back for the time being, I shut the window and slid the dresser in front of the door in this room, too. I turned off the TV and went into 5B, where Jeanny was crouched on the floor, crying. She had managed to put her clothes back on, and her hair was still tucked inside her sweater. In her hand she squeezed her father's silver cigarette case. Sophie was wailing away next to her in the makeshift bed. I set the gun down on the dresser and threw on some clothes as fast as I could. Sat next to Jeanny, put my arms around her. "It's going to be okay," I told her. "Trust me."

"No it's not!" she screamed, pushing me away. "You've gone crazy! You've got to stop all this! You're going to hurt someone."

"I won't hurt anyone," I said. "I would never hurt anyone."

Jeanny just put her head in her hands and cried. "I was wrong about you," she croaked into her palms. "So wrong about you."

I tried to hold her again, but she shrugged me off, kept crying.

"You weren't wrong," I told her.

"Oh, yes I was!" she shouted, thrashing her head up to face me. "I thought you were good. I thought you made some bad decisions because of what happened to you. I thought I could help you put things right again. But you are fucked, Dominick Pindle! Look what you're doing! You are sealing your fate!"

"Listen to me," I said. "I know you think I'm crazy. But I need to do this for my mother. For her sake, I want Roget to be held accountable for leaving her here to die."

"How is any of this going to help you prove his guilt?"

The path to answering that question came not from me but from a police officer whose voice crackled through a speaker atop one of those cars in the parking lot. "What do you want?" his amplified, electric voice asked.

I didn't walk to the window right away, because I needed Jeanny to understand what I was doing. "Look. I'm going to jail anyway. If I surrender now, then I'll never have any power to get Roget or to do anything for my mother again. Think of this as a protest. I'm protesting Roget's claim of innocence. I'm protesting my mother's death. I'm protesting for all the women who've died the way she did."

I thought that last part would make Jeanny truly understand, but she just sat there crying. Out in the parking lot that speaker crackled again. The officer's voice repeated, this time stopping between words so the question sounded mixed up and broken: "What? Do you? Want?"

"If you want to leave, then go now," I told Jeanny. "I'll move the dresser, and you can walk right out the door. I understand."

Still she sat there. "What about Sophie?" she said after a while.

"The baby stays with me. But if you want to go, go. It's your choice."

Jeanny didn't move. She looked down at Sophie, then around at the room where my mother had died, where we had fallen in love. Two things so opposite, oddly connected. I put my hand out to her then, and she let me touch her, stroke her arm. I reached over and pulled her hair out from her sweater so that it spilled down her back like something set free. We sat there awhile as Jeanny looked from Sophie to the door, then back to Sophie again. And that policeman's voice kept prodding, repeating his question. When I couldn't wait any longer, I gave up on her and went to the window. I knew that asking for money or freedom would do me no good. Once they got the baby, they'd throw me in jail, and that would be that. It was clear I needed to ask for something they couldn't take away. And I knew exactly what that something was.

"Officer Roget left my mother here to die, and I want him investigated for his connection to her death!" I called through the window. No sooner were those words out when I thought of one last wish for my mother. A fairy-tale ending that she never got when she was alive. "And I want you to contact my uncle in New York City. Donald Biadogiano. Tell him to find a way to bring me Randolph Burdan. I will give the baby to him and only him."

Once again the air was silent outside.

I knew that meeting my brother shouldn't have mattered anymore. It wasn't going to change anything after all. But if my life was speeding toward the hard, gray nothingness of a concrete-wall dead end, I might as well take this last chance to get whatever I could for my mother.

When I turned away from the window, Jeanny was talking on the telephone. I listened to her tell whoever was on the other end of the line that she was at the Holedo Motel with me and the baby. That the state and local police were outside. I kept my eyes on her as she repeated the details of our situation. Jeanny spelled my name, emphasizing each letter so there could be no misunderstanding. "*D* as in dog. *O* as in octopus. *M* as in man . . ." She did the same with my mother's name. Roget's, Edie's, and her own, too.

"Who was that?" I asked when she finally hung up.

"Channel Six. Eyewitness News out of Boston."

"How did you get their number?"

"In the phone book," Jeanny told me, pointing to the Yellow Pages on the nightstand. "If we're going to have a protest, we need to get people's attention. We do it all the time in New York."

She was going to stay. I pulled her to me and kissed her. I thought it seemed strange that anyone from a TV station would care about what was happening to us in the Holedo Motel. Then I remembered Joshua Fuller's voice saying, *You're news, kid.* I saw that swirl of headlines about my mother in all those newspaper clippings. Maybe they *would* be interested. When we broke apart, I asked, "Now what do we do?"

"I guess we wait," Jeanny said.

And that's exactly what we did. Jeanny carried Sophie in her case to the back corner of the room and got her settled in for sleep. I piled pillows on the floor by the window, fixed the curtains just enough for us to see. She sat next to me, and we watched the police out there for over an hour. All of them with their waists strapped with so much stuff—guns, walkie-talkies, handcuffs, clubs—that they looked like carpenters wearing tool belts. Different officers kept trying to talk me down—but never Roget. They took turns at the radio, telling me I should give this whole thing up and come outside. But I didn't respond. They knew what I wanted, and until they started taking me seriously, I wasn't leaving. The whole while the storm kept flip-flopping from snow to rain, rain to snow. The officers clustered around one another. Random squad cars came and went. A few of the men looked restless and bored, glancing at their watches as the minutes ticked by. A trooper in tall black boots and a cowboy-style hat kept trying to comfort Edie. Offering her coffee, urging her to take a seat in the back of his car.

But she wouldn't budge.

She just kept staring up at the motel.

The bewildered expression on her face didn't quite hold the fear I had heard in her voice during our phone conversation. I wondered—

hoped was more like it—if somehow she was beginning to understand what I was up to now that she had heard my demands.

At the other end of the lot Roget stood by his car with the door open. One arm resting on the roof, one hand fingering his mustache. He looked about ready to make a break for it, but something kept him anchored here. The scales in his mind must have weighed down on the side of confidence that he could pull out of this situation unscathed. He could still be the town hero with his shiny gold badge. After all, he was an officer with a clean record and an alibi for the night my mother died. I was a runaway. A juvenile delinquent holed up in a motel room with a gun and a baby.

Who would ever believe me over him?

That's what I was asking myself the moment I saw a white van slow down in front of the motel and turn into the parking lot.

Channel 6 Eyewitness News.

Jeanny seemed brought to life by the sight of it. Even from the window, we could see Roget watching that big blue eye painted on the passenger door. It seemed to be staring at him, taking in the whole scene, actually witnessing everything that had happened here, everything that was about to happen, too. I wasn't as confident as Jeanny that the TV news spelled victory, but something told me Roget realized he might lose control of this situation if he wasn't careful. And when five minutes later a Channel 9 Action News van pulled up, followed by a station wagon from Channel 3, I actually started to believe he was scared.

"Did you call all of those stations?" I asked Jeanny.

"No," she said, not turning her gaze from the window. "But word must be out about what's happening here."

I watched Roget rush to the back of his car and pop open the trunk. He pulled out a roll of DO NOT CROSS—POLICE INVESTIGATION yellow tape. Barked orders at his men to block off the area. But the three reporters and their cameramen were already dispersing. Two of them headed toward the state troopers. A silver-haired reporter scrutinized the lot before approaching anyone. He was a man I had seen my whole life when I flicked channels on the tube or ate at the TV tables with my parents as they watched the local news. It felt weird to see him down there, looking too tall and artificial with his beige trench coat and square face. Like he belonged more in the box in my living room than in real life. He squinted his eyes toward Roget and seemed to size up his gold sheriff's badge, different from the rest, then walked toward him. A cameraman followed, weighed down by a snaky tangle of wires and a bulging black knapsack. A white spotlight clicked on, casting a sharp glow on Roget's saggy face. I couldn't hear the reporter's question, but whatever he said must have pissed Roget off. He shouted, "Step away, sir! We are in the middle of a police action, and your presence is a direct interference. Now, step away!"

The reporter didn't move. He held a microphone extended in his outstretched arm, the light burning behind him, the square black eye of the camera watching Roget. He repeated his question, again not loud enough for us to hear. And Roget shouted one more time, "I am ordering you to step away!" His men rolled out more of that yellow tape, corralling the reporters as best they could.

But that didn't stop them.

The man from Channel 9—who I had never seen on TV but who looked a bit like Joshua Fuller only without the birthmark—positioned himself and his cameraman so that the motel was directly behind him. The reporter from Channel 6 did the same. And in an instant two lights shone on them as they spoke into their microphones.

"This must be live," Jeanny said, jumping up to turn on the TV.

I followed her, and she was right. On Channel 9 there was the Joshua Fuller look-alike. The words "Special Report" flashed beneath him at the bottom of the screen. His voice came out at a steady volume, because the TV in this room worked right. Still, it took me a few seconds to focus on what he was saying. My brain was busy adjusting to the idea that the man outside was the man I was watching from inside—that so many people were watching as he talked about me, my mother.

". . . In a strange twist, this kidnapper is not asking for money. His demands? He wants the town's sheriff—Officer Russell Roget—investigated for an alleged connection to his mother's death from a criminal abortion. The fifteen-year-old boy has accused Officer Roget of leaving Theresa Pindle to die in the motel you see behind me on January twenty-third of this year . . ."

He kept talking, but something made me reach up and switch the station. Sure enough, on Channel 6 another one of the reporters from outside stared back at us. Only this guy had already begun talking about my mother's past. ". . . The late Theresa Pindle made headlines years ago, then under the name Theresa Tierney, when she sued a Manhattan doctor on the grounds that he coerced her into giving up her child in a private adoption for his financial gain . . ."

Again my hand seemed to reach up on its own and turn the dial. On Channel 3 Edie's face filled the screen. "I want my baby," she sobbed into the hard, black nub of a microphone. "I just want my baby. That's all."

As I watched her cry, I found myself imagining all the other people tuning in to this newscast. A man who had just returned home from his job. A woman who had cooked him dinner. The two of them—and a thousand others—sitting down to eat their Hamburger Helper in front of the TV, only to find this beautiful, shell-shocked woman crying about her baby who was locked in a motel room with a fifteen-year-old boy. What were those people thinking as they stared at Edie, at this whole mess of a life?

The poor woman . . .

The poor child . . .

Maybe they felt a fleeting pang of pity. But more than that, I bet they thanked God it wasn't them on the screen, that their world was safe, secure. Tomorrow they could get up and go to work. Come home again to watch somebody else's life fall apart on the television or in the newspaper. Little did any of those people know, I thought as I gazed at Edie's grief-twisted face, how close they were all the time. That one day you could make a choice that seemed like a good one in the moment, only to end up careening down a dark road you never intended to take. Like me when I kissed Edie that first night. Like my mother when she rolled down her window and stared up at Roget's badge.

Fate.

Chance.

"So what happens next?" the silver-haired reporter was asking. "Will the police agree to this boy's unusual demands? For now we can only wait and see. And pray that this terrified mother gets her child back unharmed. We will continue with live updates as this story unfolds. In Holedo, this is Jonathan Market. Channel Three News."

All three stations returned to regular programming, and Jeanny and I walked to the window again. We had more company out there: Marnie's car, my father's truck. I scanned the lot, and my eyes landed on my father first. I pointed him out to Jeanny. He was standing away from Edie, flanked by three officers. Snow dusted his shoulders and melted on top of his hatless head. His face puzzled itself up in confusion, more lost than I had ever seen him look. It was impossible to hear what the police were saying, but I guessed that they were asking him questions.

Who gave your son the gun?

Has he ever shown signs of violence before?

Is your son a drug user?

When was the last time the two of you had contact?

I imagined those words dumped on him like snow from a plow, leaving him buried in a cold, white silence with his lack of answers. He didn't have any explanation for them as to how this had happened. How could he? And I found myself wondering for the first time what he had been doing since the night I left home. Drinking? Bawling on a barstool night after night to Mac Maloney? Telling anyone who would listen that he had lost his beloved wife?

I turned my eyes away from him and spotted Marnie standing behind the yellow tape. Gazing up at the motel, hands clasped tight, praying as if this were Mecca. Joshua Fuller was out there, too, and when I saw him, I decided that the TV reporter didn't look so much like him after all. Joshua seemed taller, skinnier to me. I thought back to him asking Roget for a lift to Marnie's place. And I wondered if he and Marnie had seen the news together and raced over here. Or if maybe they had simply driven by on their way to the bus station after their interview had been completed.

Look at all those police, I imagined Joshua saying. *Stop the car.*

I pictured Marnie's face full of alarm as she stepped on the brakes. *Oh, my goodness,* she might have said. *Oh, my God.*

I wondered, too, about Joshua's visit with Roget earlier. As cool as Roget had played it when they paced the room next door, that must have been when he realized I was hiding out in the motel. The unlocked door. Leon's car. The messy bed. The blankets over the windows. Those clues had told him all he needed to know. And as soon as he ditched Joshua, he must have begun to gather his men, maybe he contacted Edie and waited until she arrived before surrounding the place.

All that—or something pretty close to it—had been going on while Jeanny and I were having sex. Knowing that, I probably should have regretted that I'd agreed to sleep here one more night. But I didn't feel that way. Instead I felt grateful for the chance to be with Jeanny. No matter the cost. I pulled my eyes away from the commotion outside the window and slipped my arms around her waist. Kissed her cheek.

"How could you be kissing me when all this is going on?" she said. "I mean, shouldn't we be doing something more?"

I sighed and let go of her, searched for a way to explain everything I felt. My life seemed to have taken on an unstoppable energy all its own. And something told me there wasn't much else we could do right then. We had to just wait and hope that someone out there listened to me about Roget. In the meantime I wanted to be as close to Jeanny as I could. Because I knew this was it for us. But instead of telling her any of that, I simply tried to kiss her again. Just to have her a little longer. But she pushed me away so she could look out the window. "Not now, Dominick."

I gave up after that and watched outside with her some more. We were quiet until Jeanny pressed her finger to the glass. "There's my mother," she said, her voice sounding shocked and happy at the same time.

I scanned the parking lot but didn't see her. "Where?"

"Right there," Jeanny said. "Getting out of the Volkswagen. She's all by herself. I wonder who's watching my brothers."

Jeanny's mother was a frenzied-looking woman with a spray of stringy hair, dressed in a ratty nightgown with a winter coat slung over it. My mind filled with an image of her in bed when the phone rang, jolting her from a long, drugged sleep like a scream in the night. The police, or a TV station, waking her with bad news. Her daughter, her only daughter, who hadn't come home in three days, was in danger. I imagined her throwing on that coat and hurrying over here. The tires of her little car slipping and sliding along the slick roads the whole way. I watched her as she left the door to her Volkswagen open and rushed toward the swarm of policemen. One of the officers lifted the yellow tape so she could duck beneath. He led her to his car and fumbled around inside for a bit before holding the radio receiver to her mouth.

When Mrs. Garvey spoke, the sound of her trembling voice seeped into the winter air and halted the buzz of activity down in the lot. "Jeanny, baby," she said over the speaker. "Are you all right in there? Did he hurt you? Please tell me you're okay."

"What do you know," Jeanny said, holding her hand to her chin, that barely noticeable scar. She bit her lip like she might cry. "She's actually worried about me."

Jeanny took a deep breath and put her mouth to the cracked-open window, called out, "I'm okay! Just tell the police to give him what he wants and this will all be over!"

When Jeanny leaned back, we watched her mother collapse into an officer's burly arms crying. He helped her take a seat in the squad car, gave her something to drink. Meanwhile Roget kept busy. Talking into his radio. Ordering his men around. Acting as if his name hadn't been called out in connection with my mother's death once again. He walked toward my father, and I saw the two of them talking. Figuring out what to do next, I supposed. In that moment I knew my father believed Roget over me despite all the shitty things he always said about cops. And it made the anger I felt toward both of them rattle my insides. They stepped away from each other, and my father moved toward the police car where Mrs. Garvey was sitting. He gave her a sort of nod, then took the radio from the officer.

"Dominick," he said over the speaker, "it's your father." He stopped. Maybe struggling to find what he could say to me. The right words to talk me down. Make up for all he had or hadn't done to lead me here. This was all he could come up with: "I shouldn't have gotten so angry at you that night you left. And I'm sorry. I know you miss your mom. So do I. But come on now, son. What are you doing in there? Let's cut this out. Come out so we can all go home."

He made it sound like I was hiding too long in a game of hide-and-seek. Come out, come out, wherever you are. Did he honestly think we'd all have a laugh and head home? He had to be stupid to believe that. I leaned toward the window and screamed, "Do what I want! And then I will give up!"

My father looked back toward Roget as if for sympathy or advice. Then he turned toward the motel again and said, "We called your uncle the way you wanted."

"Did you tell him to bring me my brother?" I shouted.

"It's not that easy—" my father started to say, but I cut him off.

"Well, find a fucking way! And I'm telling you one last time: Roget was the one who got Mom pregnant! He was with her the night she died!"

With that I closed the window. No more talking. I wanted them to start doing something. Getting me what I wanted.

On the television a somber voice was saying, "We interrupt this program to bring you another special news update." Jeanny and I walked to the set again to find Marnie on the screen. A reporter introduced her as a close friend of the Pindle family. She didn't look weepy and worried the way she had when I first saw her in the lot. Instead she had an eager expression, sort of the way she looked on the hospital TV when she announced bingo. For a second I almost expected her to start calling letters and numbers. *B seven. N thirty-five. O seventy-three. Who's got the hot card today?* Then she said into the microphone, "I know that sheriff was with Terry Pindle the night she died. Dominick is an innocent, good-natured boy who has been driven to this horrible circumstance because of the lies that crooked police officer told. And someone needs to do what he's asking and investigate him. It's a shame Dominick had to go to these lengths for his mother's sake. But what else was he to do when the entire police force in this town is conspiring against him?"

I wanted to kiss her face on the screen. Stupid, old annoying Marnie, who I hadn't been nice enough to the last few years, was speaking up for me. She was the only one out there on my side. I remembered her voice the day of my mother's service. *I want to find a way to get Roget.* Now she had found her way. And she must have realized, too, that this was our only chance.

After Marnie's interview the newscast didn't return to regular programming. Instead the reporter kept speaking. Only with a different tone than he had used in his first report. I went from being a kidnapper to a victim. And Roget went from being the Holedo sheriff to a suspect. Jeanny and I listened as a newswoman talked about my "tragic plight" and my attempt to avenge my mother's death by bringing justice to a "crooked small-town police officer . . ." On another channel there was a discussion of a case in Texas. A woman who needed an abortion was suing because she had been refused one. The people on the news were making connections between that story and my mother's.

Jeanny and I were caught up in all that talking, feeling like we might win at this thing, the way Steve McGarrett must feel on *Hawaii Five-O* right before he says, "Book 'em, Danno." Justice served. Case closed. A giant wave curling toward the beach as the credits roll.

But then the TV went dead.

The lights, too.

The room was completely dark.

Neither of us said anything at first. And without all those voices on TV, a ghostly silence took hold. All we could hear was the sound of Sophie softly breathing in her case. Something about that quiet made me whisper when I spoke next. "They cut the power," I said to Jeanny, who was a shadow next to me.

She walked to the telephone, picked up the receiver. "The phone line is dead, too."

We stood there in the dark, letting our eyes and our minds adjust to the lack of light. Those balloons hung like apparitions around us, as if they were waiting for something more to happen now that we were surrounded by blackness. I walked to the window and peeked outside. The officers had clicked off all their red car lights. The glow was gone. Even the parking-lot light was off, too. All I could see was their silhouettes out there in the falling snow. Like those demon spots that had danced in front of my eyes when my head hit the dresser.

"They're trying to drive us out," Jeanny said, joining me at the window. Her breath made a misty white spot on the glass, which then disappeared. "And I'm scared now."

"It won't work," I told her, trying to sound brave despite the fear creeping through me as well. "We'll just keep waiting. That's all."

"But for all the talk on TV, no one's doing anything about Roget," she said. "He's still out there. Why don't they take him in for questioning?"

"I don't know," I told her. "But something's got to give sooner or later."

I could hear the storm above us now like an army of fists pounding the roof of the motel. Wind gusted and spat rain against the window. Even though the heat register was still working, the air seemed colder by the second.

"What if it's us that gives?" Jeanny asked finally.

I didn't answer her, because I was asking the same question myself. That *Hawaii Five-O* wave had been blown back into the ocean before it even hit the sand. Cutting the power seemed to have put them in control again, and I wasn't sure how to handle it. Jeanny and I stood side by side watching the nothingness out the window, until she said, "As much as I hate that gun, you could fire another shot. Tell them you want the power back on."

Something told me to hold off on that. We could get by without electricity for the time being. And I didn't want to keep bluffing with the pistol. Because the truth was, I didn't have the guts to hurt anyone—even Roget. So without any other options, we just sat on those thin pillows in front of the window. Watched their shadows out there for hours.

More cars came and went.

Two of the reporters packed up and left.

A new reporter arrived a while later.

Eventually Jeanny nodded off with her head in my lap. I stroked her hair as she slept and kept my eyes wide open, peering down at her face, then outside. In a perfect world, or at least in a fairy tale, something would have happened to save the day right about then. A fairy god-mother would have swooped down and waved her wand, making Roget melt into a puddle in the parking lot. My brother would have descended from a cloud, smiling at me. And this whole sordid ordeal would have come to a neat little end. But that wasn't my life.

Instead I waited all night by that window, as the snow turned to rain again. Then finally stopped. Oddly enough, Sophie didn't wake up, cry-ing to be fed or changed. She lay so still in the comfort of her case that I practically forgot she was there. I rested my head on the windowsill, and in spite of all that was happening or not happening, the darkness and quiet lulled me to sleep, too.

When I opened my eyes, a thin strip of sunlight streamed in through the opening in the curtains. Heat, bone-dry and dusty, gusted up through the register, making a relentless scratching sound like a deter-mined animal beneath us clawing its way into the room. Those balloons had lost even more helium during the night, and they floated a few feet away from the ceiling, their ribbons coiling on the floor. Flags slowly being lowered to half-mast. My body felt stiff and crumpled, like one of those blue tissues in Marnie's pockets. All used up but still being used.

I rubbed my eyes and looked down into the lot.

And I couldn't believe what I saw.

Twice, no, three times as many people out there as the night before. Only not just police and reporters. There was a group of women. Maybe twenty of them to one side, all carrying picket signs: WOMEN DIE WHEN THEY CAN'T CHOOSE. LEGALIZE ABORTION ON DEMAND. WHO WILL BE THE NEXT THERESA PINDLE? They stood behind that yellow tape, their faces determined and angry. I saw a girl even younger than Jeanny. A woman too old and gray to be out in the cold. The bulk of them had to be about my mother's and Marnie's age. They marched in a circle like witches casting a spell, trampling the white snow beneath their feet. Round and round. Round and round.

Across from them was a second group made up of a priest, three nuns, and a whole slew of women. One with her mouth locked into a rabid dog's snarl. Another who wore a too-placid expression on her face given what she was doing. All of them carried signs with the opposing message: BABIES DIE WHEN WOMEN CHOOSE. ABORTION IS WRONG. LET GOD DECIDE. They stood just a few feet away from the others, not in a circle but in a crowd, waving their signs.

I noticed something else that hadn't been out there the night before: two ambulances parked by the road. The way they were pulled up to the snowy curb made their boxy white bodies tilt off-kilter. I thought of an ice cream truck I had once seen sucked down into the muddy sand during a summer rainstorm. Those ambulances looked the same to me, only with a different purpose entirely.

I shook Jeanny's shoulder to wake her, because I couldn't wait for her to see all those women and their signs. She jerked her head up, startled. "Huh?" she said, dazed.

"It's morning," I told her. "And I want you to see something."

Jeanny opened her eyes and stretched her arms and legs. Let out a squeal as she loosened her body. "Happy day after birthday," she said, groggy-voiced, when she finished.

"Real happy," I told her, still not letting on that *today* was actually the big day. "Maybe we'll go to Peaceful Pizza, then catch a movie later to celebrate."

"Should we invite the police to come with us?" she said.

"And the protesters, too," I told her.

"Protesters?" Jeanny said. She sat up, brushing her hands over her eyes. Looked out the window, where one of the groups began chanting the same message that was on their signs. "Women die when they can't choose! Women die when they can't choose!" Then Marnie shouted, "Roget is a killer!" And that sent a roar across the parking lot.

I thought Jeanny would've been glued to the window, seeing as this was her type of thing. But she stood and went to Sophie's case across the room. I kept watching outside as the cameramen let their tapes roll and the reporters asked questions. Joshua was speaking to the priest, scratching notes on the pad in his hand. One at a time people ducked out of the crowd, talked to the news, then went at it again. Everyone seemed to have forgotten about the war I was waging, the battle for my mother. Even the cops seemed preoccupied by those women and their signs. And I felt dizzy staring at those words.

WOMEN DIE . . .

BABIES DIE . . .

WOMEN DIE . . .

BABIES DIE . . .

WHO WILL BE THE NEXT THERESA PINDLE?

LET GOD DECIDE . . .

All of them seemed convinced that they had the answer.

"Dominick," Jeanny was saying. "Dominick. Listen to me."

"What?" I said, turning away from the window, that separate, unending battle unfolding out there.

Jeanny was leaning over Sophie's case, palms on her knees and head cocked, like she had come across something injured on the side of the road. A broken-winged bird fallen from its nest. A kitten hit by a car but still breathing. She pressed her hand to Sophie's forehead. "I think something is wrong with Sophie."

"What do you mean?" I asked, my voice yanked tight.

"Did she wake up last night?"

"No," I told her.

"She always wakes up during the night, you know that. It's not normal for her to keep sleeping." She picked Sophie out of the guitar case, held her to her chest. "Feel her skin. She's burning up. She should be crying right now."

I went to Jeanny and put my hand on Sophie's tiny arm. Her skin felt the way it might if I pressed my fingers to an electric blanket turned on high. Like something about to catch fire. "How could this just happen?" I asked.

"She's a baby, Dominick."

The way Jeanny said it implied that I might not have realized that fact before. *Oh, that explains it,* I wanted to say. *Thanks for clearing things up.* But I didn't. "Well, did she seem all right to you yesterday?"

"I guess," Jeanny said, looking down at Sophie, whose eyes were squeezed tight. "I mean, she had a little bit of a fever when I put her down for the night. But we were leaving in the morning so there was not much I could do. I didn't tell you because I didn't want you to worry."

Out in the parking lot another clamor rose up. Shouting and chanting. The commotion down there and the sheer terror of something happening to Sophie crashed together in my mind, and I found myself screaming at Jeanny, "What do you mean, you didn't tell me?"

"Don't yell at me!" she shouted right back.

"Well, what the hell are you doing letting her get sick?"

"What do you mean, 'letting her'? You're the one who has us locked in here!"

"I told you you could go last night, and you decided to stay!"

"Well, maybe I made a mistake! Let me remind you that you'd be nowhere with this baby without me. When I first saw you on that bus, you didn't even know how to hold her!"

"I—"

Sophie opened her mouth, which shut us both up. We waited in that long pause—silently fuming as she burned up in Jeanny's arms—watching the O of her mouth to see if she might start crying, or at least open her eyes. A bubble of spit dropped from her pink lips. But no noise came.

Whatever I was going to say had flown from my mind. I took a breath and forced myself to let the argument go. Jeanny was right. I would be nowhere without her. It was all the things that had gone wrong that made me snap. And now this. "I'm sorry," I told her. "I'm really sorry. It's just scary. I don't know what to do."

"When my brothers were this small and they had a fever, I rubbed them down with rubbing alcohol," she said, her voice softening.

I raised my eyebrows and gave her a look that implied we had to think of something else, because we couldn't exactly run to the pharmacy.

"We could try giving her a bath in cool water. That will bring her temperature down." Jeanny gave Sophie a light little shake and cooed to her, "Want to go for a swim, bathing beauty? Come on, sweet pea. Are you feeling sick?"

She still didn't make a peep.

I put my arms out and took her from Jeanny. Remembered how light she had felt the first time I picked her up. How heavy she became later when I arrived in this room and she wouldn't let me put her down. I pressed my hand to her forehead. Felt all that heat, like a small fire burning beneath her skin. "Open your eyes, little alien," I said, making spider legs with my fingers and wriggling them in front of her face. "Come on, wake up."

But she wouldn't.

And that's when I heard my mother's message once more.

The

baby

may

be

in

danger

here

with

you.

Sophie was going to die.

A sick wave of terror swept over me. "I have to give up," I said to Jeanny. "We've got to get her to the hospital."

Outside, I could hear Roget's voice booming. I glanced toward the window and saw him. He was talking to the reporters for the first time, addressing the crowd, too. They had gathered around him as he spoke into the flock of microphones. "As an officer of the law with an outstanding record of fourteen years in civil service, I will remind you that there is no evidence against me. I was not with the boy's mother the night of her death. I have three police officers who will swear under oath that I was at the station with them at the time. What we have here is a runaway boy who has kidnapped an infant. You people need to remember that he is the criminal. He is holding a young girl and a baby at gunpoint."

He is holding a dying baby in his arms, I thought.

The baby may be in danger here with you.

Why hadn't I listened to her?

"We've got to get her to the hospital," I said again.

"I know," Jeanny said. "But as soon as you walk through that door, they're going to arrest you."

There was another roar in the crowd. Protesters shouting after Roget's interview. Again Marnie's hysterical voice shrieked, "Killer!"

With them on my side and with a little more time, I might have been able to bring him down. But I couldn't risk Sophie's life any longer. "We don't have a choice. I have to give up."

Jeanny and I made one last plan. I would open the door and surrender myself. She would rush the baby out behind me and get her to an ambulance. Once we settled on that, I wanted to kiss her good-bye. But everything was happening so fast, and we were both so filled with fear, that I didn't.

Jeanny took Sophie from my arms. I pulled back the dresser, and when I did, Mr. Garvey's silver cigarette case fell to the floor. I picked it up and held it in my hand the way Jeanny always did. With my other hand I turned the knob. Pulled open the door, and sunlight flooded the room, bringing a gust of cold air that made those balloons shift positions.

An army preparing for battle. I left them blowing behind me, took a breath, and stepped into that light. The sun seemed everywhere. Ricocheting off police-car windshields. Pushing down on me, charged and electric, like lightning from the sky. All that brightness made it impossible for me to see, so I stood in the doorway blinking at the outside world like a creature just hatched from the darkness of this room. A baby bird with sticky feathers stunned by the blur of beauty and ugliness it had been born into.

For a long moment no one even noticed me standing there. Too busy battling one another. Solving an unsolvable problem. Then a shrill, wild voice yelled my name, and everyone's heads turned toward the motel. Their silence was so sudden—like a collective, instantaneous gasp—that it seemed to suck all the air away from me. The complete and motionless quiet that followed pulsed in my ears. A needle pulled off a record mid-song, the beat still throbbing in my head. My eyes cleared, and I saw them.

That silver-haired reporter.

That protester younger than Jeanny.

My father.

Marnie.

Joshua Fuller.

The priest.

Edie.

Mrs. Garvey.

All their faces seemed to swirl around me like planets.

The sun blared down more, and I waved my hands in the air. Surrendering. Calling for help. But instead of letting me give up, the officers pointed their guns. In a flash I saw what they saw. The silver cigarette case that had given Jeanny so much comfort was the glint of a pistol in their eyes. And here's what they must have thought:

The boy has his weapon.

And he's going to shoot.

But not if we get him first.

Ready.

Aim.

Fire.

A deafening blast. A bullet in my shoulder. Not far from my chest, my heart. Blood spurted, and my body was knocked backward into the room. I felt a surge of heat race through my veins. My mind went white with haze, and Jeanny leaned over me. Screaming. Crying. "Please don't die!" she shrieked, still holding Sophie, a rag doll in her arms. "Please don't die!"

My mouth moved to tell her to get the baby to the ambulance, but a liquid warmth filled my throat, and I couldn't speak. My eyes flicked open and closed on their own. Blood soaked my shirt, wet and gluey. A thought floated into mind: This is the accident you kept glimpsing. It's your blood that will stain the floor a second time.

A hot rush beneath my skin again, and then the coldest cold.

I imagined myself plunged into the icy water of that pond out back. Just like my mother. I was swimming down there. Searching for her in the tangle of underwater weeds. When I shouted her name, only a stream of soundless bubbles spouted from my mouth. I took a breath, and the heavy weight of water filled me. Above my head I could hear a humming sound. A voice was calling, and I kicked my way toward it.

Jeanny.

"Can you hear me? Can you hear me? Can you hear me?" Only a second had passed, and she was talking to me still. Begging. Pleading. Then she said, "Do you remember that question?"

Question? Did I remember a question? My mind drifted again, and I heard so many questions. *Which of your parents do you like better? What were you doing out there running around almost naked in the middle of the night? If your mother is interested in the place, then why isn't she here?* I saw that church lady in St. Patrick's. She pointed her wrinkled finger toward the ceiling and said, *From here, they remind me of balloons let loose into the air, don't you think?*

After that I heard my mother.

Not the whisper of that haunted vision in the mirror or beneath the ice. But her living, breathing voice. Her question was simple: *Do you want something to eat?* I was on my bike looking up at her as she called to me from the kitchen window of our apartment. Instead of pedaling away toward Edie's, I said, *Yes, Ma. I want something to eat.* I got off my bike, clomped back up the stairs.

Another life.

Another chain of events that could have led me anywhere.

"Do you hear me?" Jeanny was saying. "Do you remember the question?"

And then I remembered. I had been waiting for her to answer that question about us when the police arrived. She pressed her lips right to my ear, a sloppy kiss that might wake me, and said, "You wanted to know if I believed we were meant to be. And the answer is yes."

Those words, and then pure blackness.

The deep heart of a forest miles and miles from anyone.

No noise, and then the whir of wings, animal sounds, teeth gnashing, crickets, and something else. Something stomping close by. My eyes blinked open to see dozens of black boots on the floor beside me. I thought of Edie's shoes in her basement. Those round rocks like skulls cemented into her walls. I looked up and saw a crowd of policemen floating above me with those balloons, staring down. Two men in white knelt beside me. The blood on their shirts made me think of a butcher wiping his hands on his apron. Chopping body parts day after day. Legs. Tongues. Feet.

Where was Jeanny?

I turned my head and could see her in the corner of the room, an officer pulling Sophie from her arms. She was screaming, "Save him! Save the baby!"

More blackness. I was laid out in that dark forest again. Safely sealed inside a box of gleaming glass. I could sleep forever. It would be so easy. Waking just once a year in the heat of summer, like a weed sprouted from the earth, growing wild for a few short days before shriveling and dying again. A ghost who boarded a bus to visit this motel, to haunt my father who owned the place. We would be together but not really together at all. He would be a ghost of his former self, too—only living, breathing. And I would be the same as those cardinals chained to the church because of their religion. The things they believed in, acted on, when they were alive.

Then I saw another future.

Someone somewhere was asking Jeanny and me how we met. City lights twinkled behind us out a wide window. Ice clinked in glasses. Smart laughter rose and fell in the next room. *On the bus in high school,* we said at the same time. It was true. But it was also our own inside joke, and we made knowing eyes at each other, because that answer conjured up images of a football player and a cheerleader, or maybe the class clown and the class flirt. High school sweethearts with a simple past. Not us. And then I saw a baby, too, only she wasn't Sophie. I pressed my nose to her skin and smelled powder. Sugary and sweet, just like her. We didn't have to give her back, because she was ours. We created her. We were meant to be.

It's your choice, I heard my mother say from someplace else. Someplace dark and distant. Farther away than even that fairy-tale forest. *Which do you want?*

Plan B, I told her.

Door number two, I told her.

I'll stay, I told her.

But she wasn't listening.

I heard a scream calling me back to the motel. A siren outside. The first ambulance taking Sophie away to save her. She would be okay. I knew. And my body was being lifted. I tried to open my eyes but couldn't. It was as if I no longer had eyes. Just an expanse of skin where they were supposed to be, like something born deformed, wrong. Just this darkness to look into. Pictures in my mind. I could feel those butcher men raising me up and carrying me out on a stretcher. My body rocked from side to side as they stepped down the stairs. When we reached the parking lot, I could sense the crowd watching me.

My father.

I knew what he was thinking. He was making a single, resolute promise to himself over and over in his mind. A bargain with God. A deal with the devil. One he intended to keep either way this time.

If he pulls out of this alive, I will change.

No more drinking. No more disappearing.

Please let him pull out of this alive.

Those men carried me across the lot, and I heard an engine start. A voice said, "IV." Then another said, "Blood loss." My eyes still would not open, and I thought, It's too late. Give up.

Only when I stopped trying could I see again.

From above this time.

Jeanny's mother was down there clinging to her, holding her. And Jeanny was watching my body on the stretcher until something captured her attention at the top of the stairs. She turned to look at the door of my mother's room. I looked, too. But no one else noticed what we saw. Those balloons that had sunk down during the night had been picked up by the wind, or something greater, and were moving out the door. Instead of drifting up, though, they descended the stairs my mother had climbed so many weeks ago.

They moved in a soldier's line. Or snakelike.

Something supernatural with a purpose, a mission.

The way the wind blew them, they seemed as alive as anyone in the parking lot. More alive than me. And at the bottom of the stairs one balloon broke away as the others lingered behind. A red one with a smaller red balloon inside drifted first to my body. Then to my father. Then to Roget, where it burst, and the tiny heart of a balloon beneath sailed upward as the others followed.

I felt myself floating farther, too, slipping away with them.

But I tried to will myself down.

Struggled a final time to push myself back into the world.

To open my eyes.

And when I did, when I opened them, this is what I saw: I saw not those balloons but my mother stepping from that room where she had died. Behind her a line of women followed. No one needed to tell me who they were and why they were there. I knew. They were women who had died the way she did. And they had come to claim her tortured soul. When they reached the bottom of the stairs, they waited as my mother walked toward me. She didn't look ghostly anymore. She just looked like my mother on an ordinary day. She could have been on her way to the grocery store or to pick me up from school. Only her face wore a different expression. More peaceful than she had been in life. And when she reached the stretcher where I lay soaked in my own blood, finding my breath, she held out her hands to me, kissed my forehead.

"I love you," she whispered.

I wanted to ask her so many questions but couldn't. She squeezed my hand and let go. Went to my father, stood before him without speaking, taking him in one last time. Then she moved to Roget. She didn't say or do anything but stare at him, a man who would get away with what he'd done despite all my efforts. My mother held first her stomach and then her heart as she stood in front of him. And then I heard a loud pop, and I was seeing not my mother and those women but the balloons again, the way I had before.

One by one, the wind carried them up and out into the blue. I kept watching that tiny red embryo of a balloon as it drifted away from Roget. As innocent as a carnival balloon slipped from a child's hand. Instead of a soul, a lost dream, a little life inside a larger one, a voice, a sign that told me my mother understood what I had tried to do for her, and we were both free.

Those men pushed me into the back of the ambulance, and I caught a glimpse of a black sedan pulling into the lot. As they were about to close the doors, I saw my uncle step from the car, and then someone familiar but not familiar at all. A tall, broad-shouldered college student. A Columbia sweatshirt and khaki pants. Thin lips. Stubble on his square chin. Wire-rimmed glasses and hair the same brown as mine.

Randolph Burdan.

My uncle had somehow managed to bring him to me. Ever since the day I'd been told who he was, I pictured him as one of those flawless, blue-blazered kids I'd seen streaming from that school on the Upper East Side. But when our eyes met, I felt as if I was looking at a version of myself; or rather the young man I might have become had none of this happened. Ordinary. Innocent enough. And all at once I saw that there was some sort of magic in that ordinariness. A magic I no longer had.

I watched him look up at the motel, then brush his fingers through his hair as he squinted toward the heavenly brightness above him. A breeze was picking up, and the ambulance was moving. He was growing smaller in the distance. And he couldn't even see me wave to him as I was carried away, just like those balloons in the sky.

Epilogue

After all of the unraveling at the Holedo Motel, it seems unfitting that my father's the one chained to this place. Not me. I open myself up to it only on these summer visits so I can tuck it back away the rest of the year, live the most unblemished life a man like me can lead. Sometimes when I'm far from here, in the middle of my day I'm filled with a fast shudder brought on by a stirred memory, a glimpse of what happened so many years ago.

But mostly I've learned to push it aside. Move on.

During the time that I stay here, I tell my father about the good things I know now. I share stories about his daughter-in-law and grandchild, the loves of my life. I show him postcards that Marnie has sent me from the senior group tours she takes around the country. The most recent one from Vegas, her swirly writing on the back says, "Dominick, I haven't won yet, but I'm still trying! Kisses—Marnie!" We talk of Sophie, who set out to *meet the father she never knew when she was in art school on the East Coast years back. And I tell my father what little I know about Rand, which I gauge from notes scratched on cards sent at Christmastime, our relationship having petered out long ago.*

Some days my father and I walk to the pond behind the motel, where he keeps goldfish stocked just like Old Man Fowler used to do. We watch them darting around, and I stare down at my reflection. With those bright fish shimmering beneath and the clear water rippling, I look almost young again in the marbled surface of that pond. Every year my father tells me how he cares for the fish, and I listen as if for the first time. Feed them regularly. Keep the water clean. Let enough algae grow so they'll have something to nourish them when the cold weather hits. I listen, too, as he talks about the early days with my mother.

Riding around on his motorcycle together.

Picnicking in the park.

How happy she was when they had me.

Only when I'm up in that room alone do I think about the rest. The way the world pinballed me that year. And the way events aligned like stars, forever reshaping the pattern of my life. Back then, I looked to those events as signs or beacons the way my mother told me to do, and I wound up in a place I never expected to be. Why? I guess Jeanny had it right our first night together when she told me, "Some things are meant to be. Fate. And other stuff is just up to chance. Who knows the reasons behind it?"

It took me a long time to give up trying to answer that question, even longer to stitch my life back together. There is no fairy-tale ending for me. If you were to see me today—say you were a guest checking into this roadside motel in a small Massachusetts town—you might spot me behind the counter during one of my yearly visits. I'd be helping my father with the guest register or handing him the keys to your room, and you might think: "There's a son giving his aging father a hand." You would never guess the history between us or the buried past of this place. You might look at me and I'd smile as you picked up your suitcase and headed out the door. You might think I was a happy man, though somewhat weathered. And you'd see in my eyes no small part of a love I learned from a girl who stayed with me long after that troubled year, a father who I learned to forgive, a mother who forgave, and two children who were lost, then found. And a part of me who will always be a boy still missing the childhood he left too quickly behind.

ACKNOWLEDGMENTS

I moved to New York City about ten years ago with all of my belongings in the back of my father's tractor trailer. My younger sister had died not long before, and sometime during the shock of it all, I had made up my mind to follow my dreams in her honor since she would never get the chance to fulfill her own. Little did I know how many setbacks there would be, how many tables I'd have to wait on, and that I'd end up becoming a books editor at a women's magazine in the process. Thankfully, there were people along the way who acted as angels in my life and helped to make my dream come true.

Joanna Pulcini is the most faithful and hardworking agent any writer could ask for. Not only did Joanna believe in this book when the only thing she knew was the title, but she also brought me to St. Patrick's Cathedral one spring afternoon and told me to look up.

I am deeply grateful to my wise and nurturing editor, Betty Kelly, who offered me unending enthusiasm during the years I spent writing this story. She also provided me with a home away from home to work on my fiction.

Patricia Burke from Paramount Pictures always seemed to call at the right moment. At first I thought she had tapped my phone, then I thought she was psychic, finally it dawned on me that she was simply an angel.

I was blessed to have Ann Hood as my writing teacher. She gave me abundant guidance early on and taught me so much about life.

The Vermont Studio Center granted me two generous fellowships where portions of this book were written on the second and third floors of Mason House.

Kate White, editor-in-chief of *Cosmopolitan*, is every writer's dream boss. She gives me constant support and even lets me sneak away from the job to focus on my fiction.

I also had the honor of working with two former editor-in-chiefs of *Cosmopolitan* while writing this novel—the legendary Helen Gurley Brown and the one and only Bonnie Fuller both offered me invaluable encouragement.

Liz Smith took an interest in me and my work, and made people pay attention in a way they hadn't before. I thank her for helping an unknown writer.

Wally Lamb was kind to me when I drove to Rhode Island from New York City to hear him read back in 1993. He offered to take a look at my writing and referred me to his agency. I am eternally grateful to Wally for his willingness to lend a hand to a newcomer.

My grandmother Dorothy believed I could be a writer ever since I showed her my first book entitled *Stories and Stories and Stories* when I was in the second grade. She never stopped believing even when other people did.

My readers: Alysa Wakin spent many late hours talking on the phone with me about this story and these characters even when she had to work the next morning. Alison Brower and Deirdre Heekin helped me immeasurably with their careful editing of this book. And Stacy Sheehan has always been an enthusiastic and gentle early reader.

I also need to give credit to Brother Dennis Sennett of the Archives and Records Department at St. Patrick's Cathedral as well as the makers of the documentary *Leona's Sister Gerri*. The family who spoke in that film about their experience, which was similar to my subject, added to my inspiration.

There are dozens of other people I would like to get mushy with but if I keep going these acknowledgments are going to turn into another book, so I'll list their names here with a huge thank-you from the heart: John Sargent, Jan Bronson, Dawn Raffel, Abigail Greene, Jen Leonard, Shira Lyons, Jenny Benjamin, Susan Seagrest, all my *Cosmo* and Breakaway friends, Sam Hood Adrain, Carol Story, Amy Ziff, Vivian Shipley, Leo Connellan, Matthew Ballast, Patrick Miller, the Gallatin School at NYU, Amy Schiffman at the Gersh Agency, Renee Bombard at Presses de la Cite, Georg Reuchlin at Verlagsgruppe Bertelsmann, Linda Michaels and Teresa Cavanaugh at the Linda Michaels Agency. Also, Linda Chester, Laurie Fox, Julie Rubenstein, Gary Jaffe, and Kelly Smith at Linda Chester and Associates. And all the great people at William Morrow: Rome Quezada, Sharyn Rosenblum, Maureen Sugden, Rich Acquan, Michele Corallo, and April Benavides.

Finally, I'm more grateful than I can articulate to Thomas Caruso, who is a soothing, loyal, and loving presence in my life every single day.

July 2000